THE CELIA KELLY SERIES
The Pact: Op One
By CN Bring

God Bless!
CN Bring

Copyright © CN Bring

All rights reserved.

ISBN-13: 978-1975919290
ISBN-10: 1975919297

All rights reserved. No part of this book may be reproduced or transmitted in any form or by any means, electronic or mechanical, including photocopying, recording, or by any information storage and retrieval system, without permission in writing from the copyright owner.

This book is a work of ction. Names, characters, places and events are products of this author's imagination or used ctionally. Any resemblance to actual events or locales or persons living or dead is entirely coincidental.

The Celia Kelly Series

The Pact: Op One

Published by
Bring Media Publishing, 2017
www.cnbring.com

Dedicated to my husband Glen and children Felecia, Melissa, Kyle and Kayla. Thank you for all your love and support!

Make a pact with the devil until you have crossed the bridge.
Romanian Proverb

PROLOGUE

The sun bounced off the instrument panel of the F-14 TOMCAT. Lieutenant Tom Kelly watched the Mediterranean Sea as he banked his fighter heading back to the aircraft carrier.

"What's on your mind?" asked Lieutenant Sam Cooper, the Radio Intercept Officer.

"Just thinking," Tom said into his mic.

"Second thoughts?" Cooper's red hair wet with sweat under his helmet clung to his rosy cheeks as the solar heat radiated in the cockpit.

Tom didn't answer as he contemplated the complexity of what he was about to do. He loved her dark green eyes and how she could always look deep into his and just know what he was thinking. At one time it had been his greatest comfort, but as of late it was his greatest fear. His thoughts interrupted with what sounded like a gunshot.

"We are losing altitude." Cooper urgently tried to get a read on what was happening.

Tom attempted to get control of the fighter. Without warning, the F-14 dived swallowing up into a flat spin. Everything around them reduced to a whirl with each revolution. The most they could distinguish was the spiraled illusion of the sea coming up to meet them.

"May Day! May Day! Flat spin!" Tom attempted to radio the carrier but there was no reply.

"Punch out!" Tom ordered Cooper as he reached to eject.

"Ejecting." Cooper confirmed.

CHAPTER 1

She felt her feet pounding the pavement as she picked up the pace. Heavy steps closed in behind her. Without looking back, Celia Kelly pressed on. She wasn't sure if the breathless gasps she heard were his or her own. Celia dug deep inside, pushing herself into longer, quicker strides. In her peripheral vision she could see him now. He was close. Faster... she had to go faster...

The last park bench along the west side of Potomac Park was in view. Celia gave it all she had and so did he. Celia won the race by less than seven inches.

"I won." Celia tried to catch her breath.

"One of these days, Kelly." Commander Frank Scott shook his head.

"In your dreams!" Celia laughed.

Every Wednesday for the last three years, Commander Celia Kelly and Commander Frank Scott raced one mile at the crack of dawn. Scott had won each race the first year. Celia gained on him, winning now and again. Determined, Celia continued to condition until she could beat him every Wednesday morning for the last ten months.

"I guess we'd better get to work," Scott said, looking at his watch. It was 0600 hours.

"Next Wednesday?"

"I'll be here," Scott assured her.

"See you in an hour," Celia called out as they separated.

The sun was just came up over the eastern horizon, cuing Washington, D.C. early morning rush-hour traffic. Celia Kelly's life was routine. She believed in rules, schedules, and maintaining precision. Celia had discipline down like a science. It was something taught to her since she was small; first at home, then at church, and later at the Naval Academy. She liked the order it gave to her life.

Celia slowed the jog to a quick-paced walk as her house came into view. In front of her house, a dark blue sedan parked the wrong way, facing oncoming traffic. The right blinker flashed. The blue sedan pulled into the left lane, crossing to the right, going on its way. Celia crossed the street to her house. A smoldering cigar was on the top step of the porch. She glanced both ways down the street, but the blue sedan disappeared.

Celia positioned the key in the lock, but the weight of her hand pushed the door open. She was certain she had locked it. Celia entered, her pulse quickening. Not sure what to expect, she searched. Calling the police was not an option. She was an intelligence officer. Check it out before checking in. Nothing was missing, and no one was waiting for her. It wasn't until she walked into the kitchen she noticed something out of place. The juice glass Celia had used that morning was on the floor instead of on the table where she had left it.

The last room she checked was the bedroom. Except for a photo album on the floor, everything was in order. Her briefcase locked. Celia's GLOCK 17 pistol was still in her top drawer, and her .32 caliber Beretta backup was still under her mattress. After putting the photo album away, Celia glanced at the clock. She needed to be at the Pentagon in thirty-five minutes. She was running late.

Skipping a shower, Celia hurriedly got into uniform. French braiding her dark brown hair, she took a moment to examine her five-foot-seven-inch frame. Good enough, she decided as she put on her cover. Looking at the cigar, Celia thought about fingerprints. Cutting off the burning end, she put the cigar in a sandwich bag to take with her.

As she walked out the door, the phone rang. She let the machine get it, then answered it, the tape recording the conversation.

"Kelly." Celia impatiently glanced at her watch.

"This is Frank. I don't have much time. I've been working on something that—Hold on." There was silence.

"Frank?" Celia wondered what was happening. He had been fine this morning. "Frank, are you there?"

Finally he spoke, softening his tone. "Celia, if I don't come into work by noon today, go into my office and remove the files. I have a safe behind the Defense manuals on the bookcase. My combination is twenty-three right, six left, seventy-six right. I have to go."

"What's going on? Do you need me to come over? I can be there in ten minutes."

"No! I'll tell you about it later." He hung up.

"Frank?" The only reply she received was a dial tone. Celia hung up, wondering what it was about. He said he'd tell her later. She threw the answering machine tape in her briefcase since it recorded the combination and went into her garage.

Celia unlocked her '57 Studebaker. It was her prized possession. The car, in mint condition, had been a wedding gift from her late husband, Tom. He had bought it from the original owner and had it restored and painted black with gray leather interior. The only thing it lacked was a radio. She had been keeping an eye out for a radio from 1957 to have installed.

As Celia pulled out of her garage, in route to the Pentagon, she thought about the phone call from Frank Scott over the blue sedan, the smoldering cigar, or someone searching her house.

CHAPTER 2

Gwen Sherwood worked in the Pentagon as a civilian contractor and had been Commander Celia Kelly's secretary four years. Gwen's day had started out in high gear. Within five minutes of walking into the office, she received a file from Admiral Lloyd's office and a phone call from the CIA. Kelly was late for the first time in the last four years she had worked for her.

When a free moment presented itself, Gwen went to the coffee pot sitting on top of the corner table to get her first cup of morning coffee. Celia walked into the office.

"Good morning, Commander," Gwen said as she stirred cream in her coffee.

"Good morning, Gwen. Hard at work I see." Celia smiled.

"I try." Gwen looked at her watch. "You're late. Was there plenty of traffic this morning?"

"I had an unexpected visitor." Celia shrugged.

"Family in town?" Gwen pried further.

"Not exactly. What's on the agenda for today?" Celia changed the subject too quickly, Gwen thought, but she let it go for now.

"The admiral's secretary handed me this as I came through the door this morning." Gwen handed Celia the file.

"What is it?"

Gwen shrugged. "I don't know, but you have a meeting with the admiral at 1500 hours this afternoon. There is one other thing... rather odd."

"What's that?"

"A CIA agent called this morning." Gwen frowned.

"What did he want?"

"He didn't leave a message. The odd part was his voice. It was gravelly. I almost thought it was a prank."

"Did he say what his name was?"

"William Dixon. I'll ask around about him at break if you'd like. The next best thing to a spy is a group of secretaries on coffee break I always say."

"And I thought that was gossip. Did he leave a number?" Celia smiled.

"No."

"If it's important, I'm sure we'll be hearing from him again." In the back of Celia's mind she had to wonder if the call had something to do with her visitor. That aside, the file in her hand indicated she had plenty to think about for now.

"Oh, I stopped by the lab before I came to the office. If they call, put them through," Celia said.

Gwen raised an eyebrow, curious.

"Will do."

Celia was about to close her office door when she paused and added, "Gwen, would you see if Frank Scott is in yet?"

"Sure."

Celia closed the door and hung her cover on the brass coat rack in the corner. If Frank wasn't there, she'd get his files at noon. Setting the admiral's file on her desk, she sank into her chair. On the wall across from her desk hung a picture of her late husband, Tom Kelly, and his RIO, Sam Cooper, standing arm in arm in front of their F-14 Tomcat. Tom had been a solid, muscular five foot eleven with sandy hair and hazel eyes. Sam was six foot and a beanpole with fiery red hair. As a pilot, Tom was calm, cool and precise. As a man, Tom had a real inner strength that Celia could always depend on and now she missed.

Gwen's voice over the speaker phone interrupted her thoughts.

"Commander, the lab on line one."

"Thanks, Gwen," Celia said and pressed line one. "This is Commander Kelly."

"The prints belong to someone from a restricted government agency. We couldn't continue without the proper clearance," the lab tech said.

"CIA?" Celia asked.

"That's my first guess." The tech had drawn the same conclusion.

"Thanks, sit on it for now." Celia decided.

"Yes, ma'am."

Celia sighed. Police involvement was out of the question if the CIA was behind her morning. Celia moved on to the file Gwen gave her from Admiral Lloyd.

Opening the file, Celia began to read.

July 31, a shipment of AK-47s, M-16s, and AIM-92s (Stingers), was on its way to Tel Aviv, Israel. Upon going through the checkpoint on the border of Syria and Israel, the shipment was intercepted. A group of eight men, dressed from head to toe in black, jumped the border guards at 0100 hours and took the shipment at 0200 hours before it reached the border.

One guard traveling with the shipment escaped, hiding in the back of the truck and jumping out when the shipment reached its destination in the desert. He reported seeing a blond-haired American remove his mask. Two days after reporting this to the authorities, the guard found dead, his throat cut.

Rumors of an American blond man exist in a clinic just outside the Syrian Desert. The blond American picked up a Lebanese boy he uses as a gopher. A short-haul Dash 8 transport plane shot down by a Stinger over Syria, killing nine people, Army rangers, who were sent to locate the blond man.

Interesting, Celia thought, the group sells weapons for five years and now they use them? This wasn't the first time Celia had heard of this group. She was sure this was the same case Frank had been working on. Frank referred to the group as the Pact. That presented a bigger question, what was it doing on her desk?

Celia shook her head, feeling uneasy. Did this have something to do with Frank's unusual call this morning? Celia thought about her upcoming meeting with Admiral Lloyd. Did Frank ask the admiral to give her this file?

Celia opened the window for some air. Her window had a full view of the Pentagon's parking lot. As she turned to her desk, a blue streak caught her peripheral vision. Celia looked out just in time to see a blue sedan pulling out of the parking lot.

* * *

It was noon. Celia was still hoping to hear from Frank. She drummed her fingertips on her desk.

"Has Commander Scott called yet?" Celia asked Gwen over the intercom.

"No, he hasn't. His secretary said he never showed up. She sounded worried."

"Thanks, Gwen. I need to do one more thing, and then we'll go to lunch."

"I'll be ready," Gwen assured her.

Celia walked the hall to Frank Scott's office. His secretary was just leaving for lunch.

"Hello, Lacy," Celia said smiling.

"Hello, Commander. I'm sorry, but Commander Scott is still not here." Lacy returned the smile.

"No problem. He called me early this morning at home and asked me to get something for him if he couldn't make it in today. Do you mind?"

"I am so relieved someone has heard from him today! What do you need?" Lacy asked.

"He asked me to take care of it personally. Please, go to lunch. I can lock up behind me."

"Are you sure you don't need me to stay?"

"No, his instructions were clear. I'll be in and out." Celia assured her.

"Ok, I'll leave you to it." Lacy got her purse and walked to the elevator.

Celia waited until Lacy left before going into Frank's office. Celia locked the door behind her. Going over to the bookshelf, Celia spied the set of Defense manuals. Using gloves from her purse, she removed the manuals exposing the safe. Still using the napkin, she tried the combination Scott had given her earlier. It opened and Celia saw a note on top.

Celia, if you are reading this, I am in trouble or dead. They will come for the files–take them. What I am asking of you is both crucial and dangerous. I have put off involving you, my friend, for I have feared that your fate would be as Tom's had been. They will be after you now. Stop them. Be careful and trust no one! Frank.

She wasn't sure what bothered her more, the word dead or the reference to Tom. Celia gathered the files and closed the safe. Returning the Defense manuals, Celia left the office.

Celia put everything into her briefcase. She tried to call Frank's house once more before lunch, but there was no answer. Now Celia was officially worried.

* * *

PETE's was a small sandwich shop that had become a favorite place for Celia and Gwen. As Celia and Gwen sat at the usual table, Pete approached them with open arms. He had a pencil in one hand and a ticket book in the other.

"What will it be, ladies?" Pete's voice boomed. He gave them a big smile.

"What is your special today?" Gwen asked him.

Pete's face fell. Celia glanced back to her menu.

"I'm not falling for that." Pete crossed his arms and shook his head.

Celia smiled to herself.

"For what?" Gwen asked innocently.

"Every day you come in here and ask what the special is, and not once in three years have you ever ordered a special. You do this only to annoy me, and I am not falling for it!" Pete stood his ground.

"I think it's only fair to point out I am a paying customer," Gwen reminded him.

Pete took in a deep breath.

"Today's special is a hot turkey sandwich on white or wheat, served with mashed potatoes and gravy, piping hot peas, and a sesame seed roll. We have a club sandwich, with roast beef, turkey, and ham," Pete finished. He looked at Gwen in anticipation.

"I'll have the club sandwich, Pete," Celia interjected.

Pete wrote it on his pad, one eye still on Gwen.

"Now on that turkey sandwich, is the gravy on the sandwich or just the potatoes?" Gwen asked.

"Both," Pete said.

"I'll have a cup of coffee. And a cheeseburger," Gwen decided.

Pete took the order and walked away shaking his head. "I knew it," he muttered under his breath.

"Now why is the cheeseburger never on special?" Gwen asked Celia.

Celia smiled. "I don't know."

Gwen smiled back. "That's the trouble with the world today, nobody wants to get involved."

Pete served them in silence, his cheerful disposition cooled. After he went to tend his other customers, Gwen dug for information.

"So what really happened this morning?"

"What do you mean?" Celia taken off guard.

"I've worked for you long enough to know when something is up. Plus, you've never been late for work. So, what's up?" Gwen asked again.

"I think someone broke into my house this morning when I went running," Celia said.

"And?" Gwen was wide eyed.

"And nothing. I found nothing missing, just a couple of things out of place." Celia took a sip of her iced tea.

"No one goes through the trouble to break into a place without a reason." Gwen frowned. "Somebody must have wanted something."

"Like what?" Celia knew Gwen was right, but she refused to panic. "I have nothing of real value, except my car."

"What about you?"

"They waited until I was gone," Celia pointed out.

"As for your car, nobody wants that car but you. There is only one other person I've ever seen driving a Studebaker, and that was Fozzie in The Muppet Movie."

"Very funny. Fozzie was a puppet," Celia said, smiling.

"Exactly. I rest my case. And Fozzie is a Muppet." Gwen then got serious, "Maybe you should stay with me."

"No, thank you. I'll find out more if I stay put."

"But they might come back," Gwen reasoned.

"Then I'll know who it is," Celia said. She was careful not to mention Frank or the files though it was all she could think about.

"What do you know so far?" Gwen asked.

"I saw a blue sedan pulling away from my house when I returned from my run."

"Get a license?"

"No, I didn't." Celia glanced out of the window of PETE's and she couldn't believe her eyes. The blue sedan! And this time it wasn't driving away.

Before Gwen knew what was happening, Celia was on her feet and headed out the door.

"Where are you going?" Gwen ran after her.

Outside PETE's now, Celia stood directly behind the sedan. She saw a bald man sitting in the front smoking. This time, Celia looked at the license plate. The man noticed her in his rearview mirror. He tossed the cigar he was smoking out of the window. He started up the sedan and peeled out of his parking space, avoiding an oncoming car. Gwen was standing next to her now. The blue sedan rounded the corner with a squeal.

"I think that may have been my visitor," Celia said, looking at the cigar. Stamping it out, she picked up the cigar. It was the same brand as the one she found on her doorstep that morning.

"Is this a new habit I should know about?" Gwen quipped as Celia walked back into PETE's.

"About this visitor," Gwen said, still following her. "This isn't someone you invite over for coffee or dinner."

"Sometimes a visitor is a surprise guest. Someone you don't expect," Celia countered. "Pete, could you give me a doggy bag?"

"Sure." Pete handed her a bag. He watched as Celia put the cigar inside and wrote a license number on the outside of the bag.

"Don't ask," Gwen advised him.

He shrugged and went back into the kitchen.

"Doesn't it bother you that in less than an hour he knows we'll know who he is?" Gwen was getting nervous.

"We need to get back," Celia said, walking out the front door.

Gwen got their purses and paid the check. Taking the rest of her cheeseburger in hand, she took a bite as she attempted to catch up to Celia.

"See you tomorrow, Pete," Gwen called out as she left PETE's.

* * *

The blue sedan moved speedily through traffic for about seven blocks and came to a stop in a side alley. The driver sighed, his heart still pounding. She had walked right up to the car and got the license. He had put himself in a bad position. He knew better than that. He was now sure she had noticed him earlier that day, long before PETE's. Beads of sweat formed on his bald head.

CHAPTER 3

The phone call he had just received changed everything. In a few minutes, Admiral John Lloyd would be giving Commander Celia Kelly the biggest mission of her career. Kelly was as trustworthy as they come and she was one of the best intelligence officers he knew—that's why she worked for him. Lloyd was about to place her completely outside of her element.

A knock on the door interrupted his thoughts.

"Come in," Lloyd said, and in walked Commander Celia Kelly. She stood at attention.

"At ease, Commander, have a seat." Lloyd waved a hand at the chair in front of his desk.

Celia sat down. She noticed Lloyd's demeanor was different today.

"Did you read the file that Maggie took over to you this morning?"

"Yes, sir," Celia said.

"You will be working on this full time. I met with the president and the chairman of Joint Chiefs of Staff, General Turner, early this morning. It was agreed that a new unit would be created in order to stop this continuing threat. We want you in charge of that unit." Lloyd looked her in the eye, waiting for a response, like he had just given her a birthday present.

"I will do whatever is required of me, sir." Celia responded carefully.

"What is it, Commander?" Lloyd was disappointed. He had expected her to be happy with this rare opportunity, yet she appeared reserved.

"I believe, sir, this is the group Commander Scott has hunted since they were first discovered five years ago. I'm curious as to why a change in command." Although questioning the admiral was hardly in good taste, it was her job to leave no stone unturned. Besides, Frank Scott was her best friend. Celia hoped the admiral's response would shed light on Frank's mysterious disappearance and unusual phone call.

"We need a fresh approach. Try it from a different angle. The plan is to go into Syria and get the intelligence firsthand." Lloyd skirted the question completely.

Celia tried again.

"Sir, I would need to work with Commander Scott. He knows the history, and his firsthand knowledge of this group would be essential."

"I'm afraid that isn't possible, Commander. That was the original plan, but that is no longer an option. I'll see to it you get everything you need."

Celia looked Lloyd in the eye. Something was definitely wrong. What? "I'll need to at least speak to Commander Scott, sir."

"Commander Scott is not available," Lloyd said.

"Why not, sir?" Celia didn't back down.

"I suppose you'll be hearing it on the news tonight." Lloyd paused.

"Commander Scott committed suicide this morning. I just received the call. I hesitated to mention it out of respect to his family. I'm not sure they have been notified."

If you are reading this, I am in trouble or dead. The words of Frank's note ran through her head. Suicide? Celia didn't believe that.

"I'm sorry to put you in an awkward position, sir." Celia struggled to keep her voice even.

"You are being thorough. That is why I chose you to begin with," Lloyd said, feeling things were smoothed over enough to continue.

"So who else is a part of this unit?" Celia's head was spinning now as she forced herself to concentrate on what the admiral was saying. She regained her composure. At least she had Frank's files; she was that much ahead. Her heart was aching for her friend, and somehow or other she must finish what he started. He deserved that much.

"I have assigned Lieutenant Commander Georgie Round to your detail. Lt. Commander Round is a weapons expert and speaks five languages: Russian, Arabic, Kurdish, French, and German. You will also be working with five Navy SEALs. The SEAL team will consist of Lieutenant Commander James Elliot, the team leader. He will be in charge of field work. Hospital Corpsman Lieutenant Christopher Perry is the medic and speaks two Middle East languages, Arabic and Farsi. Master Chief Petty Officer Henry Jeffers is the team's automatic weapons man. Petty Officer First Class Electronics Technician Daniel Ryan is the newest member of the team. Last, but not least, is Ensign Jack McDonald. It is said he can hit anything, anywhere, any distance, anytime, from any angle. It is also said he will hit on any woman, anywhere, anytime, from any angle. Keep your eye on that one."

"I'll keep that in mind, sir," Celia said, hoping he had exaggerated the case.

"You will report to Naval Air Station Oceana the day after tomorrow at 0900."

"What about Gwen? May I bring her along to my new office?"

"Of course. I'll make the arrangements."

"Who is my CO?" Celia wondered.

"Admiral Able Walton. He's a good man, solid reputation. Someone you will like."

Celia was more worried about him liking her. Working with SEALs wasn't normally considered women's territory in the

Navy. Nonetheless, it was now her job. There was still Frank. She had to find out the truth about Frank.

There was a knock on the admiral's door. Into the room walked a tall, slim woman. She was five foot ten, and her tawny brown hair was shaped in a blunt cut just at the jaw line. Her features were plain, and she wore wire-framed glasses. Standing straight, shoulders back, she saluted.

"Lieutenant Commander Round, meet Commander Kelly." Lloyd introduced them.

"Pleasure to be working with you, ma'am," Lieutenant Commander Georgie Round said formally.

"It's nice to meet you." Celia smiled and offered her hand.

Georgie took it. Celia liked Georgie at once.

"Have you been briefed on the situation?" Celia asked.

"Yes, ma'am, I have."

Lloyd glanced from Celia to Georgie. Celia sensed he was nervous.

"Well, after reviewing the file, what are your initial thoughts, Commander?" Lloyd asked, sitting back down.

"I wonder why a group has been selling weapons to the highest bidder is now using them. Are they arms dealers or terrorists?" Celia asked.

Lloyd frowned. "I'm not sure I see your point."

"I think we are missing something. Either way, we have a lead. There aren't many blond Americans in charge of terrorist groups in the Middle East," Celia said.

"Finding that trail is your job now, Commander, so why don't you get to work," Lloyd said finally. He rose to his feet and smiled. "You are both dismissed."

"Yes, sir," Celia said.

"If you need anything, Commander, no matter what or where you are, give me a call," Lloyd said sincerely. "Good luck, Commander."

"Thank you, sir."

* * *

Celia led the way into her office, Georgie next to her. Gwen looked up from her desk as they walked. There was a very plain woman next to Commander Kelly.

"Gwen, meet Lieutenant Commander Georgie Round. May I call you Georgie?" Celia asked.

"Yes, ma'am."

"Georgie, this is Gwen Sherwood."

"It's nice to meet you, Georgie. Call me Gwen. So, what is happening?" Gwen asked Celia.

"I'll be heading up an Op. Georgie will be working with us."

"Anything else I need to know?" Gwen asked.

"How do you feel about moving to Virginia Beach, Virginia?" Celia asked.

Gwen raised an eyebrow. "We're being transferred? When?"

"Day after tomorrow. Gwen, join us in my office, please."

Once everyone was seated, Celia began with the early incident that day.

"First, have you received any word on our car from this morning?" Celia asked.

"Your visitor—that is, surprise guest? The car is CIA. As to who is using the car, we aren't privy to that information. Want to wager that it was that William Dixon?" Gwen smiled.

Celia shook her head. "I'm not willing to wager anything at this point."

"Is this something I should know about, ma'am?" Georgie asked.

Celia filled Georgie in, telling her of the intruder, the blue sedan, and the message Gwen took from William Dixon.

"For now, that will have to take a back seat until we are settled in Norfolk. Our top priority is the Op and its mission," Celia said.

"Lacy called and said Commander Scott committed suicide this morning," Gwen said thoughtfully.

"The admiral informed me." Celia bit her lip. Now was not the time to give in to the emotion of losing her friend. She had work to do.

"No way!" Gwen frowned. "I don't believe it."

Celia sighed. "Neither do I."

"Excuse me, ma'am, but who is Commander Scott?" Georgie asked.

"He was in charge of this mission before it was handed to us," Celia explained.

"You're kidding me!" Gwen exclaimed. "You have been handed his mission?"

Celia nodded.

"Interesting timing," Gwen commented under her breath.

Celia turned her chair and stared out the window. She knew her friend did not commit suicide. What happened? Where was he found? Celia suddenly felt like she could have stopped it. If only she had gone to his house instead of directly to work this morning. Suddenly she had a thought.

"Gwen, call Dr. Carol Hatcher."

"Who?" Gwen didn't recognize the name.

"The D.C. medical examiner. Tell her I want to see Frank's body before it's claimed by relatives."

"Are you sure you want to do that?" Gwen was concerned. Frank Scott was one of the commander's closest friends. This had to be hard for her.

"Positive."

"Would you like me to accompany you, ma'am?" Georgie asked.

"Yes, that could be helpful. Thank you, Georgie."

* * *

Celia arrived at the medical examiner's office too late. Dr. Carol Hatcher looked frustrated as she slammed a file on her desk. Georgie and Celia walked into the room.

"Commander Kelly?" Hatcher asked observing at the emblems on their white uniforms.

"Yes, I am Commander Kelly. I requested to see Commander Scott's body," Celia said, offering her hand.

"He's gone."

"Gone?" Celia repeated.

"Some people in suits came and took his remains, without my approval I might add. Said his family requested he is buried at home. My assistant, who is new, did the paperwork."

"As an officer, he could be buried in Arlington," Celia pointed out.

"The suits said because it was a suicide, the family wanted him buried at home. I never even looked at him." Hatcher shook her head.

"I don't think it was a suicide," Celia said.

"Why do you say that?" Dr. Hatcher looked at her curiously.

"I have my reasons. Do you think it was a suicide?"

"Like I said, I didn't get a chance to even look at the body let alone examine it." Hatcher sighed.

"If I can get you on the next plane to Idaho Falls, would you do the autopsy for me?" Celia asked.

"Why is this so important to you?"

"I have my doubts about suicide. I suspect his life was sacrificed in the line of duty, and he deserves a burial with honors in Arlington National Cemetery," Celia said firmly. "If I call ahead and arrange it with his family, will you agree to do the autopsy?"

"I guess I could swing it. Besides, now I'm curious."

"You need to be discreet, Doctor."

"I will be, Commander."

CHAPTER 4

Celia buttoned up her white uniform and after French braiding her hair, put on her cover. Ignoring the nervous feeling in the pit of her stomach, she took one last look in the mirror. Celia had mastered pushing uneasy feelings way to the back. She had it down to an art form.

The last two days were a whirlwind of changes. Celia had always been more uncomfortable with change than danger. Change occurred without warning, rolling over everything in its path. She was trained for danger. Celia, in an odd way, was looking forward to the challenge of the day in spite of everything. She was anxious for introductions to be over so she could get to the job she came to do. Meeting the team and gaining their trust was going to be the hard part. Celia's gaze in the mirror was broken when there was a knock on the door.

"Come in," Celia called out. Gwen and Georgie walked in, ready to go.

"We can take my car, ma'am," Georgie offered. They left the motel in Georgie's Volkswagen.

"So, how did everyone sleep last night?" Celia decided to make small talk.

"Acceptable, ma'am, though I do prefer a good firm cot," Georgie said honestly.

"I love sleeping in motels. I don't have to move a pile of clothes off the bed before I get into it, and they have room service," Gwen said, smiling.

Arriving at the Fleet Training Center, NAS Oceana Dam Neck Annex, Celia and Georgie removed their covers as they were led to the conference room. Celia took in a breath, the only sign that she was apprehensive. The team was seated at a conference table. Admiral Walton stood at the head of the table. Celia and Georgie stood at attention upon seeing Admiral Walton.

"At ease, ladies," Walton said as he looked at the three women.

"I'm Commander Celia Kelly and this is Lieutenant Commander Georgie Round and my secretary, Gwen Sherwood," Celia said. Her tone was even and direct.

Walton introduced the members of the team; Lieutenant Commander James Elliot, Ensign Jack McDonald, Master Chief Henry Jeffers, Petty Officer First Class Daniel Ryan, and finally First Lieutenant Christopher Perry. When the introductions were out of the way, Walton invited Celia to take the lead.

Celia walked to the front of the room and stood at the head of the table as Walton stepped aside. Walton sat back in a chair in the corner and silently watched. All eyes but McDonald's were on Kelly. Although McDonald was impressed by the commander's looks, his attention was drawn to her secretary. Gwen felt his hot gaze upon her. She glanced his way and tried to ignore him. Ensign Jack McDonald came from a large Italian family, and although his mother was always trying to fix him up with a nice Catholic Italian girl, McDonald had a thing for blondes.

"Have you been briefed on the job?" Celia asked.

Elliot spoke for the team.

"Yes, ma'am, we have."

"Then we can get started," Celia said, setting her briefcase on the table and opening it. From it she took five folders. "Georgie, please pass out the files."

As Georgie went around the table, McDonald still had his eye on Gwen.

"Hello," McDonald said to Gwen, flashing his most charming smile. He intently waited for a reply. Celia's eyes darted his direction. Giving him a look of warning, Celia hoped that would be the end of it.

Walton sat back, crossed his arms, and looked at his watch. Leave it to McDonald to break her in after only ninety seconds. He decided to stay silent and let the commander handle it. She'd have to be working with the boy. She might as well figure out how to control him now. Walton could always jump in if necessary.

"Your eyes tell me everything but where you are from," McDonald said as he leaned into Gwen.

Gwen glared. "My eyes? What does that even mean? You sure they aren't telling you where to go?" This time Celia gave Gwen a look of warning.

Celia didn't know who to reprimand first, McDonald or Gwen. She decided to take care of McDonald now and Gwen later.

"Ensign McDonald, either you are easily distracted or you are not impressed by the urgency of the job before us." Celia froze her gaze to his.

"You've hardly known me long enough, ma'am, to know what impresses me." McDonald tipped back in his chair and grinned. Now Admiral Walton glared at McDonald.

Celia narrowed her eyes and in an unyielding tone laid into him. "Ensign, as you go through life you may, or may not, have approximately ten seconds or less to impress a number of people, the least of them being me, although I may be your toughest. You impress me now by sticking to the matter at hand or you are out of here." Celia never took a breath. "Are we clear?" Her eyes never left his.

"Yes, ma'am," McDonald said, sitting his chair upright. The last woman to speak to him like that was his mother, and he hadn't enjoyed that much either.

The other men sat in silence. Walton was glad to see it. It was more than he expected from her. He didn't think she had it in her, but clearly she did. Elliot, the team leader, hoped this meant he was relieved of his usual babysitting duties where McDonald was concerned.

"Now if there are no other distractions, we will continue," Celia said. Her eyes scanned the faces around the table. No one moved.

Celia continued, "Commander Elliot, you are to be in charge of the field work, so I need your input right away. Go ahead and look over the maps while I explain the objective."

Elliot opened the file and began reading as she continued.

"To stop this group, we need to find out whom and where they are," Celia said. "The intelligence work done to date suggests that an American blond man, around six foot, is calling the shots. If we find him, we find the weapons."

"We will be looking for a ten-year-old Lebanese boy who has been seen often in the company of the blond American. It is believed that the boy stays with the blond man. The boy is a regular at a free clinic run by the Red Cross at the northern edge of the Syrian Desert, just outside of Homs, Syria. The map is page two. The last known location of the group's camp is in the desert southwest of Homs. According to the latest satellite pictures, several camps are in the region. They are similar in nature, and we haven't been able to pinpoint the one. They are presumably aware of the satellite and blend in other camps. The blond man moves the camp often and has eluded us so far. The boy is the key. If we find the boy, we find the blond man." Celia paused to let them take in what she had said.

"How did a ten-year-old boy get involved with a terrorist?" Jeffers wanted to know. Master Chief Jeffers was the only black man among them.

"The boy is an orphan. He's possibly a paid gopher or messenger in exchange for room, board, and pocket change," Celia explained. "It's a common practice there."

McDonald raised his hand.

"I have a question, who has done the intelligence work on this up until now? CIA?"

"A Commander Frank Scott," Celia replied. "He, too, was Naval Intelligence."

"Was?" McDonald was making sure he had heard right.

"He's dead." She quickly continued, "The mission will be in two phases. In phase one, five of us will be going over as volunteers to the Red Cross clinic. The boy goes there a couple of times a month."

"If we find the boy?" Perry asked.

"We will follow him back to the camp. We make sure the weapons are there and we have our blond man, then comes phase two. We destroy the camp."

"Who goes in phase one?" Elliot asked.

"In phase one Lt. Commander Round will be volunteering in the kitchen as a cook. Lieutenant Perry and I will be helping in the clinic since we have medical experience. Commander Elliot, and Master Chief Jeffers, the two of you will be general volunteers."

"What if neither the boy nor the blond man show up?" Ryan wanted to know.

"Based on the information we have, we believe we will at the very least locate the boy," Celia said. "We find him, we are certain to get a lead on the blonde man."

"I'm convinced," McDonald said under his breath with a shrug, this time receiving a dark look from Elliot.

"We go in clean, no weapons beyond a pocket knife. We go in as civilians, leave your military ID at home. We blend in and make sure nothing on our person to suggest we are anything more than volunteers. A word about the camp, you should be aware of the fact that facilities are primitive. It serves the region covering the Anti-Lebanon and Hermon mountain ranges to the desert. It's neutral territory. We will be living and working in tents, no running water. Though the first priority is the mission, keep in mind we are guests. We need to take good care of these people while we're there. We'll be traveling over on a supply plane we meet up with in Germany. The rest of the team will be brought over for phase two of the mission. Any questions?" Celia asked. There were none.

"Then you are dismissed. Lieutenant Perry, Master Chief Jeffers, and Commander Elliot, have your gear packed and ready by 0400 hours tomorrow."

The room started clearing out.

"You know, we still have some unfinished business," McDonald said to Gwen.

"I no business with you." Gwen faced him. Though she had to admit he was good looking, he was not that good looking!

"McDonald!" Elliot warned.

"Don't worry, I can be a perfect gentleman." McDonald flashed a smile.

"Jack," Elliot said sternly.

"Okay, I can be a gentleman," McDonald corrected with a shrug.

"I doubt that." Gwen turned and walked away.

"I think I'm growing on her," McDonald said to Elliot.

CHAPTER 5

The desert heat engulfed him as it pulsated off the sandy terrain. A blond man wiped sweat dripping from the nape of his neck with a T-shirt. He sat baking in the heat, dreaming of a tall glass of anything with ice in it. Another man emerged from the tent to where the blond man sat. He had long red hair pulled back in a ponytail. He was clean shaven, with a two-inch scar above his left eye.

"What's the word?" the man with the ponytail asked.

"Still waiting," the other replied.

"I hope this works." The man with the ponytail wiped sweat from his brow.

"It better! I'm not wasting four years of my life for nothing."

* * *

William Dixon puffed away on his cigar. He was sitting at his desk troubleshooting, and from where he sat now there was plenty of trouble to shoot. He rubbed his bald head. Dixon was an ex-Marine standing at five foot eleven. Despite the active moments of the job, his waistline continued to spread, his pants size climbing two sizes over the last two years. Looking back over the years, it was no surprise to anyone he ended up in the CIA. His military training qualified him, and his love for the sport of secrets intrigued him to stay. Though there were questionable encounters, he enjoyed the cat-and-mouse that existed in Central Intelligence.

A woman in her early fifties, with dishwater blonde hair graying at the temples, approached Dixon. A blue scarf with green and gray sprinkled around the edge was attractively arranged against a gray dress. She waved a folded piece of paper fanning her face.

"There you are!"

"Good morning, Aggie. Again?" Dixon looked up noticing the makeshift fan.

"Hot flash. This one really has you on edge. Where have you been?" Aggie observed.

"You know how it goes, duty calls."

"Yeah, and around here it never shuts up." Aggie's smile suddenly faded as she added, "I take it, it's not going well."

"You could say that." After a brief moment, he looked up and took another puff on his cigar. Five years of his life was tied up in this thing.

"What about the commander?" Aggie asked.

"She noticed me and was right on top of me before I knew what was happening." Dixon shook his head. "Got my license number and by now knows CIA was tailing her. She has enough clearance to put two and two together. She comes up with four and I come up with nothing."

"So tell me what's really bothering you," Aggie teased. She sat on the edge of his desk.

"What did you find out about Scott?" Dixon asked.

"Not much. The body was sent back to his family. They said it was suicide."

"What did the medical examiner say?"

"She's out of town... on vacation or something."

He circled a name on a file.

"You're taking this well," Aggie said. "You worked with Frank Scott for the last five years." She waited for a reaction.

"What do you want me to do about it? He was a nice guy, but shedding tears won't bring the guy back."

"What's this?" Aggie changed the subject, reading the name on the outside of the file.

Dixon got up from his desk. "Just a little late-night reading. I'm going home. See you tomorrow," he said, dismissing her question and closing the file. He put it with his things and left.

Aggie was curious. She made a mental note of the name, Lieutenant Tom Kelly, on the outside of the file. That was the first she had ever heard of him. She wondered who he was and if he was related to Commander Kelly.

* * *

After changing planes in Germany, the team got on a direct flight to Homs, Syria, courtesy of the Red Cross. Once on the plane, they were approached by a tall, lanky man with auburn hair and a thin face. He greeted them with an extended hand and a genuine, welcoming smile.

They settled in for the long flight. The last time Celia was overseas was in Europe. She had never been to the Middle East. The hours ticked by deliberately and Celia could not sleep. She read the mission file and Frank's files over and over. Finally, she felt the plane descend as they landed.

Celia stepped off the plane and had to catch her breath. The breeze that blew through her hair was hot, dry, heavy air. It was a shock after living in D.C.'s humid summers. She looked at the four people who stood beside her, and she felt as overwhelmed by them as she did the heat. Three days ago she hadn't known any of them. Today they were standing together in Homs, Syria.

CHAPTER 6

Dixon asked to see Commander Kelly but instead found himself sitting outside the office of Admiral John Lloyd, Chief of Naval Operations.

"You can go in now." Lloyd's secretary, Maggie, hung up the phone.

"Thank you."

Lloyd didn't bother getting up as Dixon entered.

"Good to see you again, Admiral." Dixon extended his right hand. Lloyd paused before accepting it.

"It's been a while," Lloyd said.

"Yes Admiral, it has."

"Sit down, Dixon, and tell me what's on your mind."

"The reason I am here is to see Commander Celia Kelly, but they showed me to your office instead."

"What does the CIA want with Commander Kelly?"

"I need to take that up with her," Dixon said.

"Come on, Dixon, what is this about?" Lloyd pressed.

"Like I said, I'll need to take that up with the commander."

"She no longer works in the Pentagon. If you or the CIA has a message for her, I'll see that she gets it."

"How can I reach her?"

"I'm not in the position to give out that information," Lloyd said firmly.

"Then I guess I'll be on my way." Dixon got up and turned to leave.

"Dixon, we've known each other long enough to be straight with each other. You're not still chasing old ghosts, are you?"

Dixon stopped and turned to face Lloyd again.

"I'm not in the position to give out that information." Dixon smiled, walking out the door.

Lloyd shook his head wondering if Dixon would end up being a problem.

* * *

Homs, Syria, was once considered one of the few large cities in the region and part of the plains outside what was known as the Tripoli-Homs Gap. The Tripoli-Homs Gap was one of three low passes across the hill from the Mediterranean Sea. War was boiling from within its country's borders. It was just a matter of time before it came to a head. Another reason why disappearing weapons in this county was bad news.

A beautiful African American woman approached the team. She appeared to be in charge. Turning to Celia and the team, she gave them a stunning smile.

"Hi, I'm Tammy Johnson. Welcome! I'm in charge of the volunteers and supplies. I can't tell you how glad I am to see reinforcements."

"I'm Celia."

"I'm Henry." Jeffers was the first to step forward and extend his hand. Tammy took it.

"It's nice to meet you," Tammy said, still smiling.

"How long have you been with the Red Cross?" Jeffers asked, realizing he was still holding her hand. He dropped it abruptly.

"Not long," Tammy said, interlocking her gaze with Jeffers.

"This is James, Georgie, and Chris," Celia said, interrupting Tammy and Jeffers moment.

"Great! There is a doctor among you, is that right?" Tammy asked.

"Yes, that's right. I am," Perry said.

"I'll be working the kitchen," Georgie said.

"Perfect! We have a bus waiting over there, just bring your things and follow me." Tammy led the way across the field to the bus.

"Is it just me, or am I hearing fireworks going off?" Perry whispered to Elliot, chuckling.

"What?" Jeffers asked, not entirely catching what Perry had said.

"Nothing." Perry smiled.

They got onto the bus, except for Jeffers, who helped Tammy with a few extra boxes. Watching him from the window of the bus, Elliot saw Jeffers was hanging on her every word. Elliot looked over at Perry, who was still grinning from ear to ear.

"Fireworks," Perry said.

"Do you think Chief Jeffers should invite her interest, ma'am?" Georgie asked Celia.

"What does that mean to *invite her interest*?" Perry inquired.

"I can see how this can lead to distraction, but Commander Elliot will take care of it," Celia said, smiling.

"Me?"

"You are in charge of field operations." Celia reminded him.

"Passing the buck, so typical among the brass in the Pentagon." Perry smiled.

"By the way, we'd better call each other by our first names. You'd better not be caught calling her ma'am," Elliot said to Georgie.

"He's right," Celia agreed.

Tammy got onto the bus with Jeffers right on her heels. Tammy sat behind the driver. Jeffers slipped in beside Tammy.

"So did you just meet each other on the plane?" Tammy's asked. Jeffers merely nodded. "We aren't far from the clinic. Relax and enjoy the ride."

Even through the dirty windows of the bus, you could see the picturesque beauty of the desert plains. Syria's summers were blistering. Tall yellow grasses reached toward the sun, gently waving in the sweltering breeze, framed by the deep blue sky.

The clinic came into sight over the horizon. It was a lone island in a sea of grass. The clinic consisted of two large tents set in the middle with twelve smaller tents around the region. The packed sand surrounding the tents replaced the grassy terrain that had once been. The bus stopped in front of the largest tent. They grabbed their gear and exited the bus. Georgie had only a backpack.

"My goodness, is that all you brought?" Tammy asked of Georgie's single backpack.

"A well-organized person needs little," Georgie said.

"I'm sure that's true." Tammy couldn't argue that.

"I do have a small box marked kitchen, if you come across it," Georgie said. That comment had Celia's attention. What box? Celia had looked over everything twice.

"You are organized! Bringing your own supplies. At the rate we get our supplies that was very wise. I'll get it for you." Tammy was impressed.

"I'll get it." Jeffers quickly followed.

"What a gentleman," Perry said under his breath.

"Georgie, what is in the box?" Celia asked, out of curiosity.

"Three cookbooks. Beginning to Cook, So You Want to Cook, and Everything You Always Wanted to Know About Cooking. I also brought the proper measuring cups and other essential utensils."

"You're kidding," Celia blinked her eyes and gave Georgie a blank look.

"I would never kid, ma'am."

"Why did you need cookbooks?" Celia asked.

"The explanation is a good one. You see, I can't cook," Georgie said.

"Why didn't you mention you couldn't cook?" Celia asked patiently.

Elliot looked on in disbelief and shook his head.

"No need to, ma'am. A soldier is ready for anything," Georgie replied seriously.

Celia rubbed her temples. Perry laughed aloud.

"Need aspirin, ma'am? I have a bottle in my backpack." Georgie opened her pack and handed her a bottle of aspirin.

"Stop calling her ma'am." Elliot looked around them to see if anyone was in hearing distance.

"How do you propose to get through the week? You are supposed to cook for the entire camp!" Celia felt on the verge of panic, though she tried to stay calm.

"I'm a fast learner and I practiced before we left," Georgie said with confidence.

"I will take that aspirin." Celia decided.

"You could get Jeffers to replace her. He seems to be cooking," Perry suggested.

* * *

Back in Virginia, Gwen found an apartment not far from the base. She instructed the movers to set her things in the living room. Grabbing her car keys, she got into her green Chevy Nova and drove back to the office. She went to work putting things in order. She had not been working long when the messenger came.

"This is for Commander Celia Kelly." The young man was possibly eighteen. He had on a baseball cap, blue jeans, and a T-shirt.

"Thanks, let me get you a tip," Gwen said as she accepted a large manila envelope. She took money from her purse. When she turned around, the young man was gone. She stepped outside the door. Looking both directions down the hall, she saw no sign of him. Strange, she thought. Shrugging it off, she returned the money to her purse and set the manila envelope on the Commander's desk.

CHAPTER 7

Celia and Georgie were both up before the alarm. Celia got little sleep. She had spent most of the night reading Frank's files. Getting into shorts and a white T-shirt, she pulled her hair back in a ponytail. Celia's adrenaline was pumping, and she felt wide awake despite the time change and her late-night reading.

"Georgie, if you have any trouble today, come find me," Celia said.

"The books are very detailed, ma'am. I'm sure it will go smoothly," Georgie said casually as she dressed in a matching canvas shirt and walking shorts.

Celia raised her eyebrow.

"You awake?" Perry's voice came from the other side of the tent door.

"Be right out." Celia and Georgie stepped out of the tent.

The temperature continued to rise with the sun on a typical summer day in Syria. They walked toward the mess tent. Children were running everywhere, dust flying behind their feet. Most of the children had only shorts on, their dark skin soaking up the sun. Women were running after children, yelling in Arabic. Celia had to step aside in order not to be bowled over by three little boys. Watching the boys go by, she couldn't help but wonder if the boy they were hoping to find was here running with his friends. Georgie broke off from Celia and Perry and went into the kitchen of the mess tent.

After a surprisingly well prepared breakfast, the chaos began. Celia entered the clinic unprepared for what she saw. There were lines of people everywhere. She thought she detected at least two languages as patients spoke to each other, waiting to be seen. With the realization people here needed help—their help—Celia suddenly felt overwhelmed. Her foremost thought was, Lord, help us!

She spotted Perry in the back. He had the longest line, so she made her way over to him. He stood over a small girl.

"Where does it hurt?" Perry asked the child in Arabic.

The girl pointed to her ear.

Perry looked inside her left ear, then her right. He noticed Celia.

"Hi," Perry said in English. "We need penicillin. It's just an old-fashioned ear infection."

"You got it," Celia said, looking for the vial. After finding it, she prepared the syringe and handed it to Perry.

Perry continued to speak to the girl asking about her family and pets. The girl didn't attend school, and she had a goat, Celia discovered listening to their conversation. As he proceeded to administer the medication, Perry realized he should have mentioned the pain of the needle, because the look in her eyes as they filled with tears was truly heartbreaking. Perry decided not to repeat that mistake with the other children. Perry and Celia washed their hands and put on new gloves, ready for the next patient.

"Piece of cake." Perry smiled.

Celia returned his smile.

It was when they got their next patient that reality set in. Perry's face fell. Celia looked at the middle-aged man. He was too weak to speak. The smell of the wound gave away the seriousness of his condition. His right leg had a gash from the top of the foot to three inches above the ankle. The bone was exposed. Celia began speaking to his wife in Lebanese Arabic, a colloquial dialect version of Arabic to try to get information regarding his injury. Celia discovered he had cut into his leg accidentally while cutting brush away with a sickle over two weeks ago. The skin had shrunken back from the bone.

Gangrene had set in from his ankle to just below his knee. The leg was clearly beyond saving.

"How is this man even alive?" Celia asked Perry under her breath.

"Good question."

Perry set to cleaning the wound. The man winced with horrible pain. Upon further examination, the prognosis went from bad to worse. It was then Tammy checked up on them.

"How's it going?" Tammy asked.

"We've got a big problem here. He needs this leg amputated as soon as possible." Perry's tone was grave.

"What do you need?" Tammy wondered.

"I don't think you understand the situation. I can't operate under these conditions. I need to get him to the closest hospital and qualified surgeon."

"You're not going to get this man to a hospital. He has no money. This is his hospital and you are his surgeon. Now, what do you need?" Tammy repeated.

"Do you have an operating room?" Perry asked.

"We are a clinic, not a hospital."

"I thought this was his hospital." Perry repeated her own words.

"Hold on." Tammy left them and went to the other side of the tent, returning with a folded partition. She set it up around the man. "Here's your operating room. What else do you need?" Tammy asked.

Perry looked at Celia, concern penetrating his eyes. He had no choice but to do it himself. Perry felt uneasy as the inevitable unfolded before him.

"I need a saw of some kind, anesthesia, something to cauterize the veins, antibiotic, and clean dressing," Perry said.

"If I can find it, you can have it," Tammy said cheerfully, and went to fulfill his requests.

"That doesn't sound very promising, does it?" Celia frowned.

"I'm not a surgeon. I'm a medic," Perry said to Celia.

"I don't think we have options. I've read your file. You have performed emergency surgery in the field." Celia tried to encourage him. "All you have to do is saw it off, right? Seal the veins and nerve endings. How hard could it be? You can do it. I'll be right here to help you, and I'll be praying, for both of you."

Perry looked into her eyes, taken off guard. Praying wasn't something he had done a lot of in his life. He couldn't even remember the last time he prayed.

"I guess it can't hurt," Perry said. "We'd better explain what's going on to his wife."

Celia informed his wife what Perry was about to do. His wife began to cry and Celia went on in detail, pointing out the procedure would save his life. In the meantime, Perry prepared for the surgery. Jeffers had brought the requested supplies over to him. Perry held up a vial.

"Is this it for anesthesia?" Perry hoped not.

"Yeah, Tammy was hoping that was enough. The anesthesia is on the list of back ordered supplies," Jeffers said.

"I wanted enough to put his whole body under, not just his big toe." Perry was officially panicked.

"What if you injected it just around the area you want to cut?" Jeffers asked.

"It's not enough. We have to cut through the nerves in the leg."

"I have an idea," Jeffers said.

"What is it?" Celia asked.

Without another word Jeffers walked up to the man and lifted the man's torso off the table. With one swift move he punched the man in the head. The man was out cold, limp and motionless. Jeffers gently laid him on the examination table.

Celia took in a breath. Perry promptly checked his vitals. The man's wife fainted, slouching in her chair.

"That should give you at least an hour or two. Need anything else?" Jeffers asked.

"No!" Perry and Celia said in unison.

Just before Perry made the first cut, Celia prayed silently, *Guide Lieutenant Perry's hands and help our patient pull through this, Lord.* The wave of fear that had plagued them while contemplating the task before them dissipated as they began to work.

Shaking his head at the saw he was given, Perry gave it to Celia to clean. Perry worked swiftly and diligently. With a surgical knife, he cut through the skin and muscle of the upper part of the thigh. After he sealed off the main veins with a cauterizing tool, Celia handed him the saw. He sawed through the bone. When the final bandage was applied, Perry only had one final concern—the man regaining consciousness. The man not only just lost a leg, but he possibly had a concussion as well. Perry didn't think he had ever been so glad to see anyone open their eyes.

Celia explained in detail how to care for the upper thigh that remained. The wife promised her they would visit the clinic faithfully until it was completely healed. Celia feared that promise was an empty one.

When they were gone, Perry watched Celia for several minutes, and then he asked, "What you said about praying... you really believe in God?"

"Yes."

"Why?"

"Because I know Him."

Perry frowned, confused, but continued before Celia could reply, "I suppose you believe that God saved that man's life."

"I believe God was with both of you. I prayed for him and I prayed for you as you operated. He saved both of you."

That response took him off guard. He didn't know what to say. Perry threw his gloves away to prepare for the next patient.

Meanwhile, on the other side of the same tent, Elliot was giving out the polio vaccination. Jeffers had joined him. Jeffers noticed most of the children had protruding ribs and skinny limbs. There was one little boy in particular who caught Jeffers eye. This boy appeared to know the ropes, and he was different from the other children. He looked healthy.

After watching him for the day, it became obvious the boy had been here more than once. He appeared familiar with the place and the people in it. The boy walked up to Elliot and Jeffers.

"What do you need?" Elliot asked the boy.

"Nothing."

"You speak English?" Jeffers asked him.

Nodding, the boy said, "You are new here."

"Yeah," Jeffers said.

"Do you need a vaccination?" Elliot asked him.

"Na, had plenty. Since you're new, if you need anything, you can ask me," he said, pointing to his chest. He turned to go on his way.

"Hey, kid," Jeffers called out. The boy turned and looked back at them.

"What's your name?"

"Just call me Boy; everyone does."

CHAPTER 8

Everyone assembled in the cafeteria of the mess tent. Going through the line, Celia observed everything looked good. She wasn't sure if that was because she had missed lunch or if it was because Georgie turned out to be a better cook than she thought.

"It looks like real food!" Tammy exclaimed.

That comment had everyone's attention.

"What do you usually eat?" Jeffers asked her.

"It usually looks bland."

"This does look good," Perry agreed. If the truth be known, he was too tired and hungry to care. They dished up and found a seat. The boy fixed a plate and sat with them.

"Getting around all right?" the boy asked Elliot and Jeffers.

"Yes, thank you," Elliot said, smiling.

"Good." The boy was the first to take a bite. Then Tammy began to eat.

Celia prayed silently over her food and decided to go for it.

"This is really good." Celia was pleasantly surprised.

Georgie approached the table.

"I'm glad it's acceptable. The meatloaf was very challenging. I went out on a limb. I decided to dice the onions instead of chop," Georgie said.

"It's great," Tammy said enthusiastically, then added with surprise, "We have onions?"

"We have no anesthesia, yet we have onions. That figures." Perry shrugged his shoulders and took another bite.

The boy was concentrating on his dinner. It was easy to see the boy was a streetwise kid who was used to taking care of himself. That was something Jeffers knew all about. He was three years old when he was left at the orphanage in Virginia Beach, Virginia. When he was seven, he slipped out the back gate a couple of times a week to explore the city. Usually he made it back inside the orphanage grounds before anyone noticed he was gone.

"How do you like your dinner, Boy?" Jeffers asked.

"Fine." The boy looked up at Jeffers.

"Where do you live?" Jeffers asked.

"In the desert," replied the boy.

"Your ma bring you?" Jeffers continued the conversation.

"Ma?" the boy asked.

"Mother," Jeffers defined.

"No mother or father. They are dead," he said, filling his mouth with another bite.

"Who takes care of you?"

The boy swallowed his potatoes before replying. "I take care of me."

"Do you live alone?"

"No." The boy shook his head. "I live with someone like him." He pointed to Elliot. That statement had everyone's attention.

"Like him?" Jeffers repeated. That sounded a strange thing to say.

"A man with yellow hair—like him," the boy said, pointing again to Elliot's blond hair.

* * *

The day began to cool as dusk fell in the desert. The blond man entered the tent where his friend with the red ponytail was sitting at a table. He was using needle-nosed pliers to place wires inside a pipe.

"When's the boy coming back?"

"A couple of days," the blond man replied.

"Did you get ahold of your father?"

"He said she was sent to Dam Neck, Virginia. They can keep a better eye on her there. What's that?" The blond man watched his friend work.

"What does it look like?" he said of the pipe bomb he was constructing.

"What are you going to do?" The blond man looked worried.

"Someone was planted at the clinic," replied his friend, as strands of his red hair fell in his face. "No loose ends, remember?"

* * *

The western horizons orange gently blended into warm colors, turning to scarlet as the sun bowed out of the desert sky. As the quiet of the evening gave way to brilliant colors, Celia was not only enjoying the view but the cooler air that came with the close of the day. She sat on a bench along the main tent, her mind on the files. Elliot was on the way back to his tent when he noticed her deep in thought.

"Mind if I sit?" Elliot asked.

"Please." Celia smiled, glad for the diversion.

They were quiet for a long time, enjoying the view. It was Elliot who spoke first.

"Heard you had an exciting day."

"The amputation?" Celia smiled. "If Chris Perry ever got tired of the teams, he might make a good doctor."

Elliot nodded in agreement and then changed the subject. "Why did you choose Naval Intelligence?" he asked her.

"I like puzzles."

"Why the Navy?"

"I grew up in the Navy. My father is a fighter pilot. Why did you become a SEAL?" Celia asked.

"I wanted something for my country. Not just put in time on a ship somewhere. I joined the Navy and then heard about the Teams, went for it and the rest is history. What do you do for fun?" He asked.

"I read, I play the violin, and I work. Work is fun for me."

"Me too... work I mean... I don't play an instrument," Elliot said.

There was an awkward silence. Both of them were searching for something to say.

"Henry looks to have taken a liking to the boy," Celia said.

"Just the boy?" Elliot laughed.

"Well, I can hardly blame him for being attracted to Tammy. She is attractive and very nice," Celia said.

"And you won't stand in the way of true love?" he asked.

"Little early to predict that."

"How did you meet your husband?" Elliot asked, his eyes moving to the wedding band on her left hand.

"We met through my father. My husband has been gone for four years now. He went MIA over the Mediterranean Sea," Celia said, looking at her watch, feeling uncomfortable with the new line of questioning. "I'm going to call it a night." She stood up and began to walk away.

"I'm sorry about your husband."

Celia stopped, "Me too. See you in the morning."

He watched her walk away into the evening dusk.

* * *

Back in her tent, Celia waited until Georgie was asleep to begin looking at Commander Frank Scott's files. When Celia was sure it was safe, she got out a small flashlight and began to read. The information was close to the background she had previously received on the Pact. As she read further, it became obvious how complicated the case was. Scott's notes continually referred to a father and son. They fed information on weapon drops or transfer sights to the group. The group used the information to intercept and steal the weapons... a father and son? Who? Celia thumbed through countless pages trying to isolate a name. She found nothing helpful. The note Scott had left her fell out onto her pillow. Again she read Frank's reference to Tom—and Frank's plea to her to stop them. Finally she laid the project to rest for the night. Her eyes were heavy. She'd look again tomorrow.

Guilt was starting to plague her. If only she had gone to Scott's house instead of work that morning. She drifted off to sleep thinking, I can do this. I can handle it. I can fix it. I have to. Then she prayed, Please help me, Lord...

* * *

It was the dead of night when suddenly Celia sat straight up in her cot, her heart pounding as she bolted up from a deep sleep. The argument just outside the tent was heated. It was a man and a woman. Quietly, she got off her cot, tiptoed to the door of the tent, and slipped out. The voices were louder now, coming directly from behind the tent. The moon stood alone in the desert's intense black sky. The night was dimly lit as the moon reflected off the desert sand. Celia listened for the voices to guide her. She proceeded carefully, making each movement a quiet one. Without warning, a hand came on Celia's shoulder and she caught her breath.

Turning to counter the move, Celia grabbed the wrist and was face to face with Georgie. Celia's heart was in her throat. She let go of Georgie's wrist and put her finger to her lips, motioning her to stay quiet. Both continued around the tent. As they got closer, they recognized Tammy's voice. There was something different about the man's voice. It was gravelly.

"How long have you been here?" He stopped abruptly, thinking he had heard something.

"Me? What are you doing here?" Tammy was both frustrated and confused.

Suddenly he turned and grabbed Tammy's arm, pulling her closer. "What do you know? Did you find it? You'd better level with me."

"Let go of me!"

Celia could see their shadows—Tammy had a lantern. When the man grabbed Tammy, Celia instinctively rounded the corner and came to Tammy's rescue. She pulled his arm off Tammy. Georgie pushed Tammy safely away from the man. The man turned to strike Celia, but he stopped abruptly. Instead, he pushed her to the ground and ran. Georgie took off after him. Tammy went to Celia's side and helped her stand.

"Are you okay?" Tammy asked her.

"Fine. Are you?" Celia asked.

"We... I... woke you, I'm sorry."

"Who was that guy?" Celia wanted to know.

"Old boyfriend... sort of," Tammy stammered.

Georgie returned.

"I lost him," she said, out of breath.

It occurred to Tammy that what they did was unusual. Why did they pull him away from her and then try to catch him? It was beyond bravery. It wasn't a normal reaction for your average person.

"Well, everything is fine now, so why don't we go back to bed," Tammy said.

"You were in bed, too?" Celia asked.

"Yes. Well, not yet." Tammy was caught off guard. "I was about to go to bed when he came."

"I hope you can work it out," Celia said.

"Thanks. Me too," Tammy said. "Good night."

"Good night."

They went back to their respective tents. Celia sat on her cot, no longer tired.

"I think he knew you," Georgie said.

"What?"

"He knew you. Did you see his face?" Georgie asked.

Celia thought aloud a moment. "No, I didn't recognize him."

"There wasn't anything familiar about him?" Georgie asked.

"No."

"There was something in you that he found familiar, ma'am. I'm sure of it."

"Maybe I just surprised him. It's not every day a man is attacked by two women."

Georgie looked at her watch. "It's 0300 hours. Tammy's hitting the sack late, ma'am."

"Yes. And how is it you run across an old boyfriend in the Syrian Desert? He asked her if she found it. There may be more to Tammy than it seems. Whether it has something to do with our case or not remains to be seen." Celia laid her head on the pillow.

"I'll keep an eye on her, ma'am," Georgie said.

CHAPTER 9

Water slowly dripped through the coffeemaker, filling the room with the brewed aroma as Gwen began her workday running background checks on the passengers on the two planes shot down in the Middle East. On the first plane, a CIA agent named Stan Geyser died. The rest of the passengers were civilians and nothing stood out.

Gwen found out that Geyser worked with CIA Agent William Dixon. According to Gwen's contact at Central Intelligence, Geyser had been enlisted by William Dixon to find a group they called the Pact. After a long string of dead ends, Dixon and Geyser began working with Commander Frank Scott. Gwen was told Stan Geyser was not a model agent.

After four hours at her desk, she was glad to see McDonald and Ryan walk into the office. The distraction was good timing.

"We were breaking for lunch and came by to see if you've heard anything," Ryan wondered.

"No, I haven't," Gwen said as she closed her file.

McDonald moved papers aside to sit on the desk. Gwen glared at him.

"Don't do that. I have everything organized."

"You call this organized?" McDonald looked around skeptically at the piles of papers and files on the floor.

"That's precisely what I call it."

McDonald stood there, studying Gwen.

"Is there something else, Ensign?" Gwen asked.

"Where do you want to go for lunch?" McDonald asked her as though they'd made previous arrangements.

"Are you buying?" Gwen stood.

Oh boy, McDonald thought, a trick question. If he says yes, she might consider it forward and refuse. If he says no, he's cheap. He took a chance.

"Of course!" He smiled.

"No thanks. I'm busy working," Gwen said and went back to what she was doing.

McDonald was taken aback and said, "Maybe next time."

"Unlikely," Gwen said without looking up.

McDonald raised his eyebrow, considering her rejection a challenge.

"We'll see."

"Nice try," Ryan said to McDonald under his breath as they left.

McDonald and Ryan had only been gone five minutes when the phone rang.

"Commander Kelly's office, may I help you?"

"Is the commander in?" a gravelly voice asked.

"Not at the moment, may I take a message?" Gwen recognized the voice at once. It was the same man who had called that morning in Washington, claiming to be William Dixon. There was silence, and then a dial tone. He hung up. The commander's visitor from Washington had followed her. Gwen decided she had enough of this guy, whoever he was. She dialed the front desk.

"Could you please send Ensign Jack McDonald to Commander Kelly's office before he leaves today?"

Gwen decided to look up more on Stan Geyser. Who knows? They might get lucky. By the time Gwen collected her faxes, she looked at her watch to see it was after 7:00 p.m. McDonald came into the office before she could read them.

"What's up?"

"I need a phone tap and tracer put on our phone line, but I want it done discreetly." Gwen whispered as if she was paranoid of being overheard.

"I'm starting to worry about you." He crossed his arms and leaned back, looking her with concern.

"Can you help me or not? You can be discreet can't you?"

"Of course. I'm a Navy SEAL, not the CIA."

"So you can't help me."

"Ryan can. What is this for?"

"The commander has been getting strange calls. I just wanted to narrow down the source."

"We can do it in the morning. If you need more than a phone tap, let me know."

"That'll do for now."

* * *

Gwen parked her green Chevy Nova in the parking garage of her new apartment complex. She stepped out of the car and grabbed her handbag. Locking the car, she went into the complex. Once in the building, she continued up two flights of dimly lit stairs to her apartment. The hall was dark.

After grasping for her doorknob, she then felt for the lock. Gwen dropped her keys twice before she finally managed to get the key into the lock while juggling groceries and finally opened the door. She stumbled inside, pushing boxes out of the way so she could reach the light switch. Turning on the light, she could see only the kitchen. Gwen paused and looked around. It was more of a mess than usual! It was then it occurred to her, she smelled smoke... cigar smoke.

"You've got your work cut out for you!" A man's voice came from behind her.

Gwen jumped back and let out a scream. The man stepped into the light. Bald, she guessed him to be around five foot eleven, give or take an inch. He looked tired, and he had worn his three-piece suit several hours too long. Taking a puff on his cigar, he let it out deliberately before he spoke.

"I didn't mean to startle you, Miss Sherwood. Allow me to introduce myself." He extended his hand. "I'm William Dixon."

Gwen was puzzled. His voice was not the voice that had been calling the commander. That voice was gravelly though she supposed whoever it was could have been trying to disguise it. She looked at his outstretched hand but did not accept it.

"If you didn't mean to startle me, then you shouldn't have broken into my apartment, which, by the way, is against the law. It would have been just as easy to tell me what you wanted when you called." Gwen waited for a reaction.

"When I called?" Dixon repeated as his eyebrows furrowed.

"Once in Washington and once today."

"I have never called you," Dixon said quietly. He puffed on his cigar.

Gwen nearly believed him.

"Are you aware of the dangers of secondhand smoke? I must insist you put out your cigar." Gwen held up a garbage can. Dixon put it in the garbage can. He noticed that though the apartment was a mess, her garbage can was empty.

"So what do you want?" Gwen asked.

"It is very important that I speak to your boss as soon as possible."

"Who do you think my boss is?"

Dixon wasn't sure why she asked, but he decided to play along and answered it. "Commander Celia Kelly."

"Just checking," Gwen said. "After the last couple of days, you never know. So are you CIA? The guy that called said he was William Dixon, CIA."

"Yes, I am. Just what did this guy sound like?" Dixon sounded concerned.

"He had a gravelly voice, sounded like you with a cold." Interesting, Gwen thought. He wanted to know what he sounded like, not what he wanted.

Dixon knew he had to exercise caution. As if he read her mind, Dixon asked, "What did he want?"

"I don't know. He always hung up right away. It didn't make much sense. Speaking of which why were you following the commander the other day?"

"I did follow her, and the reason for that I'll discuss with her. It only took her half a day to spot me." He shook his head.

"Did you break into her house in Washington?"

"Someone broke into her house?" Dixon repeated, raising his voice. "Why would I do that?"

"You broke into mine." Gwen pointed out.

Dixon shrugged. "You got me there, Miss Sherwood."

"Why did you break into my house if you wanted to talk to the commander?"

"I understood she was transferred to Norfolk, Virginia. I couldn't find a residence for her. I did find one for you. Where is she?" He rubbed his bald head and sat at the breakfast bar.

"Not here."

"Do you mean she's out of the country?"

"I mean, she's somewhere else," Gwen said.

Dixon shook his head. Just what he needed, a secretary with an attitude.

"Why don't you talk to me instead?"

"I'm afraid I need to speak directly to the commander. I want you to give her this message for me. When she returns, she can reach me here." He handed Gwen a letter-size envelope.

"You broke into my house to give her something you could have mailed?"

"Mail and phone calls can be traced." Dixon pointed out.

Gwen picked up on it. "Oh yeah, breaking and entering is much better!"

"Do you know when the commander will be back?"

Gwen shrugged her shoulders.

"Nice to have met you, Miss Sherwood."

"Interesting meeting you, Mr. Dixon. Next time, just use the front door."

"Be sure the commander gets my message."

"Oh, I will."

He left through the front door.

Gwen took note that Dixon said mail and phone calls can be traced. Maybe he wasn't the guy on the other end of the line. Who would claim to be a CIA Agent? It would have to be someone privy to the fact that Dixon was also CIA.

CHAPTER 10

Jeffers had acquired a shadow. The boy followed him everywhere. He helped Jeffers pass out supplies and carry boxes. Everything Jeffers did, the boy did. Jeffers saw himself in the boy: alone, hungry for someone to love him. In the last two days they had become more than fast companions, they had become fast friends.

"Why does everyone call you Boy?" Jeffers asked his new little buddy as they sat on the bench near the main tent. They were having a rare moment to sit. It had been a busy day, and they were both tired. The days were hot, by the middle of the day one's strength evaporated with the heat. Jeffers watched Boy as he waited for his answer. He noticed the boy's St. Christopher medallion was gone. Boy had given it to another boy to hold for luck as he received a shot earlier that morning. He had on one of the few things he owned, a pair of brown cotton shorts with an elastic waist. His coal-black hair was thick and in disarray. Swinging tough, calloused feet as he sat on the bench, the boy looked off into the distance as he answered Jeffers question.

"The man I stay with started calling me that, now everybody does."

"What is your real name?"

"My name is Ibrahim."

"Pleased to meet you, Ibrahim. I'm Henry." Jeffers extended his hand for a proper introduction. Ibrahim smiled and shook his hand.

"How do you know English?" Jeffers wondered.

"The orphanage in Beirut. A nun there taught many of us English. For extra money we could pass information to and from the military."

"What military?"

"Military with money. Americans pay the most. That's why the nuns taught us English. The orphanage needed money." Becoming a runner was commonplace in hostile environments. It was a way of life. The boy had many nights he dodged sniper fire to give someone a piece of paper or lead a guy across town. He had to do it. It meant he could have a couple of bucks and a full stomach when he went to sleep that night. He had a reputation as the best runner at the orphanage.

"Can you tell me the name of the man you stay with now?"

"No. Don't know it." Ibrahim shook his head.

"Why do you stay with him?"

"He gives me money."

"For what?"

"Things."

Jeffers felt he had pressed Ibrahim as far as he could. This boy was a professional. Too many questions and Jeffers took the risk of giving himself away. Suddenly Jeffers felt sad. He wished for this boy something he had yet to experience himself, to be a child.

It took Jeffers a minute to even realize Tammy was standing next to them. Deep in his thoughts, he had temporarily shut out the surrounding chaos.

"My goodness, the two of you look so serious." Tammy's hands were on her hips, her eyes searching Jeffers'.

"Just taking a break," Jeffers said.

"That's nice." Tammy's face relaxed, and she flashed a radiant smile.

"I guess it's time to get back to work," Jeffers said, standing. Ibrahim stood, awaiting Jeffers' next move.

"Boy, go ahead and get something to drink, then you can meet Henry in the supply tent," Tammy said. Looking up at Jeffers, Ibrahim waited for permission to go.

Jeffers nodded, letting him know it was okay. "I'll see you in a minute."

Ibrahim ran toward the direction of the tent that held the kitchen. Jeffers watched the boy run toward the tent.

"You are wonderful with him," Tammy said.

Jeffers turned his attention to Tammy. "He's a great kid."

"He thinks you're great, too." She smiled again. "So do I. I'm glad you're here. I don't think this clinic has ever run so efficiently this. It's like clockwork. You and this batch of volunteers are the best we have ever had. Did you undergo intensive volunteer training?"

"No." Jeffers supposed volunteers from the military could be different from civilian ones.

"Where are you from? Where did you grow up?" Tammy asked him.

"I grew up in an orphanage in Virginia Beach, Virginia." Jeffers' mind went back to the days he used to go to the docks and watch the Navy ships float out on the Atlantic until they disappeared into the horizon. Jeffers promised himself that someday he would be on one of those ships. The day he kept that promise, he was finally part of a family—the Navy. There were still times that it wasn't enough. Suddenly he found himself entertaining the thought that maybe when they went back home, Ibrahim could come back with him.

"So, you and the boy have something in common," Jeffers heard Tammy say through his thoughts.

"I guess so." Jeffers looked into her big brown eyes. He had to admit Tammy was special, too. Trying to gather enough courage to see if she wanted to take a walk later that night, he couldn't find the words. She was very pretty...

Jeffers wasn't sure what happened first, the movement of the ground beneath them or the rumbling thunder of the explosion. Billows of smoke came from the direction of the kitchen. Jeffers broke into a dead run for the mess tent. Ibrahim! He caught his breath upon seeing it. It had been leveled. Fire engulfed what was left. He noticed bodies. Dead or alive he did not know. They were lying on the ground just under the outer edge of the tent. Celia, Elliot, and Perry were close behind him.

"Ibrahim!" Jeffers yelled. It occurred to him that Georgie was in there as well. Grabbing a long stick that had been blown from the tent, he began moving debris.

"Georgie!" Celia called out. She began digging through debris, burning her fingers. Her adrenaline was so high she felt nothing. The fingertips on both hands began to bleed. Elliot stopped her.

"Stay here," he said, sternly. "I'll find Georgie."

Those who were in the mess tent grabbed buckets to fill with water from a nearby well to help put out the fire. Elliot, Perry, and Jeffers covered their hands, picked up support poles left from the tent, and tried to separate the smoldering tent from what was below it. Every free hand began to pitch in to help.

Tammy covered Celia's burned and bleeding finger tips. Tammy looked from Celia's fingers to the leveled tent. What happened?

Celia felt sick as she thought of Georgie. Her responsibility! God, please let her be okay. The prayer looked impossible; the fate of everyone inside that tent had been decided. Her mind was working to calculate what had happened. Was this a kitchen accident or did someone know they were here? Accident or not, Georgie was in there, maybe hurt or dead... and how many others? She felt a lump in her throat.

"I'd suggest getting ice on those fingers, but the kitchen blew up," said a voice Celia had come to know well. She turned to see Georgie alive and well. Thank you, God!

"I thought you..." Celia was so overcome she couldn't finish.

"I had to visit the latrine. I heard an explosion, so I came right back," Georgie said with abstract calmness.

Celia, relieved, turned her attention to Jeffers as she heard him calling out again. Who was Ibrahim?

Jeffers felt heat coming through the soles of his tennis shoes, but he continued to search. His stick hit something soft as he lifted up a burning piece of tent. It was a body, a man. Jeffers pulled him from the debris and laid him by Celia and Georgie. He went back and continued looking. Celia went to check the man's vitals, but Georgie intervened.

"Might I suggest we find bandages to cover those fingers, ma'am. Burns infect easily," Georgie advised.

Celia knew Georgie was right. Going into the clinic, Celia got what she need. She administered first aid to herself and painfully pulled large-size plastic gloves over thin dressings. Gathering the more supplies into a box, she ran back to the scene of the explosion. By the time she got back, two women and three men were lying on the ground. Celia joined Perry, who was now tending to their injuries. Perry stopped. What was wrong, Celia wondered? He pulled out a small piece of pipe from a thigh injury. Celia looked back at the leveled kitchen, then back at Perry. A pipe bomb did this?

Jeffers had noticed Georgie was safe. But Ibrahim hadn't appeared as Georgie had, and his hope of finding the boy alive was fading with each passing moment. As he lifted now-smoldering pieces of tent and boards, he realized he was in the back of the kitchen. Jeffers moved pots and pans, and then he noticed the icebox was face down on the dirt. Jeffers saw a small bare foot sticking out from underneath it. An empty tin cup lay next to the icebox.

Jeffers threw his pole and lifted the large icebox off a boy's body. There lay Ibrahim, still, his face broken by the pressure of the icebox on top of him. Jeffers scooped him up in his arms.

"It's okay now. I'm here. You're going to be all right." Jeffers was overcome with emotion as he cradled Ibrahim in his arms. He gently laid the motionless child on the ground.

"His name is Ibrahim. The icebox fell on him. Can you help him?" Jeffers spoke to Perry as if he were the boy's father.

"Henry, give me a hand over here," Elliot called out.

Jeffers hesitated.

"Go. I got this." Perry nodded his head, indicating Jeffers should go. Perry looked over the boy. No pulse and no breathing. Perry cleared the airway and prepared to do CPR. As he put his hand underneath his neck to tilt the head back, it was very wet and it had the feel of chips of wood. He pulled his hand back and realized it was blood, tissue, and bone. The base of his skull had been crushed by the fall. There was nothing he could do.

After it was over, they had four survivors and ten dead. Celia looked at the body bags with disbelief. A pipe bomb! It had been a very powerful one to create such tragedy. The trouble was, in this part of the world anyone could be responsible for it for any reason.

Elliot and Perry sat, looking at what was left. The kitchen was leveled to the ground. Elliot decided to get back up to look for clues when Perry showed Elliot evidence of a pipe bomb. Jeffers came over to see how Ibrahim was doing.

"Chris," Jeffers called. "Where is he? Is he in the clinic?"

Perry hung his head a moment and then looked Jeffers in the eye.

"Henry, I'm sorry. I couldn't save him," Perry said, his eyes full of sympathy.

"Where is he? Let me see him." Jeffers started looking for the boy. Perry grabbed his arm, stopping him.

"Henry, I'm sorry. He's gone," Perry said gently. Perry put his hand on Jeffers shoulder.

Jeffers stepped back from Perry and walked away, alone again.

CHAPTER 11

After respect was paid to the dead, it was time to bury them. Elliot and Perry then helped cover the grave which was one long, deep trench on the far side of the camp. An emergency supply truck came to replace the tent, food, and supplies lost. Jeffers helped unload it, keeping to himself.

"What do you think happened yesterday?" Perry asked Elliot as they shoveled.

"I don't know. It's been on my mind all night." Elliot wiped his brow and then continued shoveling to cover the last of the long grave.

"Do you think someone knew we were here?" Perry asked, quietly.

"Why a pipe bomb? Based on the injuries, it went off next to the propane tanks by the ovens. If they knew we were here why just try to kill Georgie? What about the rest of us?" Elliot shook his head. None of it made sense.

"We could be next."

"After we have our guard is up? I don't think so," Elliot said.

"That's assuming anyone has figured out who we are." Perry pointed out.

Elliot looked over at the supply truck that had just arrived. He watched Jeffers help unload it. Perry followed his gaze.

"He's in a world of hurt over that boy." Perry observed.

"He shouldn't have become emotionally involved," Elliot said evenly. "The worst is, we've got to find that camp without the boy."

"That's the worst of it?" Disgust dripped from Perry's voice, trying not to say something he'd regret.

"We are here for one reason and one reason only," Elliot reminded him.

"I know why we're here." Perry shook his head. Suddenly he had a thought. "What if the boy was the target?"

"Maybe. If they get rid of him, we have nothing." Elliot agreed it was a likely scenario.

Finished, Elliot picked up the shovels and walked to the supply truck to put the shovels away. He noticed Celia and Georgie talking across the field by the new mess tent that had been put up that morning.

Celia's fingertips were blistered and very sore, and it looked as though she no longer have fingerprints. She had to admit the irony of that as an intelligence officer. Celia held them up to ease the throbbing.

"What do you think happened yesterday, ma'am?" Georgie asked Celia.

"I think we have a few blanks to fill in."

"Maybe the group discovered we are here."

"Maybe, but I don't think so. On the other hand, the boy is gone. The Pact may have been just tying up loose ends. That still doesn't tell us if the group was aware of us or not."

Georgie became even more serious than usual. "How are we going to find the camp without the boy?"

"I've been giving that some thought. Maybe Tammy can help us there," Celia said.

"How can Tammy help?" Georgie was puzzled.

"If the boy has spent a large amount of time here, Tammy may know where he is staying."

"Her daily phone calls are interesting," Georgie said out of the blue.

"What daily phone calls?" Celia frowned.

"Every day at 1200 hours, she makes a phone call."

"From where?"

"There was a portable satellite phone in a box underneath the cabinet, behind the pots, toward the back, on the right-hand side." Georgie was matter of fact.

"It was hidden? Why didn't you mention this before now?" Celia raised her voice.

"I thought she was ordering something. Until the day before yesterday."

"The day before yesterday?"

"She was talking on the phone as usual, and then she became angry."

"What do you mean by 'angry'?" Celia asked.

"She was yelling at the person with whom she was speaking."

Celia took a deep breath. Ask a stupid question, Celia thought.

"What did she say?" Celia rephrased.

"She was not being able to talk on the phone and to meet her in the kitchen after lunch was over, tomorrow, which of course was yesterday."

Celia became thoughtful. "The bomb went off just after lunch. If she made a call every day at noon that pipe bomb might have been meant for Tammy."

"Possible," Georgie agreed.

"Let's find out."

Elliot met everyone at the supply truck. His five-o'clock shadow was sprinkled with dust. Dark circles surrounded his eyes, and his blonde hair was tousled. Jeffers and Perry looked as if the last twenty-four hours had taken their toll. Elliot wiped his hands on his blue jeans and then took off his T-shirt to wipe his face. Celia and Georgie found the guys and joined them at the truck.

"What's going on?" Elliot asked.

"I was just going to look into that," Celia said.

"What's the plan?" Perry asked.

"We're going to talk to Tammy. I think she may have a few answers for us." Celia decided.

"And compromise our position?" Elliot didn't like that at all.

"We may have been compromised." Celia pointed out. "Maybe it has something to do with us, maybe not, but it's time we find out."

"She's right." Perry agreed. "The less we know, the more of a target we are."

"Good luck. I haven't seen Tammy since yesterday. I have a few questions myself." Jeffers was angry.

"Why?" Celia wondered what Jeffers was upset with Tammy.

"She tells Ibrahim to go to the kitchen, the kitchen blows up, then she disappears," Jeffers said.

"Come to think of it, I haven't seen her since she wrapped my fingers yesterday," Celia said, more to herself than to them, as she recalled Tammy's tears.

"I went to talk to her after Ibrahim died, to tell her. I couldn't find her." Anger turned into hurt in Jeffers' voice.

"She might be getting more supplies out of Homs," Georgie said logically.

Perry pointed to the truck. "The supplies are here."

"With the boy gone, we need another way to find the camp," Celia said. "We have to wonder, did Tammy want to get rid of the boy or did someone want to get rid of Tammy?"

"Why would someone want to kill Tammy?" Elliot wanted to know.

Celia filled in the team on the brief confrontation Tammy with her so-called boyfriend. Then Celia filled them in on the phone call Georgie overheard.

"Why am I just hearing this now?" Now Elliot was angry. "If I'm supposed to be in charge of field operations, I should have been told this right after it happened."

"I had no solid reason to think it concerned our mission until now," Celia said. "But you are right. I should have come to you. It won't happen again."

Elliot took in a controlled breath.

"What are we waiting for? Let's talk to Tammy." Perry led the way.

They went together to Tammy's tent. Celia called out to Tammy, but there was no answer. She decided to go inside first. Celia was not prepared for what she saw. Not only was Tammy gone, but everything else was too. The tent was empty. The rest of them entered.

"Looks like the lady split," Perry said with a raised eyebrow.

"Not good." Celia frowned.

Jeffers voice was tight when he said, "Maybe she knew we needed the boy and got rid of him. Maybe she was involved in the bombing."

"We can't be sure without more information," Celia said. "For instance, why was she being threatened outside her tent and by whom? Things are not always as they appear."

"I think it's safe to say she knew something. Is there anything else we haven't been told?" Elliot shot back.

"Hey, relax, Boss. She's not the bad guy here," Perry defended the commander.

"We just need to think. There has got to be another way to locate that camp," Celia said.

Elliot glared at his feet. A twelve-year-old boy walked into the tent unannounced.

"Where is Tammy?" he asked in Arabic.

"She's gone," Celia replied in his language.

"Boy took this everywhere. I hold it when I got my shot. I take it back to his camp for him. I tell Tammy I take it," the young boy said.

"You know where his camp is?" Celia was hopeful.

The child nodded, yes he did.

"If you tell me where, I'll see that it gets there." As Celia talked, she pulled twenty American dollars from her pocket. His eyes became large, and a smile formed on his lips and he nodded yes.

"Can you tell me whereby drawing me a map in the sand?"

The boy nodded, yes he could.

The rest of them stood back, wondering what was being said, except for Georgie and Perry, who knew the language. As the young boy handed Celia something small wrapped in a brown cloth, she nodded a thank you. The boy drew a map in the sand. Celia handed the boy the money, and he left.

"What are they saying? What's happening?" Elliot demanded in a low whisper.

Perry smiled and crossed his arms. "We just found another way."

Celia opened the brown cloth, revealing a St. Christopher medallion. Maybe something he got while in the orphanage. She handed it to Jeffers.

"The boy said Ibrahim took this everywhere. I have a feeling the only friend who ever cared about him was you."

"What about his friend at the camp?" Jeffers asked, staring at the medallion.

"That was a business arrangement. It should go to someone who cared for him. Besides, no one will be left at the camp when we are through with it." Jeffers found himself accepting it, closing his large fingers over it, holding it tightly in his hand.

* * *

Tammy Johnson took the planned escape route up through Turkey and caught a plane to Germany until she received further orders. Tears fell as she thought of the boy...

and Henry. Could Henry forgive her? She didn't know if she could ever forgive herself.

CHAPTER 12

Celia called Gwen to verify the information given by Ibrahim's friend and requested the latest satellite photos of the area. Celia sent for McDonald, Ryan, and gear to complete the mission. The mission was set to happen in forty-eight hours.

* * *

Ryan and McDonald got off the plane and were met by the same bus that met Celia and the others earlier that week. Georgie was there to escort them to the clinic.

The afternoon was spent going over the plan. The goal was to descend on the camp, make sure the serial numbers matched the missing weapons, and if they did, destroy the weapons and the group that had them. If the serial numbers didn't match, they walked away.

"Join hands," Celia said, extending her own.

McDonald wondered if he had heard right.

"Join hands," Celia repeated in the tone of an order. Perry looked her in the eye and smiled.

Taking her hand in his own, he said, "I guess it couldn't hurt."

The others followed his example. Celia bowed her head and began to pray, "Heavenly Father, we ask that Your hand be on all of us tonight. Help us to execute good judgment that produces a safe, successful mission." Celia raised her head and added, "I'll see you in four hours."

Darkness engulfed the clinic as the endless night began. Celia watched as the team drove off into the darkness. For Celia and Georgie it meant a long wait as the team did their job. The team disappeared into the night.

Georgie and Celia packed up everything they brought. They continued on in a jeep to the rendezvous point. Celia and Georgie waited.

* * *

Riding in silence, the team soon became surrounded by large sand dunes. The satellite pictures showed a cluster of sand dunes a fourth of a mile from the camp. That meant they were nearly there. Elliot gave the signal to stop.

The jeep was parked behind a dune and Elliot gave the signal to fall out, finishing entry on foot. Everyone double-checked their gear... twice... then three times. They put on night vision goggles. After walking roughly eight minutes, the camp was in sight. There were four tents, all dark. Jeffers took the high ground. Jeffers settled in and set up a Haskins sniper rifle. Jeffers lay on the sand sighting in the scope. Taking a moment, he touched the St. Christopher medallion around his neck.

"This one's for you, Ibrahim," he whispered aloud. In position, Jeffers looked through the thermal scope to see if there was life in the tents. Every tent was occupied but one.

"Boss, two bodies in tent one, tent two clear, and tent three has two bodies," Jeffers said into his mic. "Tent four is clear inside, two guards outside of it." Jeffers kept a watchful eye in case of a change.

"Roger that," Elliot replied quietly.

McDonald and Ryan quietly took down the guards outside of tent four simultaneously, killing them with a swift maneuver to the neck. Going into the tent, Perry saw what they came for. There were boxes and more boxes. Upon further examination, he confirmed what the satellite photos had old them. M-16s, AK-47s, and AIM-92s (Stingers), all packaged and ready to go. The serial numbers matched. He videotaped the weapons.

"Jackpot!" Perry said into his mic.

"Get it ready," Elliot ordered.

Perry put down the video camera and began to set explosives.

"Take care of the others," Elliot ordered McDonald and Ryan. They silently went into the next tent and took out the bad guys.

Working in silence, it looked like it was going to go off without a hitch, until...

"Be advised, looks like you're going to have company," Jeffers said as he watched, through his thermal scope, a body rise from the bed in tent one and go out the front flap. "He's coming out tent one."

McDonald and Ryan froze next to a tent.

Elliot quickly made his way behind the first tent and stood off to the side of the flap. When the man emerged, Elliot came up from behind, placing his hand over the man's mouth. Elliot twisted his neck in one swift move. He heard it snap, and the head hung limp. Elliot quietly laid him on the ground, finishing what he had come to do. As soon as they the situation was contained, McDonald and Ryan set explosives at the entrances of each tent remaining. Perry got a video of the face of every deceased bad guys. They rolled the det cord to the detonating box. It was ready to go.

"Blow it!" Elliot ordered.

McDonald detonated the explosives. They all hit the ground until the debris settled. It was a full three minutes before the weapons from the last tent stopped detonating. Then quiet. It took seven minutes from start to finish. Perry videotaped bodies and what was left of the scene.

"What's wrong?" Elliot asked Perry as they drove into the night. Perry seem reserved.

"I didn't see a blond man," Perry said. "The serial numbers matched on the weapons but no blond man."

"The weapons are gone, so it's over. They are out of business." McDonald shrugged.

Little did they know... it had just begun.

CHAPTER 13

Celia was so glad to be back in the States and walking into her new office. It was good to see Gwen again. Gwen happily greeted them.

"How did it go in Syria?" Gwen asked Celia. Celia and Georgie hung up their caps and jackets.

"A very long story. How did things around here go?" Celia asked.

"Another long story. So who goes first?"

As Celia and Gwen exchanged pleasantries, Georgie walked over to Gwen's desk. She was preoccupied with something and soon she was on her hands and knees under Gwen's desk. Celia and Gwen exchanged a confused glance.

"Can I help you find something?" Gwen asked.

"I noticed suspicious wires from your phone, and it appears someone has tapped it." Georgie had it disconnected and in her hand within seconds.

"You unhooked it!" Gwen exclaimed.

"No need to thank me, I was glad to do it," Georgie said.

"It took Ryan over an hour to hook that up," Gwen said, placing her hands on her hips.

"You put in a phone tap?" Celia was shocked.

"It took him forty-five minutes too long," Georgie said.

"Why did you put in a phone tap?" Celia asked.

"It was his first one. McDonald had led me to believe Ryan had done it before," Gwen continued.

"I could instruct him sometime and cut his time down considerably," Georgie said.

"Maybe." Gwen nodded.

"Excuse me!" Celia raised her voice. Georgie and Gwen turned to Celia.

"Gwen, why did you think it necessary to tap the phone?" Celia asked again.

"The guy who called you in Washington called here, twice. At first I thought it was Dixon, but I'm not sure that it was. When I met Dixon, the voice was different. He didn't seem to know what I was talking about when I mentioned the calls," Gwen explained.

"You met Dixon?" Celia asked.

"When he broke into my apartment."

Celia frowned, wondering if she had heard right. "Dixon broke into your apartment?"

"He wanted to talk to you. He asked me to give you an envelope." Gwen dug through her purse, looking for the envelope. After having no luck, she dumped her purse out on the desk. Celia waited patiently as Gwen sifted through her things. There was a roll of duct tape, scissors, can opener, and a red permanent marker along with the usual in a woman's purse. Gwen happily held up her TV remote. "I was looking everywhere for this last week."

"Where's the envelope?" Celia asked, with a sigh of impatience.

"Perhaps this is it, ma'am," Georgie said, picking up an envelope off the floor.

"Yes, that's it," Gwen confirmed.

Celia opened the envelope. First she came across a note that read, Need to speak to you. Urgent! Call Langley and ask for Dixon. What she found next in the envelope was very strange. It was a newspaper clipping of Commander Scott's suicide.

It read-Early this morning Commander Franklin Scott, US Navy, 36, was found dead. Commander Scott was discovered by a neighbor. Commander Scott reportedly worked for the Pentagon in Naval Intelligence for the past seven years.

Declared a suicide by carbon monoxide poisoning, the Navy had no comment. His picture preceded the article. Celia looked at Frank Scott's picture and felt guilty once again.

"What is it, ma'am?" Georgie asked.

Celia gave the article to Georgie. Gwen read it over her shoulder.

"Why give you this?" Gwen asked.

"Maybe because he thinks the same thing I do."

"Questioning whether it was a suicide?"

"That's my guess," Celia said.

"Maybe he wanted to convince you that it was," Georgie said.

"I guess I'll give him a call and find out. Let's go into my office. I should check in with Carol Hatcher." Celia decided.

"The medical examiner?" Gwen asked.

"Yes. I asked her to do me a favor while I was gone." Celia led the way into her office. There were files on her desk, and the large manila envelope was hidden underneath them. After looking at a number, she dialed the Washington, D.C., medical examiner's office.

"D.C. medical examiner's office," a woman's voice said.

"May I speak to Dr. Hatcher? Tell her it's Commander Kelly."

"One moment please."

"This is Dr. Hatcher."

Celia put her on speaker phone. "Good morning, Doctor. This is Commander Kelly."

"Well, Commander Kelly. I was beginning to think you had forgotten about me."

"I was out of the country. I'm sorry I couldn't get back to you sooner. What can you tell me in regards to Commander Scott's death?"

"It's not good news I'm afraid."

"What did you find?"

"The family received his body in a jar," Carol said.

"Excuse me?"

"That's right. He was cremated by the time he got to Idaho."

"How?" Celia frowned.

"Your guess is as good as mine." Carol was surprised.

"There must be record of the cremation somewhere. If it wasn't in your morgue, and it wasn't in Idaho, then where was it done?" Celia was frustrated.

"I've tried everything. Bottom line, if you suspect foul play, the evidence is gone." Carol was clearly frustrated.

"Send a copy of your report to the naval base in Little Creek, Virginia," Celia said.

"Will do, Commander." With that, Dr. Hatcher said goodbye.

Celia hung up the phone.

"Since when did you start trying to solve murder cases?" Gwen asked, crossing her arms.

"Since my best friend became a victim and the mission that may have got him killed was handed to me."

"What's really going on here?" Gwen asked with a raised eyebrow.

"Does it have something to do with your midnight reading in Syria, ma'am?" Georgie asked. She had noticed Celia reading files until early hours of the morning.

"I tried not to wake you. I'm sorry," Celia said.

"No apology necessary, ma'am. Since you went to such extremes for privacy, I figured it was none of my business. If my asking is out of line, I'm the one who should apologize."

"I'm not ready to get into any of that right now," Celia said. "In the meantime, we have another problem. Lieutenant Elliot said the blond man wasn't at the camp."

"We did get the right camp, didn't we, ma'am?" Georgie asked.

"Yes, the serial numbers matched the weapons. It was the right place. But without the blond man..." Celia sat back in her chair and sighed.

"You don't think it's over, do you?" Gwen said, looking her in the eye.

"No. I don't."

"What do you want us to do, ma'am?" Georgie asked.

"Gwen, you and I will see what Mr. Dixon has to say. While we do that, Georgie, you go to Washington and talk to this neighbor who found Commander Scott's body."

* * *

It was late afternoon in Syria. The man with the red ponytail and the blond-haired man had spent a couple of nights in Damascus after their visit to the Red Cross clinic. On the way back, they drank water cooled by ice. The camp was just over the next dune. As they rounded the dune, the redheaded man saw tracks... jeep tracks. He stopped. He walked over where it had parked.

"What's wrong?" the blond man asked.

"Someone was here. Look, the footprints go in the direction of camp." Throwing back his ponytail, hands on hips.

"Maybe someone dropped off the kid," the other suggested.

"Then why all the footprints?"

The blond man frowned. The man with the red ponytail got back in his Rover, and they headed toward camp to find out. At first, it was as if they were lost. They usually saw the peaks of the tents of the camp by now. Neither of them spoke as they realized it was just no longer there. Stopping the Rover, they haltingly got out. Speechless, neither could believe what lay before them. There were pieces of bodies, tents, and weapons scattered everywhere. The weapons were gone. While they tried to take out a mere mole, their entire camp was being destroyed.

CHAPTER 14

Celia followed Gwen out and got into Gwen's Chevy Nova. They started for Gwen's apartment, where Gwen had set up the meeting with Dixon.

"Why your place?" Celia asked her.

"He knows how to get there and it's private. Tell me about Syria."

Celia filled Gwen in on Tammy and the boy and how whom Jeffers had become attached. She included the sad ending to the boy's life and Tammy's mysterious disappearance.

Gwen shook her head. "There is never a dull moment with you lately, and it's beginning to concern me. Our biggest worry used to be getting our paperwork out on time."

"The only one who has to get paperwork out on time is you," Celia pointed out.

"That's what I said. Now I have to keep track of you, too."

Mr. William Dixon was waiting outside the door of Gwen's apartment, puffing away at another cigar, watching them walk up the apartment steps.

"Mr. Dixon, going through the door this time?" Gwen asked flippantly. As an afterthought, she asked, "How did you get in the other night?"

"Why don't you introduce us and then we'll discuss your security-system," Dixon said, looking at Celia. Celia looked at the agent in his three-piece suit, cigar in hand.

"Agent William Dixon, meet Commander Celia Kelly."

Commander Kelly was very attractive. Dixon extended his hand and Celia accepted it. It was an uneasy moment. They weren't immediate friends, but they had an immediate rapport. It was in that same moment that Gwen had the door unlocked and invited them both inside the apartment. Looking around, Dixon observed not much had changed from his last visit.

Celia stepped over a box and then backed into the living room so Gwen could close her door. Gwen held up a garbage can and Dixon put out his cigar, letting it fall into the garbage can, empty except for the cigar he had put into it previously on his last visit.

"To answer your earlier security question, the window in the bedroom opens onto the fire escape," Dixon said.

"I have a fire escape? That's nice to know." Gwen took off her high heels. "Let's have a seat. Just move something."

Celia knew the routine. She had been to Gwen's place several times before in Washington, D.C. Tidiness was not Gwen's strong suit. Deciding to take the lead, Celia sat on an empty stool at the breakfast bar. Dixon moved a coat and sat next to her. Gwen leaned on the counter on the breakfast bar opposite of them.

Celia got right to the point. "I understand you want to talk to me, Mr. Dixon."

"Yes, ma'am, that's right." Dixon looked at Gwen, wondering if she planned on staying.

"Do you want to be alone?" Gwen asked.

"Please," Dixon said.

Gwen looked to Celia. It would be up to her.

"I'll call you when we are finished." Celia gave her ok.

"Okay, I'll be right behind that door." Gwen pointed to the bedroom. She walked to the bedroom and then turned again to Celia. "Are you sure?"

Celia smiled reassuringly. "I'll be fine." While Dixon watched Gwen leave, Celia put her hand into her purse and turned on a tape recorder. Then she took out a pen and small notepad to take notes.

"I'd prefer you didn't take notes."

"Okay," Celia replied, putting the pad and pen back into her purse.

"Speaking of notes, you got mine?" Dixon asked.

"I have someone looking into it, if you're referring to Commander Scott's suicide."

Dixon nodded. "That's the one."

"I find it hard to believe you followed me all over Washington just to give me a newspaper clipping. For one thing, the clipping did not exist at that time."

"No, you're right. There's more to it," Dixon said quietly.

Too quietly, Celia thought. She looked at this man, at least ten years her senior. His forehead wrinkled into a frown. "What can I do for you, Mr. Dixon?"

"What are you working on here in Norfolk?" Dixon asked her.

"I go where the Navy sends me. Can I ask you a question?"

"Sure."

"How long have you been with the CIA?"

"Ten years this next April. Before that I was in the Marines for nine years."

"What was your rank?"

"Major." He smiled and said, "Whatever you've been working on must be big. Admiral Lloyd refused to tell me."

"My work is classified, as I'm sure yours is, Mr. Dixon."

Dixon shook his head. "I suppose."

"Did you know a Stan Geyser that died in a plane crash a while back?" Celia asked.

Dixon was taken off guard. He was here to pump her for information and instead she was pumping him.

"How do you know Geyser?" Was it her imagination or did he sound worried?

"I don't. He was killed in a plane crash and he too belonged to the CIA. I was just wondering if he was a friend of yours."

"I know who he is, and he didn't have many friends. What friends he did have didn't include me."

"Why is that?" Celia asked.

"Stan Geyser wasn't the most moral individual you'd ever care to meet. He had a ruthless flare that the agency could use now and then. He was doing work for Frank Scott." So, he thought to himself, we are working on the same thing. Her mission was Dixon's case. Dixon and Scott had been on this for over four years, and the Pentagon most likely handed it to her two weeks ago. He knew he had the ball. Dixon gave her half a grin. "You got Scott's case. You're after the Pact."

"Why have you been following me?" Celia was tiring of the game. She never liked playing games, not even as a child.

Dixon knew he had to be careful. He needed her. "If you ever want to change your occupation, you should consider the CIA."

"So you're recruiting," Celia said, looking him in the eye.

"No, I'm fishing, Commander, just like you."

"Then we are at an impasse of sorts," Celia said, not breaking her cool gaze.

Dixon smiled. "I would say so."

"What do you know about Scott and Geyser?"

"Geyser took the side with the most money, as usual. For all the good it did him," Dixon said, shaking his head. "Scott had me watching Geyser to see where his loyalty lied."

"And?"

"Like I said, Geyser wasn't much of a guy, but he was a good agent."

"Better than you?"

Dixon ignored her question and continued. "They killed him and possibly Commander Scott. Not to mention...," He stopped.

"I'm listening." Celia waited.

"Let me give you some free advice, Commander. You need to be careful. Things aren't always as they appear."

"I appreciate your concern."

Dixon chuckled.

"I'm glad you find this so amusing." Celia paused and said, "You mentioned Stan Geyser was going where the money was. What money was that?"

Dixon paused a moment, too. "Look, we both know what we are talking about here, so why don't we cut to the chase?"

"I'm all for that." Celia nodded.

"A little over four years ago, the Pact hid $20 million in a plane hangar."

"Why?"

"That doesn't matter anymore because someone discovered it and took it, and that began the search for the money."

"Did Geyser take it?"

"He was one of the many desperate to find it," Dixon said.

"And you?"

"And me what?"

"You want the money too?"

"I want the truth."

"CAN I COME OUT NOW?" Gwen yelled from the bedroom.

"Come on out," Celia said.

Gwen walked out carefully, rubbing her knees. Celia figured she had been on her knees, with her ear to the door.

"It sounds to me like you two need to pool your information," Gwen said.

"You were listening?" Dixon asked her.

"Of course, what else was I going to do in there?" Gwen shrugged.

"Why did we even bother putting you in there?" he asked.

"It seemed to make you more comfortable," Gwen said.

Celia remained serious, pondering on what to do. Why did Dixon think she wanted the money? And did he say Geyser worked for Frank? If so, why did Frank have Dixon tail Geyser?

"Trust each other already! If either one of you were in danger from the other you'd be dead by now," Gwen said.

Dixon and Celia looked at each other.

"If we died in here, nobody would ever find the bodies," Dixon said sarcastically, looking around him.

Gwen glared at him. Celia smiled.

"Well, I need to get back to work. How can I reach you?" Celia asked Dixon.

He wrote a number and handed it to her. "Ask for Aggie. She'll put you through."

"Thank you. I guess you know how to reach me." Celia stood up, putting the number in her purse and turning off the tape recorder.

"Commander."

Celia looked Dixon in the eye.

"If you don't watch your back, you'll have an obituary printed up in the paper the way Scott did."

"I'll keep that in mind. One more thing, Mr. Dixon," Celia said thoughtfully.

"What's that?"

"When you began following me that day back in Washington that means you knew what I was getting into before I did."

"I just wanted to talk to you. I was unaware of your involvement at the time."

Celia held Dixon's eyes for a long time. She didn't believe him. Dixon hadn't actually said anything yet, except that the Pact was looking for $20 million. She got the feeling he was leaving out plenty.

CHAPTER 15

Elliot came into the office to see Gwen staring at the computer screen.

"Hello, Commander. How are you doing today?" Gwen smiled as she looked up from her work.

"I am fine, thank you. I was wondering if the commander available?"

"She is. I'll let her know you're here." Gwen picked up the phone and rang the commander's office. "Commander Elliot is here."

Celia's voice came back over the intercom, "Send him in."

Elliot noticed the commander had a massive pile of paperwork on her desk as he entered the room. "I came by to see if you wanted to rent a side of my duplex. I heard you were looking for a place and so if you want to look at it."

"I do." Celia looked at her watch. The day had gone by so fast. "Let me get a few things together."

"I'm not in any hurry. Take your time." Elliot sat in the chair in front of her desk. He watched her put the papers on her desk in the proper files. Pausing a moment, she then pulled out the manila envelope.

"What's this?" Celia wondered aloud, putting it on top of the pile in her briefcase.

Unannounced Gwen walked into Celia's office.

"Sorry to interrupt, but Georgie is on line two. She says it's important."

"Thanks, Gwen." Celia picked up the phone.

Elliot watched her as she responded to the conversation. Celia grabbed a yellow legal pad from her briefcase. She began taking notes as she continued listening.

"Really?" Celia asked Georgie. She listened. "Interesting. Well, bring back what you got and we'll see what we can come up with on this end. See you in the morning, Georgie." Celia hung up the receiver, quiet a moment.

"Something wrong?" Elliot asked.

"Just work," Celia said. She looked at Gwen, who was still standing there. "Call our friend we spoke with today and set something up for tomorrow."

"Will do. Have a nice evening, Commander, and you too, Lieutenant Commander," Gwen responded casually. With that she went back to her desk.

"Are you working on something else?" Elliot asked.

"Not anymore. It's time to go home. Ready?" She snapped her briefcase shut and got up from her desk. Gwen said goodbye, then dialed the phone. Elliot and Celia said nothing as they got on the elevator and walked out of the Fleet Training Center. He led the way to his blue jeep in the parking lot. He opened the passenger door for her. Elliot got behind the wheel and pulled out of the parking lot.

"Mind taking me to my car so I could follow you?" Celia asked.

"Sure, where is it?"

"Greg's Storage, do you know it? He was kind enough to allow me to leave my car in one of his storage units."

"I know Greg." Elliot took the next left. "Why did you put your car in a storage unit?"

"I thought it was safer there."

"What do you have, a Porsche or something?"

"It's a '57 Studebaker."

They drove through the gates of the ten-foot-high fence that surrounded the grounds. GREG'S STORAGE was printed across the door of the main office. Elliot got out and opened the door for Celia. They found the office locked.

"What's happening, James?"

Celia and Elliot turned to see Greg grinning from ear to ear. Upon seeing Celia, Greg became all business. She had a sobering effect on everybody, Elliot thought to himself with a smile.

"Not much. Just giving Commander Kelly a ride to her car," Elliot said.

Greg's eyes were fixed on Celia, as if Elliot was no longer there. Greg's face became panicked.

"Commander, I want you to know this has never happened before," Greg began.

Celia's heart sank. "What's happened?" she asked evenly. Don't panic, she said to herself. It is just a car. But it was her car.

"Someone broke into a storage unit storing your things," Greg said apologetically. "It was very unusual. Someone knocked out my security guard, cut the wires to the alarms, and then broke into only one unit. I called the police to investigate. The police couldn't find any fingerprints or anything." Greg took off his baseball cap and scratched his head. His long, blond curls just touched his shoulders. His tinted glasses hid his eyes.

"Was there any damage?" Celia asked, still worried about her car.

"I don't know. The boxes were opened and things scattered. You'll need to look things over so I can report any losses to my insurance company for you."

"Boxes? Then my car is all right?" Celia repeated. It must have been the storage unit holding her furniture and personal items from her house.

"Yes, ma'am. They didn't try to go into that unit." Greg was taken aback by her question—and her response. Celia was obviously relieved.

"Well then, let's take a look," she said calmly.

"This way."

Greg led the way. After everything else over the last three weeks, Celia didn't have to wonder whether or not it was a coincidence. She knew that it wasn't. At least her car was okay. Greg pushed the door that no longer closed completely open. Celia walked in first. It appeared every box had been opened, emptied, and the items thrown back in each box. She spent a few minutes looking things over though it was nearly impossible to know for sure until she could look at it thoroughly.

"How is your security guard?" Celia asked Greg, ashamed for not asking sooner.

"He's fine, thanks. Had a nasty bump on the head though."

"Well, I'm glad to hear he's okay. That's the most important thing. All of this can be replaced." If this did have something to do with what she was working on, at least the security guard was not added to the growing list of casualties.

Greg was surprised she was taking this so well. He was afraid of everything from tears to a lawsuit.

"Is anything missing?" Elliot asked her.

"I'm not sure. Not that I can see at a glance."

"Again, ma'am, I am very sorry," Greg repeated.

"I don't hold you responsible for this. You had the proper security. You said you reported it to the police?" Celia asked.

He nodded. "That's right. They didn't find a thing."

"That doesn't surprise me," Celia said.

"What is that supposed to mean?" Elliot asked, crossing his arms.

"It doesn't matter. What's done is done," Celia said.

Elliot watched her, puzzled.

"I will get my car for now," Celia said. "I'm looking at a place tonight, and if it works out, I will send for the rest of my things."

"No hurry. Follow me." Greg took them to the next storage unit.

Elliot watched Celia's face light up when she saw her Studebaker—the same way his last girlfriend did every time she saw her cocker spaniel. Celia walked to the driver's side and opened the door. She set her briefcase on the opposite seat. Both Elliot and Greg stepped back as she backed her '57 Studebaker out of the storage unit.

"She's kind of different," Greg said under his breath to Elliot.

Elliot sighed. "You have no idea."

Celia parked in beside of the men and rolled down the window. "Can I settle with you after I get the rest of my things?"

"There's no charge, ma'am." Greg was still feeling guilty.

"We'll settle up later." Celia insisted as she took a pair of sunglasses from her glove box. "Lead the way, Commander."

Celia followed Elliot along the Virginia Beach coastline until he pulled off and parked in front of a duplex. Its deck faced the Atlantic Ocean where the grass ended and the sand sloped into a gradual descent meeting the water. The view was breathtaking. Celia knew she didn't have to see the inside of the duplex to know she could easily call this place home. Elliot parked in the driveway in front of the duplex. Celia parked beside him.

Celia got out of her car and walked toward the beach, leaving Elliot by his jeep. Stopping midway, she watched the waters advance then retreat. The cares of the day disappeared along with the receding waters.

"This is why I bought the place. Do you want to take a look inside?" Elliot asked, now beside her.

Together they walked back up to the duplex and Elliot gave her the inside tour. As Celia walked in, she saw the dining room and kitchen to the left, with the Living Room to the right. The one bedroom was off the Living Room, with the bathroom centered between the bedroom and back of the kitchen. It was perfect.

"What do you charge?"

"Nine hundred and fifty a month. Two months in advance and a hundred-dollar deposit."

"I'll take it." Celia went out to her car, returning with her briefcase. She wrote out a check.

"Thanks." Elliot folded the check and put it in the breast pocket of his uniform, making the transaction complete.

"Thank you. I think I'm going to like it here," Celia said sincerely.

"If you want, I can crash on my couch so you can have my room–"

Celia interrupted him. "Not necessary, I have a sleeping bag in the car. I've got what I need, thank you."

"I have the keys at my place," Elliot said.

Celia followed him to his side of the duplex. Elliot disappeared into another room and Celia observed his decor was simple, mostly white and black. The kitchen floor even had black-and-white tiles. The blinds were white, no curtains. She hadn't guessed him for modern. Celia took the liberty to look at pictures on a wall in the living room. There was one of him with Admiral Walton and the rest of the team. There were several others of the team. As she scanned the wall, she spotted Admiral Lloyd. Lloyd was standing in the middle of Walton and Elliot.

Celia continued to look around, noticing a black leather couch surrounded by black and white pillows. Everything was very neat and orderly, unlike most bachelors. Then it dawned on Celia, Gwen was the only person she knew that fit her idea of a bachelor.

"Here are the keys," Elliot said, handing them to Celia and interrupting her thoughts.

"I better go. I have work to do before tomorrow," she said.

"Do you want something to eat?"

"No thanks, I'll see you tomorrow."

Celia emptied out her car. She brought in two garment bags and a box with soap, shampoo, and towels from her bathroom in Washington. There were miscellaneous items she had thrown into the car at the last moment instead of boxing them for the movers. Celia even found bottled water and protein bars, which then became her dinner.

Now settled inside her new home, Celia laid out her sleeping bag and played back the tape of the conversation between her and Dixon while she ate her protein bars. She listened to it a couple of times, less convinced than ever of his sincerity. Dixon had been at her house that morning in D.C., then later at PETE's. He had to know something concerning the mission before she had known herself, even if he said he hadn't. He seemed to know of the Pact. He came right out and said Geyser was directly involved and implied Scott was murdered. Where did William Dixon come from, and how did he fit into this?

Frank Scott. Celia thought back to their friendship, the years she had known him before and after Tom's death. Did Tom know of the Pact?

CHAPTER 16

Jeffers finished up his dishes from dinner. He was wiping the counter when the phone rang.

"Hello," Jeffers answered.

He thought he heard someone take a deep breath.

"Hello?" Jeffers repeated.

Click. Dial tone. Jeffers hung up the phone, puzzled. It must have been the wrong number.

Jeffers looked at the St. Christopher medallion lying on his counter. He picked it up, holding it gently. Jeffers had seen something special in the boy, or maybe it was just that he saw himself. The boy's death was such a waste. He was going to turn in for the night when there was a knock on the door.

Jeffers opened it to find Gwen Sherwood standing there.

"Hi," Gwen said. "You're the commander's secretary, right?" he asked, wondering what she was doing here.

"That's right. I discovered we are neighbors. I saw you come in from the laundry room as I pulled into the garage. That's when I thought I should come over and borrow a cup of sugar or something to say hello." She smiled. "Call me Gwen."

"I'm Henry. Come in." Jeffers stood aside and Gwen walked inside. "You need a cup of sugar?"

"No. I'm out of tea, and I don't cook."

Jeffers smiled at that. Suddenly he realized it had been several days since he had smiled.

"Do you want to have a seat?" Jeffers moved a uniform top from the back of the couch. He hung it in the hall closet and joined Gwen.

"Thanks."

"I have tea, if you want a cup," he offered.

"Sounds good."

Jeffers fixed them both a cup. He sat next to her after serving her. He set a bowl of sugar on the coffee table and she proceeded to put in four teaspoons and stir. Jeffers watched, wondering is she going to drink it? She did.

"So, do we live in a nice neighborhood?" Gwen asked, after sipping her tea.

"I guess. I'm not around much."

"Where are you from?" Gwen was curious.

"Norfolk, I grew up in an orphanage here." His eyes flashed with sadness that he blinked away. It made him think of Ibrahim again.

"I was an only child. My father is a lawyer and my mother is a florist. Mom has her own flower shop. I grew up right outside Boston. We had a maid and a cook. The maid was okay, but our cook didn't like me."

"Why?"

"She said I was always causing trouble. I remember one day she was really upset. It was my sixteenth birthday, and I wanted to help her get ready for my party. I turned the oven up so the cake to finish sooner. Then I chilled the soda, trying to help, too." Gwen shook her head as she remembered.

"Why did she get mad when you chilled the pop?"

"I put it in the freezer."

Jeffers chuckled.

"I took it out of the freezer that night and put it on the dining room table. It was going well until it started warming up. You should have seen it! Thirty cans of soda blowing up one by one spraying everywhere! Twelve screaming girls running for cover." Gwen paused a moment. "It was the best birthday I ever had." She was smiling now. "To make a long story short, I was a spoiled brat who got everything I wanted. I didn't turn out too bad all considered. Although, my mother often points out that I'm still single."

"Sounds like you had fun."

"Sometimes, but mostly it was lonely."

Jeffers thought how two people could come from such different backgrounds yet have the same memory of their childhood. Loneliness described his childhood in a nutshell.

"I must confess, the commander explained what happened in Syria. I'm sorry. If you need to talk, I can talk for hours."

"Thanks." Jeffers nodded.

"Sure. I kept you up long enough. I'd better go. I'll see you around here if not on the base. Thanks for the tea." Gwen got up and put her empty cup on the coffee table.

"Welcome to the neighborhood," Jeffers said. Gwen left and Jeffers found himself feeling better.

Gwen went back to her apartment thinking of how clean and orderly Henry's place was. Maybe the Navy's basic training was what she needed… or her parent's maid.

* * *

Celia thought back to Georgie's call as she opened her briefcase. Georgie reported that Frank Scott's neighbor saw two men dressed in three piece suits go into his house at 0700 hours. That was an hour after their race in Potomac Park and five hours before the neighbor saw the body removed. The neighbor hadn't found the body as reported in the newspaper.

Stumped, Celia decided to move on to something else for a while and took out the manila envelope she had found on her desk. Opening the envelope, she pulled out a picture. Looking back at her were Tom and herself. It was a picture taken on her wedding day. Why send her a picture from her own wedding? She was standing arm in arm with Tom in front of the gift table. Standing next to them were Sam and Tara Cooper. Who sent it? Looking over the envelope, she found nothing. She looked at the picture again. It had been blown up into an eight by ten. Celia turned the picture over to other side. What she saw was both puzzling and disturbing. In large black letters, it read, TILL DEATH DO US PART. It made her think of the note Scott left her... *for I fear your fate would be as Tom's had been.*

CHAPTER 17

Tammy Johnson woke up upright on the park bench. She needed to check in with her handler. After spending the night in a park across the street, she was cold and tired. She couldn't go home. It was too dangerous. Tammy was relieved when she saw him park his car and enter the building.

* * *

Celia got up before dawn and ran on the beach. She showered and left for the base just as a light came on in Elliot's kitchen. Her mind kept replaying the events of the last couple of weeks. That's when she decided to look up Tom's last mission.

After stopping for a coffee and a blueberry scone, Celia arrived at the office before anyone else. She went to work, trying to bring up Tom's records. Both Kelly's and Cooper's files were inaccessible. Why? She punched in her security access code again, but it was denied.

Celia still wasn't sure about Dixon, but he might be willing to help her get information if she could convince him it could benefit both of them.

Gwen and Georgie came into the office at the same time. Celia was making the first pot of coffee for the day.

"How long have you been here?" Gwen asked, set down her purse.

"A couple of hours. I need William Dixon's number," Celia said, got right to business.

"Good morning to you as well. The number is in my purse," Gwen said.

"Let's go into my office, and bring the number, please."

"Yes, ma'am," Georgie said.

"First, Georgie, give us a full report on yesterday," Celia said as she got out her notes.

"Yes, ma'am. I arrived in Washington, D.C. at 1300 hours. I pulled in front of the home of Ted Silver no more than twenty-five minutes later. Mr. Silver claimed he saw two men in black three piece suits enter the home of Commander Frank Scott at 0700 hours. He doesn't know when they left."

"Did he have more of a description than that?"

"Mr. Silver said, and I quote, '... all government thugs look the same from the back,'" Georgie stated matter-of-factly.

"Anything else?"

"No, ma'am."

"There was no coroner's van or police vehicles there?" Celia asked as she picked up the manila envelope.

"No, ma'am, he saw the men arrive but did not know when they left."

"So, what was in that envelope?" Gwen asked. Gwen had noticed the large manila envelope on top of Celia's briefcase.

"Who delivered this?" Celia asked

"A kid, teenager I think. He was in sneakers, blue jeans, T-shirt, and baseball cap. I assumed a delivery boy." Gwen frowned.

"Here, both of you take a look at this." Celia handed the picture to Gwen first.

Gwen looked it over and then handed it to Georgie.

"Now look on the back," Celia said. Georgie and Gwen looked at the message, then at each other.

"What does that mean?" Gwen asked.

"I wish I knew." Celia sat back in her chair, sighing.

TILL DEATH DO US PART, Georgie read it again to herself. She looked over the picture closely.

"Ma'am, the quality of this picture suggests it was made from a negative—or at the very least, a high-quality photograph," Georgie said. "It isn't grainy. Do you have negatives in the wedding album you found on your floor?"

"I don't think so. Just pictures. If the picture was taken from my album, it would have been a three by five, and my photos were of average quality. I had a friend take them. She used a digital camera. We did have disposable cameras on every table. The disposable cameras had negatives." Celia was still trying to make sense of it.

"So when your house was broken into, someone took a wedding picture, had it enlarged, wrote on the back of it, and sent it to you," Gwen concluded.

"Based on the quality this came from a negative. Either the negatives taken, or the picture was sent by someone who was there," Georgie said.

"We need more information," Celia said. "Take the picture to the lab. See if they can determine for sure if it's negative or print—and if any fingerprints on it besides ours." Before she handed it off to Gwen, she took a picture of it on her phone.

"What now?" Gwen asked.

"This suggests that this has something to do with Tom," Celia said. "Maybe it's something concerning his last mission. I was trying to get into Tom's file, but I can't access it with my clearance."

Gwen frowned. "That's not good."

"What was the mission that they went MIA on, ma'am?" Georgie asked.

"I don't know. I thought I might enlist Dixon's help," Celia said.

"The CIA does have their methods. Dixon might be able to get access to them," Georgie said, then added, "Or knows someone who can."

Gwen handed Dixon's number to Celia. Celia dialed the number and waited.

"Dixon here," said a familiar voice on the other end of the line.

"This is Commander Kelly."

"Commander, what can I do for you?" Dixon asked, surprised to hear from her so soon.

"I need to see you at your earliest convenience," Celia replied.

"Where and when?"

"Langley, you tell me when."

Silence.

"Today, two o'clock," Dixon said finally.

"See you then, Mr. Dixon."

"Goodbye, Commander."

Celia hung up the phone.

"I guess now is when you find out for sure if he can be trusted," Gwen said.

That's what Celia was afraid of.

* * *

Dixon hung up the phone and sat back at his desk. He looked across the desk and into the eyes of his fellow agent.

"It was Commander Kelly."

"What did she want?" Agent Tammy Johnson asked.

"I don't know, but it sounded like she had something on her mind," Dixon said, sitting forward again and leaning on his desk.

"Will she cooperate?" Tammy knew Celia Kelly was determined.

Dixon shook his head. "I don't know."

* * *

Admiral Walton appeared into Celia's office and she stood from her chair saluted.

"At ease, Commander."

"Please have a seat, sir." Celia sat back in her chair.

"Day after tomorrow, we will be meeting with the president. He wants a personal update." He could see by the look on Celia's face that she was apprehensive.

"Yes, sir," Celia said.

Walton sensed something else had happened. "Anything you need to tell me, Commander?"

"You know the blond man wasn't at the camp."

"I know that. But the weapons are gone," Walton pointed out.

"I need to tell you a story, sir." Celia began with the day she took on the mission and William Dixon. Celia then showed the admiral the photo she had received.

"Who are these people?" he asked, the color draining from his face. He pointed to Tara and Sam Cooper.

Celia paused, noticing his strange reaction. "My husband's RIO, Sam Cooper, and Sam's wife, Tara."

"What happened to this Sam Cooper?"

"Both Tom and Sam went MIA in an incident over the Mediterranean four years ago."

"What do you think this means?" Walton asked, after reading the inscription.

"I'm not sure."

"I know her," he said finally.

"Tara?" Celia was surprised.

"She married my son two years ago. I know her as Tara Simms, not Cooper. They live just outside of Norfolk. It's amazing. Samantha, her little girl, is a dead ringer for Sam Cooper."

"Wow, though it's been a few years since I've seen Samantha," Celia said. Tara was married to the rear admiral's son?

"It's a small world," Walton said quietly.

"I have an appointment with Dixon today," Celia said.

Walton stood. "If this goes anywhere, I want to be the first to know."

"Yes, sir," Celia nodded.

Celia was left alone to think. Frank began investigating the Pact five years ago. Tom and Sam disappeared four years ago. They were pilots, not agents or even intelligence, so how did their paths have crossed?

* * *

At ten fifteen the plane landed at JFK International Airport. Passengers came into the terminal and were greeted, one by one, by loved ones or family members. A three-year-old stared at the two men behind him as his mother packed him on her hip.

A blond man in a three-piece suit smiled at the boy. Next to him was a man with red hair pulled back into a slick ponytail, in a three-piece suit. A two-inch scar was clearly seen above his left eye. Both were clean shaven. They looked as any other executives might, sharp and ready for business. That was why they were here. To finish business.

CHAPTER 18

"Please have Commander Kelly's things delivered to the left side of the duplex," Gwen said into the phone as she gave them the address. "The door is unlocked."

Gwen then called the storage unit to let them know the movers were coming for the commander's things and take care of the bill.

"Send the bill to—There is no bill? The Navy reimburses her. What? Is she aware of this? Thank you. Goodbye."

"The commander moving into a duplex?" Georgie asked. She had been eavesdropping on Gwen's conversation.

"Yes and guess what? One of the units holding her things was broken into while she was gone." Gwen shook her head.

"Interesting."

"Apparently she looked it over last night when she got her car. The guy said there was no charge and apologized. If he hadn't, I might not have known anything about it."

"If the commander thought it was relevant, she would have said so." Georgie changed the subject. "Do you know if the commander's husband was ever sent to Miramar?" Georgie asked, looking at the work before her.

"I do know the commander's father is the CO there. Why?"

"Just curious," Georgie said.

"The commander met her husband through her father at the Naval Academy."

"I noticed she still wears a wedding ring," Georgie had observed.

Gwen had always wondered why Celia hadn't taken off her ring. It had been four years. Georgie and Gwen's discussion was cut short by Celia's appearance through the office door.

"Good morning, ladies," Celia said, smiling.

"The picture is back, and it's clean. Only prints on it were ours." Gwen informed her.

"I had a breakthrough this morning, ma'am. I discovered Geyser made a special trip to the naval base in Miramar four years ago," Georgie said.

"I'll call my father and see if he remembers the visit," Celia said. She found it interesting that Geyser went there of all places.

"By the way, your belongings, or what is left of them, are on their way to your new residence," Gwen said sarcastically.

"Great. Thanks, Gwen," Celia said, noting Gwen's sarcasm and ignoring it.

"Why didn't you tell us someone broke into the storage unit holding your things?" Gwen asked, unable to stand the suspense.

"It wasn't that serious. Nothing was missing that I could see."

"If you weren't living next to a Navy SEAL, I'd have half a mind to get you a bodyguard."

"If it's just her belongings they're after, perhaps a security alarm would be more effective." Georgie suggested. Gwen rolled her eyes.

"There is one fact here you are ignoring. Whoever is behind this is getting personal. First, going through your place in Washington. Then, the picture. And now this. You don't think it's a coincidence any more than I do," Gwen pointed out.

"You're right, I don't. Until I figure out what they are looking for, I'm at a loss. They haven't found it yet. The more they look, the greater the opportunity to catch them at it. If they continue to have no luck in their search, they'll get frustrated and make a mistake. When that happens, I'll be there."

"A brilliant plan, ma'am," Georgie said enthusiastically.

"Well, now I feel better." Gwen couldn't believe her ears. They were both crazy.

"At any rate, we have an appointment to keep," Celia said. "We don't want to keep Mr. Dixon waiting. Gwen, hold down the fort. I'm taking Georgie. I want her to meet Dixon."

"When will you be back?"

"I don't know. Oh, Gwen, could you get phone and internet service to the duplex?" Celia added before leaving.

"You've got it," Gwen said.

Celia and Georgie left and headed for the parking lot. Getting into Celia's Studebaker, Georgie admired the stunning gray leather interior and superb paint job—it was clear the car was pampered.

"Nice car, ma'am," Georgie said. She was surprised that the commander drove a Studebaker. Even though it wasn't the car she pictured the commander in, it suit her.

"Thank you, Georgie," Celia said. "It is my prized possession. I saw it parked in a residential neighborhood in Boston for sale. I fell in love with it. Tom bought it for me from the original owner and had it restored."

"They did a very nice job, ma'am."

They reached the Central Intelligence Agency and went through security. They walked up the steps and Celia flashed her military ID and security pass given to her by the Pentagon. There were many times in the past she had come to Langley for Admiral Lloyd. A young woman of twenty-five, very professional, with large glasses, met them.

"I'm here to see Agent William Dixon," Celia said. The woman led the way without a word.

They walked a long, well-lit hall and took the elevator two floors down. When they got off the elevator, it was no longer white walls but light gray walls that surrounded them. They were then led into a room. The young woman left them, closing the door behind her.

THE PACT: OP ONE

A table was in the center of the room with four chairs around it, one occupied by a man with his back to them. There were no windows in the room and it was very warm. It reminded Celia of old movies where they used to tie up the enemy and set him under a big light. Celia found herself thinking how strange it was that a room without windows could make you feel like you were being watched.

Dixon turned around and saw a new face beside the commander. He set copies in a file on the table. He wiped the beads of sweat from his forehead with a white handkerchief. It was always so hot in here!

"Hello, Commander," Dixon said. "Who's your friend?"

"Lieutenant Commander Georgie Round meet William Dixon."

Dixon extended his hand. Georgie accepted it. She sized him up from head to toe. A little overweight, but one could hardly hold that against him. First impression, he was okay.

"What's up, Commander?" Dixon was very curious after her cool reception at their last meeting.

"I didn't want to get into it over the phone."

Dixon smiled. "I get that a lot in my business."

"Mind if we sit?" Celia asked.

"Forgive my manners. Please, ladies, have a seat." Dixon pulled out a chair for her, then for Georgie. Everyone sat around the table.

"I received a very strange message," Celia began.

"What is that?" Dixon was resting his elbows on the table, leaning forward.

Celia got out her phone and went to the photo she had taken earlier. She handed it to Dixon. He opened it. As he was looking at the picture, his face briefly changed expression. Georgie and Celia exchanged a look. Georgie too had noticed his reaction.

"This was on the back," Celia said, flipping to the next picture.

"What does that mean?" Dixon asked.

"Did you send this to me?" Celia asked.

Dixon shook his head. "Why would I?"

Celia explained to him how she had a photo album out of place when her house in D.C. was broken into the same day, Celia pointed out, and he was following her.

"You were sent a picture of your husband," Dixon said.

"Yes. The other couple is his RIO and wife, Sam and Tara Cooper."

"TILL DEATH DO US PART." Dixon read the words aloud then added, "Someone is really into head games."

"If that is the case, what game I'm supposed to be playing?" Celia was irritated at the thought.

"If it's from the Pact, the game is deadly, I can tell you that. You should know that it's believed the Pact has ties to the Navy. This could be saying your husband might have been one of them."

"What source indicates they have ties to the Navy?" Celia asked, narrowing her eyes.

Dixon was quiet.

"Can you get access to my husband's records?" Celia asked.

"Why not ask the Navy?" Dixon asked, back to cat and mouse.

"If the Pact does have ties to the Navy, I will be alerting them to my next move. I was hoping to be discreet," Celia said. She didn't mention the files were inaccessible.

"Let's say I get your husband's records. It could be helpful or it could be damaging to your husband's reputation. If we find anything at all," Dixon said, sitting back in his seat.

Celia looked directly into his eyes. "My husband was a man of honor. I'm not worried."

He picked up the receiver of the phone and then dialed a number. "Aggie, could you come downstairs? Thanks."

"Who is Aggie?" Celia asked, realizing the circle was getting bigger.

"My right hand," Dixon said. "If you're concerned who knows what, you should be. This thing could get ugly real quick."

"We have one dead in Washington, two planes shot down, killing eighteen between them, illegal weapons. And those are just the things we know about," Celia pointed out. "In fact, ugly doesn't even cover it."

Dixon narrowed his eyes and then lit a cigar. He took a couple of puffs off it. He couldn't argue with that. "I'm just saying you need to have a very tight lid on this. Who else knows?"

"I'm watching my back, Mr. Dixon."

He handed Celia her phone and puffed away at his cigar.

CHAPTER 19

The day was a bleak one as dark thunderclouds rolled in behind a cool wind whirling through the morning. Celia held her cover in place as she stepped into her Studebaker. Elliot came over to the driver's side of her car. Celia rolled down the window.

"Good morning, Commander Elliot," Celia said. Wind engulfed her car through the open window. She smiled.

She has a beautiful smile, he thought. "Good morning."

"If you're ready, you are welcome to ride along with me," Celia offered.

He hesitated a moment, and then he got in.

"I've never been in a Studebaker." Elliot strapped on his seatbelt.

"You'd be surprised how often I hear that."

Celia turned on the wipers as the first raindrops began to hit the windshield. She briefly glanced Elliot's way and then back to the road. She began thinking about Tom. The picture was like stabbing a knife into a nearly healed wound. She had buried her memories the day she buried him, and now she was being forced to dig them back up again.

"Can't be that bad, can it?" Elliot asked, breaking her train of thought.

Celia's face relaxed, realizing she must have appeared distracted.

"No," Celia said, leaving it at that.

"How are things going?" Elliot asked. "Do you like Virginia Beach?"

"Yes, so far. How is Chief Jeffers doing?"

"Better. McDonald made us go out last night," Elliot said, looking over at her and then back out the window at the rain.

"Really?" Celia raised her eyebrows at that.

Elliot smiled.

"Where did he make you go?"

"Dinner and bowling."

"I've heard the ensign can show someone a good time," she said, smiling.

"The rumor is true."

They pulled into the parking lot. Celia got her briefcase, and they made a mad dash to the main doors, racing the rain. They lost. Both entered dripping wet. Celia removed her cover as the door closed behind them. As they got on the elevator, a tall blond man accidentally bumped into Celia, knocking her briefcase from her hand. The blond man picked it up for her and handed it to her. He got off the elevator.

"Thank you." Celia noticed how tan he was.

"You're welcome," the blond man said and smiled at her. He nodded at Elliot.

"How's it going?" Elliot asked, extending his hand. Elliot knew him.

"Can't complain. You?" he asked, accepting it.

"The usual. The wife?"

"She's good. Sorry, James, I have to go. I'll talk later." Nodding at Celia, he said, "Ma'am." The man appeared to be in a hurry.

"Later," Elliot said.

Gwen was just taking off her raincoat as Celia came into the office. Georgie was at her desk working.

Elliot opened his mouth to say something to Celia but stopped. After a moment he continued, "I'll see you later."

Celia nodded, and he left the room. Gwen watched his awkwardness. Those strong silent types, she thought, shaking her head. She wondered if Celia had a new admirer. Celia didn't seem to notice—which was predictable.

"Tomorrow I'm going to Washington with Admiral Walton. I'll be meeting with the president," Celia said, at her door now. "Georgie, why don't you take tomorrow off and get yourself a place to get settled in?"

"Thank you, ma'am."

"What did Dixon say?" Gwen asked them.

"He is looking into it and will get back with us today if he finds something," Celia said.

Celia went into her office and closed the door, setting the briefcase on the desk. Getting out the boxes she hadn't unpacked yet, she picked up the picture of Tom. Touching the outline of Tom's image gently with her finger, she set it back on the desk. She picked up the phone and dialed her father's number.

"Hello, Admiral Mitchell here."

"Hello, Daddy," Celia said.

"Celia, it's so good to hear from you," Mitchell said endearingly. "Where are you?"

"Dam Neck naval base. How are you and Mama?"

"We are both fine, but we miss you. We haven't heard from you in a while."

"I miss you, too," Celia said, pausing.

"How did you end up at Dam Neck, Celia?" Mitchell knew his daughter well. It had been weeks since she called, and that usually meant she was working on something. Otherwise, she called every Friday night, and she never called him at the flight school.

"I was wondering if you could help me with something. Do you remember as CIA Agent Stan Geyser?" Celia waited for a reply. Her father was silent. She added, "It was four years ago."

"Yes, I do. Geyser talked with me briefly. Said he needed to speak to a couple of the pilots."

"Who were the pilots?" Celia asked.

"I had an emergency call at that time, but my second in command, Mead, took him over to the barracks. I never heard any more about it. Said he had a possible assignment for a couple of the pilots. The government hand picks guys from time to time. It didn't come to anything. I know that because I never signed off on any of my guys to go on any assignments. They don't go anywhere unless I say they are ready. If Tom was alive, you could ask him. He had lunch with Geyser before he headed back to Washington."

"Did Sam join them?" Celia wondered. She found that strange.

"No. Just the Tom and Geyser." Mitchell was beyond curious now. "What is this about, honey?"

"I'll have to fill you in at another time, Daddy. I'm afraid I need to get back to work. I will try to come home after this one," Celia promised.

"We'll be looking forward to it," Mitchell said. "Celia, your Mama and I will be praying for you. Be careful, honey." They said goodbye.

Celia picked up the picture of Tom and Sam. She couldn't think of anything at all out of the ordinary. So what had she missed? Celia decided to pay Tara a visit after she returned from Washington. Her thoughts were interrupted by a knock on the door.

"Ma'am?" Georgie opened the door.

"Come in, Georgie. What is it?" Celia asked.

"I have made a few calls concerning William Dixon. Clean as they come, ma'am," Georgie said.

"And I just called my father. He recalled Geyser and said he was there to talk to a pilot regarding a special assignment. He also said Tom had lunch with Geyser," Celia said.

"Interesting."

"I thought so. I just don't know what it means yet."

"Your husband knowing Geyser doesn't necessarily connect him to the Pact," Georgie pointed out.

"Too much of a coincidence not to connect him to something," Celia said, looking again at the picture. "That's all for now, Georgie."

Georgie left Celia alone to think. Five years ago the Pact had a great deal of money, and now it's missing. Was it taken by one of them or someone else? Whoever was remotely connected so far, that she knew of, was dead. Everyone else is missing, such as the blond man, Tammy, or the man Tammy argued with that night. Celia still didn't know for sure what Dixon knew. Now this unusual visit Geyser paid to the flight school in Miramar. The worst of it was she had little to convince the president that she should continue. As Celia put up the pictures that once hung in her office at the Pentagon, she found herself wishing she were back there.

* * *

The phone book fell to the floor of the phone booth. Tammy Johnson picked it up with cold fingers. Her body hadn't adjusted to the change in climate after living in the desert. The wind and rain were not helping much. Fumbling through the pages, she finally found the number. No address was listed. She would have to be creative. She dialed the operator.

"Operator. What city please?"

"Norfolk. I'm with UPS. We were given a phone number and a name. I need to double-check the address. Could you help me?"

"What are the name and number, ma'am?"

"Henry Jeffers, 804-555-6575."

"Thank you, ma'am, and have a nice day. The address is 14 Bender Ave, Apt. 4."

* * *

Dixon didn't need to go through Lieutenant Tom Kelly's file before handing it over to the commander. He knew the file well. Tom Kelly had received high commendations and praise by his CO. The only gray area in his file was his last assignment, which sent him over the Mediterranean Sea. Tom Kelly violated Lebanese airspace, putting them in a position to be shot down. Kelly spent ten weeks at the flight school in Miramar, coming in second. That was four and a half years ago, just before his last mission.

Aggie walked into Dixon's office.

"You were looking over this the other day. What did you find?" Aggie wondered.

"He's clean as a whistle until the last mission when he gets killed. Even at that, nothing in here implying he was involved with the Pact."

"Need anything else?"

"Not now. Thanks, Aggie." Dixon wondered about the details around the death of Tom Kelly.

One thing was for sure, Celia Kelly was going to continue until the blanks were filled in. Dixon lit up another cigar. He knew that Tom Kelly had been nowhere near Lebanese air space.

* * *

Celia looked at her watch. It was closing time, no word from Dixon. She stepped out of her office. Georgie was away from her desk. Gwen was getting her things together to go home.

"Where's Georgie?" Celia asked.

"She went to look at a place to rent. Do you think Dixon will get back to you today?"

"I thought he would," Celia said.

"No news is good news."

"I don't think that applies to intelligence."

"Do you need anything else before I go?"

"No, go home. I'll hang around and wait for Dixon's call."

"Okay. See you tomorrow."

Celia went back into her office, leaving her door open a crack. She looked over the delivered picture, wishing she could just go home and ask Tom. That wasn't an option. When the phone finally rang, it startled her.

"Commander Kelly."

"It's Dixon," answered the now familiar voice.

"What did you find?" Celia asked.

"We need a face-to-face. I want to show you something. Do you know where Town Point Park is?"

"I'll be there. What time?" Celia wrote the name and directions on a pad.

"Tomorrow, 0900."

Celia hung up the phone. When Celia looked up, Elliot was standing in the doorway. She caught her breath.

"I didn't mean to scare you," he said.

"Just took me by surprise. Looking for a ride home?" Celia put her notepad and picture inside her briefcase and snapped it shut.

"If you're headed that direction."

"I am. To be honest, I had forgotten you." Celia smiled and got her things.

"I have that effect on women." Elliot stood aside. Celia went out first and waited for him to shut the door. When the office was closed, Celia remembered the president. She had forgotten the meeting tomorrow with the president while making plans with Dixon!

"I need to see if Admiral Walton has left yet," Celia said with a hint of urgency in her voice.

"Sure." Elliot raised an eyebrow. They walked the hall and around the corner to Walton's office. Walton was just leaving, closing his door. He turned to be faced with Elliot and Celia.

"Sir, may I have a moment of your time?" Celia asked.

"Certainly, Commander." He looked from Elliot to Celia.

"Sir, I was wondering what time was our meeting set for?" She asked.

"It's at 1600," Walton replied.

"Thank you, sir. I'll see you then." She had plenty of time to meet Dixon.

"Is that all, Commander?"

"Yes, sir."

"I'll see you tomorrow," Walton replied.

"Good night, sir," Elliot said.

"I'm ready." Celia and Elliot headed for home.

* * *

The rain was now just a drizzle as Elliot and Celia pulled into the driveway. Noticing the muddy footprints on the porch, Celia knew the movers had been there. She thought of the mess that was going to be on white tile. Celia walked up the steps of the porch and inside the duplex. Even though the mud tracked in was minimal, she definitely had cleaning up to do. Her furniture and boxes were stacked in the middle of the living room.

"Wow," Elliot said, looking around him.

"I'll mop up the tile once I set up," Celia said. It wasn't the best moving job she had ever seen.

"Maybe the moving company should do that," Elliot suggested.

"They can't help the rain. I'm sure that isn't in their job description."

Elliot looked over the situation. The bed was easy access against the wall. She needed that put together by end of day. Without a second thought, Elliot got to work. He moved the headboard and footboard into the bedroom and came back out for the rails.

"I'm sure you don't want to move your tenant's furniture around after working all day," Celia protested.

"It's no problem. I can at least help you set up your bed so you don't have to spend another night on the floor." He proceeded to move the rails into the bedroom. She put her things on the counter and took off her uniform jacket. Kicking off her pumps, she followed him into the bedroom.

After it was put together, Celia stood back a moment with a thoughtful look.

"I think I want it over there," she said.

He moved the bed and centered it in the middle of the wall opposite the door. The window was to the right of the bed.

Celia smiled. "Perfect. I guess I'll see if I can find my bedding."

"I'll be right back," he said and was out the door before Celia could say a word.

Elliot intrigued Celia as he was an intense man. There was inner strength in him, but he did not appear to be happy. Suddenly it made Celia miss Tom, wishing he was still with her. Over the last few days the feeling haunted her. Maybe it was the picture... or Scott's note.

She decided to continue unpacking, trying to get her mind on something else besides Tom or the mission. Opening a box marked Bedroom, Celia found the phone. She laid it aside as she noticed the photo album. It was the same photo album that was on floor in the bedroom at her house in Washington, D.C. Celia took it out of the box. Opening it, she started looking through it. It was wedding photos. She went to her briefcase and took out the picture she had received in the envelope. It was taken during the reception. They were standing in front of the gift table. She went through the album again, finding no picture like it.

"Reminiscing?" Celia was brought back by the sound of Elliot's voice. He had returned. He had changed into jeans and a T-shirt.

"I just ran across an old photo album."

Celia slipped the larger photo inside the envelope and then closed the photo album on it. Elliot brought a couple of cans of soda with him. He set them on the counter near the opened briefcase. He glanced at it, noticing a file titled, "Agent Stan Geyser, CIA." Elliot glanced at Celia.

"Thanks for the soda," Celia said. She closed the briefcase and snapped the lock shut, picking up a soda.

"I ordered pizza. I'll get plates," Elliot said, and was out the door again before Celia could respond. His exit abrupt. Celia found it interesting he was always preoccupied with feeding her. She rarely thought of regular meals.

He was gone what seemed like a long time. Deciding to go next door and see why, Celia noticed the door was cracked open. Raising her hand to knock on the door, she overheard Elliot on the phone.

"It was open," Elliot said, and then he was listening. "I will." When he hung up the phone, Celia knocked. He immediately turned startled.

"Sorry I took so long." Elliot looked nervous.

"No problem, I thought maybe I could help."

"I got a phone call." He went to the cupboard for plates.

"Can I help?"

"I got it."

After the pizza was delivered, and they finished eating, Celia hooked up the phone in the bedroom. Elliot helped her set up her nightstands on either side of her bed.

"Do those brass lamps go in here?" Elliot asked.

"Yes, they do."

"I'll go get them," Elliot said. Celia continued to connect the answering machine to the phone.

Elliot picked up one lamp, but the cord was wrapped around something else. He accidentally kicked the photo album Celia had been looking through earlier. The manila envelope slid out. When he went to pick it up to put it back a large photo fell out. He looked at the wedding photo.

As he put it back in, he noticed writing on the back. TILL DEATH DO US PART. Quickly he returned it and put it back into the album. Elliot got the lamps and took them into the bedroom. He watched Celia as she arranged the lamps. What is going on with her? He wondered. The writing on the back of the picture was in bold black marker. It wasn't what it said. It was how abruptly the large capital letters presented the message as a threat than a romantic day.

CHAPTER 20

As Celia pulled into the base parking lot, the sun was just coming up over Virginia Beach. The brilliant light that filled the sky gave her hope. Maybe it was just the sun peeking through yesterday's gloomy clouds, but the day held promise. Hopefully, this would be the day to find answers. In the office she sat at her computer and turned on the terminal.

"Good morning, Commander." Gwen smiled.

Celia looked up from her work. "Good morning, Gwen."

"I'm going to be gone most of today. I'm meeting Dixon at 0900. Then I'm going to Washington, D.C. around 1600."

"So you finally heard from Dixon."

Celia nodded. "By the way, what is my new home phone number?"

"Just a minute." Gwen looked it up on her daily calendar where she had written it, then copied it on note paper.

"I need an address for Tara Walton."

"Who?" Gwen asked.

"She's Sam Cooper's widow, who happened to marry the rear admiral's son."

"You're kidding." Gwen shook her head. "That's an interesting a coincidence."

"I need to visit with her and find out if she noticed anything out of the ordinary four years ago."

"I'll check into it today."

"Thanks, Gwen."

Georgie walked into the office.

"Did you find a place?" asked Celia. She was surprised to see her. She thought Georgie would be moving into a place today.

"Yes, ma'am. I thought I'd work until the movers delivered my belongings. I was wondering if you needed me to go along today. I'd be happy to assist, ma'am. My things won't be arriving until 0200."

"Sure. Let's go," Celia said. "We'll be back within an hour or so I'd imagine, Gwen. See you later."

"Have fun," Gwen said as they walked out the door.

* * *

Dixon parked his car. He walked nonchalantly through the dewy grass, still damp from the rain. The sun's rays were starting to evaporate the drops of water on the benches and playground equipment. He walked over to a bench in the center of the park. He sat on the bench. Reaching in his breast pocket, he pulled out an envelope. Dixon was early.

A man and his son were in the park enjoying the sunny morning. The little boy had blond curls and big blue eyes. He ran to retrieve the large yellow ball he was throwing to his father. The ball rolled over and stopped in front of Dixon's feet.

"Hi," said the young boy with a smile.

"Hello there." Dixon returned the smile.

"Sam!" the father called out. The little boy turned and looked at his dad.

"Bye," he said and grabbed the ball and ran back.

The park was busy with Navy and civilian joggers and bike riders. A young man dressed in sweat shorts and a tank top was riding his bike around the park. His crew cut implied he was a recruit. He rode his bike behind the bench. Dixon heard a crash. When Dixon turned, he saw the recruit's day was off to a bad start as he stood his bike back up and turned two garbage cans right side up again.

Dixon's attention was shifted again as someone laid a jacket over the back of the bench and sat beside him. The man smiled and nodded. He was clean cut, in a light red T-shirt with blue jeans. Dixon nodded back.

"Beautiful day," the man said.

"Yeah." Dixon agreed.

The man opened his pocket watch. He dropped it. It ended up next to Dixon's feet.

"I dropped my watch," he said politely. "Would you mind handing it to me?"

As Dixon started to reach for it, he saw the knife out of the corner of his eye, but not soon enough to react. With one swift movement, the man slid a knife through the breast pocket of Dixon's suit, penetrating into the skin. As Dixon slumped over, the envelope fell from his hand to the grass underneath the bench. The man picked up his watch. With his clean hand, he grabbed the jacket he laid over the back of the bench, hanging it over his blood-stained hand holding the knife. He walked calmly but with a quickened step back to his black sedan. He got in and drove away.

Sam's father threw the ball to him and he missed it. Flying through the air, the ball landed on the bench next to Dixon. Little Sam ran over to get it. He picked up the ball. Sam noticed Dixon was slumping over like he was sick.

"Are you okay, mister?" Sam touched his shoulder.

"Sam, leave the man alone." The father was beside him now.

"Daddy, he's sick," Sam said.

The child's touch off-centered the body enough that Dixon fell off the bench. Dark red fluid came from his chest. Both the father and child stepped back, and Sam screamed. A police officer came to Dixon as soon as he heard the screams. The officer held everyone to stay back behind the crime scene tape. Another officer examined him, declaring him dead.

* * *

When Celia parked the Studebaker, they saw an ambulance with two attendants loading a stretcher in the back. There was no sign of Dixon anywhere. Celia and Georgie looked at each other, wondering if something had happened to him as well, and they went up to the ambulance. As the stretcher slid into the back of the ambulance, the sheet came off the face. It was Dixon! Celia began to walk closer to him, but a hand stopped her.

"Ma'am?" asked an EMT with the ambulance. "I'm sorry, but if he's a friend of yours, it's too late. He's gone."

"Gone?" Celia found herself repeating, though she knew what he meant.

"He's dead, ma'am." The EMT closed the doors.

"How did this happen?" Celia asked, confused.

"He was stabbed."

With that the ambulance drove away. The police officer, who had been talking to witnesses, walked to his patrol car, parked half a block away. The patrol car followed the ambulance.

"Excuse me." Celia stopped a man who had just finished speaking to a police officer.

"Can you tell what happened here this morning? Quite the commotion for so early in the morning."

"I heard the boy scream," said a man in sweatpants and sweatshirt with Navy printed on the front of it. "He is over there with his dad. There was a dead guy was lying on the bench and that's all I know." The man pointed to another bench where a man was cradling a young boy in his arms.

Celia and Georgie walked over to the man and his son.

"Excuse me, sir," Celia began. "I'm Commander Kelly. May I ask you a few questions?"

"I don't know, my son is very upset. I need to take him home."

"I just need to know if you saw anyone," Celia said.

"I was playing with my son. The ball rolled over there once and he was fine. A few minutes later he was... slumped on the bench."

"How long ago?"

"The first time the ball rolled over was twenty-five minutes ago."

"Is there anything else you can tell me?" Celia asked gently.

The man shook his head no. Sam looked up, raising his head from his father's shoulder. Celia turned to go.

"The other man might know," the little boy said sadly.

Celia stopped and turned back facing the boy. She knelt and looked hopefully into the little boy's eyes. "What man?"

"The blond man who sat next to him."

Celia's heart fell. It couldn't be! She needed to get them out of here and not ask any more of them.

"Have you talked to the police yet?" Celia asked. They shook their heads no. Celia wondered why the police hadn't questioned them. Certainly the jogger had told the police the same thing he had Celia. "Go ahead and take him home. The police will contact you if they need to speak to you."

"Thank you," said the father. They left.

Celia let them go, not taking the time to get their names or any other information. The father was too upset to notice Celia hadn't asked.

Celia and Georgie went over to the bench where Dixon had been found. Celia spotted the envelope and picked it up walking back to the Studebaker. She closed her eyes as she leaned back against the seat.

"Are you okay, ma'am?" Georgie asked.

"Yes," Celia said. She had liked Dixon even if she wasn't sure she trusted him. She just wished she knew exactly what it was he had died knowing.

"Ma'am? What's in the envelope?" Georgie wondered what she was thinking.

"I'm not sure, but the envelope with my name on it."

"I wonder why the killer didn't take it."

Celia thought a moment. Why was that? Unless...

"Maybe someone thought he was only going to tell me something, not give me something, and didn't notice it." Yet on the other hand why did Dixon write her a note if he had planned to speak to her? A note leaves a trail.

"Who knew you were meeting him?"

"That I don't know. I got the call after you and Gwen left. The only person I talked to was Walton. Who knows who Dixon may have talked to? Georgie, the police officer who was on scene, he didn't talk to us or the boy and his father. It was obvious to the ambulance attendants I was looking for Dixon. Not only that, but the patrol car was parked half a block away. Why so far from the scene?"

"What do you think that means?" Georgie asked. "Are you suggesting someone plans to cover up Dixon's death as well?"

"I don't know. Something just doesn't feel right."

"Now what, ma'am?"

"Call Gwen to find out Dixon's home address," Celia said, looking at her watch. It was almost 0930. She'd have at least an hour before she'd have to leave for Washington. Georgie dialed the cellular as Celia started up her Studebaker. Georgie had the information within two minutes and Celia was on her way.

"What are we doing, ma'am?" Georgie asked.

"We are going to look at his place."

"You mean break in, ma'am?"

"I don't think it's breaking in when you're dead," Celia said, knowing it was crossing the line but wanting to beat the CIA to any information.

"Can you mind reading this to me on the way?" Celia handed her the envelope.

Georgie opened it and began reading.

"What does it say, Georgie?"

"It says is Lieutenant Kelly and Lieutenant Cooper trapped. Then below that is a date, June 11th."

THE PACT: OP ONE

"That's all?" Celia asked.

"That's it, ma'am," Georgie said. "Does that mean anything to you?"

"It doesn't make much sense. They went MIA on a mission over the Mediterranean. I'm not sure what to think of that date, but I do know the mission was in September. As for June 11th, it was our wedding anniversary," Celia said quietly.

"Maybe we can see if there were missions in process on that date four years ago that your husband was attached to?" Georgie suggested.

They were now parked in the alley behind Dixon's house.

"If it looks like we can use it, take it," Celia said to Georgie. Georgie reached into her pocket, pulling out a pair of surgical gloves for each of them.

"Here you go, ma'am," Georgie said.

"You carry gloves?"

"You don't, ma'am?"

"Not two pair."

"Never know when you might have a medical emergency."

The two-story house was white with gray trim. The yard was well kept, and it even had a patio. Celia and Georgie went to the back door. Celia knocked, wondering for the first time if there was a Mrs. Dixon. No answer. Celia tried the door. It was locked.

"Allow me, ma'am," Georgie said. She took out a tool from her pocket and had it opened in seconds. Celia raised both eyebrows in surprise. Georgie did phone taps, picked locks, and carried gloves?

Celia went in first. It was evident no Mrs. Dixon existed. TV dinner trays were scattered on the counter and dirty glasses clustered in the sink. The refrigerator was practically empty. There was a half-gallon of milk, half a loaf of molded bread, cheese, wine, and moldy lunch meat.

Dixon didn't eat the majority of his meals at home. Celia nodded to Georgie, pointing to the stairs. Georgie nodded, heading upstairs.

Georgie walked into the bedroom, finding the bed unmade. Dirty clothes scattered on the bed and floor. Cigars on the nightstand. One was sitting in the ashtray, smoldering. Looking through the drawers of the nightstand, she found nothing useful. Going through the bookshelf in the corner, Georgie saw no secret compartments, nor did she find anything in the pages of the books. Hanging in the closet were four suits and ten dress shirts. There was a Ruger 22 pistol on the top shelf of the closet.

Georgie went into the bathroom. A razor and shaving cream were still at the sink. A towel caught her eye. It was dark blue with a dark reddened spot. It was blood. It was sticky as she pressed her gloved finger against it. The counter surrounding the sink was wet. Someone had been here recently. Georgie examined the razor, trying to see if there was a piece of skin or blood on the blade but there was nothing.

Celia searched downstairs for anything and everything. She took his phone bills and receipts from a desk in the corner of his living room. She noticed the answering machine was blinking. Deciding not to listen to it now, she removed the tape and set it on top of the bills. Looking for places he might have for keeping information safe, she came up empty. He was CIA and he may have anticipated something of this nature happening at one time or another. His house would be the last place he'd want an item of real value. At best, the most she could hope for is a clue to where he might keep it instead.

Georgie came downstairs with the towel in hand. Celia glanced at it briefly. Georgie went into the kitchen and found a large plastic bag to put the towel in. Celia continued to look in the living room.

"Find anything else?" Celia asked finally.

"A smoldering cigar which I left, and this towel with blood on it," Georgie said.

Celia shrugged. "It could have been from this morning. Maybe he cut himself shaving?"

"The razor didn't appear to have skin or blood on it. The sink was wet. It looks to be recent."

"We'll get it what we have tested to see if it tells us anything we use."

It had been over an hour and Celia was cutting it close. Walton was probably wondering where she was. Assembling what little they had gotten, it was time to go. On their way out, Celia noticed how bare the walls were. No pictures, either decorative or personal. He must have done his work at the office because there was little or no paperwork on the desk and it was dusty. The only sign he even had a past or present was an old photo Celia had taken from his desk of a pretty blonde woman. All my love, Sarah was written on the bottom of it.

"Let's go, Georgie."

They left. Celia drove through two alleyways before took a right on the main highway. Hopefully they would be able to piece something together. She had even more to give the president now, the death of CIA Agent William Dixon. One more to add to the growing list.

* * *

Parking in the driveway in front of Dixon's house was a black sedan. A blond man got out of it and walked up to the front door. He let himself in using a key. As he searched the house, he didn't find what he was looking for. Searching the desk, he noticed the answering machine light. He pressed the button to retrieve the message.

Nothing happened. He didn't even hear it rewind. He opened it to discover the tape was gone. Shaking his head, he left. As the sedan drove away, a man who had been sitting on the roof outside of the upstairs bathroom, lifted himself back inside through the bathroom window.

CHAPTER 21

The blond man drove back to his motel room and opened door thirteen. His friend was lying on a bed watching cable TV. The blond man sat on the opposite bed.

"It's taken care of."

"Did you go to his place?"

"Yeah, but someone beat me to it."

"Who? How?"

"It seemed empty. It didn't look like he was there very often either."

"You went there right afterwards didn't you?"

"Well, no, I stopped to clean up and change clothes. Someone might have been there long before he even went to the park."

"Now what?"

"Everything went just like it was supposed to, so relax."

His partner shook his head. Somehow he felt anything but relaxed.

* * *

Georgie drove back while Celia put the phone bills and tape in the lower section of her briefcase. She placed files on top of them. They discussed each other's findings briefly.

"Take the towel to the lab." Celia handed Georgie a baggie. "See if we can get a blood-type and an idea of the seriousness of the wound or cut. I'll keep the rest of this with me."

Rear Admiral Walton had his car waiting for them as Celia's Studebaker pulled onto the base. Walton was standing next to the car, looking at his watch. Celia and Georgie stood at attention. Walton returned the salute then opened the back door for Celia.

"Cutting it close, aren't we, Commander?"

"Yes, sir," Celia agreed.

"After you, Commander," Walton said, opening the door for her.

Celia turned to Georgie. "Georgie, go ahead and get settled. We'll get back to work in the morning,"

"Yes, ma'am."

As the rear admiral's driver started onto the freeway, Celia sighed, watching the traffic as it passed. Walton, who sat next to her, looked her over as she stared out the window. He wondered why she had been late. Celia felt the admiral's eyes upon her. She turned to him.

"I'm sorry I'm late, sir."

"Was your meeting successful?" Walton asked, wondering where she had been.

"I'm afraid not, sir," Celia sighed. "Dixon was dead when I got there."

"Dead?" Walton exclaimed.

"He was stabbed."

"Can you tell me who he was?"

"When I tell the president if you don't mind, sir," Celia said. She decided to keep the note to herself for now.

"Where did you go to meet him?"

"Town Point Park."

Walton was quiet now. He wasn't sure what he was getting into, but he was pretty sure he didn't like it. He was concerned about the shoulders of this woman. Would they be big enough or strong enough to carry this? Clearly, she was determined to carry the load, regardless. That was why he was there, just in case she couldn't.

* * *

"How did the meeting with Dixon go?" Gwen asked as Georgie walked in.

"Dixon was dead when we got there."

Gwen was speechless. She had liked him. He had reminded her of one of those undercover detectives on TV.

"He left a note," Georgie said.

Gwen raised her eyebrows at that statement. No one could accuse Georgie of being overly sensitive. Gwen walked over to Georgie's desk and Georgie handed her the letter. Gwen read it.

"Is this the date when they went on the mission?" Gwen wondered.

"No, they went in September. The commander informed me the date was their wedding anniversary."

"Let's see what we can find out," Gwen said. She sat at her desk and began working at her computer.

* * *

Inside the Oval Office now, Celia and Rear Admiral Walton saluted the president and Chairman of the Joints Chief of Staff Admiral Turner. After the formalities, everyone was seated on couches arranged around a cherry coffee table. Celia looked around the spacious room the magnified the power and dignity of the man who held the office. Celia felt a few butterflies in the pit of her stomach as it sunk in. She was in the presence of the president of the United States.

"I asked General Turner to join us," the president began. "Commander, I'd want to begin by telling you that I was very impressed with your work in Syria."

"Thank you, Mr. President. The success was a team effort, due to the SEALs, sir," Celia said, hoping she didn't appear as nervous as she felt.

"Yet I understand you think the job is not finished. Please tell us why?" The president sat back, relaxed but looking at her intently.

Turner's eyes never left Celia. He finally got to see how this woman handled things firsthand. Celia felt his eyes upon her and his uncertainty. Celia handed the file she had prepared to the president.

"Mr. President, it began the day I was asked to take on this mission. My house here in Washington was broken into two hours before I was handed the mission. A good friend of mine, Commander Frank Scott, called me and asked me to remove files from his safe if he didn't show up for work. He didn't show. I did as he asked. Later, Admiral Lloyd informed me Commander Scott committed suicide." Celia paused, uneasily.

"I'm sorry to hear that, Commander," the president said sincerely.

"In the meantime, I was briefed on the mission by Admiral Lloyd. The very mission Commander Scott had been heading up for the last five years. I then took part of the team to Syria to look for a boy who had been seen with a blond-haired man we suspected to be connected with the Pact. We discovered the boy at a Red Cross clinic where we were working undercover. We also met a Tammy Johnson at the clinic." Celia took a breath.

"Go on." The president was intrigued by her story.

"The next strange incident was the pipe bomb. I think it may have been meant for Miss Johnson. Lieutenant Commander Round overheard a conversation she had with someone she was supposed to meet in the kitchen around the time the bomb went off. The boy was killed in the explosion along with nine others. Miss Johnson disappeared as we were rescuing those survivors from the tent. Her location is unknown at this time."

"As it turned out, another young boy knew the camp where the boy had lived. We double-checked the information, calling for satellite feed to verify. The rest of the team was brought in. We destroyed the camp and weapons, but not the blond man. He wasn't there."

"If the weapons are destroyed, isn't that enough?" the president asked, looking at Turner.

"Commander Frank Scott had been on this group tail for the last five years. Commander Scott discovered an admiral and his son were involved somehow. They feed the Pact intelligence on incoming weapons and the easiest checkpoints to obtain the shipments. To complicate matters, the Pact is looking for $20 million. Someone, unknown, took it. The Pact wants it back."

"Good grief!" the president said as he realized what she was implying. "That means Scott was closer to solving it than we thought and I didn't even know he was dead." He sat back in his chair, turning to look out the balcony windows.

"Maybe even dead because of it," Celia said frankly.

"You don't believe it was a suicide?" Turner asked.

"No, sir. I don't believe in coincidences."

"Anything else?" Turner wondered.

"The planes shot down recently... We have discovered that CIA Agent Stan Geyser died in the first plane. He was working with Commander Scott," Celia said. "When I returned from Syria, I met CIA Agent William Dixon. He said that the Pact hid the money in a plane hangar, only to have someone take it. Who, I don't know."

"What about this William Dixon? What more can he tell us?" The president was facing them again. Celia's eyes dropped briefly.

"I had a meeting with him this morning at a park at Norfolk. When I got there he was dead, someone had stabbed him. A little boy saw a blond man near him just before he died." Walton gave Celia a quick look. She hadn't mentioned that.

"A blond man, the blond man you were looking for in Syria?" Walton asked.

"Like I said, I don't believe in coincidences."

"So not only do we have one of those lunatics still around to reckon with, they have a contact in the Navy?" The president shook his head, his voice thick with concern. Turner's expression was grave.

"I'd like permission to finish what's been started, sir," Celia said.

"What a mess," the president said.

"What are you going to do?" Turner asked. Any agent worth his or her salt had to have a plan.

"I'll try to find the money. If I find the money, I find the rest of the Pact. I have to consider that I might have been a pawn in all of this," Celia said. "Why I was asked to sign on to begin with should be taken into consideration. My secretary received orders for me to report to Admiral Lloyd while Scott was still alive, and suddenly I replace Scott within an hour of his death. Another reason to wonder if Scott's death was really a suicide."

Turner had to admit that he was impressed with this girl in spite of himself and surprised by her candor. He hadn't thought she was the best choice initially. If someone else had counted on that, they could have used her till they got the information they wanted, and then she takes the fall. Someone else had underestimated her as he had. This was one time he was glad to be wrong.

"Who knows about this?" Turner asked her.

"Besides everyone in this room, my secretary, and Lieutenant Commander Round." Celia added, "The team's involvement stopped in Syria."

"Commander, you will be given the opportunity to finish what you started. You will report directly to General Turner," the president said.

"No one else is to know what we have discussed here today," the president added. "If you need to use the team further, we'll discuss that then. Until then, we keep it tight."

"Yes, sir," Celia agreed.

"Here is my cell number," Turner said.

Celia and Walton left the Oval Office, leaving Turner and the president alone.

"What do you think?" the president asked him.

"If someone set her up, someone severely underestimated her," Turner said.

"So you think she was set up?"

"Either that or someone just wanted the mission to fail."

The president could see Turner was impressed with Kelly and that was all the assurance he needed. No one knew intelligence better than Turner. He had done his share of it before becoming chairman of the Joint Chiefs of Staff. President Bailey and General Turner sat in silence for a long moment. Finally Bailey spoke.

"Keep an eye on Admiral Lloyd."

Turner nodded.

CHAPTER 22

Gwen wasn't looking forward to going home alone. Starving, she realized she hadn't gone shopping yet. She drove her green Chevy Nova home. As she parked in her space, she noticed Henry Jeffers walking over to his door with two grocery bags in his arms. She picked up her pace.

"Hi!" she said cheerfully.

Jeffers looked up from his juggling act of balancing two bags and trying to unlock his door.

Gwen smiled. "Here let me get that for you." She took the keys and unlocked the door.

"Thanks." Jeffers smiled back. After the door was opened, Jeffers paused a moment.

"There you go," Gwen said. She handed him the keys.

"You want to come in?" Jeffers asked. "I was going to fry hot dogs with sauerkraut and onions."

"Sounds good, I'm starving," Gwen said and walked right in. Jeffers followed, kicking the door shut with his foot. He set the groceries on the counter and hung up his keys.

"No groceries at home?" Jeffers guessed.

"Told you, I don't cook." She spied a bowl of jelly beans on the counter and helped herself.

He shrugged. "Just a stab in the dark. Do you want something to drink?"

"What do you have?"

"I just bought milk and beer. I might have a soda."

"A soda sounds good." He handed her the soda. She pulled back the tab and took a drink. "Can I help?"

"No, thank you. How long have you worked for Commander Kelly?"

"A little over three years now. I think very highly of her."

"I was impressed with her in Syria. There is something different about her," Jeffers said thoughtfully.

"I'm not sure what you mean, but her faith is important to her," Gwen said. "She actually tries to live by what she believes."

"You sound like you don't agree."

"I'm not sure. Yes, I'd love to have that much faith in anything, but I've seen so much unfairness in the world. Remember, my father is a lawyer. I have to say, the commander has restored my faith in people somewhat."

"Not much rattles the commander, and I like that about her."

"Not even when it should," Gwen said sarcastically.

Jeffers decided not to touch that comment. He sliced the hot dogs and onions, cooking them on low. He waited before adding the sauerkraut. He mixed it together, turning it on simmer as he got out two plates. It was then they heard a crash in the bedroom. Both Gwen and Jeffers looked that direction. An eerie silence filled the apartment.

"Do you have a cat or something?"

"No."

Jeffers put his finger to his lips and quietly opened the bedroom door. As he pushed it open, he saw a shadow running for the window. Jeffers grabbed the intruder and pinned the arms to the floor. Gwen turned on the light. Jeffers gasped, shocked by his intruder's identity.

"Tammy," he said in practically a whisper. Tammy looked up helplessly into Jeffers' face, wondering what he would do next.

"Definitely not a cat," Gwen said.

"She was in Syria," Jeffers said, his eyes fixated on Tammy's face. "She was in charge of the Red Cross volunteers." His tone went from explanatory to accusing. "She disappeared after a pipe bomb went off in the kitchen."

"I heard," Gwen said.

Jeffers realized he was still restraining her, hurting her. He stood. Tammy sat up and rubbed her wrists, taking in a deep breath.

"Well, isn't this always the way? You lose something, look and look trying to figure out where it is, and then all of a sudden it's right under your nose." Gwen sighed. Tammy and Jeffers looked at Gwen with blank expressions on their face.

"Just trying to point out the bright side," Gwen added.

"Who are you?" Tammy asked.

"I'm Gwen Sherwood, Commander Kelly's secretary." Gwen smiled and extended a hand. Tammy accepted her hand. Gwen helped her to her feet. Tammy looked into Jeffers' eyes. Jeffers looked into hers. The tension was so thick Gwen figured they'd need a machete to cut through it.

"We were just about to eat," Gwen said.

"Why did you send the boy into the kitchen?" Jeffers demanded, ignoring Gwen's presence in the room. There was so much about that day that was unfinished for him. "Did you know that boy was our contact? Were you trying to get rid of him?"

"Of course not!" Tammy raised her voice defensively. A tear rolled down her cheek. "I would never have hurt that boy!"

"I can see the two of you want to talk. I'll just go check on dinner," Gwen said, meekly leaving the room. Gwen's exit went unnoticed.

Tammy and Jeffers faced each other. Henry was looking at her like she was a murderer.

"Henry, I can explain." Tammy sniffed, swallowing hard, trying not to give into her emotions completely. She didn't know where to start. The only thing she knew for sure was Henry was the last person she wanted to deceive.

It was then he took a good look at her. She hadn't changed her clothes in days. Her short hair had lost its shine. He could see there was more to this... more to her.

"You sent him to the kitchen and it blew up... Then you disappear without a word. Not one word. You weren't even there when we buried him. Can you explain that?" Jeffers' voice remained even.

"If you're asking me if I feel responsible, I do. I feel very responsible. That bomb was meant for me."

"For you? Why?"

"It's a long story. I can't say."

"Can you say why you just left? Can you say why you didn't even say goodbye?" Jeffers asked, quietly now.

"If I stayed, I could have endangered someone else. My cover had been compromised and I was required to leave immediately, no questions asked, no goodbyes." Tammy paused a moment and then blurted out, "I work for the CIA."

Jeffers was shocked by Tammy's revelation. The conversation was suddenly interrupted by a shout from the kitchen.

"Oh, help!" Gwen's panicked voice rang through the apartment.

Jeffers smelled smoke.

Jeffers and Tammy came out to a smoke-filled kitchen. The smoke alarm began sounding. Jeffers opened the kitchen window. He took flaming hot dogs and sauerkraut off the burner which was now bright red. Quickly he put the pan in the sink and ran cold water over it until the flames were out.

"This burner is on high. I had it on low," Jeffers exclaimed, still waving smoke out the window.

"They didn't look like they were cooking fast enough, so I turned them up a little."

"A little?"

"Maybe we can cut off the worst of it," Gwen suggested.

Gwen watched Jeffers climb on the table to shut off the smoke alarm, which was still blaring away every five seconds.

"Pull out the battery," Gwen advised. "That's what I did to mine. It was going off all the time."

Jeffers frowned.

Gwen shrugged. Tammy found herself, much to her surprise, smiling. After the smoke cleared, Jeffers looked at his dinner. It was covered in water. Upon the final whorl of the garbage disposal, Gwen had a suggestion.

"How about pizza?"

Jeffers smiled in spite of himself.

"I'm buying," Gwen assured him, picking up the phone. "Right after I see if the commander is back."

"The commander?" Tammy asked with a touch of panic in her voice.

"I think she should know you're in town."

"Look, I'm not sure that's a good idea. I don't think I'm a really safe person to be around right now."

"Then the two of you already have a lot in common." Gwen flashed her a reassuring smile.

"Why are you here?" Jeffers asked Tammy.

"I just wanted you to know I was sorry," Tammy said quietly.

"How did you get in here?" Jeffers wondered. He was softening; he could feel it happening and was trying to figure out how to stop it.

"Your fire escape," Gwen said as she dialed Celia's number.

"She's right. I used your fire escape."

"I know because I had someone break into my place last week," Gwen explained as she dialed the commander. They both looked at Gwen skeptically.

"Someone broke into your place?" Henry asked.

"Oh, he's dead now. Hold on, it's still ringing."

Gwen got through to Celia. "Oh good, you're back. You need to get over to my apartment complex as soon as possible. Tammy Johnson is here—Yes—We are at apartment four, Henry Jeffers place. Oh, would you mind bringing pizza? Henry burnt the hot dogs—Thanks, I'll see you then." Gwen hung up the phone.

Jeffers glared at her.

Gwen ignored him and again picked through the bowl of jelly beans. She watched Tammy. Tammy appeared to be attracted to Jeffers Gwen decided.

"Would you mind if I took a shower?" Tammy asked Jeffers.

"Sure, I'll show you where everything is," Jeffers said.

"I'll run over to my place and find something for you to wear," Gwen said. She noticed the condition of Tammy's attire.

"Thanks," Tammy said. She'd love to take the clothes she had been wearing and throw them away.

* * *

Celia had just got out of the shower and into leggings and a big sweater when Gwen called. She had hoped to relax and regroup for a couple of hours. Clearly, that wouldn't happen tonight. Her mind raced through the day's events only to have it end with yet another surprise. Tammy Johnson.

* * *

Tammy was finished with her shower. She looked as pretty as Jeffers had remembered her being in Syria. She had on blue jeans now and a white sweatshirt. Gwen was sitting at the counter still picking through the jelly beans. Jeffers had cleaned up the stove and the pan that the hot dogs had burnt in. As he wiped off the counters, he glared into the bowl of jelly beans.

"You're leaving the white and black ones," Jeffers said, his eyebrows frowning.

"Nobody likes the white or black ones," Gwen said matter-of-factly.

Tammy sat next to Gwen. Studying Gwen, Tammy saw a very professional and charming woman. She watched Gwen pick out colored jelly beans.

"How long have you two known each other?" Tammy asked both Gwen and Jeffers.

"Oh, a couple of weeks," Gwen replied.

"Are you together?" Tammy asked, carefully. Both Gwen and Jeffers started shaking their heads violently.

"Oh, goodness no," Gwen said, laughing. "That's funny."

Gwen received yet another cool look from Jeffers.

"What?" Gwen said innocently.

There was a knock on Jeffers' door. He opened it and Celia walked in with pizza. Tammy looked nervous, and Celia needed to curb that before she took off again. If Tammy disappeared now, Celia wanted to know where she was. Celia had to make sure Tammy felt safe with them, at least with her.

"How are you, Tammy? I was worried when we couldn't find you." Celia decided on the gentle approach.

"What were you doing in Syria?" Tammy was direct.

"Let's have dinner and talk later. I don't know about you, but I've had a long day," Celia said with a weak smile.

Tammy looked at Celia and noticed how tired she looked. Dixon trusted her, and he didn't trust anybody. Somewhere deep inside she must trust her, too. Otherwise why would she still be here?

CHAPTER 23

Perry had taken special pains to make sure tonight was perfect. Lighting the candles, he put them in the center of the table in the kitchen. All he had found was a light blue bath towel for a tablecloth. He used it as a table runner. Perry went into the bathroom to see if he could improve himself. He combed his wavy light brown hair. He shaved and splashed on cologne. Standing back, he looked at himself.

When he was satisfied, he cleaned up the bathroom, throwing everything in the tub and pulling the shower curtain. Perry went into the living room and dimmed the lights. Fluffing up the pillows, he set them in place on the couch. He was nervous. Maybe he could just walk out that door and run before she got here...

The doorbell rang.

Perry took a deep breath and let it out deliberately, in the same way one would do to control pain. He opened the door.

Mary looked incredible. Her dark hair was styled just right. She was wearing a black dress, just off the shoulders, the A-line skirt that barely touched the top of her ankles. At the sight of her elegance, Perry's nervousness melted away—into sheer panic.

"May I come in?" Mary asked, the corner of her lips curling upward into a smile.

"Oh yeah, come in."

Mary walked into the room, met by the aroma of spaghetti.

"It smells wonderful," she said.

"Spaghetti." Perry smiled. "It's the only thing I know how to make. McDonald does most of the cooking."

"Really? I didn't know that." Mary sounded surprised.

"It's true. Takeout Chinese is his specialty."

Mary laughed. Perry froze.

* * *

"Gwen," Celia said quietly as they had a moment in Jeffers kitchen.

"I like Tammy. A little jumpy, but she seems like a nice girl." Gwen put her glass in the sink. Celia turned the water on and left it running.

"I'm glad to hear you say that, because I have a favor to ask," Celia said, keeping her voice low.

"Why are we whispering?" Gwen asked, lowering her voice as well.

"I want you to keep Tammy at your place. You can't tell anyone. You and I will be the only ones who know. It is never to be discussed at the office or anywhere else."

"Sounds exciting."

"I'm serious, Gwen. It could be dangerous. Putting Tammy in your care would probably be the last thing someone would expect me to do, so it just might work." Celia continued, "Just do what I ask, no matter how strange."

"Everything alright?" A voice came from behind them.

Celia turned to see Jeffers standing in the doorway of the kitchen. Celia turned off the water.

"Sorry," Gwen began. "I suppose this isn't the time to get into it, anyway."

Celia stopped breathing momentarily, wondering what Gwen was going to say next.

"I had a question about... well, female problems and the commander was giving me advice. Not the best after dinner subject, I realize." Gwen sighed. "We can talk later. Thanks again, Commander." Gwen left the kitchen.

"Excuse me. I didn't mean to interrupt," Jeffers said, embarrassed, after Gwen was in the next room.

Tammy walked into the kitchen.

"Tammy, you are staying with me tonight," Celia said

Tammy hesitated. "I'm not sure if that's a good idea."

"Please, at least for tonight. If you feel you need to make other arrangements, you can do so tomorrow." Celia awaited a reply.

"I guess one night couldn't hurt," Tammy said finally.

"We need to go now if you don't mind. I ready for much needed sleep," Celia said. "Thank you, Jeffers."

"Thank you for bringing dinner," Henry said.

"I'm sorry, Henry," Tammy said, not knowing what else to say.

"We'll talk tomorrow," Jeffers said.

"I need to ask you not to speak of Tammy's arrival to anyone until we can make sure she is safe," Celia said to Jeffers. "Please trust me, especially where the team is concerned, tell no one."

Jeffers looked at Tammy and then he nodded, giving Celia his word. After they left, it was just Jeffers and Gwen.

"Well, Henry, you sure know how to show a girl a good time," Gwen said teasing.

"You are welcome to come back, on one condition."

"What's that?"

"Stay out of my kitchen." Jeffers smiled.

"That's what our cook said when I left for college."

* * *

Mary looked across the table at Perry. She just hoped his beeper wouldn't go off and spoil the evening. They were finished with dinner, and she wasn't sure, but he was acting nervous again.

"Let's go into the other room," he said.

Mary smiled. "Okay." Perry waited for her to rise, and they walked arm in arm into the living room and sat on the couch together.

"There is something I'd like to talk to you about." He put his arm around her.

"What is it?" Mary asked. He was being very mysterious.

Perry was silent. He was searching for the right words.

"Chris?"

"I just wanted to..." Perry took a deep breath.

"What is it, Chris?" Mary was getting worried. He had been acting strange all evening. Maybe he wasn't happy in this relationship anymore.

"I just wanted you to know that I love you more than life itself," Perry said finally, unable to say anymore. He couldn't believe he chickened out.

"I love you too," Mary said, relieved as they embraced.

Inside, he was kicking himself. This was supposed to be the night he was going to ask her to marry him. And he, a Navy SEAL, just chickened out.

* * *

Celia and Tammy were sitting on the bed, the only piece of furniture set up in the house thus far. Celia wanted to listen to Dixon's answering machine tape. But first she need to talk with Tammy.

"Let's get started." Celia arranged pillows and sat back.

"What do you want to know?"

"Who are you and who do you work for? What were you doing in Syria?"

Tammy appeared hesitant.

"Tammy, you have good reason to be worried, but if I'm going to help, you need to be honest with me. That means you have to trust me."

"I guess I have to trust somebody, don't I?" Tammy said with a sigh. "I'm CIA and I work for William Dixon, whom you have met."

"Did you tell Henry who you are?"

"Yes. That I'm CIA."

"When was the last time you talked to Dixon?"

"Yesterday. I'm going to try to see him again tomorrow. I was supposed to meet him tonight, but I had to see Henry."

Celia wondered if Tammy knew Dixon was dead. She decided there was only one way to find out.

"Tammy, I was scheduled to meet with Dixon this morning."

"And?"

"When my assistant and I got there, he was dead. He had been stabbed."

"No!" Tammy's eyes teared. She stood up and walked over to the bedroom window. "I can't believe they got him."

"Who are 'they'?"

"I'm not sure. Dixon kept me in the dark most of the time."

"I need to ask you something else. A note Dixon left for me," Celia said. She let Tammy read it.

"Who is Lieutenant Tom Kelly? A relation of yours?" Tammy asked, noticing the name. She dried her tears.

"He was my husband. He was shot down over the Mediterranean Sea four years ago. You haven't heard of him before now?"

"No, I'm sorry," Tammy said. "Maybe Dixon's contact knew something."

"He has a contact? Who?"

"He was the guy I was arguing with in Syria. You remember, in the middle of the night when you tried to rescue me. I don't know his name, only that he was Dixon's contact."

"Well, there's a start. How did Dixon obtain this contact?"

"I don't know that either. So where does your husband fit into this?"

"I wish I knew," Celia said with a sigh. She opened her briefcase and took out the tape. "I noticed Dixon had a message, so I took the tape from his answering machine when I went through his house. Maybe the message was from the contact."

"You went through his house?"

"Long story. I haven't had a chance to listen to this yet." Celia popped out the tape in her own machine and replaced it with Dixon's. They both listened to it.

The first message began, "This is Tammy. I'll call later." The next message was a voice Tammy recognized. "I need to meet with you at the northeast end of the docks on pier twenty-eight Saturday night at eight."

"That's him. That's the contact," Tammy said.

"The same guy I saw?" Celia wanted to make sure.

"The one and only."

"Great," Celia said happily. "Finally we are getting somewhere. Since Dixon is gone, I'll meet with the contact instead."

"He is very spooky about outsiders. Chances are if he sees you, he'll run, like he did in Syria."

"One way or another, I've got to get to the bottom of this. I'll have to take a chance,"

Celia said. "Why were you sent to Syria?"

"I was supposed to be looking for a plant in the clinic that could lead me to the Pact's camp. If I found one, I was to tell the contact."

"So you knew about the boy?"

"No."

"According to our intelligence, the boy lived with the Pact."

"That is strange. Why wouldn't Dixon tell me that?" Tammy's eyebrows frowned.

"We won't ever know the answer to that. Was the pipe bomb meant for you?" Celia asked.

"I'm not sure if the Pact found out about me or not. Dixon had me working the field there for over a year."

"Who did you argue with on the phone in the kitchen? Georgie overheard you."

"The contact."

"I see," Celia said. She realized Tammy hadn't given her any reason to trust her. In fact, for a CIA agent, Tammy was uninformed about the job given to her. Or she just wasn't sharing what she knew with Celia. Celia decided to continue with her plan and keep her alive while she checked her out.

"I want to help. Let me meet with the contact," Tammy suggested.

"I'll need your help but, my first priority is to make sure you live long enough to give it to me. I need to speak to this guy myself. As for you, it's time to get you to a safe place."

"I'm not staying here?"

"No. I need to keep you alive."

Tammy paused and tears began to fall again. "I'm not sure you can do that. You don't know these people."

"I'm well aware of what these people are capable of," Celia assured her. "Please trust me."

Tammy looked at her with large, frightened eyes.

"Now, let's get you out of here."

For the first time in a long time Tammy felt at peace.

Celia dialed Gwen and said, "Meet me at Bill's Convenience Store along Highway 4. You can't miss it. Park on the right edge of the lot, away from the streetlights, and wait for her to get into your car. One hour."

Celia pulled past the convenience store she and Gwen had agreed to. She parked out of sight behind abandoned propane store right next to Bill's. It was only a five-minute wait until Celia saw Gwen's green Chevy Nova.

"Go around behind the store to avoid the light and cameras." Celia warned Tammy.

Celia sent Tammy to Gwen's Nova, alone. Gwen did not notice Tammy until she opened the door, causing Gwen to jump.

Tammy got into Gwen's Nova. Gwen still had her engine running. She put it into drive and pulled out of the parking lot.

"Hi," Gwen said cheerfully, her heart still beating fast after Tammy startled her. "Don't worry. You'll be safe with me. Nobody can find anything in my place."

* * *

Celia got home at 2:15 a.m. The night air had chilled her. She undressed and washed up in the dark, then put on flannel pajamas. She got into bed, allowing her body to relax for the first time two days.

"Keep both Tammy and Gwen safe. In Jesus' name," Celia prayed as she drifted off to sleep.

CHAPTER 24

"So how is Tammy?" Celia asked Gwen the next morning.

"She's doing well, I think. She fell right to sleep after we snuck up the fire escape and into my bedroom. I am finding the fire escape to be quite handy."

Celia smiled at that visual image.

"Meet me at the office this morning. Take an hour or so. No hurry," Celia said.

"See you then," Gwen said.

Before Celia left for the office, she called Georgie and asked her to come to the office as well. As Celia's drove back to base, she thought about whether to share Tammy's whereabouts with Georgie. Finally decided she would just tell Georgie that Tammy was secure but not reveal the location. Georgie's input on any information Tammy can give them would be invaluable.

Celia made a pit stop at pier twenty-eight for a lay of the land. The docks of pier twenty-eight was more of a hangout for people of questionable character she concluded. Staying in her car, Celia did not want to risk being seen before tonight. She started her Studebaker and continued to the base.

Celia and Gwen arrived simultaneously, Gwen's little green Chevy Nova choking as it came to a stop. Celia walked over to her.

"I think someday I'm going to shoot this thing," Gwen said of her Nova as she pushed the lock and slammed the door shut. Her face fell as she realized what she had done. "Oh! I locked my keys in the car again."

"Again?" Celia asked, trying not to laugh.

"It's only been a couple of times this month," Gwen said, shaking her head. She put her handbag over her shoulder. "I'll worry about it later."

"You sure?"

"Yeah, I'm sure. I don't suppose you have a gun on you now, do you?" Gwen asked with a straight face. Celia smiled. They walked into the building.

"So what's up?" Gwen asked. "I didn't expect you to work today."

"I came across something at Dixon's place."

"Dixon's place?" Gwen raised her eyebrow at Celia. They got onto the elevator.

"After his death, Georgie and I looked around his place. Georgie didn't tell you?" Celia said. Gwen's mouth fell open as the elevator doors closed.

"You broke in?" Gwen asked, shocked.

Celia paused and said, "Technically, Georgie did."

"She can break into houses and does phone taps. Is it just me, or do you find that odd?"

"I'm trying not to read too much into it," Celia said.

"That doesn't sound like you at all."

"Back to your question, I'm planning an OP of my own," Celia said. She walked ahead of Gwen and opened the door.

"That doesn't sound good either." Gwen shook her head and followed Celia.

Celia's mind was speeding through other details. Taking a deep breath, she knew she'd have to pace herself and get it right.

Showing up instead of Dixon was, as Tammy said, risky at best. She'd have to be prepared to corner the contact. There was the possibility he knew Dixon was dead and would not show. Celia had noticed there was no front-page news about Dixon. In fact, it wasn't in the paper at all. Not even the

Washington Post. Someone was pulling strings somewhere. Maybe the CIA.

"I'm here, ma'am," Georgie said.

"Great," Celia said, walking into her office. Both Georgie and Gwen followed her.

"First of all, Tammy Johnson showed up last night. I have her in a safe place for now." Celia filled Georgie in on Tammy's connection.

"Interesting," was Georgie's only reply.

"I want the two of you to listen to something." Celia got right to business. She got a small tape recorder from the bottom left-hand drawer of her desk. She played the tape from Dixon's answering machine. First, they heard Tammy's message, then they heard the second message.

"That sounds like the man who argued with Tammy in Syria," Georgie observed.

"It is. Tammy confirmed that," Celia replied, nodding. "She referred to him as Dixon's contact. She doesn't know his name."

"Where is Tammy?" Georgie asked. Gwen remained silent.

"She's in a safe place until we unravel this mess," Celia explained briefly.

"A wise move I have to agree, ma'am," Georgie said.

Gwen had something else on her mind. She frowned.

"Play that again," Gwen said to Celia. Gwen's expression was intense. Celia rewound the tape and played it again.

"That's him! That is the guy that has been calling you." Gwen was excited.

"You sure?" Celia asked.

"Positive."

"I wonder why Dixon's contact called me. And why did he say he was Dixon?" Celia sat back.

"What are you planning to do?" Gwen asked. She knew Celia long enough to know she was leading up to something.

Dixon was dead, so he couldn't meet with the contact. Oh no! She wasn't! Gwen shook her head.

"What's wrong?" Celia asked her before answering Gwen's question.

"You're going to meet with the contact instead, aren't you?" Gwen frowned.

"That's right, I am," Celia said.

"Brilliant idea, ma'am," Georgie said.

"What?" Gwen looked at Georgie. Was she the only one in this office with any common sense?

"Here is the problem," Celia said. "We are running out of people who can help tie this together. I need to get my hands on this guy before someone else beats me to it. He may know some of what is going on, or he may know everything. Either way, I'm going to find out."

"What if he doesn't talk?" Georgie asked.

"I'm hoping he will."

Celia was determined. Gwen had heard that tone in her voice many times. It was obvious there was no talking her out of it.

"How are you going to do this without scaring him off?" Gwen inquired.

"I realize the unexpected variables may cause this to fall apart, but it's our best shot," Celia said, taking out a blank sheet of paper. "Here is the dock. It has a rail along here that ends just before it curves into the ocean. On this side are five buildings two meters apart. Only two street lamps. Here and here." Celia mapped it out as she talked. "Over here is a light tower. There is a clump of bushes at this corner of it."

"Doesn't look like much light," Georgie said, looking at her drawing.

"No, and it doesn't receive a lot of upkeep, a few of the street lights are burnt out," Celia said.

"How do you propose to do this without him running?" Gwen asked again.

"He took off in Syria upon seeing you, ma'am," Georgie reminded her. "And I chased him, so he might not be too receptive to me either."

"I guess I'll wait at the end of the dock and wear baggy clothes and a cap. Hopefully he'll give me at least a chance when he realizes I'm not Dixon. Since we're not sure whose side he's on, we need to be cautious. We'll wear vests and carry a gun. For protection only. I want this guy alive. Gwen, you'll be waiting in the car. We'll need someone to man the phone in case something goes wrong."

"Wrong? Who do I call?" Gwen frowned.

"Since we don't know what to expect, we will have to figure it out as we go. Not my favorite way of doing things, but I don't see where we have any choice. If he has been trying to call me, hopefully he'll want to talk to me as much as I do him."

"All due respect, ma'am, perhaps we could enlist Tammy's help," Georgie suggested.

"I'm not sure she should show herself anywhere until we know she is safe."

"So our plan is having no plan," Gwen recapped, throwing her arms in the air.

"The plan is to see what we can find out," Celia corrected. "I think we'll take your car, Gwen. It'll blend in better."

"Why? What part of town is this?" Gwen asked, alarmed.

"Let's get our things together, then we'll be on our way." Celia smiled, dismissing Gwen's question.

"No, seriously, who do I call?" Gwen asked.

* * *

Daniel Ryan dug through his locker at the Fleet Training Center. He had a date with someone he had met at the bar below his place. Ryan was glad to see that his black jeans were in there. He had thought he lost them. His date was in an hour, and they were the only nice pair of pants he owned.

Closing the locker, Ryan turned to find himself face to face with a tall blond man. Ryan stepped back, surprised. Everything in the locker room always echoed, but this guy was right behind him and he hadn't heard a sound.

"Sorry, didn't mean to scare you." He smiled, as if he had enjoyed sneaking up on him.

"That's okay. I just didn't think anyone was here."

"I'm new here." The blond man extended his right hand. "I'm Ray."

"Dan," Ryan said, shaking his hand. He was very tan, Ryan thought.

"Where you from?"

"Maine," the blond man said.

"I'm from Kentucky." Ryan looked at his watch. "I have to get going. I have a date. Maybe I'll see you around."

"Sure."

Ryan stopped at the door a moment. He realized the base wasn't getting new recruits this week.

"What team are you with?" he asked as he looked back.

The man was gone. Ryan shrugged as he looked at his watch. He needed to get going.

"Ray?"

There was still no answer. He shook his head and left.

The blond man had hidden behind a row of lockers. He knew he should take out any witness, but he couldn't risk taking out someone here. He'd have to wait till later. When he heard the door close, he climbed to the top of the row of lockers and walked to the center. He reached up and removed the cover for the ceiling duct. He climbed up and crawled into the space, securing the vent cover behind him, going quietly on his way.

* * *

Gwen had forgotten to call a locksmith. Celia and Georgie came up beside her as Gwen wondered how to get in the car.

"I'm nearly out of gas, so I'd better do that first," Gwen said. "After I figure out how to open the door, that is."

"Is there a problem?" Georgie asked.

"I locked my keys in my car."

Georgie looked inside the driver's side window. She looked across to the other side. Then she stood up and walked to the opposite door of the car, opened the passenger's door, and reached over, unlocking the driver's door.

"Fortunately for you, the other side was unlocked."

* * *

Celia looked at the lighthouse and watched the light as it bounced on top of the ocean waves, moving slowly back and forth.

"What are you looking at?" Gwen finally asked.

"Trying to figure out where the light is going to be," Celia said. "I'm going to try to stay in the shadows for the most part."

"Considering that you are half Dixon's size, the shadows won't help much, you'd better hope this guy is blind," Gwen said.

"Where do you want me, ma'am?" Georgie asked.

"The bench along the boardwalk will be the best place to see the whole dock. Settle there for now." Celia suggested to Georgie. Celia loaded her GLOCK 9mm semi-automatic and put it in a holster under her coat. She got her backup AMT .45 ready as well and left it on the front seat of the car.

"Gwen, I'm leaving this here in case you need to use it, okay?"

"A gun?" Gwen pressed her back against the car door and put her hands in the air shaking her head. "Could we go over my job description one more time?"

"It's just a precaution, Gwen." Celia set the gun on the seat when Gwen refused to take it.

"Right. A precaution," Gwen said, looking at it as if it were a snake.

"Ready, Georgie?" Celia asked.

"Hey, who was I supposed to call?" Gwen shouted out too late. They were already gone.

Gwen looked at the gun again. Carefully she picked it up and opened the glove box, put the gun inside and closed it. Then she dug through her purse until she found her can of mace and duct tape. If worse came to worst, she could spray him and duct tape him. Then if the commander wanted to shoot him, she could do it herself when she got back.

Celia started to walk to the end of the dock. She had a big coat on and decided to pull her hood over her cap. The wind was picking up, its chill blowing straight through her. As she reached the end of the docks, she looked across the Atlantic. Jumping into the water would be one way he could get away from her. She found herself wondering if she really could pull this thing off long enough to talk to him. She looked over the horizon to see a storm brewing. Dark clouds were gathering, preparing for rain. Thunder sounded in the distance.

Georgie sat on the bench. The benches looked precarious and on the verge of collapse. She took her chances with what she thought was the best one. There were older men fishing. The younger people on the docks were hanging out. There were young men, smoking, their jackets opened to their belly buttons, and young girls with thick makeup and tight pants hanging on the arms of both younger and older men alike.

The skies became darker, and evening came sooner than expected with the black clouds that covered the horizon. The darker it became, the busier the docks became. Would either hurt or hinder them? Celia wasn't sure. She was again feeling the chill again as the wind whirled. Her attire was dark and bulky, making her look much larger than she was, hopefully large enough to get a conversation in. She didn't look as tall as

Dixon, but at a distance she could bring the contact in closer. Celia waited with a knot of anticipation growing in her stomach.

"Dixon," said a man with a gravelly voice. He said it above the wind. Celia found herself jumping, her back to him.

"Dixon?" he repeated.

"I came in his place," she said, raising her voice, as he had, above the wind.

"Tammy?" he asked.

"About Dixon," Celia said.

"Who are you?" the man demanded. She wasn't Tammy. "Turn around."

Slowly Celia turned. The wind caught her hood, pushing it off her head, revealing her dark hair. A flash of lightning gave just enough light for them to see each other's face. The rain started to fall on his black hair, matting it to his head. His eyes gave away his complete surprise as another flash of lightning brightened the dock.

"You!" he whispered.

"Please, Dixon is dead. That is why I'm here," Celia said. "I need your help."

"What? My help?" he exclaimed.

She walked toward him. "I understand you were his contact."

"How do you know that?"

She was only within a couple of feet of him.

"Stay where you are," he warned.

Celia heeded the warning, with a plea. "Please, I just need to ask a few questions."

"I only talk to Dixon, no one else," he said after a long pause.

"Dixon is dead," Celia said again.

He turned suddenly and ran.

"Please!" Celia called out. She took off after him. Throwing off her large coat, she began weaving in and out of the people along the dock. He could hear the pounding of feet behind him. She was fast.

Georgie saw him take off with Celia on his tail. She got up to intercept. She ran toward him as he ran down the boardwalk. Before he realized what was happening, he saw Georgie was practically on top of him. The same person who had chased him in Syria. It was a trap! He pushed a man into Georgie's path and turned around, now facing Celia.

Celia tried to grab his arm. He blocked her and flipped her out of the way. Celia's face hit the boardwalk. She turned and lay on her back, trying to catch her breath. A trickle of blood streaming from her hairline. The contact didn't bother looking back. He jumped over the rail and into the ocean. Georgie went to Celia.

"Get him," Celia ordered Georgie, as she stood.

Georgie obeyed, jumping over the rail after him. Georgie was gone for what seemed a long time. Finally she emerged and climbed back onto the dock. She ran back to Celia, who was waiting on a bench.

"Are you alright, ma'am?" Georgie asked out of breath, her clothes and hair dripping wet.

"I'm fine. Where is he?" Celia was wet as the rain now a downpour.

Georgie helped Celia up to her feet. They started walking back to the car.

"I lost him, ma'am."

As the rain washed away the blood from her face, she felt dizzy. Gwen's face was panicked when she saw Celia.

"I've got a towel in back somewhere on the floor," Gwen said to Georgie.

"This is very unsanitary," Georgie said as she retrieved the towel off the floor.

"It looks pretty deep, ma'am. We'd better get it stitched up."

"I'm sure it looks worse than it is," Celia protested.

"It looks like stitches to me," Gwen agreed. She put her Nova in reverse and headed for the hospital.

* * *

The contact popped his head out of the water, gasping for air. It had been a long time since he had to hold his breath that long. He got out of the water and made his way back to his motorcycle. Looking around, he made sure they were gone. When he decided it was safe, he sat on the motorcycle. The rain was coming down hard now. As he pulled out of the parking lot, he wondered how Commander Celia Kelly knew he would be there if Dixon was dead.

CHAPTER 25

Gwen walked through the door of her apartment, trying to be quiet. Instead, she tripped over a rug and caught herself on a small decorator's table, knocking a vase with plastic flowers off it. As the vase crashed to the floor, Tammy sat straight up on the couch, where she had been sleeping.

"Who's there?" Tammy called out.

"It's me," Gwen said, disgusted with herself for making so much noise. She switched on the light. Gwen looked around her. Everything was in perfect order. The place was clean and everything put away, except the vase, now in pieces on the hall floor. She stood there a moment, trying to decide if she was in the right apartment. It had been a long day, but her key fit the door and Tammy was here. It must be her place.

"I got bored and cleaned up for you," Tammy explained, trying to read Gwen's expression. Tammy got off the couch and came into the hall.

"I have a rug?" Gwen asked referring the rug she tripped on.

"I found it in a box marked From Boston."

"This table?"

"Brand new, still in the box. I put it together myself," Tammy said proudly.

"All these things are mine?"

"They were in all those boxes." Tammy was concerned Gwen didn't appear to be happy.

That explained why she didn't recognize anything, Gwen thought. She'd never seen it out of the box.

"Gwen, don't you like it?"

"Oh, it looks great. It does. I'll get used to it." Gwen smiled weakly. "Go back to sleep. I didn't mean to wake you."

"I wasn't sleeping too soundly anyhow."

What did she mean, she'd get used to it? Tammy asked herself. Then she asked Gwen, "How did it go? Did he talk to her?"

"No, but he gave her a shiner and ten stitches," Gwen said.

"I should have gone with you. Is she all right?" Tammy asked, feeling guilty.

"The commander is fine. She'll live. She has so far. Where are my boxes?"

"I threw them away, why?"

"I had some of those boxes for six years," Gwen muttered to herself as she went into her bedroom.

***

Daniel Ryan climbed to the top of the stairs above the bar to his apartment. As he walked through the door, he was greeted by the familiar flashing of the neon sign right outside his window. He got ready for bed. He lay in his bed, closing his eyes, waiting for sleep to come.

Instead, his mind went back to earlier in the day when he had met Ray, the blond man in the locker room. Trying to sort it out, Ryan tried to figure out what was so strange to him. The man was very tan, like he was in the sun every day. He said he was from Maine, not exactly the sunshine state.

What was strange was how he was there and then suddenly he disappeared. Ryan tried to picture him as he tried to go to sleep.

Ryan's eyes opened and he sat straight up in bed. The blond hair! Could he have something to do with Syria? The camp had been destroyed. Ryan knew that, yet the blond man wasn't there. How could he get on base? He'd call the commander in the morning. It was likely enough nothing.

CHAPTER 26

As Celia awoke, it was obvious to her that movement would not come easily to her. She carefully rolled over as the sun peeked through the crack in the curtains. The sunshine brightened her outlook as she forced herself to get out of bed. A long hot bubble bath was what she needed. She ran water. Her head pounded with each movement. When the bath was ready, she took off her robe and sank into the bubbles. It melted away some of the tension caused by yesterday's events. She recalled the man on the docks, black hair and a black beard. He was tall, maybe six foot. His voice was gravelly, possibly trying to disguise it. None of it told her who he was.

He had recognized her, and this time, she noticed. Whether it was from the past or from that brief moment in Syria, she couldn't be sure. The only thing she did know for sure is that he was gone, and there was still nothing new. As she soaked in the tub, the phone rang. Celia never even heard it. The machine answered the call.

Celia closed her eyes and laid her head back, trying to clear her mind. After the events of the last month and a half, it was impossible. Lord, she thought, what am I going to do and how am I going to take care of this? After nearly an hour, she emerged from the tub.

Celia picked out a pair of jeans and a green cotton blouse. Tucking in her blouse, she then found white tennis shoes. She fixed herself toast and a hot cup of coffee and sat looking out her dining room window, watching the tide come in. After breakfast and two aspirin, she decided to take a walk along the shoreline.

Celia walked down the steps and onto the sand, straight for the ocean. The air was warming up as the sun's rays covered the landscape. The waves crashed against the scattered rocks as she reached the water's edge.

"Good morning," said a familiar voice from behind. Celia turned to see Elliot.

"What happened to you?" His expression was shocked.

Celia sighed. "Long story."

"I've got time," he said, concerned.

"I'm afraid it's classified."

There was a long silence as he fought the urge to press her for more information. Finally he said, "You know what you need?"

"What?"

"A free day."

"A free day? I'm not sure I can spare a day."

"Everyone needs a free day. There is a place you'd like. Interested?"

"Where is this place?" Celia felt unclear of his intentions.

"You have to trust me."

Celia wasn't sure she should, but a day to regroup might even help. On the other hand, spending this much time with a member of the team who happened to be her landlord, was inappropriate.

"I have the best intentions and I'm not suggesting anything improper," Elliot said, reading her mind.

"I'm sorry. I'm not comfortable with it," Celia said carefully.

"Afraid of me?" he asked. His eyes challenged her.

"Of course not. The Navy has rules. I have rules." Celia responded firmly.

"You are new to the area. Do you want to know a great place to go and think or not?" Elliot said tightly.

She somehow found herself talked into the sightseeing trip.

"I can only spare two or three hours," Celia said finally.

"I'll have you back in two and a half hours."

* * *

Daniel Ryan called the commander again only to get the answering machine again. He decided to leave a detailed message. "Commander, this is Dan Ryan. I think I saw the, maybe not the, but a blond man yesterday. The circumstances were strange and I thought I'd mention it."

Ryan sat at the small table that separated his kitchen from his living room and bedroom. He wondered what to do. If it was the blond man why was he in the states? Maybe the commander was outside on the beach. He'd call Elliot. When Elliot's machine came on, he left another brief message.

"This is Dan. I need to speak to Commander Kelly. Can you give her the message?" Ryan hung up the phone. He decided to go to the duplex later after his errands and see if either one of them was on the beach. If not, he'd have to wait.

* * *

Elliot drove Celia to the marina. He rented a motor boat. Once aboard, he set off for a small island just offshore. When the boat was tied to the dock, they got off with a picnic lunch Elliot purchased from a deli on the way and began to explore the island.

"What is this place?" Celia asked.

"Just a small island that the Navy at one time used for training. Still might on occasion. I personally only come here for peace and quiet."

"A perfect place for that."

"I want to show you something."

Celia followed him to a pond that the ocean supplied. It even had fish in it. They sat on the edge of the bank.

"So other than getting beat up, you settling in okay?" Elliot asked.

"For the most part. Do you know of any good churches in our neighborhood?" Celia asked out of the blue.

"Churches?" Elliot repeated, wondering if he heard right.

Celia smiled causing her face to hurt.

"Is that a tough question?"

"No. You just took me by surprise. So you are really into this praying and going to church thing. I don't spend much time in churches. Most people who go to church are hypocrites."

Celia smiled. "That's what churches are for. For people who aren't perfect."

"I guess I never thought of it like that. Sorry, I didn't mean to imply you are a hypocrite," Elliot said with worried eyes.

"You're being honest and I'm definitely not perfect."

"I can tell you're one of those people who believe your faith can move mountains. Am I right?" Elliot gave her a knowing look.

"Only God can move mountains. Though sometimes, I admit, I try to move a few on my own. That never turns out well."

"Like last night?"

"Last night?"

"Your face."

"Yeah, like last night." Celia smiled, giving him that one.

"My father left my mom when I was five. He wrote me letters from all over the world. He spent years aboard the USS Ranger. He was ranking CO and captain. Eventually he became an admiral and he died of colon cancer. In the meantime, my mom raised me alone with no money. She never remarried. I think she still loved him. I guess that's why she did it."

"Did what?" Celia asked.

"Committed suicide."

"I'm sorry."

"You know what was funny? I thought both of them were the most incredible people I had ever met. But that's not true.

She wasn't strong enough to forget and go on, and he wasn't strong enough to stay. They both checked out." Elliot shook his head. "I guess I don't see what to believe in. Life is a mess."

"It's a choice. I believe the world's chaos exists from choosing the ways of the world instead of the ways of God. I chose the job I did to improve the consequences of others' bad choices." Celia looked off into the water. "Sounds corny, I guess."

"It sounds honorable." Pausing a moment, he said, "I guess I chose the Navy because I found something to believe in there. My country. I found a new family there, in my team."

"Also honorable."

"You never had children?" Elliot asked, wanting to change the subject.

"No. I'm way past that."

"What? You're all of thirty-five," Elliot teased.

"I'm not sure I'd even make a good civilian anymore, let alone a mother, and certainly not without Tom."

"So you still love your husband," Elliot observed.

"When did you meet Admiral Lloyd?" It was Celia's turn to change the subject.

"I met him a couple of years ago." Elliot was uncomfortable.

"Where?"

"In Washington, during a briefing."

"The reason I asked is I worked for him as his assistant for three years. I noticed the picture of you with him on your wall."

"You don't miss much, do you?"

Elliot thought back a moment, remembering the briefing where he had met Lloyd. The plan had been brilliant. He had gone to Washington with Walton to get permission to rescue a couple of SEALs. Lloyd had said no, but rumor had it that his assistant had gotten wind of it. The assistant not only talked him into it but came up with a solid plan that they could execute. Could it be she was the assistant that had helped them then? He had never met the assistant and had just assumed it had been a man, but maybe it wasn't. The mission had been called the FOX Rescue.

"I was there for a briefing on a mission called Operation FOX Rescue." He looked her in the eye, watching for a reaction.

"That was your team they sent over?" she asked thoughtfully.

He nodded. Elliot liked talking to her. He knew he shouldn't be enjoying her company, but he was.

* * *

Getting into his Ford pickup, Ryan began to head toward Elliot's duplex. Glancing in his rearview mirror, he saw a car following behind him. He didn't think much of it until he turned onto the next street. Keeping his eye on it, he decided to test it out. He drove past the bar back to his apartment. He put his foot on the gas and took the next right at top speed.

So did the black sedan.

* * *

Elliot and Celia got back just before dark. Celia was tired and still had her headache, so she excused herself and went inside to settle in for the night. She needed to check in with General Turner. She was afraid to, considering what a mess she had made of the night before losing the contact.

Going into the bedroom, Celia laid her jacket on the bed. She was going to put sweats on when she noticed the answering machine light blinking. She rewound the tape and pressed play.

The first message played. "This is Dan Ryan. Please call back as soon as possible at 344-7761." The second message played. "Commander, this is Dan Ryan. I think I saw the, maybe not the, a blond man yesterday. It was strange, and I just thought I'd mention it."

Celia rewound the tape again and played it, writing his phone number. Her heart skipped a beat, thinking the blond man might have seen Ryan. She quickly dialed Ryan's number.

There was no answer. She tried again. How long ago did he leave the message? She ran next door to Elliot's. Knocking loudly on the door, Celia waited. He answered it. "I thought you'd be in bed by now," Elliot said.

"Where does Daniel Ryan live?" Celia asked with a touch of urgency in her voice.

"He left a message. He was trying to get ahold of you." Elliot now wondered what it was about.

"I know. He left me one too. Where does he live?"

"He lives above the Brite's King Bar, uptown. Why?"

"What is the quickest route there?" Celia pressed.

"What's going on?" Elliot was concerned now. What was wrong with her?

"Please, I don't have time to explain. Just tell me how to get there."

"I'll take you," Elliot said, getting his keys off the counter.

Celia nodded in agreement. They got into Elliot's jeep. He backed up and turned the jeep around.

"What's going on?" Elliot asked in a way that was meant to get an answer.

"There was a message on my machine from Ryan saying he thought he saw a blond man." Celia's voice was even but her face gave away her concern.

"A blond man?"

"You know that the blond man wasn't at the camp the night we blew it. I have reason to believe he's in Norfolk." Ryan's life could be on the line, and that counted for more now. "I'll be honest with you, James, I'm just hoping Ryan is still alive," Celia said, sighing heavily.

Elliot stepped on the gas.

"What's going on?" Elliot asked.

"I can't tell you that."

"Why won't you trust me?" Elliot raised his voice. "I know there's more to it than this. It doesn't take a genius to see that. If he's gone after Ryan, he could go after any of us. Look at you! You can't keep us in the dark."

"I have a chain of command to follow." There had always been tension between Special Forces and Intelligence, sometimes intense. It was as old as the military itself. Celia did not like contributing to it, but she was. She understood his frustration; if their places were reversed, she would be angry too.

"The Pentagon?" Elliot shook his head. "That figures."

"I understand you are angry, but it's my job," Celia said quietly.

Right now she had a bigger problem—keeping Daniel Ryan alive. Celia noticed they were in the middle of town now, and she saw the bar with its large neon sign flashing. Elliot didn't seem to be stopping. He was just looking around.

"What are you doing?" Celia asked him. "Why aren't you stopping?"

"His truck isn't here. He always parks right over there," Elliot said, pointing to the left of them.

"Where else would he be?" Celia asked him.

"Let's drive around to the spots he normally goes to."

He took them past the places Ryan might be. He even drove past Perry and McDonald's apartment. Nothing. It was midnight. The moon was full and giving plenty of light to the evening's landscape. When did Ryan leave the message?

Elliot drove along Virginia Beach but decided to start back to the duplex. Maybe he went to talk to the commander in person. It was then he noticed Ryan's Ford pickup on the other side of the freeway, speeding back toward Norfolk. A black sedan followed inches behind him, their bumpers almost touching.

"There he is," Elliot said. He did a U-turn in the middle of the freeway, crossing the viaduct and pulling his jeep onto the freeway right behind the black sedan. Celia saw that the black sedan was alongside Ryan now. Something was coming out the passenger window. A long barrel belonging to some kind of automatic was pointed at Ryan.

"Gun!" Celia warned Elliot.

"My glove box."

Celia opened it and found a .45 revolver. In the seconds it took to get out Elliot's revolver, a shot was fired into Ryan's pickup. They watched helplessly as his pickup went out of control, through a guardrail, and came to an abrupt stop against a light pole. Celia tried to get the black sedan's license but only read two letters, TA, as it disappeared into the night.

Elliot felt a surge of panic. If Ryan survived, it would be a miracle. Elliot came to a screeching stop in front of the accident. Celia and Elliot ran over to the truck. Ryan was strapped into his seat belt. His head was hanging forward.

Celia's biggest concern was if there was a bullet wound and whether she'd have to move him to stabilize him.

"Get me a blanket!" Celia ordered Elliot. He went back to his jeep for a blanket. He found one and ran it over to her. They heard a car pull up behind Elliot's jeep. Celia's attention remained on Ryan. A state patrol officer came up to them.

"What happened?" the officer asked.

"I need a first-aid kit, gauze dressing, and an ambulance," Celia ordered the officer, dismissing the question.

Celia checked over Ryan. There was no bullet wound that she could see. However, his breathing was labored. She noticed glass inside a long cut, five inches long, in his upper chest on the right-hand side. A piece of glass from the windshield was embedded in the chest cavity. The chest cavity was not expanding properly. His breathing was slow and shallow. His pulse was around 150.

Her fears were confirmed with each breath he attempted to take. Tension pneumothorax. Air was filling Ryan's chest cavity whether he breathed in or out. If the air in the chest cavity was not relieved, it would create pressure on the lungs until he would suffocate. The officer was back with the first-aid kit from his patrol car.

"I need to get him out of here," Celia said, turning to the officer and Elliot. "Do you have something we could use for a backboard?"

Elliot nodded and ran to get a piece of plywood from the back of his jeep.

Celia unfastened Ryan's seat belt and the officer slid the plywood behind him. On the count of three they had him lying flat on the ground. Elliot covered him with the blanket up to where Celia began to work. Celia went through the kit until she found a tube.

Ryan took in another labored breath. Celia removed the glass and placed a tube inside the open wound of the chest cavity and sealed off the wound around the tube. When the lungs filled, it forced the air around the lungs out the tube instead of remaining trapped in the chest cavity. As he let a breath out, she covered the tube entirely so air could not be sucked back in the cavity. She continued the procedure until his breathing was stabilized. At that point, she removed the tube and covered the entire wound.

She heard the ambulance in the distance. She looked up at Elliot, the crisis averted. If Ryan didn't have any other internal injuries from the crash, he'd be okay. Elliot read in her eyes her relief, knowing Ryan had been close to death. Ryan sounded better and his color had improved. Elliot knew she had just saved his friend's life.

The ambulance parked and ran a stretcher over to them.

"What do we got?" an EMT asked.

Celia filled them in. "Tension pneumothorax. Breathing was slow and shallow. I relieved the pressure building, and his breathing stabilized just before you got here."

"We'd better roll. May have internal bleeding," the other EMT stated.

"What about you?" the first EMT asked, as he set up an IV and put it in Ryan's arm.

"Me?" Celia asked, puzzled.

"Your face. Were you in the accident?"

"No." Celia shook her head.

"I need to ask you both a few questions," the officer said to Elliot and Celia.

"At the hospital," Celia said. She turned to the older EMT. "I'm going with you."

"Get in."

"James, meet me at the hospital and call Georgie," was the last thing Celia said as the doors closed on her and Ryan.

James went over to Ryan's truck. The bullet went in at an angle through the driver's side window and hit the right side of the windshield, shattering in large pieces. One piece had gone into Ryan's chest. The officer walked over to him.

"Did you see the accident?"

"Yes, sir."

"How did it happen?"

"Drive-by shooting. It was a black sedan."

CHAPTER 27

Celia woke up in the hospital waiting room. Gwen was sitting in a chair. Celia had fallen asleep on the couch. The sun was illuminating through the blinds into the waiting room of the Naval Medical Center Portsmouth, which was the closest naval hospital. McDonald stood looking through the blinds out the window. Celia looked to see she still had on her shirt and jeans spotted with Ryan's blood.

"And here you are again after yet another exciting night," Gwen said.

"When did you get here?" Celia asked.

"An hour ago."

Celia must have fallen asleep when Ryan was in surgery. She put her feet over the side of the couch.

"Where is Ryan?" Celia asked.

"He's taking visitors if you're interested," McDonald said.

"Absolutely," Celia said.

"I don't suppose you'll listen to me if I say you should go home and go to bed," Gwen said.

Celia and McDonald left the room.

"I didn't think so," said Gwen as she shook her head and followed.

McDonald and Gwen took Celia walked the long hall of the surgical floor. Finally they turned into Ryan's room. Ryan was sitting upright. A draining tube emerged just below the large gauze bandage wrapped around his upper chest. Elliot and Jeffers were laughing with Ryan, who was careful in his movements. Perry was sitting in the opposite corner. Ryan saw Celia come in with McDonald and Gwen.

"Commander!" Ryan said. Elliot and Jeffers looked at Celia. "You're awake!" He was in good spirits.

"I'm glad to see you looking much better, Petty Officer," Celia said. She tried to stay matter of fact though she was relieved beyond words.

"They tell me I owe it to you. Thanks." Ryan smiled. "I'm glad you guys were there," he continued, looking from Celia to Elliot.

"If I had been there when you called, the whole incident might have been avoided." Celia sighed.

It was clear that Celia blamed herself. Elliot had that same feeling himself last night – blaming her. In the light of day, after watching her work so hard to save Ryan, he knew those feelings were unfounded. She was as amazing to him as she was frustrating.

"Where's Georgie?" Celia asked Gwen.

"Georgie is meeting Rear Admiral Walton downstairs," Gwen said.

"I need to talk to Petty Officer Ryan in private," Celia said to the rest of them.

"Sure," Jeffers said, starting for the door.

"We'll be right outside," Perry said.

"I won't be long," Celia promised.

"After you," McDonald said to Gwen. Gwen went out ahead of him. Elliot started to leave when Celia stopped him.

"You can stay." Celia said to Elliot. He looked into her eyes, surprised.

He nodded and remained in the room, closing the door.

"What happened last night?" Celia asked Ryan.

"I was looking for a pair of pants for a date. I went to my locker at the base. While I was at my locker, this guy appeared from out of nowhere. He said his name was Roy and that he was new. I turned to my locker and got my pants. When I turned to ask him what team he was with he was gone. Poof! Everything in that room echoed and I couldn't hear a thing. I went on my date and went home. As I went to bed that night it just didn't set well. He was so tan, vague, stealth, the blond hair, and I guess I just had this gut feeling. So the next morning I called you." Ryan shrugged.

"An accurate feeling I'd say," Celia said.

"Sure looks that way," Ryan agreed.

"Did you see the guy who shot you?" Elliot asked.

"No. It was too dark. I noticed the black sedan following me after leaving your place. I led him on a wild goose chase for a couple of hours. I thought I had lost him and I was on my way back to the duplex to see you, Commander," Ryan said.

"Did you get the license?" Celia asked. "I only saw two letters."

"It was either a name or the letters stood for something. I read it as 43-T-A-R-A," Ryan said.

Elliot watched the color drain from Celia's face.

"What is it?" Elliot asked. "Does that mean something to you?"

"I don't know yet. Maybe. Don't talk to the police. We need a safe place for you to recover. I'll be back." Celia left the room.

"Where is she going?" Ryan asked Elliot. Elliot shrugged and then went after her.

"You are with him at all times until I say otherwise. I don't want him to be alone," Celia ordered Jeffers. Without questioning why, he went into Ryan's room.

The rest of the team watched as Elliot barely made it in the elevator with the commander. The doors closed and now alone with her, Elliot push the button to stall the elevator.

"What are you doing?" Celia asked him, taken off guard.

"I was about to ask you the same question," Elliot said.

"I need to find Georgie and Admiral Walton. I need to secure Ryan's safety and I need to find that blond man before he goes after someone else," Celia said.

"Not without me," he said firmly.

"I don't have that as an option."

"I'm not presenting it as one," Elliot replied. Taking a step closer he looked into her eyes, his determination glaring.

Celia could see there was no changing his mind. Right now she could use all the help she could get.

"I'll have to clear you," Celia said reluctantly.

"What?" Elliot asked.

"I'll talk to General Turner and clear you," Celia said. "If I let you in, I have to do it right."

"The Chairman of Joint Chiefs of Staff, General Turner?"

"Yes," Celia said, "We do it right or not at all."

Elliot stood silent, searching her dark green eyes. She was finally going to trust him.

"Okay," he said finally, stepping back. "Clear me!"

* * *

Upon seeing Celia and Elliot leave, the group followed Jeffers into Ryan's room.

"What was that all about?" McDonald asked.

"She asked me a few questions and said not to talk to the police. Then she just left," Ryan said, not knowing for sure.

"I'd better get back to the office to run interference. By the way, Commander just text me. Ryan is not supposed to be alone at any time and no one comes in or out unless it's one of us. Got it?" Gwen said to the remaining members of the team.

"Got it." McDonald nodded.

"Do you need anything?" Gwen asked Ryan.

"No, thanks," Ryan replied.

"Okay, I'll check in on you later." Gwen left.

"Hey, does anybody know what happened to the commander?" Perry asked.

"I thought maybe it was from last night," Jeffers said.

"No, those stitches are at least from a day or so ago," Perry said.

"I never even thought to ask her. I just assumed it was from last night," Ryan said.

"Why? Was she in the truck with you?" McDonald asked.

"No."

"Guess you're not the only one in danger," McDonald said to Ryan.

* * *

Celia and Elliot met Admiral Walton and Georgie at the entrance of the hospital. Walton looked at her bruised face and tired eyes. He wondered if the president and Turner had made a mistake.

"Good morning, ma'am," Georgie said to Celia.

"What happened to you, Commander?" Walton asked, with concern.

"I'm fine, sir," Celia said.

"I'm glad you are fine, but that wasn't my question. There's a reason I wasn't called before this?" Walton wondered.

"Not a good one. Things happened so fast, sir," Celia said honestly.

"So your assistant informed me, Commander." Walton raised his eyebrows looking first at Celia then at Georgie. His attention turned to Elliot. "What do you have to do with this, son?"

"Not nearly enough, sir," Elliot said, crossing his arms.

Walton sensed the tension between Elliot and Celia.

"We are going to have a chat. I'm going up to see Ryan first. I'll meet you after that in my office. You've got an hour to get your story together."

"Yes, sir," Celia said.

Walton went into the hospital.

"I could be reading this wrong, ma'am, but he may be put out with us," Georgie said. "Would you like me to drive you, ma'am?"

"No, I'm going back to the duplex with Elliot, thank you. We'll meet you at the office," Celia said. "I need to get into uniform."

"Yes, ma'am," Georgie said.

Celia and Elliot walked over to his jeep. He opened the door for her and then got in the other side. He looked over at the woman sitting next to him. Her face was still bruised and there were traces of Ryan's blood on her clothes. She was a sight, this woman who believed in a higher power. Where was her God now?

* * *

When Celia got home, the first thing she did was check the answering machine. There were no messages. Celia took a shower and put on her uniform, French braided her hair as she usually did, and completed her makeup. She stared at the sorry face in the mirror.

Celia went into the kitchen where her briefcase still sat on the kitchen counter. Her heart skipped a beat at her carelessness. Walking over to counter, she checked the briefcase. Everything was there and untouched. She put everything in place and then looked up General Turner's number.

"This is Commander Kelly," Celia said into the phone.

"What do you have, Commander?" Turner said.

"We are looking into things I acquired from Dixon's house. The night before last, Tammy Johnson surprised us. She was the woman who disappeared in Syria. Turns out she's CIA and knew Dixon's contact. I tried to meet with him but he wasn't very receptive. Then things took a turn for the worse. One of the SEAL's was shot after seeing a blond man."

Silence.

"And?" Turner asked.

"I need permission to expose the team to enough information to protect them." Celia paused. "Sir, I'd like to enlist Lieutenant Commander Elliot with full clearance."

"Just one question, Commander," Turner said. "Do you trust Elliot?"

"Yes," Celia said sincerely.

"How is your injured SEAL doing?" Turner asked.

"He'll be fine, sir. I just need to find a safe place for him."

"What about the shooting? Is there anything to go on?"

"Yes, sir, and I'm going to look into it today. I have a partial plate."

"You have your clearance, but be careful. Make sure Elliot talks to no one. As for the rest of the team, let's put it on a need to know basis. If you need to use them, then they'll need to know."

"Yes, sir."

Celia hung up the phone and put the number back in her briefcase. She snapped it shut and met Elliot outside the front door. He had showered and shaved and was in uniform. She had her car keys in her hand.

"After we meet with Admiral Walton, there is someone I need to visit," Celia said.

Elliot opened the door for her then got in the other side. Celia got settled and put her briefcase in the back.

"Who are we visiting?" Elliot asked.

"An old friend of mine," Celia said. "Georgie and I will brief you later."

"Have I been cleared?" he asked.

"You're in."

* * *

The man was sweating under the black wig. He had watched Commander Kelly drive in with the SEAL. They left a short time later. It was too open around the duplex and until it got dark, this was as close as he dared to get.

CHAPTER 28

Rear Admiral Walton was waiting in his office reflecting on the past couple of weeks. He was beginning to wonder if Kelly was deliberately avoiding him. It was starting to hit home now. If members of the team were in danger, now it was personal. There was a knock on his office door.

"Come in," Walton said.

Georgie, Celia, and Elliot began to salute, but Walton waved them to have a seat dismissing formalities.

"First of all, what happened to you, Commander?" Walton decided to start there.

"I tried to meet with Dixon's contact at the docks and met the dock instead," Celia said.

"Dixon is the dead CIA agent, right?"

"Yes, sir."

Elliot gave Celia a puzzled look.

That sounded like quite a story, but he decided to move on to Ryan.

"What happened to Ryan last night?" The rear admiral sat forward folding his hands, listening intently.

"You knew that I suspected the blond man was here in Norfolk, maybe even killed Dixon. Ryan saw a blond man in the lockers here at the Fleet Training Center. Something made him suspicious. He left a message with me. I didn't get it until it was too late," Celia explained.

"She saved his life," Elliot added.

"I also put him in danger by not checking my messages," Celia interjected.

THE PACT: OP ONE

"We are not here to talk about what might have been or place blame. What I want to know is what do you intend to do now?" Walton asked.

"I've cleared Commander Elliot to enlist his help, and the rest of the team possibly on a need to know basis," Celia said.

"That's the best idea I've heard yet, Commander," Walton approved, "Concerning Ryan, if this blond man discovers he's still alive, what's stopping him from finishing the job?"

"That is my first priority today, sir," Celia said.

"Good! What are you going to do with him?"

"I think it's in his best interest to tell no one. It's in everyone's best interest. Any knowledge on the Pact creates an automatic target," Celia said, respectfully.

"I'll allow that. Are you still checking in with Turner?"

"Just spoke to him, sir."

"Well, then I'll let you get back to work." Walton sternly looked her square in the eye. "However, Commander, if anything else comes up, I want to hear it from you. Immediately!"

"Yes, sir."

Celia had an idea forming. Hopefully it works. Celia pulled Georgie aside, out of earshot from Elliot as they walked down the hall.

"Georgie, pull Dan Ryan out of the computer. Put his file in safe keeping. See if you can erase him from the hospital computer as well." Celia went through the plan as they walked toward the office.

"Yes, ma'am," Georgie said.

"I don't want a trace of him anywhere. Pay up his rent, clean out his apartment, and empty everything out of his locker here on base," Celia said.

"Oh, one more thing. Ryan said the license was 43-T-A-R-A. Run it, though I suspect I know who it belongs to. I want Tara Walton's address as soon as possible. I have a friend who works in a caregiving facility in Boston. Here is her number. Her brother is Recon and so all we need to tell her is that we need a place for our boy to recover. We can count on her to be discreet and not to ask questions." Celia hoped she had thought of everything.

"Yes, ma'am," Georgie replied and continued on to the office.

Celia and Elliot continued out the front door to the parking lot.

"You tried to meet with a contact of a dead CIA Agent?" Elliot frowned.

"It's a long story."

"When am I going to hear this long story?" Elliot asked, as they walked up to her Studebaker.

"Soon."

"What do you have in mind?"

"Getting him out of the hospital will be the tricky part." Celia smiled as they got into the Studebaker.

"Are you going to fill me in?" Elliot asked as she started her car.

"First, we need a rental," Celia said with a sigh.

"A rental?"

* * *

Georgie entered the office to find Gwen there. Georgie acknowledged her with a nod.

"What is the plan?" Gwen asked her.

"Petty Officer Ryan's safety," Georgie replied.

Ensign Jack McDonald knocked on the door and walked in.

"What's going on and how can I help?" McDonald asked.

"Can you clean out Petty Officer Ryan's locker?" Georgie asked.

"Sure."

"Empty its contents and bring it to me," Georgie said.

"I'm on it," McDonald gave a brief salute and left the office.

"You think we should have done that?" Gwen asked.

"Time is of the essence," Georgie said.

"What else?" Gwen asked.

"You get the information on Mrs. Walton and get it to the commander and I'll work on her orders concerning Ryan," Georgie said.

"You got it," Gwen said, moving to the files she had locked in her bottom drawer. She pulled out a file labeled Tara Cooper Walton. Then she typed Tara Walton's name into her computer. She was feeling tired after being called to the hospital in the middle of the night and let out a big yawn.

"Tired?" Georgie asked. "I find getting to bed promptly by 0210 every night is just right for me."

"Then you don't go out much? No dating?"

"No, it consumes too much wasted energy searching for the right man. When the time comes, I will put forth the effort needed," Georgie said matter-of-factly.

"And here I've been wasting all my time hoping Mr. Right will appear." Gwen shrugged.

"A big waste of time," Georgie agreed. "Once you meet someone you are attracted to, you must thoroughly research commonalities, his moral compass, if he has a satisfactory job, and if you like his mother. It is a calculated process. It's unrealistic to think Mr. Right can magically walk through the door at any moment."

McDonald walked in with Ryan's things. "Here's everything from Ryan's locker," he said with a smile. Gwen shook her head.

"I see your point," Gwen said to Georgie with a sigh.

Georgie was glad to see McDonald.

"I need you to meet the movers at Ryan's apartment and oversee the moving of his things to Greg's Storage? Take the things you have from his locker with you and register his belongings under the name of Will Bear at the storage unit," Georgie said to McDonald, handing him the address of the storage unit.

"You bet. Then maybe when I get back we can have less action and more talk," McDonald said.

"I'll bet you never thought you'd being telling any woman that," Gwen quipped.

McDonald glared at her and left the office.

* * *

Celia and Elliot headed for the hospital. When they arrived Celia headed for Ryan's room and Elliot went to get a wheelchair. Celia dialed Gwen's home phone number and found an empty room to step into so she could speak freely.

"Tammy, pick up. This is Celia," Celia waited. Soon she heard a click and Tammy's voice.

"I'm here," Tammy said.

"I need your help."

"What do you need?"

"I just rented a blue van. It is in the parking lot of your apartment complex. It's unlocked. The keys are in the glove box. Meet me behind the Naval Medical Center Portsmouth in a half hour."

"Done," Tammy said. Following Commander Kelly's instructions, Tammy erased the answering machine and called Georgie.

* * *

When Celia walked into Ryan's room the doctor was with him.

"... You are making excellent progress. I should be able to move you to the medical floor by tomorrow. Your total hospital stay shouldn't exceed three days if all goes well." The doctor filled Ryan in on his condition.

It's going to be shorter than that, Celia thought to herself.

"Thanks, doc," Ryan said and smiled.

THE PACT: OP ONE

"I'll be in to check on you later," the doctor said.

"Ma'am," the doctor said acknowledging Celia as he left.

Celia stood aside as the doctor went out the door, he nodded at Celia. "How are you?" Celia asked Ryan.

"I'm better by the minute. Plenty of food and service," Ryan said with a grin.

"Glad to hear it. We are going to cut your stay short," Celia said.

"What do you mean?" Ryan was puzzled.

"It's not going to be long before the blond man tries to finish the job. He might already know you're still alive. In other words, you're leaving," Celia said. Celia took Ryan's chart. His medication was up to date. Elliot entered the room with a wheelchair. He wheeled Ryan to the back elevator and rolled him out through the maintenance hall. It was lunch hour so it would be empty. Celia had Ryan walk from the back door the rest of the way. Elliot took the wheelchair back inside and returned it to the spot where he took it. Then he went to the front parking lot to wait for Celia as planned.

Tammy pulled the van into the back lot of the hospital. Celia helped Ryan into the bed Tammy had fixed for him. She set Ryan's IV bag on a hook inside the van.

"This is very important," Celia said to Ryan. "While you are recovering, don't use a credit card or your social security number. Use cash. Don't leave the facility without telling me first. When it's time for you to check out, we'll take it from there. The less you're seen, the better."

"I don't think I'll be attending any barn dances, ma'am," Ryan said with a grin.

Celia pulled Tammy aside.

"You are going to Keyser, West Virginia. Georgie called ahead to a retirement facility called Saint Mercy. Your contact there is Jen. Make sure that he is checked in and settled before you leave." Celia handed her an envelope. "His alias is Will Bear.

Here is his chart, background information, and medical instructions. Leave him the rest of the cash after you buy gas."

"Commander Elliot has unhooked the GPS and odometer which needs to be repaired before we take the van back. So let me know when you are back. Any questions?" Celia asked.

"I'll take care of it," Tammy promised.

Celia watched them drive out of sight. She received a call from Gwen with Tara Walton's address, then she went around the outside of the hospital to the front parking lot where Elliot was waiting for her.

CHAPTER 29

"Now what?" Elliot asked Celia. He wondered who had come for Ryan. His guess was Gwen.

"Now we visit that old friend of mine," Celia said, taking the freeway to Virginia Beach.

"Who's that?"

"I guess it's time to fill you in."

"It's past time I'd say!"

"You see, my husband or his RIO may have known something about this."

"What were they supposed to know?"

"I don't know for sure." Celia shook her head. "That's why I need to see my friend."

"You still haven't told me who we are going to see."

"Tom's RIO was Sam Cooper. He was married to a girl named Tara, who is now married to Walton's son."

"Able Walton Jr.? I went to their wedding." Elliot was surprised. He remembered seeing Tara in the picture he saw the other night. That's why she looked familiar! He thought she had looked familiar to him.

"So you are friends?" Celia asked.

"Able Jr. and I are acquainted. The only time I've ever seen his wife was at the wedding. You saw Able Jr. the other day, he ran into you as we went into the elevator. I guess I should have introduced you."

Celia thought a moment, then it dawned on her. He was the tall blond man with a deep tan. Ryan had also described the blond man he had seen with a deep tan. She wondered if he was the guy Ryan saw. He was the son of an admiral, a rear admiral. However, Rear Admiral Walton did not have access to the kind of intelligence the Pact had, not here in Norfolk. Even if he were involved, there had to be someone higher.

"What can Tara tell us?" Elliot asked, bringing Celia back to the conversation.

"I didn't notice anything that I can recall when Tom was alive. I guess he acted preoccupied the last couple of months he was alive, he had something on his mind, but it didn't cause me concern at the time. Maybe Tara noticed something about Sam. Gwen said they live in a ritzy neighborhood. What does Able Jr. do?" Celia asked him.

"He was in the Navy awhile, but is now in the reserves. The GI Bill paid his tuition while he studied to become a lawyer," Elliot said.

"Why would he have been at the base the other day?" Celia asked.

"He probably went to see his father."

Celia turned left on Winchester Drive and drove up a small incline until she saw the gold numbers 115 on a two-story white house. The house was one of the largest she had ever seen. It had white pillars extending into the porch. The grounds were covered with lush green grass and flower beds. The driveway ended in a circle with a birdbath in the center surrounded by flowers and bordered with white boulders. An older man was on his knees tending the flower beds beside the stairs leading to the porch. If there wasn't an ocean in the background, Celia would have sworn she had been transported back in time to the heart of the old south.

"What kind of lawyer is he?" Celia asked Elliot, who shrugged. They parked in front of the house.

Elliot was as taken aback as Celia at the magnificent house. Together, they walked up the steps to the large double doors. Celia rang the doorbell and waited. Tara Cooper Walton was just starting the dishwasher when she heard the doorbell echo throughout the house. Tossing back her long, permed, golden-red hair, Tara looked up from her chore. Wearing a flowered sundress, she was a slim five foot five. She had gray blue eyes. Tara took off her apron and set it on the counter. Leaving her spacious kitchen, she walked through the massive dining room past a large oak table with seating for twelve. Coming to the entryway, she opened the door.

"Celia?" Tara said stunned. She looked like she had seen a ghost.

"Hello, Tara." Celia smiled. "I'm sorry to call unannounced, but I need to talk to you."

Tara said nothing. She just stared at Celia. Celia was in uniform, standing next to a man who looked vaguely familiar to her. Tara took notice of Celia's stitches and bruised face.

"This is Lieutenant James Elliot," Celia said.

"You were at our wedding," Tara said to him. He nodded.

"May we come in?" Celia pressed.

"Oh, yes. I'm so sorry. You just took me by surprise," Tara said with an uncomfortable laugh. "You're the last person I expected to see today."

Celia walked in and looked at the grand entry surrounding her. It was painted white with a white marble floor. Paintings of flowers and garden scenes graced the walls. An antique table with a pitcher resting in a bowl was just to the right of the door. In the center of the room lay a large Victorian rug with pastel colors. It was like walking into springtime.

"You have a beautiful home," Celia said.

"Thank you," Tara said. "Let's sit in the living room."

Tara closed the door. She led them into a living room that was behind two more double doors to the right of the entry way. They sank into the lush white couch. There were pastel Victorian chairs on either side of the couch and the same pastel colors in pillows that were arranged on the couch. The room was accented with light oak coffee and end tables in a Victorian design. There were many valuable things displayed around the room in the form of vases and paintings.

"So you've remarried," Celia said after they were settled.

"Yes, I did," Tara smiled. "Did you? Remarry?"

"No," Celia said simply.

"That doesn't surprise me much," Tara commented. Elliot found the statement interesting.

"How's Able doing?" Elliot asked her. "I saw him the other day, but didn't have much time to talk."

"He's fine. Busy. He's gone quite a bit," Tara said.

No sense dragging this out, Celia thought. "Tara, I am an intelligence officer for the Navy. I have been working on something lately that has raised questions about Tom and Sam. Do you recall anything unusual concerning Tom or Sam before their last mission? Anything at all?" Celia was direct and her tone even.

Tara's face drained of color. She took in a deep breath. "I'm not sure what you mean."

"Do you remember Sam talking about something called the Pact?" Celia asked.

"No, what is that?" Tara asked.

"Is your license plate 43-T-A-R-A?"

"Yes." Tara froze. Tara's face showed panic. "Why?"

Elliot's jaw tightened. Celia saw this, hoping he would not act upon what he must be feeling right now.

"Has anyone been using your car lately?" Celia waited.

When Tara didn't answer, Celia tried to continue, "Tara?"

At that moment an adorable little girl of six years came bouncing into the room. She had little red ringlets all over her head and brilliant blue eyes. She was the spitting image of the late Sam Cooper. With her was the man Celia had seen at the elevator the other day. He was dressed in trousers and a short sleeved dress shirt. He looked like he was going out for a round of golf.

"Mama, we're back," the little girl said, grinning from ear to ear.

"This is Commander Celia Kelly. Do you remember her? You were so young." Tara helped her daughter onto her lap, grateful for the interruption.

"I wasn't a commander then. Samantha, you have grown so much." Celia smiled at her.

"Able," Elliot said, standing and offering his hand.

"Hey, James." Able Jr. shook his hand. He then looked at Celia. "How are you, Commander?" He addressed her as if he knew her.

"Well, thank you."

"What happened to your face?" Samantha wanted to know.

"I fell," Celia replied.

"Whatcha guys doing?" Samantha asked.

"Your mother and I knew each other a long time ago and we are catching up," Celia replied.

"Celia was asking me if someone else had been driving my car." Tara watched Able Jr. closely.

"Really? Why is that?" Able Jr. asked.

"There was an accident last night. A car with the license plate 43-T-A-R-A was involved, but left the scene." Celia looked into his eyes as she talked. There was something about him she didn't like.

"My cousin borrowed her car, but when he returned it, there wasn't a scratch on it that I could see." His eyes were locked with hers as well. She showed no apprehension. His eyes were cold and mocking.

"It could have been a false report. When I heard Tara's name come up, I wanted to come myself," Celia said, smiling now.

"Maybe he was driving by the scene at the same time," Able suggested.

"Possible." Celia knew that wasn't the case.

"Was anyone hurt?" he asked.

"It was nearly fatal." Now Celia watched Able Jr. closely. Elliot wondered what Celia was doing. He watched them both in puzzled silence.

"I'm sorry to hear that," Able said.

"You must get a lot of sun." Celia found herself saying.

"I spend a lot of time outside," he said. Still their eyes remained locked, neither blinked. Tara decided to change the subject. She didn't like the look in Able Jr.'s eyes. She had seen it before. And Tara didn't like where this conversation was going.

"I'm so glad you stopped by," Tara said, interrupting them. Celia looked away and smiled at Tara and Samantha.

"Are you in school?" Celia asked Samantha.

"I'll be in first grade this year," Samantha said proudly.

"That is wonderful! You'll love school," Celia said.

Tara set Samantha on her feet and stood.

"We have a dinner invitation to go to in a few minutes," Tara said.

Celia could see she had exceeded her welcome. She knew it was time to go.

"We'll get out of your way then," Celia said smiling politely. Pausing, she turned to Able and added, "I want to tell you, I think very highly of your father."

"Many people do," Able Jr. replied. Tara's eyes dropped.

"We'll see you both another time," Elliot said, pushing gently on the small of Celia's back to move her before she said something else.

"I hope you both can come again," Able Jr. said.

"Count on it," Celia replied in a manner both Tara and Able Jr. knew meant this wasn't the end of it.

Elliot opened the door this time and he and Celia walked down the steps back to the Studebaker. Elliot opened the car door for her and then got in the passenger side. Celia opened her purse and turned off the tape player. Elliot noticed Tara watching them in the window of the entry way. It wasn't until the house was out of sight that either Celia or Elliot spoke.

"What was that?" Elliot asked.

"A tap dance I'd say," Celia replied.

"I meant, after Able came in?"

"That was merely a stroke of luck, him showing up like that." Celia said.

"Luck?" He shook his head. What was that supposed to mean?

* * *

The red-headed man was dressed in a business suit with a white overcoat. Hair combed back in a ponytail, he was clean shaven and wore a charming smile. He nodded to a nurse as he went behind the nurses' station to where the charts were kept. There was no chart. He walked the hall toward Ryan's hospital room. As he approached, he overheard a loud conversation between a man and a woman.

"You just let him walk out of here?" the doctor exclaimed.

"No, of course not," the nurse said. "He had to have been in a wheelchair."

"Then where is he?" the doctor demanded.

"I don't know. Maybe he was moved to the medical floor. Due to his injuries, there is no way he would have been discharged. I'm sure it's confusion with his room number and chart," the nurse said.

Walking back to the nurses' station, the red-headed man decided to search. A nurse coming from Ryan's room stopped another nurse in the hall.

"Where is that patient that was in room 413?" she asked her.

"His friend wheeled him out in a wheelchair two hours ago," the other said. "Maybe they went to the cafeteria or something."

The red-headed man continued to walk the hall and into the elevator. So the SEAL was gone. Did he see something the night of the shooting? If the injuries were severe enough, they wouldn't take him far. He'd find him. He was sure of that. The red-headed man sighed heavily as the elevator doors closed. When the doors opened, he walked out of the hospital leaving the white overcoat he was wearing folded up in the corner of the elevator.

CHAPTER 30

Gwen and Georgie were at their desks when Celia and Elliot entered the office.

"How did it go?" Gwen asked.

"As well as expected. Join us in my office," Celia said.

"Yes, ma'am," Georgie and Gwen followed Celia into the inner office.

Celia set her briefcase on the desk and opened it.

"It's time I leveled with you," Celia said thoughtfully. She retrieved the Pact file and her thinking pad from her briefcase. "James, I'll begin with you." Celia brought him up to speed on the last day she saw Frank Scott alive and how she believed Dixon had broken into her house and followed her.

"He broke into your house?" Elliot asked.

"I believe so, but he said he didn't. After we returned from Syria, I opened this." Celia got out her picture and handed it to him. "Gwen said it was hand delivered by a boy while I was in Syria."

Elliot looked over the wedding photo. He had seen the picture, of course, he knew he had to tell her. Trust was a two-way street.

"On the back is a message."

"I've seen it," Elliot said quietly.

With that, he had everyone's attention. All eyes were on him. Celia paused, then asked, "When?"

"When I went to get the lamps, I accidentally kicked the photo album across the floor. It fell out. I saw it then." He set the picture on the corner of the desk. Gwen looked at the commander for a reaction. Did she believe him? Georgie was wondering the same.

"I see," was Celia's reply.

"What does the message mean? Is it a threat?" Elliot asked her.

"I don't know. Although." Celia paused, looking thoughtfully out the window. "It is interesting that no one has tried to kill me yet. My things have been ransacked and

"I've been followed, but other than that, nothing. Yet, Petty Officer Ryan just sees a blond man and someone tries to kill him. Commander Scott is dead the day I'm handed a mission when he had been the one to investigate the Pact. Someone tried to kill Tammy in Syria. Dixon is dead. The only thing they have in common is that before their death or attempts on their lives, they were investigating the Pact and in contact with me." Celia was quiet again, thinking.

"What do Scott's files say?" Georgie asked.

"That an admiral and his son have been feeding information to the Pact since the beginning and that $20 million is missing. The Pact has been searching for it. Dixon also referenced the missing money," Celia summarized.

"An admiral is involved?" Elliot knew that was a short list.

"The thing is, Frank Scott never listed names," Celia said.

"Maybe he was afraid to," Gwen said.

"What's confusing is his files is that they don't say much more than Dixon told me," Celia said.

"If he worked on this for five years, there should be names, dates, and locations," Georgie agreed.

"Exactly, detail." Celia nodded.

"Who was the man on the docks that tried to kill you?" Elliot pointed out.

"He was running away from me. Tammy said he was Dixon's contact."

"What does he know about the money?" McDonald asked.

Celia paused a moment.

"Wait, a minute! Maybe I'm at the center of this for another reason."

"I don't follow," Gwen said, confused.

"It's the money!" Celia eyes were bright as the light dawned.

"They think you know," Georgie said, seeing where Celia was going with it.

"Yes, they think I know," Celia said nodding.

"Know what?" Elliot asked.

"They think I know where the money is."

* * *

McDonald was in the middle of town, a block from the hospital. He got in and started his red Mustang convertible. He wasn't sure what made him do a double take, but the blond guy across the street caught his attention. Maybe it was just this business with Ryan, but he thought he had seen this guy. But where? McDonald put the Mustang into gear and drove to the first stop light before when it came to him. He saw him at the base the other day. He had passed him in the hallway.

As the light turned green, McDonald cranked the steering wheel hard to the left as he made a U-turn. He dumped the clutch and pushed the throttle to the floor. Forcing his way through traffic, going the opposite direction, he nearly sideswiped a UPS truck. The Mustang's Saleen high performance 302 crate engine threw him forward. The wheels squealed while he veered to pass two other cars. McDonald lifted his foot from the accelerator as he approached the post office. He looked on the other side of the street. The guy was no longer there. McDonald considered pursuing the man, then thought better of it. McDonald shifted gears, not noticing as he passed an empty black sedan parked along the sidewalk with the license plate 43-T-A-R-A.

* * *

Elliot leaned forward in his chair, waiting for whatever came next. "We are starting over from day one, tomorrow morning," Celia said, and then she turned to Georgie. "Where is McDonald? Didn't you say he was here this morning?"

"At the post office, ma'am," Georgie replied. "He should be back shortly."

"You're letting HIM in on this?" Gwen gasped.

"He's already involved. He helped with Petty Officer Ryan's things," Georgie pointed out.

"I'm not sure what I'm doing with him yet. Did you hear from the lab?" Celia asked.

"No, ma'am, not yet, I'll check on that now." Georgie left Celia's office and went into the outer office, then sat at her desk and dialed the lab's number.

"Gwen, double-check the calls logged on Dixon's bills."

Gwen took the bills and left the office. That left Celia and Elliot alone. Sitting there a moment, their eyes locked. There were still so many unanswered questions.

* * *

Tammy drove straight through to Keyser, West Virginia, stopping only once, for gas. Following Commander Kelly's instructions to the letter, she handed off Ryan as Will Bear. After driving back to Norfolk, Tammy parked the van in the same parking lot she had found it so the GPS and mileage gauge could be reconnected.

CHAPTER 31

When Celia awoke the next morning, she was sitting at the kitchen table slumped over on a file. She lifted her head and pushed her hair from her face. She was still in yesterday's uniform. Looking at her watch, she saw that it was 0600 hours. She rose to her feet then tried to stretch out the kinks.

After taking a hot shower and drinking a cup of coffee, she gathered her work and placed it back in her briefcase. She was walking out the door when the phone rang. She went back inside to take the call.

"Hello?"

"It's me," said a male voice. Celia recognized it at once as Dixon's contact. She picked up the phone.

"What do you want?" Celia asked, after a brief second.

"We need to talk," he said. Then he added, "This time without your backup."

"You want to talk to me? Why the sudden change of heart?" Celia asked, hoping she had heard right.

"Will you meet me or not?" The voice was irritated now.

"When?"

"No backup!"

"Agreed. When?"

"Tonight, at a place called The Anchor," he paused. "Know it?"

"I'll be there," Celia assured him. She'd find it.

"Nine o'clock."

The call ended, and she felt a chill go down her spine. He knew where she lived and her phone number. Celia took the tape out of her machine and put in a new one, recording a new message. Feeling an adrenaline rush coming over her, she found herself looking forward to meeting with him. She was past reason and unwisely confident.

* * *

McDonald was gone before Perry was out of bed. McDonald received orders the night before to report to Commander Kelly at 0700. When McDonald arrived Elliot was standing next to Georgie looking over a file and Gwen was at her desk.

"Hi, what's up?" McDonald asked.

"We are waiting for the commander." Georgie looked at her watch.

"Where is she? Was she awake?" Gwen asked Elliot as she glanced at the clock above the door.

"I assumed so. I didn't see her," he said.

"The last time she was late for work, someone broke into her house." Gwen sounded concerned.

"Someone broke into her house?" Elliot asked, stunned.

"Oh, not here. It's when she lived in D.C."

"I can check on her," McDonald offered.

"She's only five minutes late," Elliot pointed out. "I think we can give it a few more minutes."

Celia entered the Fleet Training Center walking briskly to the elevator. She looked at her watch. Getting into the elevator, she pressed the button for the third floor. The elevator suddenly stalled between one and two. She pressed the button for the third floor again. There was a sound above her. Looking overhead, she thought she saw a shadow. Her attention was diverted as the elevator suddenly thrust upward. Celia got off and walked into the outer office.

"Good morning," Celia said.

"Good morning, ma'am," Georgie said.

"Everything all right?" Celia asked as she looked at their intense faces.

"Just wondering what was keeping you," Gwen said.

"Sorry, just running late. Gwen, call maintenance. I think something is wrong with the elevator. It stalled, then after a minute or so it started up again. It might be on the verge of a breakdown," Celia said.

"I didn't notice anything," McDonald said.

"Well, it could be nothing. Better safe than sorry. After you call, join us." Celia led the rest of the group into her office. It wasn't long before Gwen finished with her call and came in, sitting in the only vacant chair, next to McDonald. Celia was standing, facing the marker board that Gwen had set up for her. Celia began telling them Tammy was in town.

"So how long has Tammy been in town?" Elliot asked. Just when he thought she had been completely honest with him, there was something else.

"A few days. I thought it was the best way to keep her safe." Celia pointed out.

"What if she is involved on the wrong side?" Elliot asked.

"I trust her," Celia said, firmly looking into his eyes.

"That's good enough for me, ma'am," Georgie said, protecting Celia and hoping to break the tension.

"Ensign McDonald, I guess you're wondering what you're doing here," Celia said.

"The thought did cross my mind," McDonald replied.

Then McDonald whispered under his breath to Elliot sitting on his other side, "I didn't do anything did I?" Elliot smiled and shook his head no.

"By now I'm sure Petty Officer Ryan filled you in concerning the blond man he saw on base?" Celia asked.

"If we're going after that guy, count me in!" McDonald said with enthusiasm.

"The camp in Syria, as you know, was destroyed, but it has come to our attention that the group's attention is focused within the states. They are missing $20 million and are trying to locate it," Celia said.

"So we destroyed the camp, but not the group?" McDonald asked.

"Yes."

"Who is this leader supposed to be?" McDonald wondered.

Celia gave him the highlights.

"The blond guy..." McDonald began.

"What about him?" Celia asked.

"I think I've seen him, too," McDonald said.

"Where?" Celia looked at him intently. He had everyone's attention.

"I may have seen him yesterday as I was coming out of the post office. I don't think he noticed me." McDonald shrugged.

"Do you recall the cars parked on the street?" Celia asked him.

"No. I should have got out and looked around." He shook his head.

"It's best that you didn't." Celia paused. "There are a couple of things that are bothering me. I wonder why Admiral Lloyd chose me to finish what Frank started. I have been working at a desk in the Pentagon for three years, yet I'm chosen to go into the field, and work Intel for a SEAL team?"

"Why does that concern you, ma'am? You have proven yourself to be more than capable," Georgie said.

"I have the training in intelligence, have worked at the Pentagon and at Langley, but my field experience is limited."

"Everybody has to have that first op that they add to their list of skills," Gwen pointed out.

"Who talked who into it?" McDonald asked. Gwen glared at him. He realized he may have sounded rude. "I was surprised to see you walk in that day," McDonald said carefully.

"Really? We hadn't noticed," Gwen said sarcastically.

"If you build from that theory, someone got the president on board. Maybe Lloyd, maybe someone else, but it had to be somebody," McDonald finished, ignoring Gwen.

"If it's true, someone went through quite a bit of trouble to set you up, and maybe us as well," Elliot said, his voice trailing off as if he talking more to himself now than them. He wondered if he should. No, not yet. Not until he was sure.

"We should break down the chain of command on this one, ma'am," Georgie suggested.

"Good idea. Georgie, go to D.C. to check it out. I'll speak with Rear Admiral Walton and see if he can accompany you. You will get further with his presence," Celia said to Georgie who nodded. "In the meantime, we have Dixon's contact. He might know the parties involved or just be a paid asset. Finding out where and who he is will be a priority."

"You still don't think you know him?" Georgie asked.

"No. He's not familiar to me, but that being said, but I think he deliberately changes his voice and appearance. I want to know more about what happened to Dixon. It might help to meet with his assistant Aggie. We also need to find out who sent the picture," Celia said

Celia handed the photograph to McDonald. He looked at it. Nice wedding picture, he thought. He examined the bride in the picture closely and then looked at the commander. It was hard to believe it was the same woman. What's more, he knew the other woman in the picture as well.

"Turn it over," Celia said.

He did and read the message, TILL DEATH DO US PART.

"I received that after I came back from Syria."

"Somebody has a sick sense of humor," McDonald said.

Elliot was unusually quiet and Celia wondered why.

"Was Tara a bridesmaid or something?" McDonald asked.

"Do you know her?" Celia was surprised.

"You could say that," he said, staring at her picture.

"What does that mean?" Gwen and Elliot replied in unison. McDonald shrugged sheepishly.

"Seriously, Jack?" Elliot asked. Then he added, "Is there anybody you haven't slept with?"

"Hey, she wasn't married yet, just engaged," he said in his defense.

Elliot glared at him.

"Why doesn't that surprise me?" Gwen commented.

"Everybody stand down." Celia regained control. She asked McDonald, "When was this?"

"Two nights before her wedding day. I don't know much, except that she was upset that night and drunk, usually the perfect combination."

"She'd have to be drunk," Gwen said under her breath.

"Gwen, please," Celia said. "What do you remember about her that night?"

"It was strange. She kept referring her husband."

"Were you doing it wrong?" Gwen asked.

McDonald glared at her.

"Why did you think it was strange?" Elliot asked.

"At the time he wasn't going to be her husband for another two days. How does she fit into this?" McDonald asked Celia.

"She was married to Sam Cooper. They had a daughter named Samantha."

"The man in the picture is Cooper?"

"That's right."

"What happened to him?" McDonald asked.

"He was my husband's RIO. They went MIA in an incident over the Mediterranean," Celia said. "Did she say something in particular that struck you strange?"

"Lots of things, but the strangest was when she said, 'I can't believe he's alive'."

"Alive?" Celia was stunned. "She said 'I can't believe HE'S alive'?"

"I thought Walton just got back from a life or death mission that sent her into orbit," McDonald said.

"He's a lawyer," Gwen said.

Color drained from Celia's face. Georgie was thinking the same thing. She knew what it might mean. Georgie and Celia exchanged a knowing glance.

After a few minutes of silence, McDonald asked, "What's going on? What did I say?"

"Is it possible, ma'am? Do you think Sam Cooper is still alive?" Georgie asked.

"I don't know. They never recovered the bodies," Celia replied. Nobody said it, but they were all thinking it now. If Sam Cooper could be alive, then so could Tom Kelly. Celia paused. Then as if nothing happened, she continued.

"I guess we need to pay Tara another visit," Celia said evenly.

"Ma'am, with all due respect, perhaps Ensign McDonald and I should give it a try," Georgie suggested.

"Why?" Celia asked.

"If you were friends, on one level or another, you both are going to be factoring in the past," Georgie pointed out.

"You don't think I'll see things clearly?" Celia asked.

"I don't think she'll talk to you. She can't deny what she has said to Ensign McDonald. As for me, I am a neutral party," Georgie said.

"She's right. We already know she's not talking to you. We were there and she didn't tell us anything," Elliot said.

"That could have been because her husband came into the room."

"You even had a reaction to her husband," Elliot said, frowning.

"What do you mean?"

"I was close to getting you a whip and chair," he looked at her intently waiting for an answer.

"He fits the description."

"I don't mean to interrupt, but what are we talking about now?" McDonald asked.

She thinks Able Jr. is the blond man? Elliot wondered.

Celia tapped her fingertips on the top of her desk. She tried to remember anything at all four years ago that could help her now.

"What else do I need to know?" McDonald asked.

"Supposedly, an admiral and his son behind it," Celia said.

Elliot realized what she must be thinking. If she suspects Able Jr., that meant she suspects… no way!

"Now that doesn't sound good," McDonald said.

"If an admiral is involved, it's a short list, even if you factor in retired admirals," Celia said.

"Oh, I have a rundown on the numbers from Dixon's phone log. Most are accounted for, but there were seven calling card calls from a phone booth at The Anchor to his house," Gwen said.

"Interesting." The Anchor was where Celia was supposed to meet the contact that night. Did Dixon give his contact a calling card? She decided to leave out mention of her visit to The Anchor tonight. She was determined to talk to him one way or another, even if it meant on his terms.

"Who uses a calling card anymore?" McDonald asked.

"Let's get started. Georgie you take McDonald, and interview Tara. Take Gwen along as well." Celia paused then reinforced, "Gwen, you are just observing."

"You can count on me! Besides, I want to be there." Gwen smiled.

"Be there for what?" McDonald asked.

"What her reaction is when she sees you sober," Gwen laughed.

"Gwen, Ensign, just remember why you are there." Celia sighed.

"They are in good hands with me, ma'am," Georgie assured her.

As they left, Elliot was deep in thought. If McDonald had never seen Able Jr., then it's possible he could have stood out to him on base, where Elliot wouldn't have given him a second thought. He tried to think if any of the team knew him. Jeffers did, and other than that he wasn't sure. Elliot was the only one on the team who had gone to Able Jr.'s wedding.

Celia was thinking of Able Jr. as well. She knew she was right about Able Jr., but Iron Horse Walton was the last admiral on her list of suspects. Her gut said she could trust him.

"What are you thinking?" Elliot asked her.

"Probably the same thing you are," she said. "I'm sending Ryan a picture of Able Jr. At least then we will know if we are on the right track."

"You mean you will know. I don't see him as a terrorist," Elliot said.

"Fair enough, we will know if I'm right or wrong."

* * *

The red-headed man parked the black sedan back into the large three car garage. Able Jr. stood in the corner of the garage waiting for him. As the redheaded man got out of the driver's side door, Tara was there to confront him.

"No more. This has to stop!" Tara said through clenched teeth. She grabbed the keys.

"You're not in any position to tell me, or anyone else, what to do," he said.

"How you could do this to me, or Samantha, I don't understand," Tara said fuming.

Able Jr. came up to Tara from behind kissed the nape of her neck.

Tara turned around to slap his face, but he caught her forearm midway.

"I'd be careful if I were you. It's never wise to insult your bread and butter. You've been well taken care of, so far," Able Jr. said. He dropped her hand. "Besides you're in this as deep as anyone. It's your car that was seen. Hasn't it occurred to you that you'll be rotting in prison thanks to your dear friend Commander Kelly?" He laughed.

"I guess that depends on whether or not she figures it out, doesn't it?" Tara said smugly. "She knows. I saw it in her eyes and so did you."

"What is she talking about?" the red-headed man wanted to know.

"Kelly was here and she was asking questions," Able Jr. said.

"Celia was here?" He sounded concerned. If she got this far, it wasn't going to take her long to piece it together. "What are we going to do?"

"Get rid of her."

"We need her alive," the red-headed man protested.

"Please, stop this, both of you," Tara said, clenching the keys.

"Give me the keys!" he demanded.

"I'm not a party to this anymore!" Tara exclaimed. She refused to give up the keys. In an instant Able Jr. pinned her to the wall with a knife at her throat.

"Let her go," the red-headed man protested a hint of concern in his voice.

"You're as much a part of this as any of us. It's too late to play the hero. Give me the keys." His voice was hot on her face as he punctuated each word.

"I'll do it! I'll take care of Celia. Just let her go."

Able Jr. released her. Tara's eyes were large with anxiety. She didn't know what to do except...

"You keep quiet," Able Jr. warned her.

"All right," Tara whispered hoarsely, giving in the same way she had been doing for the last three years. As they drove away in separate cars, she rubbed her neck, trying to catch her breath, her throat tight.

* * *

The man had rented a room not far from The Anchor. After taking a long hot shower, he put on the clothes he had just bought—a new pair of blue jeans and a flannel shirt and a baggy tan jacket. He adjusted his black wig and put on the black beard. Last, but not least, he put in brown contacts.

In just four more hours he'd meet with Commander Kelly. That was never the plan, of course, but plans have a way of changing. The issue had been forced.

He wondered how things had gotten so complicated. He hadn't intended for his life to be taken away from him or for anyone to be hurt by it. Oddly enough, as time went on, it had become so easy. Too easy. Here he was, looking into the mirror of a motel room seeing what he had become. He didn't want it this way, but it was too late. He impatiently looked at his watch.

* * *

Celia sent Elliot check out the location of the phone booth where the seven calls came from while she then spent the rest of the day looking into Stan Geyser. Calling Langley, Celia talked to Aggie, asking for their version of the information surrounding the incident that caused the plane to crash. It had been shot down by a FIM92A, (Stinger), but when the plane crashed, it was landing, only thirty feet off the ground. There would have been something left of the bodies to return to families. Eight people who died in the plane were returned to their families and properly buried. One body was unaccounted for; nine people were on the plane, but only eight were returned.

Upon checking further she discovered Geyser's body was never returned to the states. His only living relative, a cousin once removed, didn't even know he was dead. Celia still needed answers. Where was Geyser? The pilot was dead. The attendants were dead. Even if he had gotten on the plane, he wouldn't have walked away from the accident.

If he got on the plane!

Who else could verify whether he was on that plane for sure? She double-checked the flight plan. It had left Germany's military base at 1435 a month ago. Celia called the airport.

"May I help you?" a friendly American voice answered.

"This is Commander Kelly, US Navy. I understand you had a small commuter plane take off from your airport two months ago—"

"Excuse me for interrupting, but you want to talk to Lowell. He takes care of the commuter planes. But you'll have to be specific. We get a lot of them. Please hold."

Celia waited.

"Lowell here."

"Hello. This is Commander Kelly, US Naval Intelligence. I understand you had a small commuter plane take off from your airport at 1435, Friday, August 7th."

"Let me take a look."

"It was shot down by a Stinger," Celia specified.

"Oh, that plane."

"I have a question concerning a passenger. His name was Stan Geyser."

"Was he the short, round, dumpy looking guy with the thin hair?"

Celia looked at the picture in his file. "Yes."

"I remember telling my wife that Stan was sure a lucky son-of-a-gun after I read the paper the next morning."

"Why is that?" Celia asked.

"He didn't get on the plane. He changed his mind at the last minute. It was too late to change the paperwork, so we never cleared his name off the computer. Didn't matter much, there wasn't time for anyone else to board and take his seat. He paid for it and never asked for a refund. Just said he wasn't going and walked out. What was your question?"

"I was just verifying passengers for body identification."

"Well, it's safe to count him out," Lowell said.

"Thank you," Celia said.

"You bet."

Could Sam Cooper be alive too? And Tom? She was afraid to hope. Celia shook her head.

Her next stop was the basement. Celia decided to pay the lab a visit before she met with Dixon's contact. She Looked at her watch and realized she didn't have much time. She wanted to know what they found on the bloody towel.

CHAPTER 32

Georgie, McDonald, and Gwen were at Tara Walton's front door. Gwen looked at the magnificent setting and the view of the ocean. The place was spectacular. McDonald knocked on the huge double doors.

"They have a doorbell," Gwen said and reached in front of him to ring it. After a moment the door opened and there stood Tara Walton. Her face went white as she faced McDonald. She didn't even look at the other two ladies. First Celia and now him?

"What do you want?" Tara said as her mouth went dry.

"Hi. How have you been?" McDonald flashed a charming smile.

"What do you want?" Tara repeated.

"Excuse us, ma'am, but I'm Lieutenant Commander Georgie Round, this is Gwen Sherwood, and I believe you are acquainted with Ensign McDonald," Georgie said matter-of-factly.

Gwen raised her eyebrow at Georgie. She had a real talent for understatement.

"May we come in?" McDonald asked, cheerfully.

Tara hesitated and then stood aside. They walked into the large entryway. McDonald looked at Tara, her long reddish hair pulled back. Tara had on blue jeans and a turtleneck sweater. Georgie noticed that her neck was bruised on either side, covered mostly by her sweater. Georgie paid attention to the detail of the house. She was sure it took a nice sized income to maintain.

Tara led them into the living room, wondering who they were and why they were here. Probably sent by Celia that much she knew. Gwen noticed wedding pictures along the wall in the hall leading into the living room. Her husband didn't resemble Rear Admiral Walton, she thought. The little flower girl was adorable with her red ringlets falling over her shoulders. Now, that flower girl was the spitting image of Sam Cooper. Gwen realized they went in the living room and she picked up her step to catch up with them.

"We need to ask you a few questions," McDonald said.

"Celia sent you, didn't she?" Tara narrowed her eyes.

"Who's Celia?" McDonald asked.

"The commander, sir," Georgie said.

"Oh, right... Yes, she did," he said, understanding.

"We need your full cooperation or we'll have to assume you're involved and we will act accordingly. I want to be clear on that from the beginning." Georgie got right to the point.

McDonald saw Georgie was taking the role of bad cop, so he'd have to compensate.

"I don't know what you're talking about." Tara caught her breath.

"Mrs. Walton?" Gwen asked gently. Tara was acting more afraid than guilty. "If you're worried about your daughter, the commander would never let anything happen to either of you. Believe me, you'll be protected." Gwen looked to McDonald and Georgie. "Right?"

"That depends on what she has to tell us," Georgie said, her eyes never leaving Tara. "Mrs. Walton?"

"What is it you want to know?" Tara asked.

"Is Sam Cooper alive?" Georgie asked.

Tara started to cry.

McDonald thought he should try.

"Listen, two days before your wedding you said you couldn't believe he was still alive. Did you mean the guy you were going to marry?"

Tara looked into his eyes and shook her head.

"No."

"Did you mean Sam Cooper?"

Tara put her face into her hands.

"We need to know," McDonald gently pressed.

She looked up again.

"Yes. Sam is alive." She sobbed.

"So how could you marry Walton?" McDonald asked.

"I didn't. Not legally. Sam was in on it. We agreed because of Samantha." Tara's eyes were sad now.

"This is very important, ma'am. You need to tell us everything. Lives are at stake, maybe even yours from the look of your neck." Georgie drew attention to Tara's bruises.

Tara touched the side of her neck automatically at Georgie's mention of it. She had her tears under control and she was considering what she should do. "You don't understand. If I don't do what they say, they will kill Samantha." Desperation oozed from Tara's voice.

"Sam Cooper would kill his own daughter?" McDonald was confused.

Tara shook her head.

"Not Sam, the others. I don't know much, but I do know I have my daughter to protect."

"Do you know anything about the money?" Georgie asked.

"I know it's missing."

"Do you know where the money is?"

"Are we sure it's not here?" Gwen asked.

"Here?" McDonald asked.

"Look at this place," Gwen said looking around them.

"No, it's still missing. That's all they ever talk about. They owed it to someone," Tara said. Suddenly fear filled her eyes. "Where is Celia?"

"Why?" asked McDonald.

"Because he was so angry." She was touching her neck again.

"He?" Georgie asked.

"He told Sam they should get rid of her." As she spoke, she became even more agitated.

"You mean now?" Gwen asked.

Tara started crying again.

"I'm not sure. Sam said he'd do it so Able would let me go." Tara touched her neck again.

* * *

Celia met Major Carl Husk in the lab.

"What can I do for you, Commander?" Husk asked. He was a tall, lanky man of thirty-nine. He had a shaved head.

"My assistant gave you a towel to look at?" Celia replied.

"Yes, ma'am. What did you want to know?"

"What did you find?"

"It was used to mop up an injury or a large cut. The blood type is AB negative," Husk said.

"Was it a shaving cut?" Celia asked.

"No, I don't think so." He shook his head. "It was more likely an open wound. If this is all you had from the scene it life threatening. We're looking at stitches. Do you need to continue with DNA testing? It could take a few weeks."

Celia looked at her watch. She needed to get going.

"Yes. Send a copy of your findings to my office."

"Will do," Husk said.

"Thank you," Celia said.

Celia got into the elevator. She pressed the button. As it went up, she reflected on the day. Maybe the contact could tell her something more tonight. Without warning the elevator stopped and went dark. Celia pressed the emergency button but nothing happened, not even the emergency lights. She tried the phone, but it was dead. Trying the alarm again, nothing happened. Did Gwen forget to call maintenance?

It was then she heard a sound overhead. Looking up, she saw a shadow. Opening her briefcase, she felt for her GLOCK. Celia pushed the magazine into place and pulled back on the slide to secure a bullet in the chamber. She depressed the trigger slightly to release the safety. The ceiling collapsed as a figure dressed in black crashed through it. Celia saw the bottom of a black boot too late as it kicked the GLOCK from her hand and it spun across the elevator going off as it hit the side wall.

* * *

McDonald was now driving at top speed as he headed back to the base. Gwen held onto the dashboard for dear life. Georgie sat up straight in back as if they were going on a Sunday afternoon drive.

"Can you please hand me my phone? It's on the dash," Georgie said to Gwen. Gwen pried her fingers off the dashboard and handed her the phone. Georgie dialed the base.

"Could you tell me if Commander Kelly is still in the building? Thank you." Georgie held the phone patiently to her ear. "They are checking," she informed Gwen and McDonald.

Gwen was holding on for dear life. Glancing at the speedometer, it was ninety-five and climbing.

"Yes?" Georgie said. "She is? Thank you. Hold her at the front desk, please. Tell her, Georgie said it's vital she waits."

"The base then?" Gwen asked. Georgie nodded.

"Get your ID's ready. We're here," McDonald said as he squealed to a stop in line to pass security.

"Watch your speed, sir," the MP said to McDonald as he waved them through the gate.

McDonald nodded and waited until he turned the corner before stepping on it once again. He suddenly reached the parking lot and stopped, pushing everyone forward in their seats. Georgie saw Celia's Studebaker was still there in the parking lot. It was 2045 and dusk was fading into darkness.

"Look!" McDonald pointed to a black sedan with 43-T-A-R-A plates. They went into the building to the front desk. They noticed a few people standing in front of the elevator.

Gwen's uneasiness was only heightened at seeing the Military Police.

"What is going on?" Georgie asked.

"The elevator is stalled and we heard gunfire come up from it. We are trying to repair it so we can bring it up to find out what is going on," one MP explained to her.

"There was a gunshot?" McDonald asked. "How long ago?"

"Two minutes."

* * *

Celia felt a stinging in her right side. Ignoring it, she tried to make out the person on top of her. The size and strength of her attacker, she was sure it was a man. Dressed in jet black clothing, gloves, and a ski mask. He covered her mouth. She bit his hand and tried pushing him away. Though he moved his hand from her mouth, she knew her teeth hardly penetrated through the glove.

Again, he tried to pin her to the floor. Celia continued to fight, pulling at the mask. As hard as she tried, she was no match for her opponent. He kneeled on her left arm, getting out a rope. That left her one hand free. He was bigger and stronger; she needed to make her next move effective. She kneed him in the groin as hard as she could. He was temporarily stunned, holding himself, letting out a scream of pain. Celia felt around for her pistol. She finally found it. Aiming it between his eyes, she tried to steady her position, fighting the pain now mounting in her side, never letting her eyes stray from her target point. In the meantime, he had recovered and as he looked back at Celia with penetrating eyes, she hesitated, unwisely, wondering whom she was shooting.

Before she knew what was happening the gloved hand suddenly produced a knife and whipped it across the elevator. As the knife sailed through the air, she pulled the trigger. The knife penetrated her left hand which she was using to support her pistol. Celia knew as the shot rang out her aim was off.

Reacting to the pain of the knife in her hand, the pistol, again, fell to the floor. The force of the bullet threw her attacker against the opposite wall of the elevator. At least she had hit something. Pulling the knife out of her hand, she looked at her attacker. He was still slumped against the wall. Celia clutched the knife in her right hand.

* * *

The second shot rang up from the shaft. McDonald began to pry the elevator doors open. Once he got it started a couple of inches, another MP jumped in and helped him pull the doors apart the rest of the way.

"You! Hold this!" McDonald called to yet another MP to take his position.

The MPs held the doors, and McDonald accessed the situation. He could see the elevator just a floor and half below him. Without taking time to ask permission, he took the MP's pistol from his side holster. He reached out for a cable and quietly scooted down the cable. When he got to the elevator, he carefully mounted on top, noticing a black figure slumped against the wall.

McDonald was about to jump in when the black figure started to rise. He saw the commander on the other side, in a white uniform, sitting on the floor leaning against the wall. McDonald aimed the MP's pistol at the back of the dark covered head and shot. A dark heap fell onto the floor of the elevator. Celia looked up, still clenching the knife. She couldn't make out the face.

"Commander?" McDonald asked. "It's me, Jack McDonald."

Celia relaxed with a sigh of relief as she recognized McDonald's voice.

McDonald jumped inside. He checked to see if the man in black was still alive, but there was no pulse. McDonald went over to Celia. He noticed her hand and the steady stream of blood running down her arm. He took off his shirt and wrapped it tightly around her hand.

"Are you alright?" he asked gently. "Other than your hand? You shot?"

"I don't think so," Celia said weakly.

"They are trying to fix the elevator. It won't take long," McDonald hoped he was telling her the truth. There was something that didn't seem right. She was too weak for just a hand wound. Standing up, he yelled up the shaft, "Speed it up, up there!"

"We're trying," was the shout back down.

"I'm late," Celia said weakly.

McDonald took her hand into his, feeling for her pulse. It was rapid and weak. Her face was very pale now, nearly the color of her uniform. He touched her face. It was cool and clammy. Though he was no doctor, he had enough training to know shock when he saw it.

"Commander?" McDonald tried to get her to respond.

"I'm late. I have to go. I'm late," Celia said so quietly he could barely make it out. McDonald searched his mind, trying to remember how to treat shock. There had been a class on it in basic training.

"Someplace else you have to be?" he asked, trying to keep his tone light. He got no response. He had to keep her warm.

"Where is that God of yours now?" he whispered.

"Right here. He sent you." Celia's eyes closed.

McDonald had to do something. He went over to the intruder and took off his black jacket. Carefully, he laid Celia on the elevator floor. He put the jacket over her shoulders. He tucked it under her body. As he tucked on the left side, he noticed it felt wet. McDonald knew what it meant even before he lifted the shirt to examine the source. A dark red spot was getting larger on her uniform jacket even as he watched. She had been shot. He took off his T-shirt and wadded it up, applying pressure as he held it against the wound. Celia flinched.

"Stay with me, Commander," McDonald looked up through the hole in the elevator. "Well, God, if You really do exist, I did my part. Now it's Your turn."

Becoming impatient, he decided to put in another plea. Standing he yelled up a floor above him, "We need an ambulance! What's taking so long?"

"It'll be just another minute, sir," said a voice from above. Finally, McDonald felt the elevator jerk as he kneeled down beside her. The cables clanged loudly as they moved the elevator up to the ground floor. Finally the doors opened and McDonald scooped Celia up in his arms, stepping over the body in the center of the elevator. McDonald was met by two EMTs with a gurney who laid Celia onto the stretcher. Gwen looked on in horror.

"She was shot in the lower right side," McDonald said.

"What happened to her hand?" one EMT asked.

"A knife. She spaced out on me and we didn't get much conversation in," McDonald said.

"What about him?" The EMT asked, looking at the body in the elevator.

"He'll need the coroner."

* * *

It was 2100 hours. He couldn't believe she didn't show. Shaking his head, he glanced around the dim room. He finished his drink then paid up his tab, leaving The Anchor. He felt anxious as he walked back to the motel. Something felt wrong. Commander Celia Kelly always showed up and always kept her word. Where was she?

* * *

Able Walton Jr. waited for Sam. He was in a parking lot across from the base. He saw an ambulance and a Coroner's car go onto the base. But Sam never came. Sam was to bring the commander so they could get the information and kill her together. Able knew as time ticked away that Sam was the one who was dead. That meant Able would have to get creative.

CHAPTER 33

McDonald was sitting in the waiting room, hunched over, staring at the floor as Perry came off the elevator onto the surgical floor. His eyes were ablaze with worry. The commander had grown on everyone.

"What happened?" Perry asked.

"The commander was shot," McDonald said without looking up from the floor.

"I know that," Perry said as he sat beside McDonald. "I want to know how it happened."

McDonald filled him in on what he knew so far. Perry listened intently. Gwen came into the waiting room. Georgie joined them with news.

"She's going to be okay," Georgie said. "They have repaired a flesh wound on her side and sewn up her hand. The only real danger that she encountered was going into shock."

"When can I-we see her?" Elliot asked Georgie.

"They said it will be a few minutes," Georgie said. Gwen looked pleased with the good news.

"Have you called Walton?" Elliot asked him.

"Not yet. I will do that after I see the commander," Georgie said.

"I'm going to check with the doctor," Elliot said, leaving them.

McDonald's mind went over the night's events. He thought about what the commander said. She was late. Late for what?

"What is it?" Gwen asked sitting beside him. "You looked like you were having a rare moment."

"What?" He looked up at Gwen.

"You looked like you were thinking." Gwen smiled.

"Did the commander have an appointment tonight?" McDonald asked.

"Not that I know of," Gwen said, looking at Georgie.

"She didn't inform me of an appointment," Georgie said.

"She kept saying she was late."

* * *

Tammy looked at the clock. It was after midnight. Gwen still wasn't home. Tammy dialed the commander's number, only to get the machine. She called the base, but found out nothing. When Tammy had no luck trying Gwen's cell phone again, that disturbed her even more. She walked around the living room, feeling helpless.

"God, what should I do?" Tammy prayed aloud. She knew that something was wrong. Suddenly she had the overwhelming feeling that she must get out of the apartment. Tammy soon found herself knocking on Henry Jeffers' window.

Jeffers answered in less than a minute. He was shocked as he looked out the window at his guest.

"Tammy!"

"May I come in?" Tammy asked.

Jeffers opened the window and stepped aside, giving her a hand as she climbed in the window.

"Gwen didn't come home. I'm worried," Tammy said.

"Gwen? You are staying with Gwen?" Jeffers asked, again surprised.

"Now that I've blown my cover, I won't be there for long. Have you heard from Gwen or the commander?" Tammy asked anxiously.

"Let me try Georgie." Jeffers called Georgie.

When Jeffers' hung up, his expression was enough to tell Tammy the news wasn't good.

"What has happened?" Tammy asked.

"The commander was shot tonight," Jeffers said.

Tammy's eyes filled with tears. "Is she going to be okay?"

"Yes. I just talked to Georgie and the commander will be fine. She asked me to stay with you rather than come to the hospital."

They just stood there a moment. Then Jeffers stepped forward and took her in his arms giving her a comforting hug. Suddenly she broke away and stepped back.

"Who did it?" she asked him. The agent in her was at work, her fear gone.

"I don't have any details, just that McDonald took the guy out," Jeffers replied.

* * *

Celia opened her eyes to find herself focusing on Gwen's smiling face. She felt very tired.

"I would say I told you so, but I'll wait until you're feeling better," Gwen said, still smiling.

"Maybe I'll have to start listening to you," Celia said weakly.

"I won't hold my breath," Gwen said.

"Where's Jack?" Celia asked.

"I'm right here." McDonald stepped forward standing next to Gwen. "Feeling better?"

"I will be," Celia said. "I just wanted to say, thank you."

"Anytime." McDonald grinned.

"Who was it?" Celia asked.

"Looked like Sam Cooper to me," McDonald said.

"Didn't you see him?" Elliot asked Celia.

"No he had a mask." Celia sighed.

"I have them running his fingerprints as we speak, ma'am," Georgie said.

"Where is he?" Celia asked. She wanted to talk to him. "He was injured, wasn't he?"

"Ma'am, it was worse than that. He's dead," Georgie informed her. Gwen rolled her eyes. Subtle as usual, she thought.

Celia closed her eyes and shook her head. Another one.

"And he won't hurt you or anybody else again!" Gwen pointed out.

Celia looked to the ceiling. Not only had she missed meet with Dixon's contact, but Sam was dead. He was most likely a main player. With Sam gone, it left her right where she had started. Nowhere.

"There will be a lot to do in the morning," Celia said, closing her eyes.

"You are in the hospital. I'm glad I wasn't holding my breath," Gwen said sarcastically.

"The doctor said I am free to leave in the morning. My injuries were not serious. I'm fine."

"I'm going home. This is an argument I know I can't win." Gwen yawned.

"Me too," Georgie said. "It's four hours and twenty-nine minutes past my bedtime and I still have to call Admiral Walton. Good night, ma'am."

"Tell him I'm fine, Georgie."

"Yes, ma'am."

"I'm getting a cup of coffee," Elliot said, following Georgie out.

"Jack, stay a minute," Celia said to McDonald as the room cleared.

"I was supposed to meet with Dixon's contact tonight at 2100 at The Anchor. Have you heard of it?" Celia lowered her voice.

"Yeah, I've heard of it. Been there. You didn't mention that earlier today. Were you going alone?"

Celia nodded.

"You were bound and determined to check in here tonight, weren't you?" McDonald said, shaking his head. "What do you want me to do?"

"Go there. See if he's still around. He has black hair, a black beard, brown eyes, and wears contacts. He's around five eleven, maybe six foot. If he's there, tail him. I want to know where he goes."

"I'm on it. Good night, Commander," McDonald turned to leave. He left the room and ran into Elliot, nearly spilling his coffee.

"Going home?" Elliot asked.

"Yep. You?" McDonald asked, already knowing the answer.

"I'll just crash here tonight," Elliot said casually, without looking him in the eye.

"Ah huh? See you tomorrow." McDonald grinned.

Elliot nodded.

CHAPTER 34

As Gwen parked her Chevy Nova, she realized that she hadn't called Tammy. She put her phone in her jacket pocket and went up to her apartment. When she reached her door, she heard a noise on the other side. Tammy was up pacing the floor, Gwen decided. Shaking her head, she unlocked the door. She stepped into darkness. It struck her as strange. Maybe Tammy wasn't up.

Gwen went to turn on the light switch only to have a gloved hand suddenly on top of her own. She gave a startled scream, but it was interrupted by another hand over her mouth. Gwen struggled, taking her elbow and sticking it hard into the intruder's ribs. Getting loose enough to slip out of his hold, she tried to open the door. The man grabbed her arms as she kicked at him blindly, losing her balance and slipping underneath his legs. He tried to pull her up by her hair but she grabbed hold of his knees to stop herself. He pulled harder and she bit him on the kneecap as hard as she could. In reflex to the pain, he let her go.

Gwen immediately sprang to her feet and ran out the front door. She started running down the stairs. He took out a bottle of chloroform and quickly poured it over a handkerchief. He threw the bottle behind him landing in the apartment, running after her. Gwen heard footsteps at the top of the stairs. Heavy breathing was becoming louder as he closed in on her.

She was not quite to the main door in the foyer when her intruder grabbed her and placed a handkerchief firmly on her mouth and nose. Gwen faded into unconsciousness as she pulled off his mask looking into his conquering eyes. Him. Her eyes closed and her body went limp.

***

Jeffers walked Tammy across the complex to Gwen's apartment. As they walked up the stairs they heard tires squealing out of the parking lot. When they reached the top of the stairs, Tammy saw the door to Gwen's apartment was wide open. Tammy rushed inside.

"Wait!" Jeffers ran to catch up with her.

"Gwen?" Tammy turned on the lights.

Right away they noticed a strong odor was in the air. Jeffers and Tammy looked at the mess in the entry way. The table was knocked over on the floor and broken. Gwen's purse was on the floor, her keys nearby.

Tammy went into the bedroom. "Gwen?"

Jeffers spotted a spilled bottle of chloroform on the floor. Jeffers closed the door. As it closed, he saw a note on the other side with a knife through it holding it firmly to the door.

"Tammy."

Tammy came back down the hall.

"What is it?"

Jeffers ripped the note off the door and handed it to her. "Look at this."

Tammy took the note from Jeffers hand, *'Your secretary for the money'*.

"I'm guessing this was meant for the commander," Jeffers said, stating the obvious. "And this must have been for Gwen," he said, picking up the empty chloroform bottle.

Tammy was suddenly very quiet.

"What?"

"He protected me," Tammy said quietly.

"Who?"

"God. I asked Him what I should do. I had this overwhelming feeling to leave. He really is with me," Tammy said with tears in her eyes.

"Too bad He wasn't with Gwen," Jeffers said sarcastically.

Now she needed to ask God to help Gwen.

"Since the commander is temporarily out of commission, we'd better get a hold of Georgie," Jeffers said.

Jeffers watched Tammy. He suddenly realized she now had that same look the commander had, a look of peace. How does someone get that, he found himself wondering? Tammy was a changed person from the other night in his apartment.

* * *

Wiping the sweat from his forehead, the man leaned against the door to catch his breath. She was heavier than he thought. The chloroform would be wearing off soon and then she'd start moving. Trying to balance her while he opened the door was impossible, so he had to lay her on the ground. Concealed in a large tarp, he picked her up and continued carrying her inside the stucco building. He laid her on the floor. He moved a rug to the center of the room and opened the trap door in the floor. He began descending the ladder, pulling her over his shoulder. Gwen stirred. Carefully, he felt for each step. Somehow, he made it to the bottom. She sat hard as she slid from his shoulder to the chair. Gwen's eyes opened, but she couldn't move. She noticed the concrete floor, with a layer of dirt over it. She wondered why her body was so limp. He removed the tarp and tied her hands. Then he tied her waist to the chair. Gwen's head drooped forward.

"You know, Miss Sherwood, you're more of a fighter than I had thought you'd be," he said smiling.

Gwen raised her head now. She struggled to focus her eyes.

"I know who you are," Gwen said. "I've seen you before."

"You have?" He said surprised. "My partner was supposed to take care of your boss."

"I don't think that went very well," Gwen said weakly. She looked at her surroundings. She knew they were in a basement. What basement?

"So now we need to negotiate."

"You and your partner?" Gwen asked.

"Don't tell me! You've seen him too," he said with a touch of sarcasm.

"Never know," Gwen said, looking smug.

"So, you've seen me. Where?" he said sitting in a chair at a small table. There was a phone in the middle of the table. He played with the cord.

"A lot of pictures have been floating around."

"Is that a joke?" he asked, looking at her intently.

"I have a fairly good sense of humor and I don't think that qualified as a joke," Gwen said sarcastically.

"You mean you saw my picture?" he asked concerned, ignoring her last comment.

Gwen watched his jaw tense. "Don't feel bad. Pictures make a lot people are self-conscious. I personally think I look hippie."

He took in a deep breath as if to gain self-control. He looked at his watch and began pacing the floor. Gwen wondered if he were waiting for the man who had attacked the commander.

"Maybe your buddy is in a body bag."

He glared at her.

"Now that was a joke."

* * *

It was 0100 hours when McDonald pulled up to The Anchor. He got out of his car and walked up to dimly lit doors. It was closed. He walked along the dock and saw no one that fit the description the commander gave him. In fact, he saw no one. He got back into his Mustang convertible and took a moment to look out across the parking lot. Seeing nothing of interest he started up his car and went home.

CHAPTER 35

McDonald was sleeping soundly when Perry shook his shoulder. He blinked as his eyes adjusted to the light.

"Hey, up and at 'em," Perry said impatiently.

"What time is it?" McDonald said as he sat up and put his legs over the side of the bed.

"It's 0600. Let's go," Perry said. "The admiral called and said to meet at the hospital. It didn't sound good."

"Is the commander okay?" McDonald asked concerned.

"Didn't say." Perry shrugged.

McDonald made his way to the bathroom and splashed cold water on his face. He looked into the mirror. He looked felt like death warmed over after only two and half hours sleep.

"How did it go with Mary?" McDonald asked from the bathroom, raising his voice over the running water.

Perry appeared at the bathroom door. "I chickened out again."

"You're a Navy SEAL! What are you afraid of?" McDonald chuckled, as he ran water for a shower.

"Nothing!"

McDonald smiled. "Afraid she'll say no?"

"No. Maybe."

"Afraid she'll say yes?"

"And what if she does?" Perry asked. The only reply was a roar of laughter from McDonald. Letting him have the last laugh, Perry went into the kitchen. He had just finished making a pot of coffee when the phone rang.

"Hello," Perry said into the receiver, as he poured himself a cup of coffee.

"This is James," Elliot's voice came from the other end of the line.

"We're coming. We'll be at the hospital in twenty minutes." Perry looked at his watch.

"Then you know?" Elliot asked.

"I know about the commander's attack last night." Perry detected something else in Elliot's tone.

"No, it's not that."

"Then what?" Perry asked. McDonald emerged from the bathroom wearing only a towel. He poured a cup of coffee.

"Who is it?" McDonald asked Perry.

Perry motioning McDonald to be quiet.

"The commander's secretary, Gwen, was kidnapped and they want the money," Elliot said finally to Perry.

"Gwen? What money?" Perry repeated.

"What about Gwen?" McDonald asked.

"I'll fill you in later. Just hurry," Elliot ordered.

"We'll be right there."

"What?" McDonald could tell something was wrong.

"Gwen was kidnapped and somebody wants money." Perry was confused. "What money?"

"I don't know what is harder to believe. That they took Gwen on purpose or that they think we'll give them $20 million to get her back." McDonald shook his head.

"Twenty million dollars! What $20 million? Why am I always the last to know everything?" Perry frowned.

* * *

Admiral Walton joined Celia and the team in the hospital room. Celia saw that Georgie had something on her mind.

"What is it, Georgie?" Celia asked.

"It's Gwen, she's been kidnapped. They want the money." Georgie kept it to the point.

"Kidnapped? When?" Celia asked.

"Miss Johnson and Chief Jeffers found this note in her apartment." She handed Celia the note. Celia read it. Thank God Tammy was alright!

"How can we be sure Tammy Johnson wasn't involved?" Admiral Walton asked.

"I trust her, sir," Celia said.

"So do I," said Jeffers.

Elliot hoped that they were right.

"That favor I asked you to do Ensign McDonald, How did that go?" Celia asked.

"He was gone and The Anchor was closed."

"Who was gone?" Elliot wondered.

"Dixon's contact. I was going to meet with him last night," Celia said.

"By yourself?" Elliot frowned.

"Like she was safer in the elevator," McDonald said, jumping to her defense. He winked at Celia and she found herself break into a slight smile.

"Gwen is top priority now. Is the note all we have? No instructions of any kind?" Celia asked Georgie.

"No, ma'am," Georgie said.

"Everyone else who has crossed paths with these guys is dead," Celia said quietly.

"They just want her for leverage. If she cooperates, ma'am, she should be fine, at least for the time being," Georgie pointed out.

A hush went across the room. Everyone was thinking the same thing. Gwen? Cooperate?

"We need to find her as soon as possible," McDonald said evenly.

"I imagine we'll be getting a call soon. Ma'am, there is something else."

"What's that?"

"Your attacker was Sam Cooper. The fingerprints confirmed it," Georgie said, handing her the report.

"That doesn't explain how Sam became involved with the Pact in the first place. I need to get out of this place. I want to take a look at Gwen's apartment." Celia was becoming frustrated feeling helpless in a hospital bed.

* * *

Gwen was still sitting upright tied to a chair when she awoke. She was alone. Light came in from the basement window. She heard a car horn. No, it was a ship. The basement she was in was by the water, maybe a dock. Gwen was glad for a moment to be alone. She could relax. She remembered she had her cell phone in her jacket pocket, but her hands were tied and she couldn't reach it. Luckily she had put it on vibrate in the hospital. Her cheek was sore as she realized it was cut. It probably happened struggling with him at her apartment. She wished at least one hand was free to wipe a tear from the cut on her face so it would stop stinging.

* * *

Celia had Elliot and Perry take her by Gwen's apartment. Gwen put up a fight. As Celia looked around, she noticed that this place was much cleaner than she had ever seen any of Gwen's apartments. The incident took place in the entryway and hall. It must have taken him time to catch up to her with the chloroform.

"What are we looking for?" Perry asked.

"Besides Gwen, what else is missing?" Celia asked.

"You tell us," Elliot said.

"Look for her purse, keys, and phone." Celia decided to search out the obvious first.

"Here's her purse," Perry said, bent to pick it up off the hall floor.

"Her keys are still in the door," Elliot said.

"No phone in her purse," Perry announced.

They search the apartment and still didn't find her cell phone.

"She always has her phone with her. Let's take a look in her car," Celia said.

Elliot took the keys and they found her Chevy Nova in the parking lot. Upon a search of her car, there was no phone.

"I need someone to check the office, to make sure she didn't leave it there. If she didn't, maybe we can activate the phone's GPS to find her," Celia said.

"If it's on," Elliot said.

"And if her captor didn't find it," Perry added.

CHAPTER 36

Celia decided to work out of the duplex. Gwen, Georgie, Tammy, and the team met her there. McDonald had been watching Elliot's actions and reactions toward the commander. Something wasn't quite right.

"Ma'am, Admiral Walton and I will be leaving for D.C. shortly." Georgie informed Celia.

"Give this to General Turner," Celia said, writing a message. She folded it and placed it in an envelope.

"Yes, ma'am," Georgie said and left the duplex to fulfill her mission.

"How are you doing?" Perry asked Celia.

"By tonight I'll be as good as new." Celia smiled.

"You think so?" Perry asked skeptically.

"I guess I'll see," Celia said. Her moves were still careful, but she felt better as the day went on.

As Celia went into the bedroom, she stopped. Noticing her strange reaction, Elliot and Perry followed her. The window was wide open and her closet was wide open. The clothes were to one side. McDonald was right behind them.

"You had a visitor," McDonald said.

"Looks like it." Elliot sighed.

"He left a note, how thoughtful." McDonald picked up a note from the pillow at the head of the bed.

"What does it say?" Celia asked, walking over to him.

"'I got her, meet me at The Anchor with the money. Tomorrow, 9:00.' He signed it Mot." McDonald raised his eyebrows. "That is a very popular place!"

"Who is Mot?" Perry asked.

"This is the first I've ever heard of Mot." Celia shrugged, frowning.

Elliot looked at the answering machine. It was blinking. He pressed the button. McDonald handed Celia the note as the first message began to play, *"You didn't show, you'd better have a good reason"* The second message played, *"It's Tammy, call me"* The third message, *"Celia, it's Tara. I hope you're okay, I just called to say I'm sorry."*

"So now what?" Perry asked.

The first message was from the contact, Celia knew that much. Tammy might have tried to call when Gwen didn't show up and as for Tara, poor Tara! It had just occurred to Celia that now Sam was dead. Tara might not be aware that he's gone. Lord, please be with Tara. Please help her, Celia silently prayed.

Celia began to speculate. Mot maybe Dixon's contact, but the contact was waiting for Celia at The Anchor. Why would the contact take Gwen? Did he want the money too?

"Do you know Mot? Is he the contact?" Celia asked Tammy.

"No. I didn't know the name of the contact. Dixon just called him the contact," Tammy said.

"Tomorrow, when I meet with Mot—" Celia began.

"You're not going," Elliot protested.

"Excuse me?" Celia frowned.

"Sounds like she's going," McDonald said, crossing his arms. "I don't mean to burst anyone's bubble, but aren't you forgetting one small thing?" McDonald asked.

"What is that?" Perry asked.

"We don't have the money. Weren't you supposed to bring that?" he pointed out.

"I have a plan instead," Celia said.

"Instead?" McDonald asked, wondering how she could maneuver that one.

"What's the plan?" Elliot asked skeptically.

"I don't know Mot, but I do know the Pact. If they are the same, I must draw the conclusion that they have no intention of keeping Gwen alive," Celia began.

"And?" McDonald said.

"Once they have the money, there is no reason for them to keep any of us alive. We need to rescue her before the trade even takes place," Celia said.

"Since we aren't really trading anything, I can get on board with that." McDonald shrugged.

"We won't need the money. If we find Gwen, her safety won't depend on it. If we can turn the tables and control the narrative."

"That is if we find her," Elliot pointed out.

"He's right. We don't know where she is," McDonald pointed out.

"We'll find her. I have a call into tech to locate her cell phone," Celia said. "We still need more information about what happened last night on the base. They need ID to even get on, let alone in the building where we have our office. Find out if we can see Sam on the cameras entering the base. Commander Elliot and Ensign McDonald go look over the elevator."

"What are we looking for?" McDonald wondered.

"Anything."

"I need to do something first. I'll meet you out front." Elliot left McDonald standing on the porch.

"Sure." McDonald nodded and James left and went to his side of the duplex. McDonald walked out of Celia's front door and noticed Elliot's door was opened a crack. He saw Elliot was on the phone. McDonald at the door when he overheard part of the conversation.

"I've been watching her like a hawk! I moved her in the duplex. I can't get much closer than that. I'm telling you I don't think she knows where the money is," Elliot insisted. He paused, listening. "Yes, sir. I will, sir." Elliot went to hang up the phone.

McDonald quietly went down the front steps and leaned on the hood of his red Mustang as if he had been waiting awhile. He took in a deep breath. Elliot came out of his side of the duplex.

McDonald thought about what to do as Elliot walked toward him. If he did nothing, McDonald could keep an eye out and confront Elliot if there was reason. He decided that nothing might be the best thing to do for now. He'd keep an eye on him, hoping it wasn't as bad as it looked, hoping he had misunderstood.

"Ready?" McDonald asked casually. He got in the driver's side.

"Let's go," Elliot said reluctantly. He jumped in the passenger side.

"She's fine. I wouldn't worry about her." McDonald started the car.

"I'm not," Elliot said.

McDonald was beginning to think that might be true. On one hand Elliot seemed to care for her. On the other hand… there was the phone call. He had worked with the guy now sitting beside him for over five years. Elliot was the best SEAL he had ever met. McDonald had great respect for his work and for Elliot himself. What was that phone call? In any case, McDonald's guard was up and he was watching.

***

Gwen realized for the first time that her legs weren't tied to the chair. She managed to stand, carrying the chair on her back, bent at the waist, and walked in the direction of the window. Only able to see the floor as she proceeded forward, she miscalculated, hitting her head on the cement wall, setting her off balance and causing her to tip backwards. Trying to keep herself from falling, she set her chair down harder than she wanted. At least she landed on all fours again. Her attention went to her hands tied behind her back. *How did they loosen ropes up in the movies, she wondered.* It was then she realized her watch was gone. Great. Gwen shook her head. She lost the watch her parents had given to her for Christmas. Her mother was going to kill her if she lived that long. Gwen heard voices. They sounded far away. She scooted her chair now closer to the window to get a look, but the basement window was too dirty. She called for help at the top of her voice. No response. If she could hear them why couldn't they hear her?

In despair, not knowing what else to do, Gwen began to pray. If You really exist, help me now. If it works for the commander, Gwen thought, maybe it could work for her. Her chest felt tight. It didn't help. She was alone in a basement, still tied to a chair, unable to use her phone.

CHAPTER 37

McDonald and Elliot walked through the front door to find a repair crew working in the elevator shaft. Elliot paused a moment before walking down the stairs, looking toward the elevator. McDonald was not one to analyze, but he had to wonder what Elliot was thinking. McDonald followed Elliot into the basement. Pipes lined the ceiling as they followed a long narrow hall leading into a huge open room with furnaces running and hot water heaters clustered in the center.

"Look." McDonald picked up a long black wig.

"Interesting. So what does that tell us, besides that the guy who did this might not have any hair?" McDonald asked, letting the wig dangle from his finger.

"Cooper wanted to make his hair a different color," Elliot said.

McDonald gave Elliot the wig. They split up with McDonald searching the office and Elliot continued searching the rest of the basement. McDonald left the office and found a broom closet full of tools with gadgets lined along the wall.

"Find anything?"

McDonald jumped and turned to see Elliot.

"Well?" Elliot waited for an answer.

"No," McDonald said. "Did you?"

"Not a thing," Elliot said.

"What did you do with the wig?"

"I set it on the steps," Elliot said.

They walked back to the stairs but the wig was gone.

"It's gone," Elliot said, frowning.

"I think that's why investigators hold onto evidence," McDonald said. It was on the step. Now it was gone. Did Elliot take it?

"Help me find it," Elliot said after walking into the office.

They split up again to continue the search. McDonald noticed there was a door at the bottom of the stairs that opened up to the elevator shafts. He looked back to see Elliot talking to the MP's. He opened the door and went inside unnoticed, quietly closing the door behind him. This could be how Cooper got on top of the elevator. McDonald decided to climb the ladder and see what he could find.

He took a miniature flashlight out of his breast pocket and looked around. McDonald saw his own T-shirt; it must have fallen off the commander when they removed her from the elevator. The MP's hadn't done much of a mop-up job yet. Everything was as it had been the night before. It bothered him to see the blood stain where the commander had been lying. He picked up his shirt and as he bent over he saw a small square piece of paper. Putting his shirt over his shoulder, he picked up the paper. When he had it in hand, he saw it was a wallet size photo. It was two guys in front of an F-14 Tomcat. The commander had this photo in her office hanging on the wall. He put it into his breast pocket.

Climbing out of the elevator, he noticed next to the shaft was a vent. The cover was off. He climbed into it and followed it. He could hear voices and lockers slam shut. The vent went into the locker room. McDonald quietly crawled back. McDonald saw Elliot across the hall and he walked up to him.

"Where have you been?" Elliot asked him.

"Just looking around," McDonald said.

"Find anything yet?" Elliot looked at him skeptically.

McDonald lied, shaking his head no.

* * *

Rear Admiral Walton and Georgie were just outside Washington, D.C. Georgie had spent the trip catching the rear admiral up to speed. Suddenly he turned to Georgie.

"Georgie, does the commander suspect any admiral in particular?" Walton asked.

"The commander has great faith in the Navy and those she serves under. I think that whoever the admiral is behind it, she'll have to see it to believe it. We are not even sure what is true."

"Tara." Walton said.

"Excuse me, sir?" Georgie asked.

"Seeing that picture of Tara has been bothering me. I'm amazed Able ever married. And Tara came out of nowhere." Walton looked back out the window.

"In what way, sir? If you don't mind my asking," Georgie said.

"He went away for a weekend and came home with a fiancé. Even though it was a surprise, we thought marriage would be good for him. We wanted him to have someone." Walton sighed, then continued, "Most people are unaware of this, but Able was adopted. My wife, Sarah, and I tried for years to have a baby. When we had the chance to adopt, we jumped at it. I couldn't have wanted that boy more than if he were my own flesh and blood."

"When did he bring Tara Cooper home?" Georgie asked.

"A week before the wedding. Both my wife and I fell in love with little Samantha right away. Little Samantha spent a lot of time with us before my wife died. Sarah loved having a granddaughter to spoil. Tara was always very devoted to the child. Sammy, that's what we called her, was her whole world."

"He is a lawyer, correct?"

"Yes. He's been doing well the last few years. D.C. has him working big cases," Walton said proudly.

"He works in Washington?" Georgie asked.

"The Pentagon, I think Admiral Lloyd has enlisted Able's help on an advisory board."

As odd as that sounded to her, Georgie. "The commander went to see Tara yesterday morning. Then Lieutenant McDonald and I talked to her later. She was the one who clued us in that the commander might be in danger."

"So Tara is involved in this too?" Walton sounded shocked.

"Apparently, sir."

"You still haven't said who attacked the commander." Walton waited for her reply, looking at her now.

"Sam Cooper, sir, Tara's first husband. It was believed that he went MIA along with Commander Kelly's husband, until yesterday."

Walton looked away. If Tara's husband had been alive, Tara wasn't married to Able. He sat in silence, wondering if he knew his son at all.

* * *

Once at the Pentagon, they took the elevator to the second floor. The Chairman of the Joint Chiefs of Staff was standing in the hall talking to the FBI special agents. Walton gave Georgie an uneasy look. The FBI walked past them into the elevator.

General Baxter Turner noticed them at the end of the hall. He recognized Walton and he met them halfway. Walton and Georgie stood properly at attention. Turner returned the salute.

"At ease," Turner said.

"Message from Commander Kelly, sir." Georgie handed Turner the envelope.

Turner's smile faded. This couldn't be good.

"Let's go into my office." They followed him.

Georgie and Walton sat silently as Turner read the note. I was attacked, my secretary has been kidnapped and they will return her for the money, which I still haven't found. I suspect Lloyd's involved. Turner shook his head.

"How is Kelly?" he asked Georgie after reading the message.

"Home now, sir," Georgie replied. "She had a gunshot wound on her right side, and a knife wound through her left hand. Nothing serious, sir." Both men looked blankly at Georgie, who remained matter of fact.

"When she was here last, she didn't say it but I know she had doubts concerning Lloyd even then. Her instincts were correct. Lloyd was involved," Turner said.

"Sir, we have also discovered CIA Agent Stan Geyser never got on the plane that supposedly killed him. As for Cooper, he is permanently out of the picture," Georgie said.

"Lloyd was possibly their man in Washington," Turner said leaning forward.

"Did you say he was?" Walton asked him.

"His car blew up this morning in his driveway, with him in it."

"If he were behind it–" Walton began.

"Then why is he dead?" Turner finished Walton's question. "Good question. Someone else got greedy, I'd say. We suspected him after the commander's last visit. We put a tap on Lloyd's line. Interestingly enough, he received a call from Lieutenant James Elliot just before someone took him out. In fact, Lieutenant Commander Elliot checked in on a regular basis. And you might want to look at the other calls." Turner handed a log of call details to Walton. As Walton read the log in front of him his worst fears confirmed.

Log six: call from Norfolk 555-6768, Able Walton Jr. to Admiral John Lloyd.

Walton: I took care of it.

Lloyd: Then why is she on our tail?

Walton: Legally it can't be traced to us. Cooper and Kelly will be blamed for everything.

Lloyd: Celia Kelly is smarter than that. You be careful.

Walton: Right now we need her to lead us to the money. Tara just got back, got to go.

Log nine: call from Norfolk 555-6768. Able Walton Jr. to Admiral John Lloyd.

Walton: Cooper is sure she either has it or can get it.

Lloyd: To get his family back?

Walton: something like that.

Lloyd: After we get the money, we get rid of all of them, including Cooper.

Walton: I hear Samantha, can't talk now, gotta go.

Walton had read enough. How did Able get involved in this? This made it appear as if he avoided Tara. His face was white, his hands felt clammy. This couldn't be happening. It's not that he didn't know the boy had problems, but this? His son was committing treason. Georgie gently took the print out from his hands. She began to read the first page. Turner waited for a response.

"When you read the next page in the log, you'll notice Geyser has checked in with Lloyd as well," Turner said sitting back.

Georgie flipped the page. Walton scooted his chair closer to read it with her.

Lloyd: It's about time you checked in. It's been over two weeks.

Geyser: I see your commander took out the entire camp.

Lloyd: All I care about is the money. The plan is working perfectly.

Geyser: Look, this isn't the plan we discussed. You tried to kill me.

Lloyd: Meet me at my place 0800 tomorrow. We'll talk.

Geyser: Talk?

Lloyd: She's smart. I've had to change a few details. She doesn't even trust the Lieutenant as I had hoped.

Geyser: I am detail you had to change? Sure it's not just you and that son of yours wanting the money for yourself?"

Lloyd: 8:00 tomorrow morning.

"This implies Geyser had something to do with Lloyd's death, if he were to meet with him this morning," Georgie said.

"It sure looks that way," Turner agreed.

"Wait a minute," Walton said looking concerned. "You said James Elliot called Lloyd?"

"Yes, that is right." Turner nodded. "His was the next call as you can see."

"As you can see the dialog is questionable on whether Elliot was involved in the same way your son was. Elliot might have had full knowledge of what they were doing or maybe none. That must be determined. The last call doesn't make Elliot look good."

Georgie turned the page and looked at the conversations between Elliot and Lloyd. Both sides of the conversations were guarded. She couldn't make heads or tails of Elliot's involvement from the log. If the intention was to set up the commander, it was not too unlikely that they assigned someone to keep an eye on her. If they were lucky, he might witness a mistake. Yet, the general was right, the last conversation was strange.

Lloyd: Have you found anything yet?

Elliot: I've been watching her like a hawk. I've moved her into the duplex. I can't get much closer than that.

Lloyd: Don't be too sure.

Elliot: I'm telling you I don't think she knows where it is.

Lloyd: Don't get soft on me boy, there is too much at stake.

Elliot: Yes, sir.

Lloyd: I want you to find out where that money is.

Elliot: I will, sir. Yes, sir.

Walton sat back in his chair. His jaw was tense now. One person he thought highly of was James Elliot. It was inconceivable that he could be wrong about James as well as his son. Walton knew his son wasn't perfect, but James Elliot?

"An admiral and his son are supposed to be involved in this, right?" Turner reminded them.

"But Able is my son and Lloyd has no children. He didn't even marry until after Sarah and I had adopted Able," Walton said, puzzled by the reference to Lloyd's having a son.

"There is no record of Lloyd and his wife having anything other than that annoying bulldog," Turner agreed.

"It could have been before his wife, sir," Georgie suggested.

"An affair," Walton added. If he wasn't beyond cheating on his country, he could be cheating on his wife.

"It could be we have another member floating around out there. Look into it," Turner ordered Georgie.

"Yes, sir." Georgie looked at her watch, "We best get back. If Geyser is responsible for Lloyd's death, he might be on his way to Norfolk. May I take a copy of the log, sir?" Georgie asked.

"I'm sure the commander will want to look at the call logs."

"Absolutely, I'll have my secretary make a copy of it," Turner said.

"Could we look at Lloyd's office before we leave?" Walton asked.

"No, the FBI is in there now. I want Kelly to handle things on her end before we hand over everything on the Pact to FBI," Turner said.

"Does the FBI have these logs?" Walton wanted to know.

"Not yet. You tell Kelly her window of time to solve this is very small."

CHAPTER 38

"We found a black wig."

"You did? Where is it?" Celia was encouraged. She suspected the contact wore a black wig.

"And then we lost it. It was laid on the steps when we went into the basement. Unfortunately, it disappeared," McDonald said.

"I set it down and we separated to look around, but when we came back, it was gone," Elliot said.

"I see." Celia was disappointed.

"But I found something else." McDonald pulled out the picture. "I found this picture in the elevator."

Elliot frowned at McDonald and said, "I'm getting some air."

Celia took the picture, not noticing Elliot's reaction. Sam and Tom both kept this picture in their wallets. Sam must have lost it last night while they struggled. Sam still carried it with him after all that time. It was so hard to picture Sam trying to hurt her, knowing him when Tom was alive. It was then it occurred to her. Maybe Sam had no choice. Maybe he was simply keeping Tara and Samantha safe. This posed another theory. Was Sam a bad guy? Celia knew she'd never know the answer to that question. It died with Sam.

Celia's cell phone rang.

"Kelly."

"Hey, just letting you know I showed that picture you texted me to Will Bear and he confirmed that it was the man he saw." Celia's friend called from the retirement home where Ryan was staying.

"Thanks. Is he okay?"

"Good as new!"

Celia hung up the phone and looked at the rest of the group.

"Able Walton Jr. was the man Ryan saw. He confirmed his identity from a photo," Celia said.

"So we are on the right track," McDonald said carefully.

"Something else you want to ask me, Ensign?" Celia saw the look of concern in his eye.

"Do you think it's Admiral Walton?" McDonald asked.

"No, I don't," Celia said.

* * *

Tara Cooper packed two suitcases, one for her and one for Samantha. Taking all the cash she could find, she called a cab. Putting Samantha inside the cab first, she sat beside her. She asked the driver to stop at her bank and withdrew nine thousand dollars in cash. Amazingly enough, the bank did not question it. Able had large deposits or withdrawals here more than once. Tara got back into the cab and took Samantha's hand in her own.

"The airport please," Tara instructed the cab driver. Within fifteen minutes, they were in front of the airport. The driver parked and got out. He took their bags from the trunk and accepted his fee from Tara. He got back in the cab and drove away.

"Where are we going, Mommy?" Samantha asked her mother.

"Someplace better, I promise!" Tara looked into Samantha's frightened eyes and led her into the airport terminal, each carrying their suitcase. Tara walked up to the ticket desk. The lady behind the desk smiled sweetly.

"May I help you?" The lady behind the desk smiled sweetly.

"Yes, I am taking my daughter on a surprise overseas trip which we are selecting today for the fun of it. Can you tell me the available flights going out today? Are you running any specials?" Tara asked casually.

"We have a special flight going into Ireland."

"Perfect."

The tickets were soon processed and ready. Tara accepted them, never letting go of Samantha's hand. They waited until it was time to board the plane. When their flight was called, they walked through the boarding tunnel and found their seats on the plane. Tara put her arm around her daughter's shoulders and gave her a squeeze. She then looked out the window. Tara had left a note for Able saying she had gone shopping.

* * *

Tammy and Jeffers were about to leave the duplex to go to Langley when Jeffers noticed Elliot leaving and clearly upset.

"I'll be right back," Jeffers said to Tammy.

"No problem. I'll wait in the car," Tammy said.

Jeffers was concerned for Elliot. He had recently had an experience with getting too close himself. He wondered if maybe somewhere along the way Elliot was having the same problem with the commander. Jeffers decided to check on him. It didn't take long to spot him walking along the beach.

"You're starting to care more than you should, aren't you?" Jeffers asked.

Elliot was quiet.

"Do you love her?" Jeffers asked him.

"What?" Elliot was floored.

"Is that what you think?"

"I'm asking," Jeffers said carefully.

Elliot looked Jeffers in the eye. "Hasn't anyone else noticed that since she came to Dam Neck, people have been dropping like flies?"

"Maybe so, but I don't think she's responsible. Why do you?"

"She hid Tammy, didn't she?" Elliot pointed out.

"And she's alive because of it. So is Ryan," Jeffers reminded him.

Elliot caught himself. He felt himself was losing control. He had to get it back. "I'm sorry. I guess I'm just blowing off steam."

"You know I've been watching her too. There is something different about her. I was afraid of it too, at first, but now I'm thinking she has something I'd like to have," Jeffers said. After pausing, he continued, "She has a peace about her–"

"Peace, is impossible, otherwise there wouldn't be a Navy SEAL team in the first place. I'm not afraid of her God," Elliot countered.

"I didn't say anything about God, you did," Jeffers said.

CHAPTER 39

Celia walked along the beach, Perry beside her. She was beginning to regain her strength. Other than watching out for the stitches, she was feeling good. At least the stitches on her hairline were gone.

"I've heard through the grapevine that you are thinking of proposing to your girlfriend. Is that true?" Celia said as she began to walk.

"Afraid so," Perry said, nodding, walking beside her.

"It has to be easier than cutting off somebody's leg," Celia smiled at his response.

"You'd think so, wouldn't you?" Perry returned the smile.

"Maybe she's not the right one."

"She's great, perfect," Perry said, more to himself than Celia. "I bought a ring and everything."

"So."

"I to be married and having children, but," his voice trailed off. "I guess I'm afraid of leaving her alone too much. That might not be what she wants."

"Trust your heart and let her speak for herself. I'll pray about it for you." Celia smiled again.

"It isn't always that easy, pray and then everything works out," he replied.

"If things were easy, we wouldn't need to pray in the first place, Lieutenant," Celia said.

Perry stopped a moment and replied, "I've never thought about it like that before."

Celia's cell phone rang.

"Kelly."

The call was brief. She looked like it was good news.

"Who was it? Good news?" Perry asked.

"We have a location on Gwen's cell GPS."

They went back up to the duplex where McDonald was sitting on the porch reading Frank Scott's files.

"You were right, there is not much detail in these files after five years of work. Why?" McDonald wondered out as they came up the stairs.

"Good question, but we'll talk later. They have a location on Gwen's phone. I need you and Perry to come with me and check it out," Celia said.

"We got this. You are supposed to be recovering," Perry protested.

"I am fine." Celia was getting tired of reminding everyone.

"Can you run?" McDonald asked.

"If I have to."

"Can you be someone else?" McDonald asked next.

Perry frowned and Celia looked puzzled.

"Whoever took her is watching for you, not us. If you want us in and out right under his nose, we go in alone," McDonald said.

Celia knew he was right.

"Okay. Let's see where the location is," Celia said.

Inside they brought up the map on line. Celia recognized it right away.

"This is where I first tried to meet the contact." Celia frowned.

"Where you got the stitches and shiner?" Perry asked.

"Yes."

"Let's go."

"You are not going." McDonald was firm.

"I will stay in the car." Celia heard herself say it, but she didn't believe it either.

"No," Perry and McDonald said in unison.

"We meant, no, ma'am," Perry rephrased.

Celia rolled her eyes.

"Look, just get Gwen. I need Able Walton Jr. in play if I'm going to get the rest of them." Celia was firm.

"Just Gwen, got it." McDonald nodded.

They took her GLOCK and her back up and Celia watched them drive away.

* * *

"Let's get back and see what we can do to finish this mess," Elliot said as he watched McDonald's red Mustang drive away. Jeffers followed Elliot's eyes. Elliot's jaw tensed. Pressure didn't usually surface in Lieutenant James Elliot. Jeffers found himself wondering what Elliot was struggling with, the mission or his feelings. Elliot began to walk back to the duplex.

Jeffers stayed behind taking in the majesty of the ocean, reevaluating his own life to this point. Jeffers had always been alone, from the earliest age he could remember. He had always been searching. Searching for something real to fill the big hole left in his heart. God was one thing he hadn't tried. Jeffers had always depended on himself and then he depended on his team. Depending on someone you couldn't see and only believed to exist was a frightening concept.

* * *

"What's going on?" Elliot asked Celia.

"We have a fix on Gwen's phone. Perry and McDonald went to check it out," Celia sighed.

"I should have gone with them."

"Me too, but I let them talk me out of it." Celia sighed.

"Considering the last couple of days, that's probably wise."

"With you here, they have backup to call on if needed." Celia added, "I'm glad you are here and I don't have to wait alone."

"Let's go inside so you can sit," Elliot said relaxing his demeanor. Maybe he was right where he should be.

* * *

Gwen's stomach started to growl. Her host lowered the ladder into the room. He stepped off the ladder onto the cement floor. She noticed he was carrying a black wig. She found that curious. He didn't have it the day he brought her here. She decided to dig for information.

"I don't think it's you," she commented.

This brought her a glare.

"Did you bring something to eat?" Gwen asked, hopefully.

* * *

"There he is." McDonald nodded toward the docks.

"You are sure he doesn't know who we are," Perry said.

"He possibly knows who all of us are. I just don't think he'll be as apt to look for us. He has no way of knowing that the commander temporarily changed our job description from SEALs to Intel investigators," McDonald said.

"Intel investigators? Is that even a real job?" Perry asked.

"It is today."

McDonald and Perry walked to the docks from McDonald's car. They watched as Able Walton Jr. walked to a building. Waiting until he was a safe distance ahead, they followed.

They watched him go into the last cement, stucco building at the end of the dock. Once in front of it they stopped. McDonald noticed a watch on the ground and picked it up.

"She's here. This is Gwen's." McDonald tried the door. It was locked, so he went behind the building. There were two basement windows along the bottom back side. At 1700 hours, dusk was upon them. It could be an asset. As they came up to the first window, they noticed the second window was opening.

McDonald heard a man's voice.

"There! Happy now? You've got your air," a man's voice growled.

"I'm as happy as I can be. What's the wig for?" they heard Gwen ask.

McDonald was above them now, Perry sitting next to him, listening on either side of the window.

"How long do you plan to drag this out?" Gwen asked.

"Until I get my money back," he said.

"Now, technically, that money wasn't yours. You stole those weapons. That means you obtained that money illegally," Gwen pointed out.

"You are possibly the most annoying person I have ever met."

"I'm curious. What made you think I would be worth $20 million to the commander?" Gwen said.

McDonald gave Perry the "I said that first" look.

"Certainly your services must be worth something."

"I'm a secretary, not a paid escort," Gwen said sarcastically.

McDonald shook his head.

"Do you always have to have the last word?" Able was becoming impatient and angry.

McDonald could hardly blame him. Whether he was a bad guy or good guy, a guy could only take so much. McDonald had to remind himself that he was here to rescue her.

"No I don't. So seriously what's the wig about," Gwen said.

"I'd take time to kill you now, but I need to use you to meet your boss. For your sake, she'd better have that money. After I get the money, killing you will be the next thing on my list."

It sounded like the man was gathering things and hopefully was leaving, McDonald thought.

"Why do you think she knows where the money is?" Gwen asked.

"Because he was her husband," the man said as clenched his teeth and fists.

"You are uptight. You might consider a vacation. Cuba is nice this time of year," Gwen said.

McDonald put his face in his hands. Perry shook his head.

"I'll deal with you later," he said hotly as he climbed up the ladder and unhooked it from the pegs on the floor. He took it up with him as he opened the door, then slammed it and locked it shut.

Gwen muttered to herself, "The last word, I don't do that."

Perry slipped around the front to make sure he was leaving. When he saw the man drive away, he gave McDonald the high sign. McDonald decided to let her know he was there.

"You do," McDonald said through the opened window.

"Who's there?" Gwen asked, looking up startled.

"It's me, Jack McDonald."

"I hate to admit it, but am I glad to hear your voice." Gwen smiled. So God sent her McDonald. He must have a sense of humor.

He put his head in the window. "We are going to get you out of here."

The opening of the window was big enough so McDonald jumped in, landing on his feet.

"We?" Gwen asked.

"Chris and I."

"Where am I?"

"The docks of ill repute," McDonald said.

"Oh, well, that explains why no one has paid any attention to me."

"I don't think I'll touch that one," McDonald said. His attention went to Gwen. She had a black eye and cut with a large bruise around it. "Are you okay?"

"Yes." Gwen was glad to see him. "Are you just going to stand there or are you going to untie me?"

McDonald took his knife and cut the ropes that had been tied so tightly that her wrists were red and sore from rope burns. Then he helped her off the chair after the ropes were removed.

"I found this near the door."

Gwen smiled. "My watch! Thanks."

"Would you two cut it out and get out of there?" Perry said.

"He's right, let's go. Take your shoes off and stand on my shoulders." McDonald first moved the chair over to the window. He stood on the chair and kneeled allowing Gwen to climb onto his shoulders. Gwen awkwardly put her feet on his shoulders. She was squatting at first, trying to figure out how to balance to stand.

"Just balance and I'll stand up. Move your skirt, I can't see." McDonald was irritated. Gwen saw for the first time that as she straddled her legs her skirt went over his head. She pulled it off and behind his head. Perry stuck his head out of the vent opening.

"When I stand up grab Chris's hands. Piece of cake. Got it?" McDonald asked her.

"Got it," she said.

Gwen reached up and Perry took her hands and pulled her through the window. Gwen put her elbows on either side of the opening and pulled herself the rest of the way. McDonald then jumped up and grabbed Perry's hand. Soon, they were on the other side of the window.

"How did you find me?" Gwen wanted to know.

"GPS on your phone," Perry said.

CHAPTER 40

Tammy showed her CIA credentials and Jeffers showed his military ID as they passed through Langley's security. When they reached the second floor and came to a door marked Area 4, Tammy put her right eye close enough for the scanner to read and the door opened. Jeffers followed her inside where Aggie was waiting for her.

"How can I help?" Aggie asked.

"Who is Mot?"

"The code name for Dixon's contact," Aggie said.

"Who is Dixon's contact?" Jeffers asked.

"I don't know, I never met him." Aggie shrugged.

"What do you know about the money?" Tammy asked.

"The money was intercepted and hidden instead of being paid to the seller of the last weapons bought by the Pact. The Pact has to find the buyer's money to continue to do business."

"They haven't done any buying or selling since?" Jeffers asked.

"That's why you were planted in Syria at the camp where the boy spent most of his time. Dixon was hoping you would hear chatter," Aggie said to Tammy.

"So what went wrong?" Jeffers asked

"It became a race to information when Commander Kelly showed up," Aggie said honestly.

"What does the commander's husband have to do with this?" Tammy asked.

"I don't know. I do know that Dixon had Tom Kelly's file on his desk. I don't know why," Aggie said.

* * *

"You are supposed to be relaxing," Elliot said.

"I need to be doing something," Celia replied.

"You are doing something, making me nervous."

Georgie and Rear Admiral Walton drove back to the duplex. When they entered the duplex, Celia was still pacing. Elliot was sitting at the table looking at the files. Tammy and Jeffers returned from Langley.

"I'm glad you're back. What do we know?" Celia asked.

"How are you feeling, ma'am?" Georgie asked.

"I'm fine, thank you. I was having a little trouble waiting," Celia said.

"A little?" Elliot raised an eyebrow.

Jeffers smiled.

"Where is McDonald and Perry?" Walton asked.

"We got a location on the GPS for Gwen's cell phone. They are checking it out," Celia said. "What did Aggie have to say?"

"She said that Mot was Dixon's contact," Tammy said.

"Who is he?" Georgie asked.

"Aggie didn't know, she has never seen him," Tammy said. She filled them in on what Aggie said concerning the Pact, the money, and Tom Kelly's file.

"Daniel Ryan confirmed Able Walton Jr. to be the blond man he encountered. I'm sorry, sir," Celia said to Admiral Walton.

"Thanks for your candor, Commander. We have answers and unexpected news. Lloyd is dead," Walton said.

"What?" Celia couldn't believe it. "How?" She hadn't expected that.

"Well, ma'am, can we speak to you privately a moment?" Georgie asked.

"I could use some air. Let's go outside," Celia said.

A wise move, Walton decided. Georgie opened the door and they walked to the water's edge. She pulled out the copies of the logs that Turner had allowed her to take. She explained how Turner had suspected Lloyd and put a tap on his phone.

Celia read the log where Georgie had asked her to start. She read the conversation with Stan Geyser. So, Geyser was still alive as she suspected.

"It looks like Geyser could have taken advantage of the meeting and killed Lloyd," Celia said.

"Yes, ma'am, he'd be my top suspect." Georgie agreed.

"It gets worse, Commander, for both of us. Keep reading," Walton said, a sadness in his tone.

Celia read the conversation between Able Walton Jr. and Lloyd. That didn't surprise her, but she wasn't prepared for the log of Lloyd and Elliot. Since Lloyd was dead and Sam was dead, that left Able Walton Jr., Stan Geyser, and possibly Elliot, to go after the money. She still wasn't one hundred percent sure where Mot fit into the equation.

"What do you want to do, ma'am?" Georgie asked.

"I think we should confront James," Celia said. "What do you think, sir?"

"I agree, and I'd need to talk to Able," Walton said.

"All due respect, sir, let's see what James has to say first," Celia said.

She already knew Able Jr. was dangerous. They had to figure out what side James Elliot was on. Then she paused and asked, "If Lloyd was the admiral who is the son? He had no children. According to the log, his only correspondence is with James, Geyser and your son, sir."

"I've given that some thought, ma'am," Georgie paused, looking at Walton.

"What do you think, Georgie?" Walton was anxious to know her theory.

"It's something you said on our way to Washington, sir. You mentioned that Able Jr. was adopted."

"Are you saying we adopted Lloyd's son?" Walton shook his head.

"Let's see how much Elliot knows before we jump to any conclusions." Celia could see Walton was overwhelmed.

"Yes, ma'am," Georgie said. "Oh, the FBI is investigating Lloyd's death. Turner said you have a small window of time to find the Pact before he has to hand everything over to them."

"Then we'd better get to work," Celia said.

They started walking toward Elliot's side of the duplex and as they reached the front deck, McDonald's red Mustang pulled into the driveway. Celia looked over at the Mustang. Perry got out of the back seat. He leaned back into the car and took out four large boxes. As McDonald opened the door to get out, Celia thought she heard arguing. Gwen and McDonald got out of the car, simultaneously, disagreeing over pizza.

"Everybody likes pepperoni," McDonald said as he shut his door.

"Only if it has pineapple," Gwen said back, shutting the other door.

"Nobody puts pineapple on pepperoni," McDonald replied frustrated.

Perry walked up to Walton, Celia, and Georgie carrying a pizza. He was smiling.

"She was hungry," Perry said, rolling his eyes.

McDonald managed half a grin when he saw Celia.

"Here she is, just like I promised, in one piece."

"Thank you. Well done," Celia said to both McDonald and Perry.

"If wasn't for me, he might have taken her back," Perry chuckled.

Celia smiled.

"He doesn't know we have her back?" Celia asked Perry.

"We let him walk away just like you asked us too." Perry hoped she knew what she was doing.

Gwen walked up to them. Celia saw her face was bruised and her wrists were still rope burned and she took in a breath. At least Gwen was safe now.

"Boy, do I have a story to tell you." Gwen smiled then added, "Did you miss me?"

McDonald shook his head and walked into the duplex.

* * *

Able Walton Jr. parked in his three car garage. Tara's car was still gone. Did Cooper still have it? Getting out of his Ford Bronco, he went into the house through the garage.

"Tara," he called. No answer. She must be upstairs he decided. He went into the kitchen to pour himself a glass of juice. As he looked into the refrigerator, a beer looked better. He needed to unwind. Closing the refrigerator door, he noticed the note stuck on the refrigerator with a bunny magnet.

So she went shopping again. Able drank his beer and decided he was hungry. Opening the refrigerator again, he took out fixings to make a sandwich. After he made his sandwich, he sat at the kitchen table to eat and read the paper. He was particularly interested in the article on the front page. It had a huge picture of Admiral John Lloyd. The article went on to say that the chief of naval operations was dead. That he had been victim to a car bomb in his driveway. Able suddenly felt sick and nearly choked on the last bite of sandwich he had devoured. Lloyd? Dead? It couldn't be true. He went to the phone and began to dial when...

"Hang up the phone."

Able hung up the phone as he turned to face his unknown guest.

CHAPTER 41

With Gwen's arrival, Celia's conversation with Elliot was put on hold. Instead of interviewing either Gwen or Elliot, Celia decided pizza was a good idea. A break might be just what everyone needed.

"Wow, you really like pizza don't you?" Jeffers said to Gwen.

"Who doesn't?" Gwen replied.

Celia decided she wasn't hungry. She slipped out to the deck of the duplex to think. Elliot followed her.

"Can I talk to you?" Elliot asked her.

"Eat. We can talk later." Celia managed a weak smile. She didn't want to talk to him now. She didn't to prepare.

"We need to talk now," Elliot insisted as he sat beside her.

"What is it?" Celia was curious now.

"First, I'd..." Elliot paused, avoiding eye contact. "There is something I need to tell you. I thought about telling you a couple of times, but..."

Celia waited. James was quiet. Was it concerning his phone calls with Lloyd? Celia was hoping it was an explanation she wanted to hear. Even more than that, she hoped it was one she could believe.

"I have been required to check in with Admiral Lloyd since we came back from Syria," Elliot said evenly.

Walton came out of the duplex at that moment. He had seen Elliot follow Celia out and thought he should check it out.

"Everything okay out here?" Walton asked Celia.

"Yes, sir," Celia said.

It was then Elliot realized they were both being guarded. Celia thought she saw a moment of panic in his eyes as he looked at Walton, then back at Celia. One thing was for sure, Elliot was right. They did need to talk.

"Let's continue this conversation with Rear Admiral Walton present."

"Maybe we could go over to your place, Lieutenant Commander," Walton suggested.

"I think that is a good idea. I want both of you to know," Elliot said looking into Celia's eyes. He appeared sincere.

"I'll be right back." Celia was polite as she got up and went back into her living room.

Gwen came out of the bathroom then, her blonde hair was wet and straight instead of the usual low ponytail. She was wearing Celia's sweatpants and a sweatshirt with a Navy logo across the front.

"Feeling better after a shower?" Celia smiled.

"Yes, much," Gwen said.

"Gwen, I'm going next door to go over new information. Maybe you could keep everybody entertained."

"Sure. McDonald makes it a tough room, but I'll do my best," Gwen said. This brought a grin to Perry's face as he overheard. He enjoyed Gwen and McDonald's banter.

"We'll just be next door. Georgie, please join me," Celia said.

"Yes, ma'am." Georgie responded at once getting her attaché case.

* * *

Celia, Walton, and Elliot sat around the kitchen table. Georgie remained standing. Elliot looked at her. He hadn't expected Celia to ask Georgie to join them.

"Have a seat," Elliot offered Georgie.

"I prefer to stand, Commander," Georgie said. It was as it Georgie was standing guard. Even after time getting to know the team, Georgie was unaffected by any personal connection, if any existed for her. She remained the ever ready soldier. Celia found this very hard. She had come to care for the members of the team. They were her responsibility. She didn't want to back Elliot into a corner.

"We have come across information–"

"Before you say anything else, please."

Elliot paused.

"Please just hear me out," Elliot said, paused, then continued.

"When we were in Germany on our way home from Syria, Lloyd asked me to keep an eye on you. He said to follow your orders but to watch you closely. He even suggested I have you move into the duplex. He mentioned the money. He suggested that you either knew where it was or could lead the government to it."

"So you're saying he thought I was part of the Pact and assigned you to check me out?" Celia asked astounded.

"Lloyd led me to believe that he wasn't sure if you were involved directly or not. He wanted to be sure. I was supposed to report every move you made. I was following orders. As things continued, I knew there was more to it, and that I was wrong." Elliot waited for their response.

"To say you were wrong is an understatement. Boy, as acting CO, I should have been informed if there were any doubts concerning Commander Kelly's credibility," Walton said sternly.

"Didn't you find it strange the same man who sent me here wanted you to spy on me? I realize you didn't know me well enough to trust me, but you certainly could trust Admiral Walton. If Lloyd was questioning me why didn't Lloyd express his concerns to Admiral Walton? He wanted a spy that's what you were." Celia tried to sort out the pieces.

Elliot said nothing.

"James, are you aware that an hour after you talked to Lloyd this morning, he was killed by a car bomb?" Celia asked, her eyes not leaving his, looking for any clue she could. The color drained from his face. Lloyd was dead? How did she know about the phone call this morning?

"No."

A hush came over the room.

Celia thought James Elliot was a good man. Now she had to face the possibility James Elliot wasn't the man she had come to know. A rush of panic swept over her. Other than Gwen, she hadn't known any of these people longer than two months. She felt alone. Mot had said to watch her back. Dixon had said to watch her back. Were they right? Celia got up from the table and went past Georgie out the front door.

"Ma'am?" Georgie asked, confused.

"I'll be back," Celia said on her way out without looking back. She closed the door behind her hoping no one would follow.

Celia walked quickly to her Studebaker. Using her spare key from underneath the floor mat, she started it up, and backed out. In her rear view mirror she saw Elliot and Walton running after her. She stepped on the gas. As she drove onto the highway, she realized she felt something else. Fear. Celia drove until she spotted a small church just off the highway. Without a second thought, she pulled into the church's parking lot. The plaque near the door read Virginia Beach Assembly. Celia walked up to the door and tried it. It was open. She walked into the sanctuary and up the main aisle. Sitting in the front pew, a tear run down her cheek. Her prayer life had been lacking, only talking to Him when nothing else was working. She realized that was exactly what she was doing now. Instead of depending on Him every day, twenty-four hours a day, she only called on Him when she got stuck? Celia was stuck now and losing focus. Celia knew it was time to give the control back to God.

Celia bowed her head as tears fell freely, "Lord, forgive me for the mess I've made of things. Show me the direction I need to go in. Give me the power to discern who I can trust."

After getting back on the road, Celia called Turner's number. It was time to check in.

"This is Commander Kelly," Celia said into the phone. Feeling a big weight had been lifted from her shoulders, she knew God was with her.

CHAPTER 42

McDonald and Gwen were the first outside to see what the commotion was about. Gwen watched Celia's car disappearing into the distance. *Now what is she doing?* Gwen thought. Elliot started getting into his jeep. Before Elliot knew what was happening, McDonald grabbed him by his collar, pulling him from the driver's seat, pushing him against the side off the jeep. Walton and Georgie were too surprised to do anything but watch.

"You are not following her," McDonald said through clenched teeth.

"What's wrong with you? Let go of me." Elliot was taken off guard.

"Why? So you can watch her like a hawk? So you can see how much closer you can get?" McDonald increased his force with each word.

Elliot looked him in the eye. He knew McDonald was referring to the phone call. Neither man flinched. Neither of them noticed Gwen taking the keys out of the jeep's ignition.

"That's right. I overheard your phone conversation this morning," McDonald said.

"It's not what you think," Elliot said.

"Let go of him, Ensign," Walton said finally to McDonald. "Let's go inside." McDonald held firm. Pushing him against the side of the jeep one more time, he released Elliot's collar. Elliot got into the jeep, but Gwen was in front of it holding up his keys. She wasn't sure what was going on, but she figured she'd help detain him until she found out.

"If you're looking for these, you'll have to get them from the admiral." With that Gwen tossed them up to Walton. Walton caught them right on cue. "Inside," Walton repeated opening Celia's front door.

"You can't just let her go," Elliot said. "Not after everything that has happened. It's not safe."

"She's safer with you?" McDonald crossed his arms.

"What's going on here?" Perry wanted to know.

"We have dissension in the ranks," Gwen said.

"Why? What happened?" Jeffers asked, looking at Elliot. Elliot had been acting strange all day. Now McDonald and Elliot were at odds.

"In light of recent events, LT. Commander Elliot, why don't you inform the team of what you shared with us earlier," Walton instructed.

"Admiral Lloyd wanted me to keep an eye on Commander Kelly in case she dealt directly with the Pact," Elliot simplified. "He gave me orders. I followed them."

"He suspected Commander Kelly? Of what?" Perry asked. He found that hard to believe.

"And she had someone attack her on the docks, then in the elevator to throw us off the trail. Brilliant!" McDonald said sarcastically.

"This is outrageous. Celia Kelly is one the finest officers I've ever worked for!" Gwen was on her feet and in Elliot's face. Of course Kelly was the only Officer Gwen had worked for, but she decided not to mention that. "And let me tell you something else, she saved Lloyd's butt in that office more than once. I realize you didn't know her from Adam when we came here. But, if you really knew Admiral John Lloyd, you should have processed any order from him a couple times through that thick skull of yours before taking it seriously. I don't doubt for one minute Lloyd could have set her up, but in choosing Commander Kelly, Lloyd made the same mistake he always did, he miscalculated. He didn't think she could do it. He thought she'd fail and he could put the blame on her, but as usual he was wrong." Gwen ended, her voice hot with anger, her finger firmly poking into Elliot's chest. The room was waiting for a response, any response.

"You don't think she wanted the money for herself?" Elliot asked.

"If you ask me, I'm not sure that money even exists. And if it does, whoever was dumb enough to leave it lying around instead of using a Swiss bank account like a normal terrorist, deserved to lose it." Gwen crossed her arms.

McDonald narrowed his eyes. She had just made the dumbest comment he had ever heard make sense. He admired her loyalty and her spunk as annoying as it may be. Even as an outsider looking in, he didn't think the commander was involved with the Pact. Commander Kelly had caused the Pact the most grief.

No one was aware that the door had opened. No one had even heard the car. Celia had come in and had heard most of what Gwen said. Gwen was not only counting on her to solve this, she was sure that Celia could. It served both as pressure and encouragement. For Celia that was the right combination, only this time she was doing it with God's help.

"Sorry I left so abruptly. I talked to General Turner." All eyes turned to the door.

"Oh, hi," Gwen said, changing her tone, relieved to see that Celia came back. Gwen led Celia to the door. "Can I talk to you a minute outside?"

"Sure, excuse us," Celia said to the others.

After hustling Celia outside, Gwen didn't waste any time. "Where did you go?"

"I needed space," Celia said carefully. "I found a church up the road and–"

"You panicked?" Gwen finished Celia sentence.

"I felt closed in."

"You mean, afraid?" Gwen raised her eyebrow.

"Just for a split second. I haven't known any of these people longer than two months."

"So you left *me* alone with them?"

Celia wasn't sure how to respond to that, so she decided to change the subject. "Since I've got you alone now, who kidnapped you?"

"Able Walton Jr.," Gwen said.

"So he did do his own dirty work," Celia said.

"With Sam Cooper dead I guess he didn't have much choice," Gwen said. "There is something else. Walton Jr. had this black wig. I don't know why. He was planning to wear it I guess. I tried to get something out of him, but I just seemed to make him mad."

"That's hard to believe," Celia said quietly with a smile.

"That's what I thought," Gwen agreed shaking her head. "As kidnappers go, he was completely unreasonable."

"Mot." Celia said thinking aloud.

"Who is this Mot?" Gwen asked.

"The name of Dixon's contact," Celia said.

"You think Able was Dixon's contact?" Gwen frowned.

"No, he had a black wig to make it look like he was Dixon's contact. Why? I don't know."

* * *

"You killed him?" Able Jr. exclaimed.

"He made it so easy." The older man laughed. "We are so close now. You haven't screwed it up with Kelly have you?"

"Cooper is dead, but I have her secretary. I'm hoping to trade." Able explained.

"Her secretary?"

"Look, I was going to call Kelly and let her talk with her secretary. The only hope of Kelly cooperating, will be proof of life," Able Jr. said.

"Mind if I come along? Sounds like fun."

"Trust me, it's no fun. Fun is the last word to describe that woman," Able Jr. said. He looked at his watch. Tara was taking a long time shopping. It was way past dinner time.

* * *

"I'm sorry to have to tell you this, sir." Celia paused as she faced Rear Admiral Walton. "Your son was Gwen's kidnapper."

"Did he do that to your face, Gwen?" Walton asked with compassion showing now in very sad, tired eyes.

"I'm okay, Admiral," Gwen said with a smile.

"Able Jr. checked in with Lloyd as well as CIA Agent Stan Geyser," Celia said.

"Geyser was supposed to be killed on the plane that was shot down in Syria," Gwen said. She remembered checking him out.

"At the last minute he didn't get on the plane."

"The Pact owed that money to another set of bad guys for the purchase of weapons. Who?" Celia asked.

"Maybe Geyser," McDonald suggested.

"You might have something there. Maybe killing Lloyd was getting rid of a loose end," Celia agreed.

"Where does that leave us?" Jeffers asked.

Celia pondered that very thing. Elliot was telling her the truth, and she believed him, but Turner wasn't ready to count only on her gut concerning Elliot. Too many lives were at stake, Turner said. Celia knew she had to address that first.

"James, while I stepped out, I called General Turner. We discussed you at great length. I think both of us ended up just where Lloyd wanted us. We were both set up. If Lloyd could pin this on me, then you have the best seat in the house to see it play out as a witness to testify against me. A perfect witness."

"So you believe me?" Elliot asked her.

"It makes more sense to me that you were as much a pawn in this as I was. I want to believe you," Celia said carefully.

Celia took a breath and continued.

"The General has agreed to allow you to stay on with the condition I know where you are at all times," Celia said.

"I see," Elliot said quietly, dropping his eyes. "I'm still part of this team."

"That hasn't changed," Celia said.

"You can trust me," Elliot said to her, with pleading in his eyes.

"Like you trusted me?" Celia pointed out, regretting saying it as soon as it was out. For the first time he detected hurt briefly in her eyes. He was speechless. He wanted to say he was sorry, but that just didn't cover it. Walton shook his head. To think his son had contributed to this mess and maybe behind it.

"Jack will be hanging with you, that's how I'm handling it. You are still a part of the team and the Op. In the meantime I can assure Turner I have an eye on things," Celia said.

"I guess we're bosom buddies for a while," McDonald said to Elliot, stepping up to the job.

"That should be punishment enough for anybody," Gwen said sarcastically. McDonald glared at her.

Elliot knew she was in a bad position and he was lucky to still be here. He still didn't like it.

"Admiral, can I get Able Jr.'s cell number?" Celia asked.

Walton gave it to her.

"Georgie, I want tech on it and run down every number he called in the last year," Celia said.

"I will get right on it, ma'am."

"Even when after we stop the Pact, we still have another arms dealer they did business with to stop. In the meantime, I have an idea," Celia said.

"What are you going to do?" Elliot asked.

"I'm calling him myself to set up a meeting."

"A few flaws in that plan isn't there?" Gwen asked, crossing her arms. "First, they don't have me and second, you don't have the money."

"So we go to Plan B," Celia said.

"We have a Plan B, ma'am?" Georgie asked.

"Did we really have a plan A?" Gwen frowned.

* * *

Able Jr. kicked the chair across the room. It was the chair he had tied Gwen up in a couple of hours earlier. His fellow companion leaned against the wall and laughed. Able Jr. wasn't laughing.

"How did she get away?" Able asked, frustrated.

"Did you search her?"

"Search her? All she had on her were the clothes she was wearing."

"Did she have a phone in her pocket?"

"I don't know," Able admitted.

"Now what?" The other man said.

"I'll find another way to get what I want from Kelly. I intend to get that money back, one way or another."

"I got here just in time. You have to be patient or you risk losing everything."

* * *

"We have a few loose ends to tie up before I contact him. Once Able discovers Gwen is gone, he'll be desperate. I think he will have to pull the other players together," Celia said.

"I'm guessing you are counting on that," Walton said.

"It would be nice to take them at once."

"How?" Elliot asked.

"On our terms. I'm going to set up a meet on the island. I want to control the location. While Georgie and I fill in a few blanks, you start putting together options," Celia said.

Elliot nodded.

"Georgie, we need to go the office," Celia said.

"What do you need me to do?" Gwen asked.

"I want you and Tammy to stay here. You'll both be safe with the team," Celia said.

Celia and Georgie left. Georgie closed the door on the passenger side of the Studebaker. She looked over at Celia.

"Do you have any idea where the money might be, yet, ma'am?" Georgie asked her.

"No, Georgie, not a clue," said Celia. She started her car, backed up, and drove out of the driveway.

"But you have Plan B?"

"I'm working on it," Celia said.

"Have you ruled Admiral Walton out completely, ma'am?" Georgie asked.

"I haven't ruled out anything completely. When we're at the office, you can double-check the adoption," Celia said.

"Will the Pact meet with you without a pawn?" Georgie asked.

"Hopefully, if they think I have the money," Celia said.

CHAPTER 43

"What are you doing?" Celia asked.

Georgie was hard at work on her computer.

"Trying to get into the state birth records, ma'am. And I'm in." Georgie typed in what she wanted to know and waited. Soon Georgie had her information.

"Seven pound baby boy, twenty inches long. March 15, 1970, named him Able John Walton Jr. Mother, Sarah Mabel Banks Walton, and father, Able Michael Walton," Georgie read aloud.

"So Able is their son?" Celia questioned.

"Not necessarily, ma'am," Georgie said. "From what I know of adoption, when a child is adopted, there are two birth certificates. The first certificate is made out when the child is born, and then a new one is made when the child is adopted, naming the adoptive parents as the mother and father. The original certificate is sealed."

"So the certificate may not tell us anything?"

"If you see here, ma'am, the certificate names the date of birth and the hospital the child was born. Now, the date of the birth is usually only a few days different from the date the certificate was issued. When a child is adopted, the variation in the issue date can be months. However, the hospital where he was born is more than likely accurate."

"Where was he born, Georgie?" Celia said.

"He was born in a private Hospital in upstate West Virginia," Georgie said. "I'll look up the hospital."

"Well?" Celia asked after a few minutes.

"I'm not sure what to make of this," Georgie said finally. She continued scanning the website.

THE PACT: OP ONE

"What is it?" Celia asked.

"The only patients at this hospital are women, pregnant women. It is a joint home and hospital for unwed mothers."

"Get the address and phone on it. We'll check it out." Celia was curious.

Georgie printed out the address and contact information for West Virginia Women's Hospital in Berkeley Springs, West Virginia.

"What happened to Mrs. Walton?" Celia wondered.

"We know she is deceased. Let's see what she died of." Georgie began punching away at the keyboard again. They read it together, silently, as it appeared on the screen. Sarah Mabel Walton died in a car accident after her car went out of control and into the bay. It took two days to recover her body. What was interesting was the date. It was one month to the day before Celia came to Dam Neck to go after the Pact. The rear admiral was a recent widower.

* * *

Chris Perry stood outside Mary's apartment. He couldn't believe how he was dreading this. She was smart, beautiful, and she'd make a wonderful wife and mother. So what was wrong? He rang the doorbell. It took a while for her to answer. Finally, the door opened.

"Chris!" Mary ran her fingers through her wet hair. She was in sweats. "This is a surprise. I thought you were going to be gone for a while. I called the base, they said you were unavailable."

"Can I come in?" Perry asked.

"Of course." Mary stepped aside. She sensed something different in him.

"Is everything okay?" She asked as she shut the door.

"Things have been crazy." Perry stalled.

"Is everyone okay?" Mary asked.

"No, everyone is fine," Perry said. He stood there, staring at her.

"I can see something is wrong, Chris. Just tell me what it is."

Perry felt the ring in his pocket. He walked into the living room and sat on the couch. He patted the cushion next to him and Mary sat beside him.

"Chris?" Mary asked him, wondering why the long silence.

"It's about us."

"What about us?" Mary asked. She was trying to predict what he was going to say next. It made her nervous. "Have I done something?"

"No, no!" Perry paused. "It's just that I've been thinking, well, I'm a Navy SEAL for one thing."

"I know that," Mary said. She gave him a puzzled look.

"I can be called anywhere at any time. I might even be transferred at any time. That's one thing I want you to understand," Perry said, pausing for a reaction.

"Have you been transferred?" Mary asked, trying to guess at what he was trying to say.

"No," Perry shook his head. This wasn't coming out right. "It's not fair to you. To have a husband who's gone all the time, maybe raising the kids by yourself half the time. It just isn't right."

"What are you saying?" Mary narrowed her eyes.

"If I ask you to marry me, it's not always going to be that great. For you, I mean. It would be great for me because you'd be here when I got back from... wherever. But if you and the kids are always having to move around... and then be alone." He paused realizing he was digging himself into a hole.

"Are you asking me to marry you?" Mary's eyes lit up, but she showed nothing in her tone of voice.

"Yeah. Yes, I am." Perry's heart sank. This wasn't exactly like he had planned it.

"Are you trying to talk me out of it first?" Mary smiled at him.

Perry laughed.

Mary took his hand in both of hers. "Chris, I love you and I would go anywhere with you. It is lonely without you, but the time we are together has always made up for it."

Perry looked into her eyes, his fears were calmed and he knew. He just knew. Perry kneeled on one knee in front of her, taking the small box holding the ring from his pocket. He opened it and asked, "Will you marry me?"

Mary's eyes sparkled as she nodded her head yes. Just as he was about to put the ring on her finger, she quickly pulled her hand back.

"How many kids?" Mary asked him.

CHAPTER 44

"The interesting thing about the wig Elliot found, is it was longer hair, shoulder length."

"The contact on the docks had short black hair. What do you think it means, ma'am?"

"Maybe Able Jr. just simple used a disguise. I may be wrong in thinking he knew about Mot. That towel you found, the lab determined it mopped up a wound."

"Any other evidence found on the towel, ma'am?"

"No. The blood was AB negative. The lab is going a step further and running a DNA analysis. Let's find out the blood types of everyone involved thus far, even if they are dead," Celia decided.

"Yes, ma'am," Georgie said accessing service records of who they knew to be involved to date.

"Maybe I'll have Tammy and Jeffers bring by the answering tape from my house. Maybe the techs can filter Mot's voice."

Celia called Tammy. After she hung up, she noticed Georgie had something on her mind.

"What happened earlier today, are you okay, ma'am?"

Celia knew Georgie was referring to Celia's drive to the church.

"Yes, thank you, Georgie. In fact I'm better than I have been in a long time."

"How so, ma'am?"

"I took time to pray. I found a church just off the highway, pulled in and regrouped." Celia smiled.

"I have to tell you, ma'am, I am quite fascinated by your commitment to religion."

"It's not just a religion. I have a relationship with God."

"I find it very interesting. I studied African religious cultures in college, but that is the extent of my knowledge."

"If you're interested, you can attend church with me if you'd wish to see a service in person."

"I'd like that, ma'am. I will take you up on that."

The phone rang. Celia answered it.

"Commander Kelly?" the familiar voice said from the other end of the line.

"Yes, this is Commander Kelly."

"This is Petty Officer Daniel Ryan, ma'am," he said.

"How are you? Where are you?" Celia asked.

"I'm good. I'm checking in. Do you need any help? I'm going crazy here."

"As a matter of fact, yes I do. I'd need you to go to a special hospital upstate in West Virginia not far from where you are," Celia said.

"Why?"

"I need you to check out the birth of a baby boy. He was born March 15, 1970, seven pounds, twenty inches long. Did you get that?"

"Just a minute." Ryan tore a page out of the back of the phone book hanging from the booth he was in. He took a pen he found on the floor and wrote the address. Celia gave him the name and maiden name of the mother who adopted him and where the hospital was located.

"We are trying to find out the birth parents," Celia said.

"Okay, I'm on it," Ryan said enthusiastically.

"When you know something, give me a call."

"I'll be in touch," Ryan said.

Celia hung up the phone.

"Daniel Ryan is going to check out the hospital for us. That should speed things along somewhat." Celia hoped Ryan could fill in a blank.

Tammy and Jeffers entered the office. She handed Celia the tape and Celia placed it into her briefcase.

"How are things on the home front?" Celia asked them.

"We have a couple of scenarios in place. Is this considered a hard target?" Jeffers wanted to know.

"Yes, a sanctioned hard target."

"Okay, I'll get what we need," Jeffers said.

"Maybe we'll have one answer by tomorrow, ma'am," Georgie said.

"The money is still hanging over us. For them to believe I know its whereabouts suggests Tom was involved, but how? The only thing that makes sense to me is the money was stashed his plane hangar. Tom finds it. The Tom I know, wouldn't take it, so he confides in someone."

"His RIO, Sam Cooper," Georgie said.

"Okay, who put the money there to begin with?" Celia wondered.

"There is only one person who was reportedly at Miramar and involved with the Pact," Georgie said.

"Stan Geyser."

"How did Dixon get involved and when did things go south for Sam?"

"So why did they wait four years to involve you? Why not right after Tom's death?" Georgie asked.

"Maybe to wait and see if I went on a spending spree. Or to wait and see if Tom turned up with it?" Celia sighed.

"When neither of those things happened, they had to find another way to find it, get the money, and set up the dead pilot and his wife," Georgie concluded.

"It still doesn't tell us how Mot fits in or who sent the picture," Celia said. "Can you take the tape to the tech? When you get back, we'll make the call to Able Jr."

Celia left to get them each a coffee and Georgie went into Celia's briefcase to get the tape. There were two tapes that looked the same. She took them both. When Celia returned with their coffee. She picked up the picture of her and Tom standing in front of the gift table. She looked at the day that was one of the happiest days she had ever known. *TILL DEATH DO US PART.* What does that mean now?

Celia called Elliot and together they discussed the options and finalized the plan.

* * *

McDonald was sitting on the couch with his feet up on the coffee table. Elliot was sitting across from him. The plan was set. Orders were for everyone to get rested, sleep if they could.

"Why did you trust Lloyd?" McDonald asked.

"I had no reason not to. He was Chief of Naval Operations." Elliot looked past McDonald.

"We've worked together for what, five years now?" McDonald asked. Elliot nodded.

"Throughout these five years we've had an understanding, you don't like the way I live and I don't think you live at all. That was personal. As a SEAL, I don't think I've ever had more respect for anyone than I have for you. When I overheard that call…" McDonald's voice trailed off.

"I would never do anything to hurt her," Elliot said suddenly and sincerely.

McDonald looked him in the eye. "I believe you."

"I followed an order. I don't have to prove anything to anybody," Elliot said.

"Not even to her?" McDonald asked.

Commander Celia Kelly. James Elliot's life had been simpler before she had come into it.

* * *

"Okay, Georgie, this is it," Celia said feeling nervous all of a sudden.

"We are ready, ma'am," Georgie assured her.

Celia dialed Able's number.

"Hello," Able answered cautiously.

"This is Commander Kelly."

"What do you want?"

"It's what you want. I understand you are missing $20 million. I think I can help you with that," Celia said.

"How?"

"There is an island north of Norfolk, I will give you the quadrants," Celia said.

"I pick the place."

"I will be there waiting for you, don't be late, 2000 hours." Celia hung up the phone.

"Think he'll be there, ma'am?" Georgie asked.

"At the very least he may consider ways to try get rid of me on the island. We just have to get him to take the bait." Celia pointed out.

"How do we know if he takes the bait?"

"He won't call back."

* * *

A knock came on the door. Elliot got up to answer it.

"Hi," Gwen smiled. "Mind if I come in?" she asked as she passed by him entering the room before he invited her.

"What do you want?" Elliot wasn't in the mood for idle chatter.

"The commander wants you to meet her on the beach," Gwen said. McDonald started to rise. Gwen added directly to McDonald, "She wants to see him alone."

"There is your chance," McDonald said to Elliot. Elliot ignored him and went out the front door.

"His chance to what?" Gwen asked.

"It was a private conversation," McDonald said to her crossing his arms.

"Men have conversations?" Gwen asked raising an eyebrow.

"I'm going to pretend I didn't hear that." McDonald glared.

"Now, that is the conversation I'm used to having with a man," Gwen said.

Elliot stood at the top step of the porch and looked at the beach. Celia was running. He noticed she had changed into running clothes and her hair was pulled back in a ponytail. He watched her until she stopped. He walked toward her. The sun began to set, spreading color across the horizon. She was framed in by waves gently rolling in behind her and the red rays shining through her dark hair. He wished they had met long before now. He was still a few feet from her when she turned to face him. She was out of breath.

"Take a few days off running and it's like starting all over again. Let's walk over to the rocks and sit a minute," Celia said. It was the furthest point she could see on the beach and she decided to push herself into going on.

"Are you sure you feel up to it?" he asked, estimating it was at least one fourth mile. It wasn't even in view of the duplex.

"Positive, let's go before it gets dark on us," Celia said.

They walked side by side in awkward silence. Celia watched the sunset over the ocean.

"When did you first meet Admiral Lloyd?" Celia asked him.

"So, the reason you wanted to talk to me was to further analyze my relationship with Lloyd." Elliot was disappointed.

"These questions are not accusations. Just working on the timeline."

Celia paused.

"Somewhere along the way I thought we may have become colleagues. I just want you to tell me what you know."

Celia looked sincerely into his eyes as she spoke. Elliot's eyes were locked with hers in emotional turmoil.

"Do you trust me?" Elliot needed to know. If she didn't, anything he said would be a waste of time.

"Yes," Celia said without hesitating. Then she asked, "An even bigger question is, do you trust me?"

Elliot paused then said quietly, "I think I always did."

They continued walking to the rocks. Celia led the way climbing up half way. When she found a wide enough spot she sat and breathed in the sea air. There wasn't a cloud in the sky. Elliot looked out over the ocean and when he spoke, mesmerized by the waves crashing into the rocks below them.

"I met Lloyd two years ago. Our team was chosen to work on the FOX Rescue. It was intense. We had a couple of SEALs being held prisoner in Beirut. We nearly lost them to the politics of the whole mess. The government thought getting them out might cause more trouble than they were worth. After all, we are paid to die if necessary. Someone who worked in his office fought to send in a rescue with an idea that worked. It made both sides look good. Lloyd presented it, the president went for it and we got them out."

He took in a breath. "Lloyd called me a year before you came to Dam Neck. He said he had beach property he wanted to get rid of and asked me if I wanted to buy it. I looked at it and he gave me a good price. I took it." Elliot stopped and shook his head. "I didn't think too much of it. Not even when he suggested I should offer to rent the other side of the duplex to you."

"When was the first time he asked you to watch me?"

"Lloyd called me the night of our debriefing in Germany. He called and said he thought you knew more about the Pact than it appeared. At first, he was vague. The rest you know," Elliot said.

Vague was the Admiral Lloyd she had come to know well over the last three years. In climbing the ladder to the top of life, there were two types of people. Those who worked hard to get there, and those who made you think they did. Maybe Lloyd had been more of an illusionist than she thought. It always looked right, but it never felt right. Celia had worked so closely with Lloyd that she had convinced herself it was just politics. Looking back, maybe she should have seen this coming.

"Lloyd was the one who said your husband was a pilot. He said your husband had been involved, he didn't say how. I was required to find out whatever I could. I was required to find out if you could be trusted." Elliot looked at her now.

"What did you find out?" Celia asked.

He looked into her eyes, silent for a moment.

"Now and then, I wondered. Just when I thought it could be possible, something would happen to change my mind."

"Like what?" Celia asked.

"Like the night you saved Dan's life. Or the night you were shot." He took in a deep breath.

The evening sunset was fading into dusk. Celia stood.

"It's time to get back. I'll race you," she said.

"That's not much of a race is it?"

"Are you saying just because I was shot two days ago, I can't beat you?"

"Pretty much." He stood.

"We'll see." Celia started climbing down the rocks.

Elliot followed.

* * *

Georgie looked at her watch. They had been gone a while. She wondered why they were out of sight of the duplex. She got out binoculars. McDonald and Gwen stood on either side of her watching for Celia and Elliot as well.

"It's getting dark," McDonald announced.

"It never ceases to amaze me how observant you are." Gwen rolled her eyes.

"Thank you." McDonald merely gave her a charming smile.

"Here they come," Georgie said as she looked through her binoculars, satisfied. Pausing, she added, "They are racing."

"How can you see them?" Gwen asked. Even binoculars didn't do much good in the dark.

"Night vision," Georgie said, pointing at her binoculars.

CHAPTER 45

Tammy was very quiet. Jeffers looked across at the woman he had met just a few weeks ago. He had gone from wondering if he loved her, to hating her and now he just didn't know. They had lived an entire lifetime in those past few weeks on a runaway freight train. Jeffers was getting to the point where he wanted to get off at the next stop for a while.

"This whole thing is unbelievable." Tammy sighed.

"I'd have to agree with that," Jeffers replied.

"The Bible says 'All things work for good' if you believe. Sure doesn't feel like it right now," Tammy said, putting her head in her hands, resting her elbows on the table.

"You doubting God now?"

"No. It has made such a difference. The..."

"Peace?" Jeffers wondered.

"Yes, peace. I just wish I could the plan He has in this," Tammy said.

"It can't last forever. Everything has a beginning and an end. Everything." Jeffers stopped short.

"What about us?" Tammy looked up and into his eyes. "Is it the beginning or the end?"

Jeffers was surprised by that question and didn't know what to say.

"I guess we'll have to wait and see."

Jeffers drove her back to the apartment complex and walked her to Gwen's door. Without warning, he gently touched his lips to her forehead.

"The beginning, I guess," Jeffers said softly and got back into his car and left.

Tammy stood watching his car disappear from sight.

* * *

Celia was supposed to be resting but she couldn't help going through every file again and every piece of the puzzle they had so far. Gwen was still staying with Celia and she came out to get a cup of tea.

"I'm curious," Gwen said, leaning on the table.

"What is it, Gwen?" Celia asked.

"Are you so sure you should trust Lieutenant Elliot?" Gwen asked carefully.

"Yes, as sure as I can be." Celia took in a breath.

"Why?"

"My gut feeling is, he's telling the truth," Celia said with conviction. There was a moment of silence as Gwen and Celia's eyes locked.

"Your gut feeling has always been good enough for me," Gwen said sincerely, smiling.

Taking up where she had left off, Celia returned to the opened the file. Gwen went into the kitchen and put on the tea kettle. Gwen poured the hot water into a cup draped with a tea bag.

"Can I get you a cup?" Gwen asked Celia.

Celia, realizing Gwen was speaking to her, looked up briefly. She shook her head no and then gave her attention back to her planning.

"Is there something I can do?" Gwen asked.

"No, thank you, Gwen. I'm good," Celia said.

Celia didn't even flinch when there was a knock on the door. Gwen answered it, to find Georgie had returned after checking on her dogs.

"I'm back, ma'am. I had to feed my Dobermans," Georgie said. She sat on the other side of the table facing Celia.

"You have Dobermans?" Celia asked.

"They guard my gun collection, ma'am."

"How many do you have?" Celia asked.

"Three Dobermans and a 35 piece gun collection."

"Wow, that's impressive."

"And disturbing," Gwen said, frowning.

Celia handed the plans over to Georgie.

"I'm going to bed," Gwen said, grabbing a bagel with her tea.

"Are you wondering if he will show up tomorrow?" Georgie asked.

"Yes, I've been second guessing myself."

"Is this the note from Mot?" Georgie asked, turning the note around so she could read it.

Looking at the note upside down, Celia noticed something she hadn't noticed before. Suddenly what Celia saw made her jaw drop. Mot was Tom spelled backwards.

CHAPTER 46

Petty Officer Daniel Ryan drove the long driveway that led to the West Virginia Women's Hospital. As he parked his rental car in the large parking lot of the facility, he noticed how nice it was. The grounds were covered with lush green grass with white benches set next to flowered gardens. He walked up the sidewalk leading to the steps of the front doors. He saw two pregnant women. No, they were young girls, practically children themselves. They were sitting on a bench talking. They noticed him and their eyes followed him as he walked passed. He nodded politely and smiled.

Entering the building, he came across more pregnant women. Ryan encountered more stares as he walked to the front desk. Obviously they didn't get many men through here. Considering everyone's condition, a man was the last thing any of them wanted to see.

"Excuse me, ma'am," Ryan said quietly to the nurse behind the desk.

"Can I help you?" The older redhead gave him a smile.

"I sure hope so. I recently found out I had a brother who was given up for adoption when he was born. I have reason to believe he was born here." Ryan hoped his cover story would get him somewhere.

"That information is confidential," the redhead said.

"Please, he is an adult now. My mother can't change her mind. She died last week. She told me about my brother on her deathbed. Can you help me?" Ryan pleaded, secretly enjoying himself. The nurse was silent, deciding what to do.

Finally, she said, "Wait here."

She disappeared around the corner at the end of the hall. She was gone a long time. While he stood at the front desk waiting, a girl of sixteen or seventeen approached him. When she spoke, she had a thick southern accent.

"Was your mama real sorry?" she asked him, looking at him with eyes searching for answers.

"Excuse me, ma'am?" Ryan asked taken off guard.

"Was your mama sorry she gave up your baby brother?"

"I..." Ryan stopped, realizing that his answer may be telling this young girl what to do. "She missed him very much, but I think she thought she did what was best for him at the time. She valued his life enough to allow him the chance to live it, even if it was with someone else. Because of that, I may have the chance to meet him."

"For that, your mother is to be commended, Mr.?"

Daniel turned to see a large woman with grey hair. She was wearing a long while coat.

"I'm Will Bear," Ryan smiled and extended his hand. He liked her right away.

"I'm Frances Bossier. I run this place. Follow me."

Frances gave him a warm smile, shaking his hand. Ryan followed her.

Frances opened the door at the end of the hall. It was her office. She sat in a large soft chair on wheels behind her desk. She looked directly into Ryan's eyes.

"Please have a seat," she said, nodding at the chair in front of the desk.

Ryan sat across from her.

"What can I do for you?" Frances leaned forward.

"I'm looking for my brother. My mother told me on her deathbed that she gave birth to a baby boy here. She gave him up for adoption," Ryan explained.

"We seal our records here to protect the birth mother," Frances replied.

"My mother is dead, ma'am, and I want to find the only family I may have left," Ryan said, thinking that sounded good.

"What did your mother tell you?" Frances asked.

"She said he was born on March 15, 1970. He was seven pounds and twenty inches long."

"And her name?"

"Sarah Walton."

"She didn't go into admitting under the name Walton. It's common to use maiden names." Frances smiled then.

"I guess you're right," Ryan said, realizing his mistake. "Her maiden name was Banks, if that helps," he said off the top of his head. He knew that she wasn't going to find either of those names, but he'd cross that bridge when he came to it. Frances pressed an intercom on her phone.

"Bridgette, could you come in here please?" A slim brunette with big glasses came into France's office.

"Bridgette, can you help this young man? He needs information from records, the sealed ones." Frances ordered Bridgette.

Bridgette looked surprised by the request, but nodded in obedience. Without a word, Bridgette led Ryan to a door. They continued down a long flight of stairs that ended in the basement. They walked into a library of files. Long rows labeled with the letters of the alphabet. Ryan found himself wondering how many women came here. He hoped the children in these files found someone to love them.

Ryan was starting to have a respect for Frances Bossier though they had just met. He had heard and seen enough to know he had just met a woman of great integrity. He felt guilty deceiving her to get this information. Still, he had a mission to do.

Bridgette looked for a while under the name Sarah Banks. After a half hour she turned to Ryan. "Can you give me the date of birth?"

"It was March 15, 1970," Ryan said.

"I'll need to cross reference. Sometimes, the woman will check in under an assumed name. I'll look up the date and see if I can find a baby boy and to whom he was born, then we can have a name. When I get the name, I can pull the file," Bridgette said explaining what she was going to do.

She went to a corner of the basement that had an older version of a microfilm screen. She looked through several labeled slides. She searched through the dates of 1970. When she got to March, she read each entry carefully. She finally found something.

"What was the baby's size?" Bridgette asked him to verify.

"He was seven pounds and twenty inches long."

"I found him. There were three babies born that day. A girl and another boy, but the other boy was nine and a half pounds, so we can rule him out," Bridgette concluded.

Ryan followed Bridgette as she down the W aisle. She stopped at the beginning of it, picked up the file, and looked puzzled.

"What's wrong?" Ryan asked her.

"This is going to be easier than I thought. It's not sealed." Bridgette looked back up to see if there was another name. There wasn't.

"I don't get it," Ryan said.

"If a child is adopted, the record is sealed," Bridgette said frowning. "If the file isn't sealed, it means the mother took the baby home. There was no adoption, at least not by us, or we made a mistake and neglected to seal your brother's file," Bridgette said perplexed. There was no other explanation.

"I wish she was alive to ask," Ryan said, not knowing what else to say.

"You can look at the file, I suppose, but it won't tell you where he is now."

Bridgette handed him the file and left him a moment. Reading through the file it said the baby had AB negative blood. He then saw the name of the mother is what the commander wanted. Sarah Walton. He took a picture of the file with his phone.

CHAPTER 47

Rear Admiral Able Walton Sr. spent the night in the attic of the home he shared with his deceased wife Sarah. He hadn't confided his doubts with the commander, but he had a feeling she was doing her own research on the same thing, Able Jr.'s parentage. He had thought about nothing else since he returned from Washington. He wanted to talk to Able Jr. hoping it was bad dream, simply a misunderstanding. The longer he put off confronting him, the longer he could hold on to that possibility. He shook his head and looked back. All those years ago when he had come home to a brand new son and Sarah after a year's deployment, what did he miss?

Walton looked fondly at the pictures of Able Jr. playing in the sand box when they were stationed briefly at a base in Florida. Walton continued to turn each page to the right, going back in time, seeing his son graduate from college, then high school, then toddling around the kitchen in diapers. Turning back to when Able Jr. was so small he was wrapped in a blanket lying in his arms, a newborn.

John Lloyd had been around a lot then. Jack McDonald reminded him of John Lloyd from time to time. Lloyd had been a real lady's man and had a girl at every port in their early days in the Navy. He even flirted with Sarah on occasion. Walton had noticed a change in Lloyd after Able Jr. was born. Gradually they saw John less and less. John married just under a year later and Walton always figured that seeing them as a happy family made John want one of his own. Lloyd's marriage was a rocky one and they never had children. Maybe Lloyd had gotten a girl pregnant and Sarah decided to help him out and take the baby.

Walton began to turn the pages to the left now as he was at the beginning of the book. He wished they were back in that small house on that base. As he searched through the trunk, he noticed something on the bottom. It was two hospital bracelets: one read baby boy Walton, and one read Sarah Walton. He knew one thing for sure, if Sarah had given birth to Able Jr., the boy was not his. The Walton's had discovered years before that he was sterile. Who was the father? Could it have been John? If he and Able Jr. were the head of the Pact, maybe both of them had known they were father and son.

Suddenly, he was glad Able wasn't his, that it was not his blood flowing through his evil veins. Then he felt sorry, sorry he could quickly disown the boy, just like that, after the years of loving him as his son. Then he thought of Sarah's car accident. Suddenly, he knew it wasn't an accident. She was just one more loose end that had been tied up. He returned the photo album and descended from the attic. There was only one thing he was sure of, he would do everything in his power to help Commander Kelly end this once and for all.

Walton began to sob bitterly.

* * *

Celia had just arrived at the base when she answered her phone. She talked as she continued inside to her office.

"Commander, Daniel Ryan. I got that information. According to the hospital records that baby wasn't adopted. It was taken home by the mother Sarah Walton."

"Anything else?" Celia asked.

"The blood was AB negative," Ryan said. "Hope that helps."

"It's more help than you know. How far away are you?" Celia asked.

"An hour, ma'am." Ryan glanced at a mileage sign for reference.

"Come directly to the Command Center," Celia said.

"I'm on my way," he said.

As Celia hung up the phone, she realized what this meant for Rear Admiral Walton. His wife had been lying to him. She had an affair and passed off the baby as one they had adopted. Now, possibly, his so-called adopted son may be involved with his birth father. He had been one of the biggest victims in this web of deceit. What was interesting was the AB negative blood. AB negative blood was on the towel from Dixon's place. Could Able Jr. have been in Dixon's house before her and Georgie? It is common for an assailant to cut himself while stabbing someone else. If so, why clean up at Dixon's? Celia called Turner.

"Hello, sir. We going to execute them tonight." Celia informed Turner.

"I'm very glad to hear that. What is the plan, Commander?" Turner asked.

"There is an island just northeast of Little Creek. We are supposed to meet there. I hope to end it."

He didn't need to ask what she meant by that. He knew.

"The FBI confirmed that Admiral Lloyd was the body in the car when it detonated. I have the autopsy report in front of me."

"Does it mention his blood-type anywhere?" Celia asked.

"O Negative, why?" Turner wanted to know.

"He's not Able Jr. father." Celia was confused.

"Maybe Frank's Intel was wrong. Maybe it was the son of an admiral and not an admiral and his son involved," Turner suggested.

"Maybe, but Frank didn't think so."

"How does that change things?"

"It leaves big questions concerning who else we might be looking for and I still don't have the money."

"What about Lieutenant Elliot? Have you determined his involvement?" Turner asked.

"I don't think he's involved with the Pact, sir."

"Even so, be careful, Commander," he cautioned, hoping she had solid ground to stand where Elliot was concerned.

"I intend to be, sir. Hopefully, I'll be on my way to Washington in the morning for a debriefing when this whole thing will be behind us."

"I hope you're right. I'm looking forward to that debriefing sooner rather than later, Commander." Turner was ready for the whole thing to be done.

"I'll call later, sir, and give exact coordinates to secure the backup plan."

"I'll have notified SECNAV. We agreed the FBI will back you up and take the over investigation after your part of the Op is over."

"Yes, sir. I'll check back at 1400 hours, sir."

"I'll be here."

Celia ended her call with Turner, she saw Georgie enter the outer office and sit at her desk.

Celia looked over at the picture of Tom and Sam hanging on her wall. Everyone thought Tom had the money. Where would Tom hide it? As often as she had moved from one station to another, it's strange she hadn't come across it or a sign of it, not even a safety deposit key or a storage locker bill. Where it would $20 million in cash fit? How large or small are the bills?

Celia sat pondering. She looked again at the wedding picture delivered to her. The four of them Tara, Sam, Tom, and herself were standing in front of the wedding gifts. There was a large mirror behind them. Celia had noticed the mirror in the picture before but never looked at it. She had spent most of the time focusing on the four people in front of it. In the mirror was a reflection that for the first time caught her attention. Celia got out a magnifying glass from her top desk drawer. It was a guy taking a drink. It was hard to see his face because of the drink and the reflection of light from the flash, but Celia was sure she knew who it was. The cigar positioned in his right hand as he held up the drink and the bald head gave him away. Agent William Dixon was at her wedding.

"Georgie!" Celia called out.

Georgie immediately came into Celia's office.

"What is it, ma'am?"

"Come here. Look in the mirror." Celia handed Georgie the picture.

"When a picture is taken the mirror in the background, it reflects the light and ruins the picture. That didn't happen here, it was taken at the right angle."

"Look at the reflection of the man in the mirror. Who does that look like to you?"

Georgie saw right away what Celia meant.

"Is that Dixon, ma'am?"

"Yes. I don't remember him being there. To tell you the truth, the only thing I remember clearly on my wedding day was getting out of bed. The rest was a blur, until we finally got away for our honeymoon," Celia said, thinking back. She also remembered feeling very happy. Her wedding had been a large one. Since her father was acting CO at Miramar.

"I have a feeling if Dixon didn't want to be noticed, ma'am, he wouldn't be," Georgie speculated.

"You're right about that. This means Tom and Dixon knew each other from the beginning."

"Do you remember anything else?" Georgie wondered.

"No." Celia sighed. Even in the picture she was looking at Tom, not the photographer. It was then she noticed Tom was looking at the photographer. Tom was facing her but his eyes were looking in the direction of the camera. Had he noticed Dixon?

"What else happened that day?" Georgie asked.

"We got married, had the reception, and went on our honeymoon."

"Where did you go for your honeymoon?"

"Tom chartered a plane and we flew to Catalina Island. It was a stormy weekend. We spent the weekend watching the storm." Celia remembered the weekend fondly.

"Anything else, ma'am?"

"We exchanged gifts there. I gave him a gold dog tag to put with his Navy tags. It had an inscription." Celia suddenly stopped.

"What is it, ma'am?"

"The inscription was 'Till death do us part'." Celia paused and then said, "I know where the money is!"

"Where?" Georgie asked.

"I mean no disrespect, Georgie, but it's safer to leave that unsaid for the time being. Believe me, when the time is right you'll be the first one to know." Celia stood putting her things away and snapped her briefcase shut.

"I trust your judgment, ma'am," Georgie said, unaffected by her commanding officer's decision.

"The only thing that bothers me is who took the picture and why was I sent the photo?" Celia wondered.

"Let's go see if Admiral Walton is in yet. I want him to know what we found out about Able Jr." Celia was concerned she hadn't heard from Walton yet.

They approached the office of Rear Admiral Walton and found his secretary was gone, so Celia knocked on his door. There was no answer. She opened the door.

"Sir?" Celia said in the form of a question announcing her presence. As she opened the door and scanned the room, she could see he wasn't there.

"May I help you?" a voice asked from behind them.

Celia turned to see his secretary. "We are looking for Admiral Walton."

"He said to cancel appointments, Commander. He won't be in today. I'm sorry, I forgot to inform you. He asked me to," the secretary said apologetically.

"Did he say why?" Celia asked puzzled.

"He sounded sick or something." She shrugged. "He didn't give me a reason."

"Thank you," Celia didn't like this new turn of events. It wasn't until they were in the elevator that either of them spoke.

"What do you make of that, ma'am?" Georgie asked.

"I don't know, Georgie, but I'm getting a bad feeling. While I begin the briefing with the team, you get over to Admiral Walton's place and check on him. Just be careful."

"Yes, ma'am."

CHAPTER 48

Georgie drove into Rear Admiral Walton's driveway. She proceeded to get out of the car and go to the front door. She rang the door several times with no answer. Going to the back of the house, Georgie tried the sliding patio door. It opened, and she walked inside, closing it behind her. The silence was deafening. Pulling out her GLOCK, she pulled back the slide. A bullet secured in the chamber. She went through every room looking carefully, leading with her weapon.

She walked upstairs. There were only two rooms, the bedroom and the bathroom, and a hall closet. The bed was made. There were no signs of the admiral changing clothes. The bathroom looked virtually untouched. The whole house showed no sign that he had been there the previous night. Georgie decided to open what she assumed to be the hall closet. She saw it was a set of stairs leading up to an attic.

Georgie went up the stairs. At the top she entered a large room full of boxes and shelves holding the usual things stored in an attic. No one was there. There was a trunk open. Georgie looked at the picture album lying on top in the open trunk. She continued to look in the trunk. She found an adult and a baby hospital bracelets saying Walton. Georgie realized Admiral Walton had put a few things together himself.

That still didn't explain where he was. She gathered the photo album and hospital bracelets and headed downstairs. Georgie heard voices. She set the things gathered quietly on the floor and listened, her pistol drawn. It was coming from outside the window. Quietly, she went to the window and looked out, staying out of sight.

Able Walton Jr. was holding a 9mm Parabellum Specter, with a 30 round magazine in it. Able Jr. had it aimed at Rear Admiral Walton. A black sedan was there but Georgie couldn't make out the driver. They wanted Walton to get in the backseat. As Walton got in, Georgie made an attempt to help him. She decided to shoot the machine-gun out of Able Jr.'s hand. There was no way she could get downstairs in time to get a closer shot. Georgie aimed. Her finger squeezed the trigger and a 9mm bullet left her GLOCK, aiming for his bicep so his fingers spread on bullet impact instead of making a fist and possibly squeezing the trigger. Able Jr. dropped the Specter, looking up in the direction of the window, stunned.

Georgie heard someone yell, "Get in!" Able Jr. stood there yet another second looking into Georgie's eyes. Georgie put pressure on the trigger and shot again. Able Jr. dropped to the ground and the black sedan took off down the alley and out of sight. Going downstairs, Georgie went outside into the back yard. She checked Able Jr.'s pulse. He was dead. He had been shot in the heart. Georgie noticed a shot had grazed his head. Someone from inside the car shot him.

***

Gwen felt awake after her shower. She saw that the commander was gone and left her a note to ride to the base with Elliot and McDonald. She went next door and knocked. McDonald answered.

"Can I help you?" McDonald asked.

"I just need a ride to the base," Gwen said.

"Are you supposed to go?" Elliot asked.

"I have a note and everything," Gwen said sweetly as she handed him the note.

"Oh, well in that case," McDonald said. Elliot read the note.

"We'd better get going," was Elliot's only reply.

***

Tammy was exhausted after taking a long bath and getting dressed. She then went into the living room to cleanup. It was still a mess after Gwen's kidnapping. Tammy was folding the blankets she used on the couch in the living room when she heard a sound coming from the bedroom. As she walked the hall to check it out.

At that moment a man in a black wig and beard emerged from the bedroom. Startling her, she screamed.

"Sorry," He said. He removed the wig.

"How?" Tammy was surprised.

"I can explain," he assured her.

* * *

Celia was in the briefing room. A map of the island was on the table. She looked at her watch, wondering if she should have sent someone along with Georgie. Daniel Ryan came in the room. He saluted and Celia returned it.

"At ease," Celia said.

"Where is everybody?" Ryan asked.

"Coming. How did you get here so fast?" Celia asked

"I might have exceeded the speed limit, ma'am." Ryan shrugged sheepishly.

* * *

Gwen, Elliot, and McDonald entered the building at the same time as Perry and Jeffers. They gathered at the front desk.

"Excuse me, sir," said a chief petty officer from behind the desk. He was speaking to Elliot. Elliot looked his way.

"Commander Kelly is using briefing room two, sir."

"Has anyone else gone up to the briefing room?" Elliot asked.

"Yes, sir, a petty officer first class. I didn't catch his name."

"Thank you," Elliot replied.

"Petty Officer Daniel Ryan must be here," Georgie said as she joined the group. The group looked at her and then each other.

"Something wrong, Lieutenant Commander?" Georgie asked Elliot.

It was hard to decide what to ask first because Georgie was holding a photo album and a Specter automatic machine-gun.

"Why do you... never mind," Gwen said, shaking her head.

"Ryan's back?" Perry decided to ask about that instead. Georgie merely nodded and shifted the specter to her other hand.

"I need to stop by the office and I will join you shortly," Georgie said.

"Follow me, gentlemen. You too, McDonald," Gwen said.

McDonald glared at her.

Gwen was the first off the elevator as the door opened. Everyone else followed in anticipation. They walked in to find Celia in deep discussion with Ryan. Celia and Ryan ended the conversation as they entered the room.

"We're here," Gwen announced to Celia.

"I don't suppose you happened to see Georgie?" Celia asked hopefully.

"She'll be here. She had to go up to the office for a moment," Gwen replied. "Possibly to unload her little machine gun."

Celia didn't know what to think about that.

"Everybody take a seat." Celia handed Gwen the folders, and she dispersed them to each SEAL, including Ryan.

"How are you doing?" Jeffers asked Ryan.

"As good as new." Ryan gave him his farm boy grin.

"Good to have you back," Perry shook his hand.

"Anything exciting happen since I've been gone?" Ryan wanted to know everything.

"Where do we begin?" Gwen said. She threw up her hands.

"How about good news?" Perry asked.

"I'm all for good news," Jeffers replied.

"I do. I'm getting married," Perry blurted out, beaming.

"Congratulations. That is good news," Celia said.

Celia then looked at her watch, waiting for Georgie before she began. The guys exchanged their congratulations.

"So when's doomsday?" McDonald asked.

"We haven't set a date yet," Perry said.

"That will give you time to change your mind," McDonald said with a grin.

At that moment, Georgie entered the room much to Celia's relief. Georgie and Celia exchanged a glance and Georgie shook her head no. Celia's eyes dropped to the table. So she hadn't found Walton. Then she looked up at the team. Georgie did not have Walton and Celia knew something was wrong. Georgie walked to the head of the table holding a photo album and something in the palm of her right hand.

"Does what happened this morning affect the plan?" Celia asked Georgie.

"Yes, ma'am," Georgie said.

Celia pondered whether she should speak to her in private or not. She looked around the room. If it affected the plan, it affected the team. "Fill us in, Georgie."

"Yes, ma'am," Georgie replied. "I arrived at Admiral Walton's home at 0800. I rang the bell several times. When there was no answer, I proceeded to go around back and enter the premises. As I searched the house, there was no sign of the Admiral Walton even having slept in his bed. I discovered a stairwell leading up to an attic. Going up the stairs, I looked over the attic. The only thing I found of interest was a photo album and these hospital bracelets." Georgie handed them to Celia.

"This supports the information Ryan got earlier," Celia said looking at the bracelets.

"What information is that?" Elliot asked.

"Well, in the shorter version, Admiral Walton's wife had someone else's child. She passed him off as an adopted child," Celia explained.

"Able Jr.?" McDonald wanted to clarify.

"That is correct." Celia turned to Georgie. "Gwen mentioned you had a machine-gun? Why?"

"I think you'll find that very interesting, ma'am," Georgie began. "As I came from the attic, I heard voices. I determined they were coming from the back yard. When I looked from the upstairs window, Able Jr. had a 9mm Specter aimed at Rear Admiral Walton, instructing him to get into the car. The car was the same black sedan. I then proceeded to shoot Able Jr. in the bicep to release the Specter without the risk of firing it. The rear admiral was already in the car. I took the opportunity to shoot Able Jr. before he could grab the Specter and shoot Admiral Walton. Another shot came at him from within the car and grazed his head. I believe mine was the kill shot. The car sped away before I could see the driver."

Celia was quiet a moment, then sighed. "So now they have a hostage."

"Didn't we need Able alive?" Elliot asked.

"He could have been a good source of information, but Admiral Walton's life is more important," Celia agreed.

"Is anybody going to show up?" McDonald asked.

"Somebody still wants the money and Walton is their insurance," Celia said.

It was time to get on with it. There was no reason to believe they would keep Walton alive.

"This is the latest satellite view of the island. There is a road used as a landing strip on the northwest side. I don't want them knowing you're there. A Chinook is taking new recruits up for a night jump one mile east of the island. I have arranged clearance for you guys to catch a ride. You will be the first ones off the Chinook and will take gear and two rigid hull inflatable boats and go to the island. The CO in charge of the recruits thinks you are participating in training of your own," Celia said as they looked at the map.

"Master Chief Jeffers, you will be positioned here. It is the highest point on the island and you should have a three-sixty view. Petty Officer Ryan you will be here at the docks waiting for the boats, theirs and mine. When they arrive, your job is to plant explosives under the stern of each boat, ready to detonate on my order."

"Lieutenant Perry, you will continue going inland to the pond, position yourself in the brush along the pond, right there," Celia said using a pointer.

"Lieutenant Elliot and Ensign McDonald, you will be positioned in areas of cover here and here." She pointed to the west and east of the road often used as an airstrip. "The meeting place is here, on the edge of the landing strip."

"They are only meeting with you for the money," Elliot pointed out. "What do you think they'll do when they discover you don't have it?"

"Stay with me. I think you'll understand," Celia said.

"Why blow both boats?" McDonald asked.

"They have new leverage, Admiral Walton, to insure my cooperation. When we arrive, I will suggest they leave the admiral on the island while I take them to the money. I'll leave Georgie with the admiral. I will tell them unless they leave the admiral and come with me, they will not get the money. They'll agree because not only do they have a shot at the money, they now have me for insurance. I am easy enough to dispose of after they get what they want."

"I'll get in the boat. I'm not sure which boat they will choose. Whether they choose my boat or theirs it won't matter, both will be ready. When I give the signal, which will be 'high tide', give me ten seconds to jump from the boat. Then detonate your charges. I'll go under until the debris is clear and the bad guys are gone," Celia finished, made it sound simple.

The team sat in silence, taking in what she had said. Perry looked at his fellow teammates. Jeffers' eyebrows had gathered into a frown. Ryan looked as if he were going to say something but he closed his mouth and sat back in his chair. Jeffers looked at Elliot, figuring if anyone was going to object it would be him. McDonald cleared his throat. Elliot looked at Celia in disbelief. It was Georgie who spoke first.

"Excuse me, ma'am, but have you been trained for such a maneuver?"

"I'd like to know that myself," Gwen said, sitting forward.

"Look, I have given this thought. If someone is going to take them to the money, it'll have to be me. They aren't going to buy anything else. If I get into the boat, they aren't going to suspect that anything is wrong with it," Celia replied.

"What if you don't clear it?" Elliot asked her in an even tone, referring to the debris.

"I'll die doing my job. It is my job to see that they are stopped and they will be." Celia wasn't afraid, she knew what had to be done.

"I'm against this plan," Gwen said.

"Gwen, go get everyone coffee," Celia said. She didn't want to argue with Gwen. Celia needed to have absolute authority. Gwen's questioning it could cause division and now was not the time.

"Coffee?" Gwen looked at Celia, frowning.

"Gwen, go," Celia said firmly, not wishing to be distracted further.

With Gwen out of the room, everyone else was speechless.

"Any questions?" Celia asked.

No one responded.

"Okay then."

"What about Mot?" Georgie interrupted suddenly.

"I guess I'll have to deal with him after I deal with them," Celia said.

Elliot glared at his boots. The fact that she was willing to sacrifice everything showed just how deep her integrity was. Though it strengthened his admiration, it concerned him.

"You will leave for the drop zone at 1200 hours. Georgie and I won't be there until 1700. I want you to have plenty of time to position yourselves and to secure the area," Celia said.

Elliot looked at his watch. There was an hour and a half to prepare their gear.

"Do you know where the money is?" Elliot searched her eyes.

"As of this morning, maybe," Celia nodded.

"What is the line of command?" McDonald asked looking at Elliot.

"The same." Celia was firm.

"Elliot is still team leader?" McDonald making sure he heard right.

"Is that a problem?" Elliot asked McDonald.

Celia interceded. "You guys are a team. You were a team long before the Pact and you will be a team long after the Pact is gone. I realize Lloyd created a scenario that put Commander Elliot in a bad light. You must trust what you know to be true." Celia paused then continued. "You need to stick together now more than ever. I, for one, trust each one of you. And later today I will trust each of you with my life. The line of command is the same because you are the same team that you were before you ever knew who I was. Once on the island, Commander Elliot calls the shots. I'll let him know when I jump and you blow the boat when you hear the 'high tide' command."

Elliot and Celia's eyes locked briefly as the guys conversed.

"There's just one more thing," Celia said.

"What's that?" McDonald was almost afraid to ask.

"I want everyone to come up here with me," Celia instructed. The team came to her, Georgie stood on her right. "Join hands."

They came together knowing she was going to pray. They joined hands and bowed their heads.

"Heavenly Father, put Your hand upon us today as we prepare for the job we must do. Keep us safe. Let Your will be done. Guide our thoughts and actions. In Jesus name we pray, amen. Dismissed," Celia said.

CHAPTER 49

Tammy poured two cups of tea. She made a couple of sandwiches and sat at the kitchen table. Gwen came through the door at that moment. She walked into the kitchen and spied the two cups and sandwiches.

"You are so terrific. I am famished," Gwen said, throwing her purse on the counter and sitting next to a surprised Tammy. "How did you know I was coming home?"

"I didn't," Tammy stammered. "What are you doing home?"

"I got kicked out. What a morning. I had to ride to the base in the same car as McDonald, had to listen to somebody *else* announce their engagement, and then I got kicked out of the briefing room because I didn't think the commander should go on a suicide mission. Can you believe that?" Gwen shook her head as she took another bite. "Can I have a glass of milk instead of tea? Another thing, is it me, or is it smoky in here? Which reminds me, I forgot to tell the commander what I found in her driveway."

"The commander kicked you out?" Tammy asked, trying to keep up with what she had said.

"You wouldn't believe the plan she's got. She might as well put a big sign on her back that says, 'Here I am, shoot me.'" Gwen shook her head, still rambling. She didn't notice that someone else was in the kitchen pouring her a glass of milk.

"She thinks after getting her hand stabbed and a gunshot wound in the last three days, she can jump from a boat before it explodes. Can you believe that?" Gwen accepted the glass of milk.

"Thank you." She took a long drink. It was then that she noticed a black wig on the table. That can't be good, she thought.

"You're welcome," a man said from behind, crossing his arms.

Gwen's every muscle stopped, slowly she turned and was immediately to her feet. After getting a good look at her guest, her mouth fell open.

* * *

Celia and Georgie sat in her office going over last minute details. Celia's cell began ringing.

"Commander Kelly," Celia said as she continued to look over the map from the morning briefing.

"This is General Turner. Georgie left a message," the chairman of the joint chief's voice came on the line.

"Yes sir, I was about to call you again," Celia replied.

"I found out something interesting," he began. "We discovered from a phone tap on Able Walton Jr. home phone that his wife left him. The call came from New York, a phone booth in the airport, to the answering machine."

"She's running. Possibly the safest thing for her to do," Celia observed. "The one thing I don't need is another hostage."

"I don't follow, Commander. What else has happened?" Turner asked.

"They took Rear Admiral Walton, sir, at gunpoint. Georgie witnessed it and killed Able Jr., but was unable to stop the kidnapping," Celia explained.

"I can't say I'm sorry. Is the body still there?"

"Yes, sir."

"I'll send the FBI to collect the body."

After she hung up with Turner, Celia looked at the hand still bandaged from the knife wound. She began to unwrap it.

"Isn't it too early to take off the bandage, ma'am?" Georgie asked.

"It'll be too hard to use wrapped up. I'm going to put a thinner bandage on it," Celia bandaged her hand. "Get us bulletproof vests to wear under our uniforms."

"Yes, ma'am." Georgie went to carry out the order.

As Georgie walked out Lieutenant Elliot walked into the office.

"Got a minute?" Elliot asked her, sticking his head inside the door.

"Sure," Celia said as she tried to re-wrap her hand. Elliot took the gauze from her and helped her as they talked.

"About later today, maybe one of us, one of the guys can…," Elliot paused, trying to figure out the best way to approach it. Celia stopped him.

"I appreciate the fact you chose to disagree with me in private. I understand why you'd question my judgment on this one," Celia said.

"So, let one of us do this."

"Lt. Commander, I don't even want them to know you are there. I'm harmless. They won't be expecting anything until we reach the money. That's where they'll think the trap is. That's when they'll have their guard up. If I get in the boat, they'll think they've still got bargaining power. Trust me. They won't know what hit them."

He would hardly describe her as harmless. "Still, I'd want to go on record as saying, Commander that I don't approve."

"Noted, Lt. Commander. I guess we'll just have to be successful, won't we?" Celia said smiling.

"I need a piece of tape," Elliot said.

"On the desk."

Elliot taped the gauze and let her hand go.

* * *

Elliot and the rest of the team checked over their gear once, twice, then a third time. Secured and loaded were the inflatable boats, explosives, weapons, and communications in waterproof packs. The team was set with LAR V Dräger breathing apparatus to use after parachuting into the water. They boarded the Chinook taking them to the drop zone, getting on one by one and sitting along the side of the plane. They were in their hooded wetsuits and Dräger breathing systems attached to their chests ready to use when they hit the water. As the plane approached the DZ, Elliot and McDonald moved the inflatable boats to the back of the plane.

"Two minutes," the pilot called to Jeffers at the top of his lungs, trying to be heard over the loud whining of the engines.

"Two minutes," Jeffers yelled over the engines to of the team, also signaling two minutes. Two minutes passed and the side door of the Chinook opened. Elliot pushed the boats off and watched the boats fall, the chutes open automatically.

He motioned everyone to begin jumping. One by one they went out of the Chinook. They pulled their chutes, gliding into the Atlantic Ocean. Elliot emerged closest to one of boats and Jeffers grabbed the other. They pulled the tap on each boat and they inflated, exposing their gear. Soon they were loaded into the boats and headed toward the island.

On the way they put on their headsets and mics. They secured their small arms, and Jeffers had his sniper weapon of choice, a Mark 11 equipped with an infrared/thermal scope, flung over his other shoulder.

Once on the island, Jeffers went to high ground to set up his rifle and scope. Ryan gathered the explosives and found a place in the brush back from the beach watching the dock. Everyone else got into position. Once the island was secured, they waited.

* * *

"I can't believe this," Gwen said, shaking her head. "I need to call the commander."

"No," he said standing between Gwen and the phone.

"I can't let you do that." He grabbed her arm.

"Why not? What's going on here?" Gwen frowned.

"I need to know where she went," he said.

Gwen looked at Tammy with questioning eyes. Tammy looked just as confused.

* * *

Celia looked up at Georgie.

"You know, Ryan said the baby's blood was AB negative," Celia said.

"Maybe it was Able Jr.'s blood on the towel," Georgie concluded.

"Maybe," Celia agreed. She paused then said, "Let's go through and check everyone's blood type. Walton's, Geyser's, even Dixon's, since he lived there."

"Yes, ma'am, just need to look up their files."

Georgie went to her desk to work on her computer. She typed out what she wanted and ordered the computer to print out two papers. Thinking a moment, she typed another name in and waited.

They were about to gear up when Celia's cell rang.

"Commander Kelly," Celia said.

After a moment of silence, a voice she knew well came over the line.

"I suppose you know by now Geyser has me," Walton sounded tired.

"Yes. Are you alright, sir?" Celia asked.

"I'm fine, Commander."

"I will give the quadrants for an island. I have a condition," Celia got right to the point.

"What is it?"

"The trade will be you for me and I take them to the money."

"I won't let you do that," Walton said quietly. There were muffled voices in the background.

"It's the only way I'll do it. Tell them to be on the island in the clearing. Two hours." She gave the quadrants and hung up the phone.

Georgie looked at Celia with admiration. "I just want to say, ma'am, it has been a pleasure to work for you. I hope we have other assignments in the future."

"Thanks, Georgie. Me too," Celia said.

* * *

Rear Admiral Walton was tied to a kitchen chair. He was looking at Stan Geyser sitting across from him who had heard the whole conversation on speaker. He tipped back his chair and then sat forward leaning his elbows and forearms on the table.

"Lloyd made a mistake in talking the president into putting her on this," Geyser said and shook his head. "She's smart." He looked over at Rear Admiral Walton.

"Sorry was nothing more was a loose end. His death was inevitable," said Geyser.

Walton said nothing

CHAPTER 50

Looking over the blood types, Celia frowned. Rear Admiral Walton was O positive. They knew Admiral John Lloyd was O Negative. The big surprise was that William Dixon was AB negative. Celia's cell phone rang.

"Commander Kelly," Celia said, still pondering the information in front of her.

"This is Agent Ted Baker from Langley. I was given tapes to analyze."

"Yes. What did you find?" Celia asked, switching to the speaker so Georgie could hear.

"Well, it was interesting. Two different men were trying to camouflage their voices. I kept mixing and matching the different possibilities you gave me with your recordings. I finally came to a conclusion. One voice belonged to Able Walton Jr. and the other voice belonged to Commander Frank Scott," Baker said.

"You're sure?" Celia was surprised. That couldn't be right.

"Positive."

"Thank you. Could you document those conclusions and send a copy to me and the FBI?" Celia asked.

"Yes, ma'am."

"What's wrong, ma'am?" Georgie asked after Celia hung up.

"I'm not sure." Celia proceeded to tell Georgie what Ted Baker said.

"Not only do the blood tests suggest Dixon is Abel's father, but one of the Mot voices belongs to Commander Frank Scott."

"It doesn't make sense," Georgie agreed.

"If Frank had been Mot all along, he might have come up with the idea to use Tom's name backwards since Tom was his best friend. I didn't even know we sent a tape of Frank's voice." Celia sighed.

"I just gave him the tapes from your briefcase, ma'am."

Celia thought a moment. "The morning Frank called I picked up the phone after my machine went off, then I threw the tape in my briefcase."

"Did anyone ever find out what happened to his body, ma'am?"

"No," Celia said.

* * *

Celia and Georgie boarded a speedboat. Georgie manned the wheel. Stray hairs from her French braid escaped as the boat went into the wind skimming across the top of the water. Celia took in the sea air being forced into her nostrils. Her mind sorted out the final details, thinking back to the beginning. It was then she thought of the picture sitting on Dixon's desk in his house. It was signed 'All my love, Sarah'. It was Dixon who had an affair with Sarah Banks Walton, not Admiral Lloyd. Where did Frank fit in? They rode the next ten minutes in silence. They each put their earwigs in and hooked the mics to the underside of their lapels.

"This is the commander. Is everything set?" Celia decided it was time to check in and waited for Elliot's response.

"Roger that," Elliot replied over the headset.

Georgie pushed the boat while Celia secured the rope. Celia tied the rope to a bush. The boat was now sitting on ten-feet-deep water. Ryan went under the boat with explosives in hand. No sooner did he finish when another boat could be seen on the horizon.

Ryan waited under water until the second boat docked. He wired a two-and-a-half-pound block of composition C-4 to the underside of the second boat. He carefully wired the charges, double-checking the work.

Two men began to walk to the meeting site where Celia and Georgie were waiting. Celia felt her stomach drop as she came to the realization that this was it. Stan Geyser and Rear Admiral Walton walked toward her and Georgie, who was out of Geyser's line of sight.

When the two men were approximately ten feet away, Georgie stepped into sight. Rear Admiral Walton's upper body was tied up, and he was led by a rope. His hands were zipped tied and his face bruised.

"I assumed you'd be alone," Geyser said, eyeing Georgie.

"You assumed wrong. I said we do it my way, remember? Georgie is my assistant. She is assisting me," Celia said calmly, even managing a smile. The team could hear everything she was saying. Elliot did not have a clear view.

"I'm moving in closer," Elliot said.

"Boss, you want me to follow?" McDonald asked.

"Not yet, over," Elliot replied.

Celia listened to the team's exchange and in the meantime made small talk. "It doesn't appear that you take very good care of your hostages."

"I don't care about your opinion of how I treat anybody. Now let's talk money." Geyser got to the point.

"Not so fast." Celia shook her head. "First, let the admiral go."

Geyser pulled a .22 caliber Ruger pistol from his jacket and aimed it at her head.

"I assume you're wearing a vest, so you should know I won't be aiming there."

"We got a problem. He's pulled a gun," Jeffers said looking through his sights.

"I can see that. Jack move in closer, wait for my cue," Elliot ordered McDonald.

"Go ahead, shoot me and then you'll never know where the money is," Celia said without blinking an eye, looking directly into his. "Now, release the rear admiral to Georgie's care and I will take you to the money."

"Commander, watch yourself," Elliot advised in her ear.

"Why should I trust you?" Geyser asked Celia.

"You don't have a choice," Celia said to Geyser.

"Okay." Geyser put down the gun.

"Release him," Celia said again.

"You both lay down your weapons. He can go," Geyser said.

Celia and Georgie exchanged a glance. Celia nodded and simultaneously they both gently laid their weapons on the ground. Then Georgie laid down a second weapon, then a third, and then a fourth. Jeffers rolled his eyes as he watched through his scope.

McDonald and Elliot closed in on either side hiding behind the brush, not making a sound. Perry, without a word even to Elliot, had moved closer. Watching and waiting they were relieved to see Geyser put his gun down to his side. It looked as though the commander had convinced him, for the moment.

"Boss, the gun is down," Jeffers updated, moving his finger off just enough to take the pressure off his trigger but still letting it rest on it. Elliot gave a sigh of relief.

"Go!" Geyser pushed Walton toward Georgie.

Walton tripped and lost his balance. He fell at Georgie's feet. Celia stepped forward and beside Geyser.

"Did you figure it out? Your husband's death?" Geyser asked Celia suddenly.

Celia did not respond, so Geyser continued, "Your husband was going to nail us right after he got back from the mission. We had no choice but to get him first. He contacted his buddy, then Lieutenant Commander Frank Scott, Naval Intelligence."

Geyser laughed. "We threatened Cooper's little girl, so his job was to make sure the F-14 they were flying that day went down. The F-14 is prone to a flat spin in an extremely stalled position due to its center of gravity. He placed a timed device to go off in the intake to destroy the engine to cause it to stall out. It worked beautifully, causing the flat spin. Cooper, after they ejected, tried to get the location of the money."

"But something went wrong after they ejected," Celia said.

"Cooper ended up getting hurt. Funny thing is, Kelly's only concern at that point was to save Cooper. Go figure. We discovered Cooper had shot Kelly before Cooper had the location. So there we were, expecting Cooper to lead us right to it, but he couldn't. We made it look like they both were MIA and Cooper convinced us he could figure it out. The only thing Cooper ever got out of him was Kelly hid it in a wedding gift."

"This trip down memory lane is touching, but I'm ready to get on with it," Celia said trying not to react to the news that Tom was left for dead.

"Well, I guess we are ready then. Where are we going?" Geyser asked with a smile.

"Off the island. We take my boat," Celia said.

"Okay," Geyser agreed too quickly, Elliot thought.

Celia stepped forward. Geyser grabbed her arm, pulling her close, using his other arm for a choke hold. Georgie stepped forward going for her weapon now lying on the ground. Geyser decided not to take any chances. He turned his weapon on Georgie. Geyser shot Georgie in the head and put the gun back on Celia. The force of the bullet caused Georgie to collapse hitting the ground. The Admiral Walton kneeled beside her.

Celia didn't try to disarm him because she wanted him in the boat.

"Admiral, help her. I'll be fine," Celia said for the team's benefit more than her own. She knew Perry was close by to step in and treat Georgie.

"Boss?" McDonald probed.

"Let him take her. Perry, go to Georgie as soon as his back turns. We follow the commander," Elliot said after a twenty second silence.

Geyser pushed Celia ahead of him and put the gun to her back. They began to walk to the boats.

"Perry with Georgie. McDonald, with me. Ryan in the water and be ready to disarm whatever boat they don't use. Go!" Elliot ordered.

"Roger that," Ryan said.

"On your six," McDonald said.

"With Georgie now." Perry informed Elliot. Then to Georgie, Perry said, "Georgie, talk to me." Suddenly, they heard a moan. She was alive.

"Boss, be advised, another boat is coming in on the other side of the island," Jeffers said.

"Keep eyes on it," Elliot ordered. What now? Who? Elliot thought to himself.

"Roger that," Jeffers said.

Elliot watched as Geyser made Celia get into his boat. The Commander had predicted if she suggested her boat, he would insist on taking his. Ryan began pulling charges off Celia's boat. When Geyser's boat pulled away Ryan was out of the water and getting into the commander's boat. Ryan laid the unconnected charges in the bottom as McDonald jumped in starting it up and followed Geyser's boat.

"Where to?" Geyser asked.

"The mainland," Celia said.

"McDonald, don't lose them. Perry, report." Elliot needed more information.

"Hold on, Boss," Perry said.

McDonald and Ryan had Geyser in their sight. Geyser looked back and saw them on his tail. He grabbed Celia and hit her. Then he searched her, found her mic, ripped it off her collar, and threw it in the water. He ordered her to take out her earwig and toss it. She threw it in the water. Geyser then realized the boat was gaining on them. He chained her to the side.

Meanwhile, Perry was at Georgie's side assessing the damage. There was quite a bit of blood, Walton thought. For the amount of blood, Perry found minimal damage. The frame of her glasses was imbedded into the side of her head. There was no sign of a bullet entry. The bullet must have been deflected from the frame. Perry smiled and shook his head.

"How is she?" Rear Admiral Walton asked.

"The stem of her glasses ricocheted the bullet. She'll be okay," Perry said.

"Did I hear that another boat is approaching?" Georgie asked weakly.

"Do you know who it is?" Perry asked.

"He hit her and ripped her collar," Jeffers said.

"McDonald," Elliot said.

"We are almost on him." McDonald was not letting this guy go. He had the boat at full throttle.

"Mot is in the other boat," Georgie said slowly still feeling woozy as she sat up.

Suddenly Jeffers broke into the chatter.

"Boss, we got a problem," Jeffers said with a haunting sound entering his voice. "He chained the commander to the boat!"

Elliot's heart sank. Celia was there, and he was here. He ran toward the inflated boats.

"McDonald, move it and DO NOT blow the boat! DO YOU COPY?" Elliot said with firm authority.

"Copy that." McDonald acknowledged the order.

Celia hadn't said a word since she had gotten onto the boat. Why? He knew her well enough by now to know she would have given the signal chained or not. Something was wrong!

"What can you see? Can she hear us? I don't hear her anymore. Anybody?" Elliot asked impatiently.

"Her mic was on her collar, Boss. It was ripped off," Ryan said.

"Boss, What about the boat coming in on the other side," Jeffers said.

"See who it is and get back to me. I'm in the inflatable. Jeffers keep eyes on the island. Perry help Jeffers secure the island!" ordered Elliot as he started up the inflatable boat and sped toward Geyser's boat to assist McDonald and Ryan.

CHAPTER 51

"This is the island," Gwen said, looking at the map. Tammy giggled and took the map.

"Then it's a miracle we got here. You have the map upside down." Tammy replied.

Dixon laughed. He loaded his gun and put it in the holster. Tammy wondered what was going on, something wasn't adding up.

"Can't I do something?" Gwen asked. "I want to help." She felt left out.

"Just wait in the boat," Dixon said.

"I want to help," Gwen repeated.

"I will give you the signal when I need you." Dixon docked the boat onto the sandy side of the island. Both he and Tammy got out. "Now remember wait for the signal."

"Okay. The signal," Gwen agreed.

Dixon and Tammy disappeared into the brush.

"Wait. What signal?" Gwen called out. There was no answer.

Jeffers looked through the scope, hardly believing what he was seeing.

"Boss, it's Tammy, Gwen and... a bald guy?" Jeffers frowned as he updated Elliot.

"I copy. Keep them out of the way. Perry, help him out," Elliot answered tensely, his eye on Geyser's boat.

"Affirmative," Perry replied.

* * *

Celia's head hurt from the blow she took just before Geyser found her mic. She still had a knife hidden at her ankle. It was unlikely that the team would blow the boat, for two reasons. A, she hadn't given the order and B, they never wanted to go along with it in the first place. Celia had to admit that now that she was chained to the boat, she wasn't too crazy about the idea either.

She looked behind the boat to the speedboat and a Navy issue inflatable headed at top speed their way. She was as relieved by that and Geyser looked worried. He recovered. Geyser opened the compartment on the floor of the boat and produced a MK-19 40mm grenade launcher. Celia's heart sank. It could only shoot once, but that one shot could kill a member of team. She had to think of something. Fast.

"Excuse me," Celia exclaimed. She sounded strange even to her. She had his attention.

"What?" Geyser asked.

"I suggest you put that away," Celia said.

"You suggest I put this away? What are you going to do?" Geyser laughed.

"Yes, I do," Celia looked at the slack she had in the chain.

Geyser relaxed his grip as he laughed. He then turned to aim at the boat behind them. As hard as she could, she swung the chain hitting Geyser across the back. As he lost his balance, and the launcher. Celia watched the launcher fall into the ocean.

"Grenade launcher," Ryan said.

"It went overboard," McDonald said.

McDonald and Ryan saw Geyser hit the commander again. They were nearly side by side now with Elliot not far behind them.

Geyser's eyes ablaze with anger, he towered over her, slapping her across the head and against the boat. He was to strike her again, but held himself back. Not only did he have a SEAL team on top of him, but she was still the only one who knew where the money was.

Celia had to get rid of this chain. Geyser was at the wheel again trying to pick up speed. She reached for her knife. The chain was attached to the side by a simple screw plate. At every given opportunity she worked on the three screws until they were finally out. She was standing now, ready to jump. Geyser looked straight ahead, the boat at full throttle.

* * *

Elliot caught up to McDonald and Ryan. They saw her stand in the boat.

"Boss, she's going to jump," McDonald said.

"Boss, from where I'm sitting, she's still got a chain around her wrist, but no longer attached to the boat," Jeffers said, zooming in his scope.

"I copy that. Get ready on my count," Elliot ordered McDonald.

"Roger that," McDonald said.

"We're still doing that?" Ryan whispered McDonald.

Celia jumped over the side, but the chain hooked onto the side of the boat, dragging her. She held on with both hands. Elliot was side by side with Geyser's boat now. Geyser went for his weapon and Elliot jumped into the boat and shot Geyser simultaneously. Elliot stopped the boat. He pulled Celia back into the boat. He removed the lock from the chain with his knife.

"Are you okay?" Elliot asked her. He brushed her hair away from her bruised face.

"I'm good. Looks worse than it is," Celia said.

"Hey," McDonald said as they pull alongside. "What about the bald guy?"

"Bald guy?" Celia repeated.

"Another boat arrived with Gwen, Tammy, and a bald guy," Ryan explained.

"Dixon. Dixon was Able Jr.'s father," Celia said.

"The dead CIA Agent?" Elliot asked. Celia nodded.

"And it keeps getting better!" McDonald said as they loaded onto Celia's boat. The inflatable had stopped a few yards away, so Ryan swam out to it and brought it back.

"Now," Elliot nodded to McDonald.

They were far enough away so McDonald detonated Geyser and his boat.

"So is this Dixon a good guy or bad guy?" Ryan asked.

"I'm not sure. Georgie is okay?" Celia said honestly.

"She's fine, the bullet ricocheted off her glasses." McDonald smiled.

* * *

Gwen looked at her watch. Certainly they had given her the signal by now. She just couldn't see it. She had gotten out of the boat and started walking inland. She saw dinghies come back toward the island. She'd meet them she decided.

* * *

Perry had Georgie and Admiral Walton at the water's edge waiting for the boats to come back. Admiral Walton was watching the boats come back when Georgie looked over at him, concerned.

"Are you alright, sir?" Georgie asked Walton.

Walton turned to her and smiled. "I think the question here is, are you?"

"Turns out being nearsighted was a stroke of luck. That and stainless steel frames," Georgie said.

"Hey Chief, where are the bald guy and Tammy at now?" Perry asked Jeffers.

"Nearly to your location," Jeffers said.

"Anybody know if he's a good guy or bad guy?" Perry asked.

"Still don't know. Keep your guard up," Elliot said. "We are almost there."

"The commander thinks its Agent Dixon," Elliot said.

Gwen appeared first.

"Where's Dixon and Tammy?" Gwen asked.

"Coming as I understand it," Perry said.

"What are you doing here?" Walton asked.

"Long story."

It was then Gwen noticed Georgie's injury. "Georgie, what happened?" Gwen asked.

"I was shot, but I'm fine," Georgie said, hurrying past Gwen.

Gwen was confused, pausing momentarily, thinking how weird she could be. Georgie got her weapon ready.

"Boss, the bald guy and Tammy have reached the others," Jeffers said.

"I copy that, so have we," Elliot said.

Gwen stopped Georgie. "Georgie, there's something you should know. Dixon is–"

Georgie interrupted her. "Dixon is alive. I know."

"Why am I even here?" Gwen said in frustration.

"That is a good question," McDonald said as he joined them.

Gwen and the others turned to see Elliot, McDonald, Ryan, and a once again beat-up commander.

"Really? Again?" Gwen went up to the commander and inspected her wounds. Perry was right behind Gwen.

"Are you alright?" Perry asked.

"It's just cosmetic. I'm fine," Celia said.

"I don't think cosmetic means what you think it means," Gwen said sarcastically.

"So I thought we had visitors. Where are they?" Elliot said.

"We are here," Dixon said as he and Tammy stepped out of the bushes.

Celia watched Tammy and Dixon approach the group.

"Commander, he's alive," Tammy said happily.

"I can see that. Agent Dixon," Celia didn't know what to ask first.

"You are amazing, Commander," Dixon said.

"How so?"

"You have figured this out and found the money." Dixon shook his head and smiled. "I'd say that is amazing."

"What are you saying?" Tammy looked at Dixon confused.

"Now, let's negotiate."

Dixon grabbed Tammy holding a gun to her head.

Immediately weapons were drawn.

"There is no way you are walking away from five Navy SEALs and the rest of us." Celia was suddenly tired.

"I can't get a shot," Jeffers said in Elliot in his ear.

"The world already thinks I'm dead," Dixon reminded her.

"I am not letting you have the money unless the team and Tammy go free."

"I will kill her right here right now if you don't." Dixon's eyes locked with hers.

"Then you'll kill Tammy, we'll kill you," Celia said.

"This is the worst negotiation ever!" Gwen crossed her arms.

Tammy's eyes became horrified as she watched Dixon and the commander call each other's bluff.

"If I don't get the money, they will kill him like they did Sarah," Dixon said.

"Kill who?" Celia asked.

"My son," Dixon replied.

"When did you become involved in this?" Celia asked.

"I was at your wedding, invited by the groom's side. I knew Tom's father. That's when I had the idea to hide the money. I never dreamed Tom would find it."

"You hid the money?" Georgie asked.

"Sarah had just told me what Able had gotten himself into. She begged me to help," Dixon explained.

"I'm guessing that didn't go very well," Gwen said then.

"When I found out he was dealing arms with the Pact, I figured if I could stop the money, I stopped the sale. I just created another problem."

"Why didn't Sarah come to me?" Walton asked Dixon.

"I don't know. I didn't even know Able was mine until five years ago." Dixon sighed heavily now.

"Tell Jeffers to stand down," Celia said to Elliot.

Elliot and Celia exchanged a glance. He decided to trust her.

"Stand down," Elliot said to Jeffers.

"Okay. Copy that." Jeffers was confused.

"Do you know who the Pact is?" Celia asked.

"Not the top guy. I've tried. Look, I have to undo what I did. I need the money back." Dixon was pleading with her.

"It won't undo anything. You have to know that. Please let Tammy go." Celia countered with a plea of her own.

"I can change Able's mind if I just have a chance to talk to him and explain what happened. You promise me that, I'll let her go," Dixon said.

"Able is dead," Walton said to Dixon.

"He's dead?" Dixon asked Walton.

Dixon looked to Celia. She nodded that it was true.

Dixon dropped the gun and released Tammy. Perry took Tammy away from Dixon.

"Now what?" Dixon asked Celia.

"Boss, someone else is on the island," Jeffers said puzzled.

Those who had earwigs looked around to see who was missing.

"Someone else just docked on the island," Elliot said to Celia. Celia knew the FBI was set to arrive, but they would send more than one person.

CHAPTER 52

"You said that you didn't know who the leader was, do you know where he operates from?" Celia asked.

"Beirut. I was only able to figure out the players here, tracking Able's movements and cell phone, and that's how I knew Lloyd was involved."

"When Tom found the money, did he contact you?" Celia asked.

"He called me."

It was then Frank Scott appeared from the trees. Weapons now drawn and turned on Frank Scott. McDonald who still had Dixon in his sights.

"Hello, everyone. Looks like I'm late to the party," Scott said.

Dixon was as surprised to see Scott as anyone.

"I thought you were dead." Dixon frowned.

"Does anyone really die?" Gwen asked.

"Who are you?" Elliot demanded.

"Frank?" Celia was in disbelief.

"I can explain." Scott put up his hands after laying his own weapon on the ground.

"Did you two get together and plan this or what? I have to say both of you faking your deaths, that's suspicious," Gwen said crossing her arms.

"Celia, I'm sorry." Scott gave her a pleading look.

"This is Commander Frank Scott," Celia's said.

"Let's relax, I can explain my part," Scott said, his arms still in the air.

McDonald produced zip tie cuffs for Dixon and put his arms behind his back. Once Dixon was secure, Jeffers left his post and joined them. Celia in the meantime gave Turner a call. Turner let her know the FBI was in route to the island.

"Tom called me the day he found the money. We needed to know who put it there, so we had Tom move it and waited for someone to show up for it. It was weeks, and nothing. Finally one day there was a visit from Stan Geyser. I started looking into him and asked the CIA for a liaison. They gave me Dixon. Tom said his family knew Dixon, so I felt comfortable using him to help me in unraveling the mess."

"I was keeping an eye on Kelly so when he contacted Scott I knew, and when Scott contacted the CIA I volunteered. By then I realized the money was gone. I was worried someone might be looking into Able's involvement," Dixon said.

"When did the Pact find out you hid the money?" Celia asked Dixon.

"I didn't tell anyone. Scott and I had been working together for about a year and suddenly they contacted me and threatened to kill Sarah if I didn't find it for them," Dixon said.

"By then Dixon had told me and I had updated Admiral Lloyd. That's when things began to go south," Scott said.

The private briefing was over as FBI took over the island. FBI Special Agent Harold approached the group and introduced himself.

"We will be interviewing each of you separately. I need a Commander Kelly first," Harold said.

"I'm Commander Kelly," Celia said stepping forward.

"You need a Doctor?" He asked.

"I'm okay. What do you need?" She asked Special Agent Harold.

The interrogation of the team and recovery of Geyser took up the next five hours. Dixon was taken into custody. Gwen looked trouble as the FBI took him away.

"Gwen, are you okay?" Celia asked.

"He was just trying to help his family. What's going to happen to him?" Gwen asked her.

"FBI will hand him over to the CIA. He did, at the very least, interfere with an investigation, giving a terrorist organization free reign for the last five years," Celia said.

"You make it sound like treason," Gwen said as crossed her arms.

"It is treason," Celia said.

"Still," Gwen sighed.

Elliot joined them.

"Still too many unanswered questions," Elliot said to Celia. He looked over at Frank Scott who was speaking with an FBI Agent.

"I know," Celia said watching Frank Scott as well.

"But we got them, right?" Gwen asked.

"Right, except for whoever is running things in Beirut," Celia said. She walked over to Frank Scott.

"Please tell me she did not just say that," Gwen said to Elliot.

Elliot just smiled and followed Celia. McDonald and Perry joined Gwen.

"What's wrong?" McDonald asked Gwen.

"She's crazy." Gwen pointed at Celia.

"We knew that. It's a good kind of crazy," McDonald said trying to point out the bright side.

"Celia, you did great work. Tom would have been proud of you," Scott said to Celia.

"It's not finished though. The money is still missing and there's still an arms group running out of Beirut," Celia pointed out.

"But they no longer have sources to use in the Navy. That is huge. Sometimes it's one problem at a time. You guys did great work as well. Thanks to keeping her safe," Scott said to Elliot after reassuring Celia.

"Somebody had to," Elliot said. Scott knew what he meant by that. Though Elliot thought Scott disappearing and dumping it on Celia wasn't the right way to go about it.

"I'll talk to you tomorrow," Scott said to Celia.

As the FBI escorted the rest of the team off the island, Celia and Elliot hung back. Elliot knew she was not done working, he knew that look she got when things didn't add up.

"What's wrong?" Elliot asked her.

"I'm not sure," Celia said.

"Me either," Elliot agreed.

"Something isn't setting right with you either?"

"Nope."

"I guess it's out of our hands now, it's an FBI investigation," Celia said trying to convince herself to walk away.

"There are plenty of other bad guys out there," Elliot reminded her.

"I know, but we are missing something." Celia couldn't put her finger on it.

Admiral Walton walked up to them.

"They say we can go," Walton announced.

"I know," Celia said.

"I feel it too," Walton said. Walton could see she wasn't satisfied with the ending either.

CHAPTER 53

It had been a couple days since Celia had her final showdown with the Pact. Frank stayed in Norfolk and they took care of the last of the paperwork as Gwen shoved page after page in their face. Elliot and Scott were in Celia's office helping with the reports.

"Fewer bodies next time would definitely cut this in half. Just something to think about," Gwen said. Both Scott and Celia looked up from the table and glared at her. Elliot smiled.

"Your friend here was right what he said," Scott looked to Elliot.

"What did he say?" Celia asked.

"I really dropped the ball with you. I was supposed to protect you but instead I put you in more danger. Tom would kill me if he were here," Frank said sadly.

"I would have preferred to know you were alive." Celia smiled and got a twinkle in her eye. "However, when you least expect it..."

"Fair enough," Frank smiled back.

"Now we need to do one last thing," Celia said.

"The money?" Elliot asked her.

Celia nodded.

"Let's go back to the duplex," Celia said. Gwen joined them so she could get her car which had been parked there since the day of the mission. When they pulled in front of the duplex, Gwen got out and got the key from Celia.

"Leave my keys on the counter when you are done, we will be working out here." Celia walked over to her car. Elliot and Scott look at each other wondering what work Celia was going to do.

Celia stood in front of her beloved Studebaker. This was the logical scenario. Celia opened her trunk and began the search. Scott was wondering why she was taking everything out of her trunk.

"So are you going to let us in on what we are going to do?" Scott asked.

"I think we might be looking at it," Celia said looking up from the trunk.

"We are looking at your car." Elliot stated the obvious.

"And maybe the perfect hiding place." Celia crossed her arms.

Scott laughed. "That sounds like the Tom we both know and love."

"Your car?" Elliot asked.

"This was my wedding gift from Tom," Celia said.

"The picture sent to you, you were standing in front of the gift table." Elliot saw where she was going with it.

"We just start looking." Celia in pain just thinking of tearing into her prized possession.

Scott rolled up the sleeves of his flannel shirt and went to work, anxious to get started.

"Grab the other side of the carpet, would you?" Scott asked Elliot.

Elliot looked to Celia. He wasn't doing anything without her okay. Celia nodded the go ahead.

Together, Elliot and Scott pulled out the carpet in the trunk. Staring at bare metal, there was no money.

"I guess we'll look inside of it." Celia sighed. Scott nodded.

After an hour and a half, the carpet from the inside lay on the ground beside the Studebaker, along with the door panels, glove box and dashboard. Nothing.

"That just leaves the seats," Scott said frowning. He looked at her skeptically.

"Let's take them out," Celia said sadly. Her prize possession was now in pieces.

Elliot carefully removed the front and Scott removed back seat. Celia's heart sank when they found no money. The only thing they found was a clothes hanger under the back seat.

"I was wrong," Celia said.

"Where else could it be?" Scott asked her.

"I don't know. I was so sure." Celia looked around at the various parts of the Studebaker.

"Did he give you anything else?" Elliot asked.

"No, just the Studebaker. Although on our anniversary the year he died he did have my seats recovered." Celia stopped suddenly, realizing what that might mean.

Scott shook his head as he admired the gray leather.

Celia looked over the seats carefully.

"They are not removable covers," Celia said, slowly looking up the two men. Scott got out his pocket knife.

"This is going to hurt me more than it'll hurt you."

"Somehow, I doubt that." Celia sighed again.

"You want to join in?" Scott asked Elliot.

"I'm good. I'll just watch," Elliot said not wanting to add to Celia's trauma.

Sticking the knife into the edge of the seat cover, Scott slowly moved it down the full length of the seat. With anticipation, Celia waited, hoping their efforts weren't in vain. It took only thirty minutes to dismantle the seat covers and stuffing. Again no money!

Celia was quiet as she picked up the hanger and sat on the porch steps. She played with it a few minutes then put her face in her hands. Scott shook his head and sat beside her. After a moment's hesitation, he put his arm around her.

"I'm sorry," Scott said, not knowing what else to say.

Celia looked up and threw up her hands, "I can't believe I destroyed my car. Look at it." She looked at her watch. "It took three years to restore it. I tore it apart in less than two hours."

"We helped." Scott tried to make light of it.

"Thank you so much." Celia was past having a sense of humor.

"I can fix it." Elliot promised her.

"My seats." Celia watched stuffing fly through the air as the breeze picked up.

"You can fix that?" Scott asked Elliot. Elliot nodded that he could.

Gwen chose that moment to walk out the door. She looked at them and then she looked at the dismantled Studebaker.

"I don't even want to know." Gwen shook her head, threw a bag into the backseat of her car, got into her Chevy Nova, and drove away.

Celia watched as Elliot started to put the dash back inside the car. Still playing with the hanger, Celia began tearing off tape that held paper rolled around the bottom in place. Someone had taped it on the hanger.

"Frank, let me see your knife," Celia said urgently.

"There's nothing left to take apart."

"No, not that. The hanger."

Both Elliot and Scott came over to see what she had discovered. Carefully she cut through the tape, and then she unrolled the paper. It read 'It's back in the airplane hangar'.

Celia smiled. "Of course! Where is the one place no one would look?"

"Where?" Scott asked.

"The place it originally was to begin with." Celia read them the note.

"We should check it out ourselves. If you're wrong, the General might not like having to send a crew over two thousand miles."

"I'll call Turner. He can have NCIS or the FBI check it out to keep it in a chain of custody. I'm not going behind his back," Celia said.

"Okay, we'll call him," Scott agreed with hesitation.

Elliot thought it was a good call.

"If they find it, we can accompany the money back to DC. You could visit with your parents," Scott suggested.

"We'll see if General Turner wants us to see it through to the end," Celia said.

"If so, you're going to need a ride to the airport," Elliot said looking at the car.

* * *

Celia and Frank Scott were led to her father's office.

"Frank, it's good to see you in one piece, son." Mitchell smiled. Looking past Scott, he looked warmly at his daughter. Celia and her father met halfway and embraced. "Why didn't you tell us you were coming?"

"I wanted to surprise you."

"General Turner called me this morning," he said and smiled. "It's a good thing we spend of time on our knees for you."

"I'm glad that you do too, Daddy," Celia kissed him on the cheek.

"So what can I do for you two?"

"We need to see Tom's old hangar."

"The FBI is on site. I'll take you over there."

* * *

Mitchell led the way to the plane hangars. The pilots were up doing maneuvers and the hangers were empty. They watched as the FBI looked for loose panels in the floor, finally finding one. The agent gently lifted the floor panel.

"It's all here," the agent said.

"You were right," Scott said, smiling.

*　*　*

General Turner arranged for a security team to go with the money to Washington, D.C. Scott insisted on traveling with the team. When it was signed over to the proper authorities, Mitchell insisted Celia spend the night before going back to Dam Neck. Celia's mother, Grace Mitchell, greeted her with open arms. Celia had always thought her mother to be the most beautiful woman she had known. Even though grey was peeping through her dark brown strands, age truly agreed with her. The Mitchell home overlooked the Pacific Ocean.

They ate dinner on the patio as the sun set. Celia played with her salad as her parents caught her up on the base gossip. After dinner Celia's father suggested they take a walk.

"What's wrong? You are somewhere else," Mitchell asked her.

"I haven't been home like this since Tom died."

"It's okay to move on, you know that don't you?" Mitchell asked his daughter.

"I'm not ready yet." Celia shrugged her shoulders.

"When you are... it's okay."

*　*　*

The plane carrying the money landed at Kennedy National Airport at midnight. The FBI had it in hand the entire trip. Their orders were to give it to FBI Agents in D.C. The chain of evidence document was signed and the exchange was made. The money then was passed off to three men in three-piece suits and taken to a black limousine with government plates. The three men got into three separate black sedans and drove in opposite directions.

CHAPTER 54

Opening her closet, Celia looked for the white high heeled pumps she had just bought. She heard her front door open.

"We're going to be late," Elliot's voice traveled to the bedroom.

"I'll be right there." Celia finally found her pumps. With one last look in her full length mirror, she grabbed her shawl. Celia came from the bedroom dressed in a teal chiffon hitting her mid-calf. Putting on white gloves matching her shoes, Celia attempted to latch a string of pearls around her neck. She looked stunning and Elliot had to remind himself to breathe.

"Ready?" he asked.

"Ready," Celia said as she looked at Elliot. He looked exceptionally handsome in his white tux.

"Let me help you." Elliot went behind her and securely latched her pearls.

"Thank you," Celia said, taking a deep breath.

They walked out of the duplex to find Chairman of the Joint Chiefs General Baxter Turner waiting for them. He was standing against a long black limo. Celia and Elliot walked over to him.

"Commander, you look lovely," Turner said, saluting back.

"Thank you, sir." Celia smiled.

"I'm glad to see that you are back on your feet." Turner smiled. "How are you Commander Elliot?"

"Fine, sir."

"By the way, Commander Kelly, the White House will be announcing it later today, but I wanted you to be the first to know. The nomination was approved overwhelmingly. Walton is now not only a three star admiral, but the new chief of naval operations."

"That is wonderful news, sir." Celia smiled. "I can't think of anyone more deserving or better qualified."

"I wanted to come and thank you personally." Turner smiled at Celia.

"For what, sir?" Celia smiled.

"For the excellent work you did on this mission and retrieving the money. It was a pleasure working with you, Commander. That's why I am here. I'd want you back in the Pentagon to work for Walton." Turner waited for her reply.

"I'm honored, sir."

"I hope that is a yes, Commander."

"Yes, sir."

"Would you both like a ride to the wedding?" Turner asked.

"You're going, sir?" Celia asked.

"Wouldn't miss it," Turner said.

"Thank you, sir, we accept." Celia smiled.

* * *

It was a twenty minute drive to the church. Celia thought back over the adventures of the last couple of months. Celia was going to miss Dam Neck and the team.

"This sure isn't the wedding I thought I'd be going to," Celia commented.

"Me either." Elliot nodded.

"I never knew he proposed," Celia said.

"It just goes to show, you never know." Elliot smiled.

"Kind of like the last six months."

Once at the church, Elliot and Celia separated and Turner was seated inside the sanctuary. Celia went back into the room where the bride and bridesmaids were fussing over the bride.

"Where have you been?" Gwen asked her franticly. Gwen was dressed in a similar style to Celia.

"Sorry," Celia explained.

"I think I ripped my dress," the bride said anxiously.

"I'll fix it," Gwen said as she bent and looked at the damage. She got her purse and then went back to the dress.

Celia went over to the bride and gave her a brief hug. "I am so happy for you. He's a good man."

"He is, isn't he? I am so lucky. No, I am so blessed. If it hadn't been for what we've been through in the last couple of months, it might never have happened! God really does work things out for the best, doesn't He?" The bride beamed.

That is when they heard a sound as if someone was pulling off Velcro.

"What was that?" the bride asked.

"Fixed it," Gwen said.

"Fixed what?" Celia asked.

"I fixed her dress," Gwen said.

"Thanks, Gwen." The bride smiled.

"Don't mention it."

"It's time," Celia said, glaring at Gwen over the bride's shoulder.

The bride was too nervous to notice. The ladies filed out one by one. They met the groomsmen in the hall. The groom and his best man, Elliot, were waiting at the front of the church. McDonald walked Gwen down the aisle first. Then Perry walked with Mary. Celia, the maid of honor, walked and stood opposite of Elliot. Admiral Walton, the new Chief of Naval Operations, walked the bride to the groom.

After Walton was seated, the bride and groom, Tammy and Jeffers, joined hands and looked into each other's eyes as they prepared to take their vows. Celia glanced briefly to the back of Tammy's long white train. She thought she noticed silver. She looked again as Tammy moved up the stairs of the altar. Celia did see silver! It was duct tape! Celia raised her eyebrow at Gwen, who gave her a thumbs up.

EPILOGUE

Celia unpacked her things, now back in her home in Washington, D.C. As she put a few stray things for the office in her briefcase, she came across the files from Frank Scott's office. She began reading them again. There was so much that wasn't explained.

Geyser's words echoed in her head: *Your husband was going to nail us right after he got back from the mission. We had no choice but to get him first. He contacted his buddy, Commander Frank Scott, Naval Intelligence. We threatened Cooper's little girl...*

So that's why Tom is gone...

"I was at your wedding, invited by the groom's side. I knew Tom's father. That's when I had the idea to hide the money. I never dreamed Tom would find it." Dixon shook his head.

How did Dixon get the money to begin with? The Pact didn't even know he had taken it until he began working with Frank Scott... makes sense. Frank did report to Lloyd, Lloyd reported to the Pact.

Then there was Mot. According to Aggie, it was the codename for Dixon's contact. Aggie knew the money was intercepted and hidden. Is there still another guy out there?

One thing is for sure, the Pact is bigger than what she thought. Why didn't Frank mention Beirut in his files?

The other thing that nagged at Celia was, who sent the wedding picture?

* * *

When he opened his eyes they were out of focus. The blurry outlines and distorted colors gradually began to become clear. A nurse put on a new IV bag. She adjusted the drip, decreasing it. He felt weak and dizzy. He tried to sit, but the nurse objected and made him lie back, speaking to him in an unknown language.

Where was he? How long had he been here...?

CN Bring is the author of The Celia Kelly Series, The Jack Sleuth Series and Co-author of Laundry Ladies: The Stain Gang. CN Bring, originally from Montana, now makes her home in Oregon with her husband Glen.

Made in the USA
San Bernardino, CA
07 September 2017